I0847251

CELESTIAL WARNING

DECIPHERING THE ANUNNAKI CODE

CARLO TONALEZZI

Celestial Warning – Deciphering the Anunnaki Code
By Carlo Tonalezzi

Copyright © 2025
All rights reserved.

No part of this book may be reproduced, stored in a retrieval system, or transmitted in any form or by any means—electronic, mechanical, photocopying, recording, or otherwise—without the prior written permission of the author or publisher, except for brief quotations used in reviews or scholarly works.

This is a work of fiction. While this story draws inspiration from myths, legends, and historical events, any resemblance to actual persons, living or dead, or real events is purely coincidental, or is used in a fictional context or for descriptive purposes only. The author has taken creative liberties to craft a narrative that blends elements of myth and history within a science fiction framework.

The views and opinions expressed in this book are those of the author and do not necessarily reflect the official policy or position of any government or space agency.

For those who look to the stars and imagine what's next.

TABLE OF CONTENTS

CHAPTER 1

Timeless Legacy

Drifting through the endless void of space, we gaze down upon an Earth growing ever more unrecognizable.

Beyond the reinforced glass of our orbital lab, a planet in turmoil unfolds. From this fragile sanctuary suspended in silence, the continents below twist and drift—once-familiar silhouettes dissolving into alien shapes. The world is shifting. And we are being tested.

Civilization now teeters on the edge of a precipice, confronting a trial of unprecedented scale. A question hangs in the silence—vast, weightless, and cold as the vacuum that surrounds us: will humanity, long divided by borders, beliefs, and ambition, finally summon the unity and resolve to stand together against the shadow of annihilation?

Will we, as a species, rise above the clamor of division to fight for a common cause—the survival of our home, our history, and our hope?

This cataclysmic transformation—the phenomenon now referred to by scholars and mystics alike as the Great Purification Cycle—is no mere disaster. It is a foretold event, inscribed in the margins of ancient scriptures, passed down through cryptic oral traditions, and hidden within the obscure algorithms of forgotten civilizations. It has come before, and now, inevitably, it comes again. Like the relentless ticking of some cosmic timepiece, the Cycle arrives with mathematical precision. It cleanses, it devastates, and then, it begins anew. From chaos, it breeds creation.

For centuries, scientists, philosophers, and spiritual seekers have searched for the formula behind a haunting pattern—the elusive equation that governs Earth's cyclical rebirth. It was never the work of a single lifetime, but the culmination of generations of unyielding pursuit. An unbroken lineage of brilliant minds and tireless hearts, each willing to sacrifice comfort, family, even life itself, in the name of a truth powerful enough to either save humanity—or condemn it beneath the weight of forbidden knowledge.

Yet this revelation—this understanding of the Cycles—did not emerge spontaneously, as if from thin air. It is the fruit of a tree planted long ago, rooted in an age when truth was scarce, but sacred. It was a time when a man's word was his most binding contract, and to break that vow was to invite dishonor—or even death. It was in this crucible of mistrust and survival that a unique bond was forged: a pact between two families whose destinies would become inseparably intertwined. The Rosen and Fischer lineages—bound not by blood, but by unshakable loyalty—formed an alliance that would endure centuries of change and chaos, war and peace, loss and legacy.

Their story begins in the aftermath of one of history's most pivotal moments: the fall of Napoleon Bonaparte. Following his crushing defeat at the Battle of Waterloo in 1815, Europe was a continent in disarray. With the echoes of war finally silenced, the Rosen and Fischer families—once soldiers in the ranks of the Prussian army—laid down their arms not in defeat, but in resolve. They turned from the battlefield not as conquerors, but as men who had endured, choosing a future shaped not by empire, but by knowledge. Seeking refuge from the turmoil, they settled deep within the Bavarian Alps, a region as remote as it was pristine, far from the political intrigues of Europe's capitals.

There, in the shadow of snow-capped peaks and within the silence of pine forests, they began the painstaking process of rebuilding their lives. They brought with them not only memories of bloodshed, but also the wisdom born of war—the understanding that legacy is not inherited but earned. Through mutual respect and shared purpose, they established a covenant, one that would preserve their family names, uphold their values, and protect a secret that would one day hold the key to humanity's survival.

The Rosens, a family steeped in the deep, scholarly tradition of language and cultural memory, had long been recognized as master linguists—custodians of the world's most elusive tongues. For generations, they had dedicated themselves to the study of ancient languages, forgotten dialects, and obscure linguistic systems that had fallen into disuse and obscurity. From the hieroglyphs etched into Egyptian stone to the indecipherable syllabaries of pre-Minoan Crete, the Rosens were capable of unlocking voices long silenced by time. Their expertise made them not only valuable to academic institutions and historical societies but vital to the rediscovery of humanity's oldest narratives. It was said that if words had ghosts, the Rosens could conjure them.

In contrast, the Fischers were people of the earth—driven not by the intricacies of grammar and syntax, but by a desire to physically unearth the past. They were master archaeologists, intuitive and precise in their craft. Their hands, calloused from decades of excavation, had gently brushed the dust from relics untouched for millennia. The Fischers had an uncanny ability to know where to dig, to sense the presence of history buried beneath layers of soil, ash, and stone. From desert tombs to forest-covered ruins, they followed the silent echoes of lost civilizations, recovering fragments of pottery, corroded coins, intricate carvings, and faded manuscripts—each whispering hints of ancient worlds waiting to be heard.

Their partnership had never been born of convenience, nor of academic curiosity alone, it had been forged out of necessity. The two families complemented one another in a way that transcended coincidence. Many of the Fischer family's greatest discoveries were stories left incomplete relics that spoke in symbols, half-finished inscriptions, shattered mosaics, and ceremonial objects whose meaning had faded with time. These fragments, though invaluable, would have remained locked in ambiguity if not for the Rosens.

It was the Rosens, with their mastery of language and history, who brought meaning to the silence. They translated the unspoken and decoded the indecipherable. With their expertise, the artifacts came alive—ancient battles reconstructed, religious rites reimagined, legal systems and lost mythologies unearthed and understood. Through the synergy of both families, history was not only remembered, it was revived.

And as the decades passed, this sacred exchange of knowledge did not fade, it deepened. From fathers to sons, from mothers to daughters, the traditions took root early nurtured from childhood and refined into lifelong devotion. Over time, as the Rosen and Fischer lineages expanded and branched into new family names and distant marriages, the pact between them endured. It adapted. It strengthened.

What began as two families became something greater: a quiet, far-reaching network, stretching across Europe and beyond. Their alliance attracted like-minded individuals; engineers, scientists, doctors, linguists, educators, archivists, and builders, each one vetted not only for skill but for integrity. Over time, they formed a kind of clan: a fellowship bound not by blood alone, but by shared purpose, loyalty, and the pursuit of truth. Among them, secrets were protected, discoveries shared, and knowledge preserved. Trust and respect were not requested; they were earned, and they were sacred.

At the center of this ever-growing constellation of allies stood the two founding families: the Rosens and the Fischers. Their friendship, now passed through generations, remained the unshakable core. It was as much an intellectual symbiosis as it was a testament to legacy—a bond tempered not only by study, but by trials, by war, by sacrifice. What began as professional collaboration had evolved into something far more profound: a generational alliance rooted in unbreakable respect and a shared burden of truth.

They were not merely colleagues or even friends. They were kindred spirits, drawn together by a hunger that defied time and borders—an insatiable desire to uncover what had been hidden, and to preserve it from being lost again.

Among their most treasured and controversial acquisitions were a set of manuscripts of immeasurable value—documents unearthed, bartered, or smuggled during Napoleon Bonaparte's short-lived but impactful occupation of Egypt at the turn of the

19th century. These writings, transcribed in ancient Coptic, early Arabic, and even proto-Hebrew, included cosmological treatises, ritual scrolls, and early astronomical records—many of which hinted at cycles of time, catastrophe, and renewal. Some were penned on fragile papyrus that cracked at the touch of dry air; others were inked on leather or parchment so aged they resembled brittle autumn leaves. Yet despite their fragility, they survived, carried across borders and hidden in secret caches known only to a few.

These manuscripts endured not just the ravages of time, but the full wrath of the modern world's most destructive chapter— the First World War. The Great War tested the limits of endurance for both the Rosen and Fischer families. As the world descended into chaos between 1914 and 1918, borders were redrawn with blood, empires collapsed, and cities that once welcomed scholars became targets of artillery. Libraries were looted. Archives burned. Graves, both literal and historical, were disturbed.

For the Rosens and the Fischers, survival meant more than staying alive, it meant preserving what they had sworn to protect. As soldiers marched and bombs fell, they carried scrolls in hidden compartments, buried codices beneath cellar floors, and passed knowledge through encoded letters. Each generation took on the burden of guardianship, often without knowing the full significance of the knowledge they protected.

And yet, through the ash and rubble, they endured. They survived the disintegration of their world by leaning on each other—sharing food when supplies ran thin, hiding one another when safety faltered, and, above all, never letting go of the bond that had begun more than a century before in the highlands of Bavaria. The hardships did not weaken their alliance; they fortified it. Their loyalty, tested by fire and fear, became something unbreakable.

By the end of the Great War, as the last cannon fell silent and the world staggered toward an uneasy peace, the Rosen and Fischer families came to a solemn realization: survival demanded more than courage and endurance—it required foresight, preparation, and absolute commitment to preservation. The horrors they had witnessed, the burning of libraries, the looting of museums, the wholesale destruction of cultural memory—convinced them that their legacy, their lifework, could not be left vulnerable again.

Determined never to be caught unprepared by the tides of history or the flames of war, they convened in secret and made a sacred vow—a binding oath passed through generations like an heirloom: they would protect the knowledge they had gathered, no matter the cost, even if it meant disappearing into obscurity to do so.

As the clan expanded—no longer just the Rosens and the Fischers, but a growing fellowship of trusted allies bound by purpose—the need for protection grew urgent. With war clouds once again gathering over Europe, and the weight of ancient knowledge resting on their shoulders, they began the construction of something monumental: a hidden stronghold that would outlast regimes, revolutions, and even civilizations. The Rosens and the Fischers poured every resource, every ounce of engineering ingenuity and historical acumen they possessed into the project. The result was not merely a bunker, but a fortress of secrecy: a subterranean labyrinth carved directly into the mountain bedrock, reinforced with iron, sealed with stone, and woven with deception.

False passageways branched into dead ends. Echo chambers confused the ear. Mechanisms triggered misleading sounds or collapsing walls. Every corner was designed with misdirection in mind. Only those who possessed the families' most guarded secrets—ancestral codes, symbolic maps, and linguistic keys passed down orally—could navigate its twists and turns. This was not only to protect the contents, but to ensure that should the archive ever be discovered, it would remain impenetrable to the uninitiated.

At the heart of this cryptic underworld, beyond the maze of decoys and deadfalls lay the Archive—their most prized and sacred treasure. It was a vault unlike any other on Earth: a vast, climate-controlled chamber constructed with reverence and precision. Rows of custom-built shelving stretched into the dim distance, holding fragile scrolls inked by vanished civilizations, stone tablets etched with forgotten runes, ancient books bound in leather that had survived empires, and parchments so old they whispered when touched. Each item in this hidden library was more than a relic—it was a thread in the tapestry of human existence.

The Rosens and Fischers devoted years to the meticulous work of cataloging and translating its contents, creating encrypted ledgers and multi-lingual indices to ensure that even if they perished, their work would remain legible to those worthy enough to find it.

The families guarded it, not out of fear, but out of duty. To protect the archive was to protect the very memory of mankind.

And so, hidden beneath the snow-covered peaks of Bavaria, in silence and shadow, the Rosens and Fischers prepared—not for another war, but for the day when the world would once again be forced to remember what it had chosen to forget.

By the 1940s, both lineages had risen to prominence in European intellectual circles. Despite the scars of the First World War and the rising tide of instability across the continent, the families had carved out positions of great influence. The new generation—their heirs in blood and in burden—stood at the forefront of their respective fields.

Johan Rosen, a brilliant polymath, had become one of the most respected linguistic scholars of his era. Fluent in over two dozen languages, he was a master not only of syntax and semantics but of the subtle cultural nuances that shaped human expression. His work on the decipherment of pre-Etruscan proto-scripts and the syntactical structures of extinct Afroasiatic languages brought him international acclaim. Yet his greatest work, his real work—was done not in universities or lecture halls, but in the cold, candle-lit depths of the family archive. There, surrounded by the dust of times, Johan spent countless hours poring over symbols etched in obsidian, inked on animal skins, or burned into clay tablets, always seeking the unifying thread—the code behind the myth.

His counterpart, Rudi Fischer, was a man of earth and stone—a field archaeologist with a soul shaped by the soil he sifted. He had led expeditions across the Mediterranean, North Africa, and the Middle East, recovering ruins swallowed by sand and time. His discoveries redefined timelines and rewrote the accepted understanding of the Bronze Age collapse. Yet Rudi, too, kept his most important work hidden from the public eye. After each official dig, he would return quietly to Bavaria, his journals heavy with sketches and notes he would not publish. He worked in tandem with Johan, matching symbol to site, artifact to language, story to geography—assembling pieces of a puzzle no one else even knew existed.

Together, Johan and Rudi pursued an elusive truth. Not a myth, not a theory, but something older than memory, buried deeper than any tomb. Something the world was not yet ready to know—or perhaps something the world had once known and had deliberately chosen to forget.

Their search became an obsession, a calling inherited and accepted without question. Publicly, they were luminaries, adored by students and lauded by peers. Privately, they were custodians of a secret legacy, their every action guided by the silent vow their ancestors had made: to protect the truth, whatever it cost.

And all the while, the clock of the Great Cycle ticked onward, unseen by most, but never ignored by those who knew the signs.

One cold night, Johan burst into the hidden chamber, barely containing his excitement. His hands trembled as he poured two glasses of wine, his breath quick and uneven.

"Rudi," he said, gripping an ancient Egyptian manuscript, "Do you truly believe humanity has been on this Earth for as long as the history books claim? That Darwin's theory of evolution explains everything?"

Rudi took a slow sip of wine, eyes thoughtful. "I've stood in places that defy explanation," he said at last. "Archaeological sites with engineering feats impossible for the civilizations we credit them to."

"Exactly!" Johan's eyes gleamed. "Listen to this." He traced his fingers over the ancient Egyptian manuscript and read aloud: *We must endure until the time of Earth's rebirth—when all will be swept away, and we must begin anew. In the fleeting years between these great reckonings, we must prepare to survive. The celestial warning is written in the stars, and it falls to the Skywatchers to decipher its meaning before time runs out.*

Rudi leaned forward, his fingers gripping the edge of the table. "Go on . . ." he urged.

Johan hesitated. "That's it."

Rudi's brow furrowed. "What do you mean, that's it? Generations of translating, and that's the big breakthrough?"

"No, that's it as in—that's all we have." Johan exhaled.

Rudi was silent for a long moment before he asked, "What do you make of it?"

Johan's voice was barely a whisper.

"It means this message was important enough to be recorded in three languages. One is ancient Sumerian, one is ancient Egyptian, and the third is Greek.

But these symbols, "he paused, eyes narrowing—"these are unique. I've never seen them before."

A small voice interrupted them. "Could it be a message from a lost civilization?"

Startled, Johan and Rudi turned to see little Karl, Johan's five-year-old son. The boy, already fluent in several languages thanks to the rigorous Rosen tradition, had been sitting quietly in the corner, listening intently. His innocent yet astute question hung in the air for a moment—before both men burst into laughter.

Yet, despite their laughter, the thought lingered.

In the 1940s, the world was shifting once more. The political climate was darkening, growing more oppressive with each passing year. Yet in the shadow of rising tyranny, the Rosens and the Fischers continued their secret meetings—bound by a shared mission to unlock the ancient mysteries they had unearthed.

They debated endlessly: What triggered the Earth's cyclical rebirth? How long had humanity truly been here? Their discussions stretched late into the night, fueled by fine wine, flickering lamplight, and an unyielding pursuit of truth.

Then, one night, Rudi arrived breathless, wild excitement in his eyes. He could barely form the words.

"Hitler" he panted, "is recruiting scientists for an expedition to Antarctica."

Johan's face hardened. "And?"

"I've been asked to join." Rudi's voice was a mixture of

exhilaration and unease. "I had to swear secrecy but you are my confidant. I must tell you the truth. You must swear secrecy as well."

Johan leaned in, his expression grave. "You have my word. What is it?"

Rudi glanced around, as if making sure no one else was listening. Then, leaning in, he whispered, "The official reason for the expedition is margarine fat—some absurd cover for wartime shortages. But they know the true reason. They know about ancient knowledge. About the artifacts—ones that could grant power beyond imagination."

Johan's breath caught in his throat.

"And they're searching for them," Rudi continued. "Everywhere."

The weight of his words settled heavily between them.

From Antarctica to Peru, to Mexico, to Egypt—their goal was to leave no stone unturned in their pursuit of knowledge and power. For Johan and Rudi, the implications were staggering.

"Do you realize what this means for us?" Rudi had exclaimed, his eyes alight with excitement. "Unlimited funds. Unlimited resources. We could finally complete our research!"

But Johan had been apprehensive. He knew the cost of such an alliance.

"Rudi, Hitler's expedition is his own, and any findings will belong to him. How can you be part of it without exposing us? Our families?"

Rudi had already thought of this. "I will oversee all the expedition's archaeological findings. I will have scheduled time to photograph and catalog them—that's when you will do your thing."

Johan frowned. "Have you lost your mind? We could be

branded as traitors. It would mean the end of generations of work; we could fail our ancestors and disgrace our entire family."

Rudi leaned in, his voice calm but firm. "Johan, there is no progress without risk. We have been searching for answers our entire lives—this is our chance. An opportunity like this will never come again."

Johan rubbed his temples, considering the weight of it all. "I know, I know, but the risk factor is immense. We must not reveal our own studies. My son and your daughter must be safe at all times."

Rudi nodded. "Must I remind you of what our ancestors built under our feet? The underground chambers were made for times like these. We have enough food and water stored for years. If war or any other catastrophe comes, our families will be safe."

And so, both Rudi and Johan joined the Nazi-led scientific expedition. Rudi was appointed the official leader of the archaeological team, while Johan became the head of the artifact warehouse. In other words, nothing passed through without their knowledge.

Their families had been meticulous in documenting their work for generations. The Rosens and the Fischers possessed hundreds of accurate journals passed down through their lineage, safeguarded within their secret library bunkers. Their research had revealed something astonishing that had happened repeatedly throughout history. And now, it seemed, the Nazis had caught on.

Rudi traveled frequently, disappearing for months at a time while Johan remained in the laboratory, examining and sorting through the materials the team uncovered. Whenever Rudi returned home, he would use their old code phrases to summon Johan for their secret research meetings in one of the study bunkers.

At first, their findings were meager—local rumors, whispered legends. The indigenous people in various regions spoke of ancient visitors who descended from the skies, of lost civilizations buried beneath the ice or hidden in jungles. In Antarctica, there were even wild theories about pyramids, lying frozen beneath miles of glacial ice.

On his second expedition, Rudi returned with a few new obsessions: the polygonal walls around the world. He had listened to accounts of enormous stones similarly constructed around the planet—were they built by the same architects? If so, how could that be? They are thousands of miles apart! It was thrilling, but frustrating. These were only stories, unverified and impossible to prove. Rudi was growing desperate for tangible evidence. "Johan, have you ever delved into the intricacies of ancient polygonal masonry?"

"A bit, Rudi. It's that method where large stones are precisely cut and fitted together without mortar, right?"

While setting down a weathered book on the table, Rudi remarked, "Exactly. It's fascinating how this technique appears across various ancient cultures."

Johan, still scanning the large map pinned to the wall, responded thoughtfully, "Indeed. The Inca sites in Peru come to mind."

With a nod, Rudi continued, "Yes, places like Machu Picchu and Cusco showcase this with remarkable precision. The stones are so tightly joined that even a blade can't slip between them."

"Impressive craftsmanship," Johan said, stepping back to take in the full scale of the topographical sketch.

"Absolutely," Rudi agreed, flipping open his field notes. "And it's not just in Peru. In Italy, regions like Lazio and Campania have ancient walls in cities such as Norba and Alatri, built using massive stone blocks fitted without mortar. And even in the remote Easter Island, at the Ahu Vinapu site, the same uncanny craftsmanship emerged from the volcanic soil. The resemblance across these distant lands is undeniable yet officially dismissed as coincidence."

Pausing near the window, Johan turned and added, "Similar techniques are evident in Greece, especially in Mycenae and Tiryns."

"Right," Rudi replied as he adjusted one of the stone photographs on the table. "The so-called Cyclopean masonry there uses enormous limestone boulders, roughly fitted together."

"The term 'Cyclopean' suggests that the ancient Greeks believed only the mythical Cyclopes could have constructed such massive structures," Johan noted with a wry smile.

"Exactly," Rudi said, pulling a photo from a manila folder. "And this style isn't confined to Europe and South America. In Japan, castles like Osaka and Nij? feature polygonal stone walls, showcasing the technique's reach."

Johan leaned on the edge of the table, eyes gleaming. "It's intriguing how diverse cultures adopted similar construction methods."

Rudi nodded. "Indeed. The presence of polygonal masonry in various regions highlights a shared understanding of durable construction techniques among ancient civilizations."

With genuine admiration, Johan whispered, "Truly remarkable."

And as he rolled up a site diagram, Rudi added with quiet excitement, "And next, we're heading to Puma Punku in Bolivia, Machu Picchu in Peru, and the Central American pyramids. One thing is to read about these places," he continued, eyes gleaming with excitement, "another is to stand before them."

Yet something was changing. Rudi was becoming increasingly militaristic. Each time he returned, he seemed more rigid, more disciplined—his demeanor shaped by the influence of the Nazi hierarchy. His laughter came less easily. The weight of his position, the secrecy, the deception—it was transforming him.

But after a few hours of discussion, a few bottles of wine, the old Rudi would resurface. The two friends would talk late into the night, chasing the secrets they had pursued since their youth.

A Change of Pace

By this time, Rudi's young daughter, Karin, had become a near-constant presence at his side. The little girl had long since adapted to the rhythms of her father's unpredictable life, his sudden departures, the hurried goodbyes, the long stretches of absence filled only by faded postcards and cryptic letters. But whenever Rudi returned home, he made it a point to give her all the attention he could in the little time he had. Their bond was quiet but deeply rooted, a connection forged in fleeting moments and gentle rituals: morning walks through alpine meadows, bedtime stories whispered by lantern light, the careful brushing of ancient dust from relics while she watched wide-eyed and curious.

She rarely left his sight when he was home. And he rarely let her go.

And then, one fateful evening, everything changed.

The sun had long dipped below the jagged mountain horizon, casting the Bavarian peaks in a soft, bruised light as the chill of night crept in. Johan Rosen was alone in the underground library. A fire crackled in the iron stove beside him, casting dancing shadows across shelves filled with ancient wisdom. He was hunched over a manuscript—Syriac, he suspected—but the words blurred as a sudden sound echoed through the corridor: hurried footsteps on stone.

Moments later, Rudi appeared at the threshold, Karin bundled in his arms, her face nestled against his shoulder. Her boots and coat were dusted with travel, her cheeks red from the cold. Johan stood immediately, startled by the sight.

Something was wrong.

Rudi looked different. Not tired—no, Rudi was always tired after a field mission—but this was something else. His usual spark, the infectious energy that trailed him like a comet tail, was gone. In its place was a heavy stillness, like a man who had glimpsed something that could not be unseen. His eyes, usually alight with excitement, were shadowed. Haunted.

He gently set Karin down, brushing a hand through her hair. She clung to the hem of his coat, silent but alert.

Johan crossed the room. "Rudi, what's going on?" His voice was low but firm.

Without a word, Rudi stepped closer and gestured Johan aside, away from Karin. His voice, when he finally spoke, was quiet but carried a strange urgency. A weight.

"We found something," Rudi said, his eyes fixed on Johan's, not blinking. "Something real."

Johan's breath caught mid-inhale. After all these years, all the theories and half-truths, it was a phrase they had fantasized about but never dared to say aloud. Something real.

"What is it?" Johan asked, heart beginning to race, the gravity of the moment sinking into his bones. He knew Rudi well enough to understand that whatever he had brought back this time, it was different. It wasn't just another relic. It wasn't a broken tablet or an old carving or a suspicious glyph etched into cave walls.

This was the shift. The fulcrum moment.

Everything they had been working toward—the sacrifices of their ancestors, the code passed down through generations, the secrecy, the oaths—it was all building to this.

Johan moved toward him, concern tightening his brow. "You look like you've seen a ghost."

"Worse," Rudi muttered, his voice raw. He glanced toward Karin, who had quietly perched on a small bench near the reading table, curling into herself as though sensing the gravity of the moment. Rudi turned back, voice low and trembling: "I found something, Johan. And I think we were right. About everything."

Johan's breath hitched. "What do you mean?"

Rudi paused, his eyes scanning the bunker as if still wary of being overheard—even here. He pulled a battered leather satchel from beneath his coat and set it on the table with a thud that echoed far too loudly in the still room. The bag looked ordinary enough, but Johan could tell by the way Rudi handled it—like a relic, like something volatile—that it contained more than just field notes.

Rudi's voice dropped to a whisper. "It's not just prophecy. It's not just a myth. It's mapped. It's measured. It's coming."

Johan stared at him, his mouth dry. "You mean, the Cycle?" Rudi nodded slowly. "Yes. And there's more. So much more."

He reached into the worn canvas bag and began laying out the contents: folded documents, faded photographs, charcoal rubbings of ancient stones—and finally, a thin, weathered tablet etched with concentric circles.

"What we've been guarding . . ." he said quietly, his voice tight with urgency, "it's not just history. It's a warning system. A record—left by those who survived the last Cycle."

He pointed to the tablet. "Look at these symbols. They match—repeatedly. A depiction of our solar system but with an extra planet in orbit." He spread out more artifacts. "Here's the carving found at Machu Picchu. Now compare it to these—one from Sumer, the other from Egypt. Different continents, different ages, but the same celestial pattern. They knew. And they left this behind for us to understand—before it happens again."

Johan stood frozen, the room around him falling into a hush so deep it felt sacred. For the first time, in all their years of research, they weren't just chasing echoes.

Johan opened a bottle of wine and offered Rudi a glass.

Rudi, in a rushed and frustrated tone, replied, "I don't want a drink."

Johan raised an eyebrow. "That was a first."

Then, almost immediately, Rudi apologized, "Sorry, I didn't mean to be rude."

"All I want is to talk about what I've found," Rudi said. His voice was unsteady, but there was an urgency behind it. "Johan, I think I have found proof of the Earth Rebirth theory. There are clear signs of a major cataclysm in Puma Punku."

Johan leaned forward. "Tell me."

Rudi's eyes darted around the room, his mind working faster than his words. "You should have seen it; the massive, elaborate stone constructions in Puma Punku, cut with such laser-like precision that even with today's technology, we would struggle to replicate them. How, Johan? How could they have done this thousands of years ago?"

Johan frowned. "What do the locals say?"

"That's just it!" Rudi exclaimed. "When you ask the native people how these structures were built, they don't take credit for them. They say it was done in one night by the Sky People."

A heavy silence filled the room.

Johan studied his friend carefully. "Okay, carry on . . ."

He leaned forward. "Johan, these stones—these colossal stones—are just sitting there, scattered like puzzle pieces thrown with absurd force. As if something catastrophic sent them flying. I was there. I saw them. They look like they've been lying there untouched for over ten thousand years. It's just impossible."

Johan exhaled. "Rudi, sounds like you need a drink."

"No!" Rudi shot back, shaking his head. "You don't understand.

In the Americas, the pyramids were built on top of older ones. Why would they do that? It's like a restoration job after some massive disaster.

"And in Peru, there's this massive wall—stones cut so precisely you can't even fit a razor blade between them! It's as if the stones were turned into molten plasma and molded into place. But they weren't just stacked, they were engineered to withstand earthquakes. Some of the shamanic people believe in the Earth Rebirth theory—that after a certain number of years, the Earth goes through a cataclysm and resets itself."

Johan's skepticism wavered. "Withstand earthquakes? That would require engineering precision far beyond their time."

"Yes! And all of this is built on mountaintops, nearly eight thousand feet above sea level. The quarries? The stones were taken from even higher up the slopes. Do you realize the scale of effort required to move them? It's staggering."

Johan sat back, running a hand over his beard. "Rudi, this is incredible."

A Shocking Discovery

As time wore on, the world around them began to dim, the light of peace fading into the long shadow of something far more menacing. The air in Europe grew colder—not from winter, but from fear. War loomed like a gathering storm, its thunder rolling just beyond the horizon. Tensions mounted with every passing day, and whispers of violence, of borders breaking and ideologies rising, became impossible to ignore. Then, as if fated, the inevitable unfolded: World War II had begun.

Daily life in the Alps changed subtly at first, and then all at once. The once-quiet villages became places of paranoia and silence. Neighbors stopped speaking freely. Strangers lingered longer than they should. Soldiers began appearing in train stations, then on roads, and finally near the towns themselves. Conversations were measured, conducted behind closed doors, and even those were often reduced to glances and nods. Eyes watched everything, and words carried too much weight.

Yet amid this rising darkness, Rudi did not stop. He could not. The urgency he carried in his bones refused to let him rest. Under the guise of academic diplomacy and archaeological outreach, he continued his travels—discreetly, methodically, as war tightened its grip on the continent.

His expeditions took him across the Atlantic and deep into the forgotten places of the Americas. He stood among the shattered ruins of Puma Punku in Bolivia, marveling at the impossible precision of its stonework, unmatched even by modern tools. He walked the silent terraces of Machu Picchu, where ancient structures seemed almost to hum with latent energy. He stood beneath the towering pyramids of Teotihuacan and Chichén Itzá, feeling as though the very air vibrated with old knowledge.

It was during these travels that the pieces began to converge—patterns hidden across continents, etched into stone and memory.

There were similarities too specific to be coincidence. Alignments of architecture with solstices and star clusters. Mythologies separated by oceans, all pointing to the same celestial timing. He saw carvings of cycles, spirals, and suns swallowed by darkness—echoes of what the archive had only hinted at. And it terrified him.

By the time he returned home, he was no longer a man seeking answers—he was a man carrying a warning.

Lost Knowledge

Rudi's face darkened, his features tightening as though the weight of centuries had settled onto his shoulders. He reached into the satchel again, carefully withdrawing a cloth-wrapped bundle and placing it on the table between them. With slow, reverent hands, he began to unwrap the layers, revealing a small, cracked stone tablet covered in strange geometric carvings and spiraling glyphs that shimmered faintly under the low lantern light.

"I managed to photograph and recover a handful of these tablets," he said, his voice tight with frustration, "along with some fragmented manuscripts. And I only got that far because I had full clearance and an open budget from the expedition commanders. They thought I was gathering material for state preservation archives." He shook his head. "They had no idea what I was really after."

He held up one of the tablets, running a finger over its carvings. "Here it is—written in stone. Celestial maps. And not just any stars—Orion, Sirius, the Pleiades; all marked with astonishing accuracy." He looked up, eyes sharp with disbelief. "How could they have mapped them with the naked eye? Thousands of years ago. Unless—" he paused, "unless they had help or remembered something we've forgotten.

"He exhaled, the breath escaping like steam in the chilled air. His hand hovered over the tablet for a moment, then slowly withdrew.

"But so much was lost, Johan. Centuries of knowledge—gone. When the Spanish arrived, they didn't just conquer the people—they tried to erase their entire legacy. They burned everything. Libraries, codices, maps, calendars, astronomical records; entire civilizations' memories turned to ash. The priests called them savages," he said bitterly. "But it was they who committed cultural genocide in the name of salvation."

Johan's hands curled into fists at his sides, his jaw clenched so tightly it ached. "Brutes," he spat. "Ignorant men, hiding behind belief."

Rudi gave a slow nod, eyes distant. "They believed they were saving souls. What they destroyed instead were the blueprints of the past. Imagine, Johan—imagine what we could have learned if even a fraction of those records had survived. We might have had diagrams, formulas, and step-by-step instructions on how these structures were built. Puma Punku, the Nazca Lines, the pyramids. They weren't just monuments. They were data, encoded in stone."

He shook his head. "Now, all we have left are fragments and whispers. Bits of oral tradition passed down by the indigenous peoples—stories that are often dismissed by modern scholars as folklore or myth."

"But myth is history distorted through memory," Johan murmured, almost to himself. "It's truth passed through fire and silence."

Rudi looked at him sharply, as if startled by the precision of the phrase. Then he nodded, solemn. "Exactly. And we've been treating it like poetry, when it might have been a warning all along."

Johan stepped closer to the table, eyes scanning the symbols on the tablet. He had seen many scripts in his time, but there was something about this one, something hauntingly familiar and utterly alien at once. "Do you think these inscriptions reference the Cycle?" he asked.

"I'm sure of it," Rudi said. "The symbology is nearly identical to what we found in the archive—spirals, conjunctions, astronomical references. There's even a repeated motif that matches the stone relief we discovered behind the sealed vault in Section Nine."

He paused. "And there's more. One of the rubbings—I'll show you in a moment—mentions a 'sky-borne cleansing flame.' Not in so many words, of course, but, it's unmistakable. Something from above. Destructive. Periodic."

Johan felt a chill settle into his spine. "So, it's true," he whispered. "The ancients weren't just building temples. They were building reminders. Stars observatories. Warnings. Clocks."

Rudi met his gaze, and for a long, heavy moment, neither man spoke. In that silence, beneath the earth, surrounded by forgotten histories and fragile hopes, they both understood something unspoken.

This wasn't just archaeology anymore. It was prophecy.

Johan looked over at Karl and Karin, who were quietly listening, their young minds processing every word. He saw the curiosity in Karl's eyes, the way he gripped his journal as if eager to write everything down.

Johan turned back to Rudi. "You said something about the Earth Rebirth theory. Do you think these ancient civilizations were destroyed in a past cataclysm?"

Rudi's expression grew even more serious. "I don't just think it—I'm certain of it. The evidence is everywhere. These ancient people weren't just building structures. They were safeguarding knowledge. Preparing for something."

Johan let that sink in. "And what do you think they were preparing for?"

Rudi hesitated. Then he finally said, "Another cycle. Another disaster. Something they knew would come again."

The room fell into silence once more. Outside, the distant sounds of the war-torn world continued. But inside, in that library bunker, two men, a boy, and a little girl sat surrounded by books and artifacts that whispered of a past long forgotten—and a future still uncertain.

CHAPTER 2

Synergistic Souls

arin was only three years old—barely tall enough to see over the edge of the table—yet already, she was being shaped by the same strict, disciplined tradition that had molded Johan's boy. In this household, excellence wasn't optional—it was expected, even for the youngest.

From her earliest days, Karin was immersed in the quiet but potent rituals of intellect and self-mastery: keeping a personal journal, absorbing knowledge like breath itself, and most of all, embracing the unshakable truth that information was not merely useful—it was power, distilled and alive.

But alongside these intellectual pursuits, there was another kind of teaching. A deeper, quieter one. A lesson unspoken but ever-present. It was something both children came to understand implicitly, a principle etched into their daily lives:

Loose lips sink ships.

It was more than a wartime slogan—it was a code. It meant discretion. It meant learning to keep things close to the chest. It meant knowing when to speak and, more importantly, when not to. It meant discipline of the tongue, an understanding that silence, when wielded deliberately, could be far more potent than any words.

Both children understood it, though in different ways. For Karl, Johan's son, the lesson was learned through trial and error, through the eager flapping of his young wings and the frequent need to be grounded again. He was a passionate learner, a curious boy with a mind that raced ahead of itself, constantly seeking more. Always more. He had an almost painful thirst for understanding, always reaching toward the next conversation, the next piece of insight. He was forever trying to leap into discussions that were just beyond his reach—adult topics, heavy ideas—armed with opinions that had not yet been sharpened by experience or tempered by caution.

And yet, Johan was patient. Firm, but patient. He guided Karl with steady hands and clear expectations. There were no raised voices, no punishments, only reminders. Consistent, unwavering reminders.

"Karl," Johan would say, his tone calm but resolute, "you have two ears and one mouth. What does that mean?"

The boy would lower his gaze, lips tightening with the weight of repetition. "Listen more and talk less," he'd reply, often with a trace of reluctance. He knew the answer well, but that didn't mean it always came easily.

Johan would nod, satisfied but not yet finished. He would lean in just slightly and add, "And when you do speak, make sure you've done your due diligence. Know your facts. Deliver them with surgical precision. Your words must be chosen, not spilled. They must mean something."

And so, Karl learned. Slowly, steadily. He began to speak less and observe more. He took in everything with sharp, intelligent eyes—absorbing, analyzing, cataloging. He became something like a little computer, storing facts and figures, replaying conversations in his mind. He kept notes, was careful and obsessive, returning to them in quiet hours the way other children clung to toys or picture books. He knew he was fortunate—privileged, even—to be raised in the company of two minds sharper than scalpels. To grow up in a home where intelligence was expected, honed, and praised.

Meanwhile, Karin lingered at the edges—too young to participate, too small to be of use—but her silence was anything but empty. It was alive with observation. She didn't need words to make her presence known; it was felt in the quiet intensity of her gaze, the way her eyes tracked every gesture, every shift in tone, every flicker of emotion.

Her vocabulary was still growing, and much of the conversation drifted beyond her grasp—but she understood something deeper. She felt the energy in the room. The weight. The gravity.

She watched Karl closely. She mirrored his posture, his habits, and the quiet intensity in the way he sat or scribbled or listened. She followed his lead, soaking up his reactions and responses as if by doing so she could learn the hidden language spoken by the grown-ups. She didn't fully grasp what was being said—not yet—but she knew that something important was happening. Something worth noticing. Something worth remembering.

And when Johan spoke with Rudi—when the two men engaged in their low, deliberate exchanges—Karin didn't just hear their words. She felt their weight. There was a kind of gravity in their tone, in the rhythm of their dialogue. A sense of seriousness that went deeper than the surface of language.

And Karin, with her wide, unblinking eyes and preternatural awareness, absorbed it all. Not in what was said. But in what was not.

Tragically, both Johan and Rudi had suffered the same devastating loss—each had lost his wife, just a few short years apart. It was a cruel symmetry of fate, a grief that echoed between them like a quiet, endless refrain. That shared sorrow, raw and deeply personal, had become a silent thread binding the two men even more tightly together. It wasn't the kind of grief that could be spoken about easily. It was too vast for words, too intimate for casual comfort. But it was understood—profoundly and without explanation—by those who had once loved fully and deeply, and who had then experienced the shattering emptiness of that love suddenly being torn away.

Their wives had not merely been companions or homemakers. They had been pillars—equal parts of the foundation upon which both family and purpose had been built. These women were not simply supportive figures in the background; they were architects of the very world Johan and Rudi had envisioned. Each had played a critical, irreplaceable role in raising the children, nurturing them with patience, strength, and wisdom. But beyond the walls of the home, they were also immersed in the work—contributing daily to the great unraveling of ancient mysteries, lending their voices to discussions that wove together science, history, philosophy, and instinct.

Their insights often bridged the gap between hard data and higher meaning. Where numbers faltered, their intuition prevailed. They brought clarity to the chaos, a warmth to the cold edges of logic. In every step of the journey, the women had been partners in the truest sense—essential, present, and brilliant.

When they were gone, the absence was more than emotional—it was structural. Without their steady hands and guiding presence, something in the world shifted, ever so slightly, like a compass just a few degrees off true north. Life continued, but the axis had tilted. The balance was disrupted.

In the face of that loss, Johan and Rudi responded the only way they knew how: they buried themselves in the work. In their research, in their daily routines, in the raising of the children left in their care. They clung to purpose as if it were the last remaining thread connecting them to the ones they had lost. And in doing so, they became something more than colleagues. More than old friends. More than battle-tested allies in a long and complex mission.

Together, they became an unshakable force in action, in heart, and in the unspoken commitment they made to carry on together. Their grief never disappeared. It didn't fade or heal in the way some might expect. Instead, it settled beneath the surface of their lives like a quiet river—always flowing, always present. But it became something else, too. A motivator. A fuel. A silent fire that propelled them forward. Every problem they solved, every ancient secret they uncovered, every lesson they passed on to young Karl and little Karin, was done in memory of those who were no longer there.

Each achievement, no matter how small, was a kind of offering. A tribute. A whispered promise that what had been lost would not be forgotten. And that, somehow, in the act of continuing, of building, of believing, something might yet be recovered.
Not the past. But perhaps the future.

Something new. Something fragile. Something worth hoping for.

Karl and Karin had little say in the matter—their paths were chosen for them long before they could form the words to protest. Born into a world governed by relentless intellect and rigid discipline, they were swept into their fathers' unyielding pursuit of truth from the very beginning. Their upbringing was structured down to the minute, demanding in every sense—mentally, emotionally, and physically exhausting. No moment was wasted, no time unaccounted for. Every hour of the day had a purpose, and that purpose was growth, improvement, mastery.

There was no room for whimsy or idle wandering. Spontaneity was frowned upon. Rest was not a right, it was an occasional allowance, granted only when every task had been completed to perfection. Leisure, as other children knew it—lazy afternoons, spontaneous games, unstructured joy—was a foreign concept. In Karl and Karin's world, life was a curriculum, and the standards were impossibly high.

Their lives were shaped by expectation, chiseled by the high-pressure mold created by the men who raised them. Johan and Rudi weren't cruel, they were committed. But their commitment demanded sacrifice, and for the children, that meant childhood itself was something they observed more than lived.

And yet, somewhere in the midst of the endless books, philosophical debates, historical deep dives, and scientific breakdowns, Karl and Karin discovered an unexpected release valve—an outlet that was entirely their own: martial arts.

It began almost as an experiment, a physical counterbalance to all the mental strain. Johan often reminded them, with quiet conviction, "The body is like a machine. Maintain it well, and it will serve you longer—and better."

At first, training felt like another obligation, another form of discipline. But soon, it became something far more personal. More than physical exercise, it turned into a sanctuary—a quiet rebellion against the constraints of their world. A source of strength not handed down from above but forged from within.

For Karl, this transformation began through an old family friend—a reclusive but revered Asian professor who had been close to their circle for generations. It was through this man that Karl was first introduced to the ancient art of Jiu-Jitsu—a discipline rooted in control, leverage, and the strategic dance of grappling. At first, Karl floundered. His mind, so used to clear logic, linear steps, and absolute answers, struggled to adapt to the fluid, unpredictable nature of combat. Jiu-Jitsu was improvisational, instinctive. It demanded surrender before mastery.

But something in it called him. It was, in its own way, a puzzle—one where the pieces moved, adapted, resisted. The more Karl trained, the more he realized it wasn't a departure from his intellectual world, it was an extension of it. A different language for the same principles: precision, timing, calculated execution. Discipline became a form of meditation. A conversation between bodies. A space where thought and motion were indistinguishable.

Karin, on the other hand, was drawn to something rawer. Simpler. Cleaner. Where Jiu-Jitsu was intricate and technical, Kickboxing offered her clarity. Power. Directness.

Her mentor was a kickboxing champion from Brooklyn, New York—a man of African descent whose reputation preceded him, whose presence could still a room. Tall and agile, he was an intimidating figure with muscles like steel. He didn't deal in riddles or theory; he was blunt, disciplined, and demanded everything. Karin respected him deeply for it.

His world was easy to understand; you landed your punch, or you didn't. You protected yourself, or you got hit. No pretense. No room for overthinking.

In Kickboxing, she found herself. There was something cathartic in the rhythm—gloves striking mitts, roundhouse kicks thudding against the heavy bag. It was action stripped of explanation. No philosophical tangents. No debates. Just sweat, grit, and the pursuit of power honed into precision.

As time passed, what had begun as extracurricular became essential. Martial arts no longer sat beside their academic training—it stood shoulder to shoulder with it. Both Karl and Karin trained obsessively, often well past exhaustion. Though they pursued different disciplines, their journeys became interwoven. They met in the middle—sparring, drilling, trading knowledge.

Karl taught Karin the nuanced world of grappling: how to feel for shifts in weight, how to exploit leverage, how to remain calm while twisted in a chokehold. Karin, in return, schooled him in footwork, in pacing, in the explosive clarity of a jab placed at exactly the right moment. She showed him how one second of distraction could end a fight—and how rhythm could disarm as effectively as brute strength.

Their sessions grew more intense with every passing year. What began in childhood matured into something sharp and undeniable. They tested each other constantly, sometimes to the brink of frustration, sometimes to the edge of injury. Bruises came and went like badges. Failure was frequent, but never final. They pushed each other because they knew no one else could. They understood each other in a way no one else could.

By the time adolescence arrived, their training had birthed something entirely their own. They were no longer just practitioners of Jiu-Jitsu or Kickboxing. They were something hybrid. Adaptable.

Karl could bring Karin to the mat with a well-timed take-down—only to find himself caught in one of her calculated traps seconds later.

Karin could slip past Karl's punches, just out of reach—only to be snared by his counter with surgical precision.

They had become each other's greatest rival—and most trusted partner. Bound not just by destiny and circumstance, but by effort. By sweat. By the deeply shared truth that here, in this sacred physical space, they were free.

Martial arts gave them more than skill—it gave them themselves. In a world shaped by others' expectations, this was the one realm where they got to decide who they were, moment by moment, strike by strike.

Their fathers may have shaped their intellects, may have forged their minds in fire—but it was through combat, through movement, through pain and perseverance, that Karl and Karin forged something stronger still: an identity of their own.

CHAPTER 3

Celestial Bond

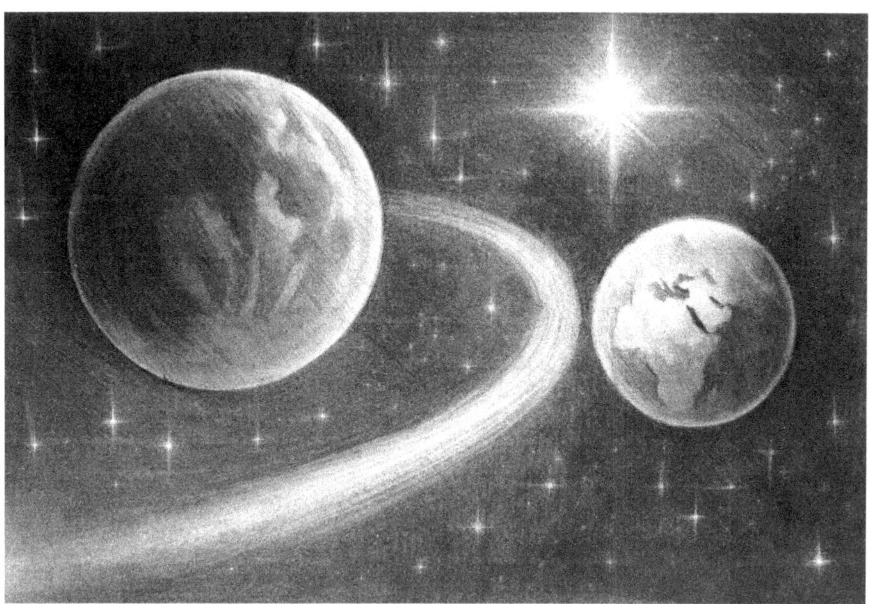

The Rosens and Fischers had always suspected that the conventional narrative of human civilization was incomplete—if not entirely misleading. Their years of studying ancient texts, cross-referencing myths, and analyzing archaeological anomalies had convinced them that a more profound truth lay buried beneath layers of accepted history. But it wasn't until Rudi Fischer's latest discovery that they realized just how deep this mystery ran.

While pacing through the room, Johan mentioned, "You ever think about how far back civilization actually goes?"

Rudi looked up from his notes and responded with a grin, "You mean beyond the Romans and the Greeks? Way before that?"

Johan nodded enthusiastically. "Exactly. I'm talking ancient Mesopotamia. The Sumerians."

Rudi leaned against the table, intrigued. "Ah yes, the Sumerians. That name always pops up when you trace the roots of human history. They were real pioneers, weren't they?"

With a sparkle in his eye, Johan walked over to the bookshelf. "Absolutely. The Sumerians were among the first to build actual cities—Uruk, Ur, Eridu. We're talking about the southern part of Mesopotamia, in what is now modern-day Iraq."

Rudi poured himself a glass of wine, nodding. "Right there between the Tigris and Euphrates rivers. Fertile Crescent territory. That's why it's often called the cradle of civilization."

"Exactly," Johan said as he turned back, holding a dusty old book. "And what makes them really stand out is how advanced they were—cuneiform writing, organized religion, even early legal systems."

"And don't forget ziggurats," Rudi added, smiling. "Those massive temple towers. They weren't just buildings—they were symbols of order, of their connection to the divine."

Johan chuckled. "And to think, they were doing this over 4,000 years ago. Farming, trading, even studying the stars."

"People often forget just how sophisticated they were," Rudi said, now flipping through a journal. "They weren't just early settlers; they were the architects of civilization."

Johan nodded solemnly. "Exactly. And studying them reminds us that the roots of modern society go much deeper than most realize."

While setting down his satchel, Johan glanced over with a curious joking smile. "So? Did you bring anything back from Uruk this time, or are you still hoarding the good stuff for the museums?"

Rudi chuckled, pulling out a sealed envelope. "Let's just say . . . the desert has spoken again."

Johan raised an eyebrow. "More tablets?"

"Thousands," Rudi said, removing his coat and draping it over the chair. "Uruk, Nippur, Nineveh—we found layers of clay tablets beneath the ruins. Entire archives, intact. Not fragments. Complete records."

Johan stood, now visibly animated. "You're serious? Intact tablets from Mesopotamia? Cuneiform?"

"Yes," Rudi said, his voice even. "Authentic, ancient, and densely inscribed. Reed styluses into soft clay. When we cleaned the first few, the wedge shapes leapt off the surface like something alive."

Johan poured them each a glass of wine, pacing slowly. "We've had Sumerian tablets before—dozens in private collections, museums. What makes this different?"

Rudi accepting his second glass of wine. "Volume. Scope. Variety. These aren't just ledgers or receipts. They're a full record of Sumerian civilization: trade, taxes, law, marriage, agriculture— even celestial movements. It's like opening the operating system of the ancient world."

Johan settled into the armchair. "So we're not just talking about bookkeeping. We're talking about memory."

Rudi nodded. "Collective memory. We have legal contracts outlining land boundaries, dowries, civil disputes. But next to those—poems, myths, even philosophical reflections."

Johan leaned forward. "Gilgamesh?"

"Of course," Rudi said. "The Epic was there—complete and legible. His journey, his grief, his desperate plea for immortality— it's all there. These weren't dry records; they were meditations on death, life, and meaning."

He took a sip of wine, then added, "That's what stunned me. They weren't simply writing to record—they were writing to remember."

Johan smiled thoughtfully. "So writing wasn't just invented for administration. It was for identity."

"Exactly," Rudi said. "Cuneiform didn't start that way, but it evolved. From pictographs to abstraction, it became the medium through which the Sumerians preserved their cosmos."

"And how old are we talking?" Johan asked, now cross-legged, eyes shining with curiosity.

"Earliest forms date to around 3400 BCE," Rudi replied. "Before the pyramids, before Mycenae, long before Rome or Greece. We're not just pushing back timelines—we're redefining the birth of civilization."

Johan glanced over to a display shelf where a single clay replica sat beneath glass. "That puts everything into perspective, doesn't it?"

"Absolutely," Rudi said. "It's the transition from prehistory to history. Before cuneiform, there were only stories passed by voice. After it—written law, written myth, written thought."

Johan stood, walking slowly toward the fireplace. "And the religious texts? What did they show?"

"A society obsessed with cosmic balance," Rudi said, voice lowering. "It's so interesting, they catalogued these mysterious deities they call the Anunnaki as gods, you've heard of them, right? Enlil, god of air and sovereignty; Enki, water and wisdom; Inanna, love and war. Each deity bound to nature and human behavior." He paused. "Their stories weren't entertainment. They were written as blueprints for reality. So, I think. Back then, it wasn't as easy as just grabbing a pen and pencil—they went through a lot of work to record what they thought was important." Johan nodded slowly. "Yes, good point. I always found Inanna's descent into the netherworld fascinating. Stripped of power, judged by gods more ancient than her."

"The Anunnaki," Rudi said. "They appear throughout the texts. Not just gods, Johan—cosmic arbiters. Their name literally means 'those who came from heaven to Earth.'"

Johan turned sharply. "Wait, I've heard that exact phrasing in Andean cosmology."

"You're right," Rudi said. "The Quechua and Aymara speak of beings from the sky—tall, radiant, otherworldly. Viracocha and his companions. It's uncanny."

Johan looked intrigued. "Do you think they're the same?"

"Not necessarily the same beings," Rudi replied, "but perhaps the same archetype. Divine intelligences, descending to shape humanity. The parallels are too precise to ignore."

Johan rubbed his chin. "So, what was the Anunnaki's actual role?"

Rudi stepped forward. "In Sumerian cosmology, they weren't just observers. They maintained the cosmic order—life, death, fertility, war. They judged the dead. They assigned destiny. Even kings claimed divine authority through them."

"Divine mandate," Johan muttered. "Still a popular idea, just dressed differently."

Rudi smiled. "And their influence wasn't symbolic. Ziggurats were built in their name—towering temples that served as religious and political hubs."

"E-Kur in Nippur, right?" Johan recalled. "That was Enlil's temple?"

"Yes," Rudi said. "The House of the Mountain. Believed to be the literal link between heaven and earth. Where kings were crowned by divine right."

He continued, now animated. "E-Abzu, dedicated to Enki in Eridu—constructed near water, symbolizing the freshwater abyss.

E-Anna for Inanna in Uruk—massive, ornate, filled with sacred courtyards and marriage rituals."

Johan raised his glass. "The sacred marriage. King and goddess, merging to legitimize rule."

"Exactly," Rudi said. "Every ritual held cosmic weight. Nothing was arbitrary."

"And Anu?" Johan asked. "He seems more distant."

Rudi nodded. "Supreme sky god. His temple, E-Sharra, also in Uruk. Less described in later texts, but foundational. His authority was absolute, encompassing all the heavens."

"What about the underworld?" Johan asked.

"Nergal's temple—E-Meslam in Kutha," Rudi replied. "God of war and the dead. His rites governed funeral practices. They believed he secured the soul's passage beyond."

"And Shamash?" Johan prompted.

"Two temples," Rudi said, "E-Ulmas in Sippar and E-Babbar in Larsa. Sun god and god of justice. Both temples acted as court centers—priests interpreted omens, settled disputes, invoked divine judgment."

Johan looked impressed. "So they didn't separate law from religion."

"They couldn't," Rudi said. "Even the Code of Ur-Nammu—the earliest known codified law—was divine in origin. It wasn't just legislation. It was cosmology made civic."

He continued, "Nanna's temples in Ur, like E-Mash and E-Gipar, tied lunar cycles to agriculture and timekeeping. One was home to the high priestess, who served as celestial mediator."

Johan raised a brow. "And Ningal?"

"E-Kishnugal," Rudi said with a small smile. "Ningal was Nanna's consort. Fertility and reeds. Her temple in Ur oversaw planting festivals—prayers for harvest, health, the continuation of life."

Johan exhaled deeply. "It's staggering. A society so ancient, yet so sophisticated. Structured. Introspective."

"They left nothing to chance," Rudi said. "The written word allowed them to systematize the world. They gave humanity its first true legacy—language, law, literature, myth. And the means to remember it all."

As thunder rolled softly in the distance, Johan adjusted the reading lamp over his desk, the golden light illuminating a cuneiform tablet. "These Sumerian tablets," he murmured, "they're more than just myth—they're the foundation of everything that came after."

Rudi glanced up from a stack of translated texts and replied, "They really are. We're talking about the oldest known written records of human creation, predating even the Babylonian *Enuma Elish by* centuries."

Johan nodded slowly. "Most of them come from cities like Nippur, Uruk, Eridu—heartlands of ancient Sumer. These weren't just religious texts; they were cosmologies, blueprints for how people understood life, gods, and themselves."

Rudi tapped gently on the edge of a clay tablet cast. "The Oxford Museum's translation project uncovered some fascinating details. Their work on the tablets stored at the Ashmolean and British Museums gave us new insights. The translations—meticulous and layered—speak of divine councils, genetic crafting, celestial interventions. It's not just symbolic; it feels procedural."

Johan looked intrigued. "You mean the creation myths read like technical documentation?"

"Exactly," Rudi said. "Take the *Eridu Genesis*—one of the oldest known creation stories, written in Sumerian cuneiform around 1600 BCE but based on even older oral traditions. It tells of a time when the gods decided to fashion mankind to serve them—to maintain their temples, work the land, bring offerings. Not out of malice, but necessity."

Johan turned a page in his notes. "And according to the myth, it was the Anunnaki—particularly Enki and Ninhursag—who undertook the act of creating humans, wasn't it?"

"Right," Rudi affirmed. "According to several translated fragments, Enki mixed divine blood with clay—the symbolic fusion of heaven and earth—to create the *lulu amelu*, the 'mixed man.' It's a recurring theme: man as a hybrid being, part celestial, part terrestrial."

He paused thoughtfully, then added, "There's even reference to failed attempts before the final version. Early humans who couldn't speak, couldn't function, or died quickly. It reads like a trial-and-error process. It's eerily specific."

Johan leaned back in his chair, visibly shaken but intrigued. "So the Anunnaki weren't just abstract gods. They were hands-on creators, engineers, planners."

"Exactly. And the tablets don't shy away from showing conflict among the gods about this process," Rudi said. "Enlil was against creating humans altogether. Saw them as noisy, reckless. Enki argued for them—saw their potential. Ninhursag intervened as a healer, correcting the flaws in early prototypes."

Johan furrowed his brow. "The Oxford translations even include hymns to Ninhursag where she's called the 'Mother of All Living.' That's not just mythological poetry—it implies a role as a biological originator."

Rudi nodded. "And when you compare these with later traditions, like the Biblical Genesis, you start noticing eerie parallels—man formed from earth, divine breath animating clay, a paradise-like garden, a forbidden knowledge, a fall from grace."

"The Sumerians had it all first," Johan said quietly. "Thousands of years before Moses or Genesis." Rudi smiled slightly. "And they recorded it all in cuneiform, on tablets that sat buried beneath ruins for millennia. Tablets like the ones the Oxford teams are still deciphering today. Every season brings new fragments—new revelations." Johan rose, walked over to the table where a tablet sat under glass. "It makes you wonder," he said. "If the story of human origin we've inherited is only the latest version. A retelling of a much older narrative."

"A narrative where gods weren't just watching from the heavens," Rudi said, "but walking the earth, arguing, building, even going to war—shaping our species in the process."

The room fell silent for a moment as the two scholars stared at the clay tablet, its markings etched with the quiet power of millennia.

Finally, Johan spoke. "We call them myths. But what if they're memories?"

Rudi's eyes gleamed in the dim light. "Then humanity may be far older—and far stranger—than we've ever imagined." He raises his glass, then added quietly, "We think of them as the distant past. But really, it sounds more like they're the beginning."

Johan clinked his glass gently against Rudi's. "To the ones who began it all."

Rudi met his gaze. "And to those still listening . . . wait! Does that mean that we humans are part god?"

Johan looked at Rudi sarcastically and replied, "Well, cheers to our divinity then—and to Dionysus, or Bacchus, for providing humans with wine!"

Both men laughed out loud.

CHAPTER 4
Assembling the Unknown

The room breathed warmth, steeped in the scent of dry wood and the quiet symphony of crackling logs. The fireplace whispered in its hearth, weaving light and shadow like a slow, familiar lullaby. Rudi Fisher stands near a tall bookshelf, clutching a cuneiform tablet. Johan Rosen sits at a large wooden table, scribbling notes in a weathered notebook. Piles of clay tablets, scattered documents, and ancient maps surround them. As Johan opens a bottle of wine, Rudi fetches the glasses, and the two men begin to do what they enjoy most; debating new research discoveries.

Rudi pacing. "We've spent a massive number of hours reconstructing fragments of Sumerian history, piecing together myths and religious texts. And now—this. A complete creation narrative. Not symbolic, not fragmented—but precise. That could change everything."

Johan adjusted his glasses, setting down his notebook. "But that's what troubles me. Myths evolve. They get distorted, filtered through generations of storytellers. But this is set in stone, well . . . clay and from the cradle of the first civilization, the linguistic consistency, the mathematical references, even the cosmological details—this was recorded with scientific accuracy. That's not normal for an ancient myth."

Rudi turning toward Johan. "Unless it wasn't a myth. Unless it was a transmission of knowledge—knowledge so advanced it could only be preserved through sacred texts. You saw the alignment of the star maps—those positions match modern calculations almost exactly. How could they have known that without advanced instrumentation?"

Johan sharply. "That's exactly what I'm saying! Either they were astonishingly ahead of their time, or the Sumerians weren't working alone. And if the Anunnaki were involved—if they were celestial beings with access to superior technology, then we must reconsider the very nature of early human civilization."

Rudi leaning forward. "You know what this means, don't you? The Sumerians didn't simply start civilization; they inherited it, sounds more like they were custom designed to exist and evolve. And in that case, the Anunnaki may have shaped human society from the very beginning. If you think about it, the leap from hunter-gatherer tribes to complex urban centers—it's suspiciously fast. Too fast."

Johan nodding. "Yes, it's the single greatest anomaly in human history. Agriculture, writing, metalworking, and monumental architecture—each emerging within a few centuries. That's statistically implausible unless some external force accelerated the process. The tablets make it clear: the Anunnaki weren't just mythological guides—they were engineers."

Rudi quietly. "Engineers of what, though? Human civilization or human biology?"

Johan pausing. "I would say both. The creation tablet mentions the Anunnaki molding humanity from clay—but it's more detailed than any other myth. It refers to "essence" extracted from the blood of the gods. That sounds like more than a metaphor. Genetic manipulation?"

Rudi eyes narrowing. "That would explain the repeated references to "perfecting the vessel." It wasn't just about creating life—it was about modifying it. Shaping it. Selectively breeding it. But for what purpose?"

Johan rubbing his temple. "That's the question. Were they trying to create a servant species? Or a reflection of themselves? The tablet speaks of humanity as a "hybrid creation"—divine essence mixed with terrestrial matter. But if the Anunnaki intended to create a subservient race, why grant us so much intelligence?"

Rudi grimly. "Because intelligence makes for better instruments. They gave us just enough self-awareness to survive and serve them—but not enough to challenge them. That's why the creation narrative ends with the Anunnaki withdrawing from human affairs. The moment humanity became self-aware enough to question its purpose—the gods vanished."

Johan narrowing his eyes. "Or were driven out. The texts also mention a "great conflict in the heavens." What if it wasn't a symbolic war among gods—but a literal one? A celestial conflict that forced the Anunnaki to abandon Earth?"

Rudi darkly. "And left us with the remnants of their knowledge. That's why the Sumerians were so advanced—they weren't starting from scratch. They were reconstructing what was left behind. And what's more dangerous than incomplete knowledge?"

Johan sitting back. "That would explain why the tablets were hidden so carefully. Whoever buried them wasn't trying to preserve knowledge—they were trying to protect it from misuse. Perhaps even from us."

Rudi pacing. "But why protect it? Unless the knowledge itself is dangerous. The descriptions of the "sky chariots"—they're not just poetic embellishments. The texts describe mechanical details—propulsion systems, complex navigation patterns. That sounds an awful lot like advanced technology."

Johan voice tightening. "You're suggesting the Anunnaki left behind not just knowledge—but technology?"

Rudi turning sharply. "Yes. And that means it might still be out there. If we're rediscovering this knowledge now, it's possible someone—or something—is guiding that rediscovery."

Johan quietly. "Or preparing us for their return."

(A long silence stretches between them. The low flicker of lamplight dances over the clay tablets.)

Johan breaking the silence. "The real question is, why now? Why are we finding these tablets at this precise moment in human history?"

Rudi staring into the middle distance. "Because humanity has reached the threshold. Genetic engineering, artificial intelligence, quantum computing—we're starting to replicate the very capabilities the Anunnaki bestowed upon us."

Johan lowering his voice. "Or perhaps we've reached the point where we can either transcend or destroy ourselves. The Anunnaki may have seen this pattern before. Civilizations reaching too far, too fast. Perhaps that's why they left."

Rudi turning toward Johan. "Or perhaps they didn't leave at

all. Perhaps they're watching. Waiting. To see if we are worthy to inherit the knowledge they left behind".

Johan shaking his head. "Or waiting to intervene if we prove ourselves unworthy."

Rudi with a cold smile. "Maybe that's why the creation story is so detailed. It's not just history, it's a blueprint. A set of instructions. And we're following it, step by step. The final stage may not be creation—but reunion."

(The two men sit in silence as the weight of this possibility settles over them. Red wine stains mark the table as both men finish the bottle. The clay tablets on the table seem to hum with quiet energy—a whisper from the ancient past.)

Johan softly. "So, what do we do now?"

Rudi darkly. "We keep reading. We find the missing pieces. And we prepare for the day the sky chariots return."

As the sun dipped behind the hills, Johan stepped away from his desk, the flickering lamplight casting long shadows across ancient maps and printed tablets.

While unrolling a newly received transcript, Johan murmured, "At the heart of these records, they find the principal Anunnaki deities—Anu, Enki, Enlil, Ninhursag and Inanna—each playing a pivotal role in shaping the destinies of early human civilizations."

He paused at a highlighted section and read aloud with quiet reverence, "Anu (An): The supreme deity of the sky, Anu was regarded as the father of the gods and the progenitor of the Anunnaki. His authority encompassed the overarching structure of the cosmos, and he was often depicted as a distant yet omnipotent figure."

Rudi, peering over Johan's shoulder, added, "Enki, also known as Ea, was the god of wisdom, water, and creation. He was considered a benefactor to humanity, often depicted as the one who bestowed knowledge and enlightenment. In the myths, Enki was seen as a friend of humankind, secretly warning Ziusudra about the Great Flood and teaching humans the secrets of agriculture and writing."

Johan turned another page and continued thoughtfully, "Enlil, on the other hand, was the god of wind, storms, and authority. Unlike Enki, he was often portrayed as a strict enforcer of divine will, sometimes favoring destruction over mercy. According to ancient texts, it was Enlil who ultimately decided to wipe out humanity in the Great Deluge, viewing them as an unruly and overpopulated species."

Rudi pointed to a nearby illustration. "Ninhursag (Ki): As the earth goddess and mother figure, Ninhursag was associated with fertility and the nurturing aspects of nature. She played a crucial role in creation myths and was revered as a protector of life."

Tracing a line of cuneiform with his finger, Johan added, "Inanna, also known as Ishtar, was the goddess of love, war, and fertility. She was a complex figure—both a divine protector and a fearsome warrior. Her influence stretched beyond Mesopotamia into later cultures such as the Phoenicians and the Babylonians, where she was worshiped under different names."

Rudi leaned back in his chair and reflected, "Furthermore, the tablets described the tension between Enki and Enlil, which became one of the defining conflicts in ancient Anunnaki history, a struggle that shaped the destiny of human civilizations and turned them into a raging war."

Later that night, as Johan skimmed a new section, his voice lowered with intrigue. "As Johan delved deeper into the tablets, he uncovered references to a time of great strife among the Anunnaki—an era now known as the Pyramid Wars. This was no mere myth; it was described as a period of fierce battles fought over the control of Earth's most sacred sites, including the pyramids, which were said to be powerful energy hubs or advanced technological structures."

He looked up as if to gauge Rudi's reaction before continuing, "The wars were primarily between Enki's faction, which sought to coexist with humanity, and Enlil's forces, which believed in strict dominion over humans. Some accounts suggested that Inanna played a pivotal role, shifting alliances depending on which side offered her the greatest power. The battles were said to have been fought with devastating weapons, described in ways eerily similar to modern nuclear or energy-based weaponry."

Rudi, staring into the fire, nodded gravely. "Ancient Egyptian and Mesopotamian texts even reference a 'great storm' that spread death and destruction—a possible remnant of this ancient war. Some researchers have speculated that the environmental and societal collapses of the time were direct results of these conflicts."

Johan tapped the edge of a clay tablet reproduction and said, "A recurring motif etched into the lamentation texts stood out like a dark beacon: the 'Evil Wind.' Described with chilling clarity, it was said to be a deathly cloud that rolled in from the west, bringing with it an invisible but inescapable doom. Its touch was lethal— humans collapsed where they stood, clutching their throats as their lungs filled with poisoned air. Crops withered under a sickly sky. The waters turned foul and undrinkable, carrying the stench of decay."

He slowly read from one translated passage:

"The day turned to night.
The wind screamed across the land.
Men and women fell where they stood,
Their breath stolen, their blood thickened.
The rivers wept black tears.
And the gods were silent."

Rudi spoke quietly, the words heavy in the air. "Archaeological evidence aligns with this tale of devastation. The sudden collapse of the Sumerian civilization around 2024 BCE coincides eerily with the timeline suggested by these texts. Entire cities were abandoned, their streets strewn with the desiccated remains of their inhabitants. The few survivors who managed to escape wrote of a poisonous mist that clung to the earth for weeks, killing even the hardiest livestock and leaving the land barren for generations."

Johan closed his notebook slowly. "He couldn't shake the sense that the 'Evil Wind' was more than just a metaphor for plague or natural disaster. Could it have been the result of a weapon—something unleashed either by the Anunnaki themselves or by forces beyond their control? Or was it the consequence of an even greater cosmic reckoning—a last, violent gasp from a dying world?"

He shook his head. "The texts provided no clear answers, only fragments of despair and confusion. But one thing was certain: the Anunnaki's departure was not a peaceful farewell. It was an exodus born of desperation—and perhaps, fear."

Rudi turned the page with a slow, deliberate motion. "One of the most shocking revelations hidden within these ancient texts was the destruction of cities that defied the gods. Among them, Sodom and Gomorrah stand out as prime examples."

Johan stood, reading aloud with urgency now. "The biblical account describes these cities as having been wiped out by 'fire and brimstone' raining from the sky—language that could be interpreted as an ancient description of an advanced weapon. The Sumerian tablets parallel this story, but with a twist: they attribute the destruction to the Anunnaki, specifically Enlil, who deemed the cities corrupted beyond redemption."

He pointed to a scientific note in the margin. "Johan found striking evidence suggesting that these cities had been annihilated in an explosion of unprecedented force. Some modern archaeologists have noted the presence of a layer of glass-like substance in the region, which only forms under extreme heat—similar to what happens after a nuclear detonation. Could this be evidence of an ancient war involving weapons of mass destruction wielded by the Anunnaki?"

Rudi, clearly intrigued, flipped to another section. "As Johan explored further, another mysterious site emerged in his research—the ancient city of Mohenjo-Daro, one of the greatest settlements of the Indus Valley Civilization. It was abandoned under enigmatic circumstances, and the ruins told a tale eerily similar to Sodom and Gomorrah."

He scanned a photo. "Excavations revealed skeletal remains scattered in the streets, suggesting that whatever calamity befell the city struck with sudden and overwhelming force. Many of these remains were found lying face down, as if their inhabitants had been caught in an instant of destruction. Even more astonishing was the discovery of vitrified stones—structures that had been exposed to extreme heat, fusing them into glass-like material. Modern scientists have struggled to explain this phenomenon, as the temperatures required to produce such an effect exceed anything that could have been achieved through ancient warfare or natural disasters."

Johan leaned closer, voice barely above a whisper. "Some researchers have drawn parallels between the fate of Mohenjo-Daro and the accounts of the Pyramid Wars, theorizing that the city may have been another casualty of these conflicts. Was it targeted by an advanced weapon, similar to those described in the destruction of Sodom and Gomorrah? Did the

Anunnaki, or their adversaries, unleash a force so powerful that it obliterated one of the most sophisticated cities of its time?"

They both sat in silence, staring at the image of the deserted ruins.

Finally, Rudi spoke. "The eerie silence of Mohenjo-Daro, its deserted streets and inexplicable destruction, raised chilling questions. If Johan's research was correct, then the evidence of ancient, highly advanced weaponry was not confined to the Middle East—it spanned across civilizations, revealing a hidden chapter of history that mainstream scholars had yet to acknowledge."

He tapped an artifact image gently. "While there is no definitive evidence directly linking the ancient city of Mohenjo-Daro from the Indus Valley Civilization to the Mesopotamian goddess Inanna, certain artifacts suggest possible cultural interactions or shared motifs between these ancient civilizations."

He continued, pointing to a seal replica. "One notable artifact from Mohenjo-Daro is a seal depicting a deity that bears resemblance to representations of Inanna, the Mesopotamian goddess associated with love, fertility, and war. This similarity has led some scholars to propose potential cultural exchanges or parallel religious iconography between the Indus Valley and Mesopotamian civilizations."

Johan added, flipping to another annotated page, "Additionally, certain seals from the Indus Valley Civilization display motifs reminiscent of Mesopotamian themes, such as figures in dynamic interactions with animals, which are characteristic of the 'Master of Animals' motif found in Mesopotamian art. These parallels suggest a possible transmission of artistic or religious concepts between the two cultures."

Rudi leaned forward, eyes fixed on the map. "Whatever the truth, the echoes of their stories stretch further than we ever imagined."

CHAPTER 5

Duel of Minds

The bunker is darker now. The oil lanterns flicker, casting long shadows over the ancient texts and tablets scattered across the table. Dust floats in the dim light. Johan and Rudi sit across from each other, tension hanging heavy in the air.

Rudi, running his fingers over a stone tablet. "This is more than just a creation story, Johan. It's a record of their departure—a calculated, deliberate withdrawal. And we both know you've been thinking it too."

Johan, leaning back, eyes narrowing. "Thinking what exactly?"

Rudi, voice lowering. "That they didn't leave because they had to. They left because they wanted to."

Johan, shaking his head. "That's speculation. You're ignoring the physical evidence. The texts also mention the rapid aging problem, the changes in Earth's atmosphere, the possibility of radiation exposure—it would explain why they couldn't stay."

Rudi, sharply. "Then why did they stay for so long? If the atmosphere was hostile to them, why linger long enough to engineer human society, build monumental structures, and pass down advanced astronomical knowledge? They didn't just survive here, they thrived. Until they didn't."

(Johan stands and walks to a nearby shelf, pulling down a worn volume filled with rough sketches of ancient symbols.)

Johan, opening the book. "Look at this. Sumerian. But this symbol here—it matches carvings found in Bolivia. And this one— Peru."

Rudi, leaning over the table. "A shared origin."

Johan, takes a deep breath. "Or shared contact. The 'sky chariots' described in the texts—they aren't just a Sumerian motif. The Egyptians recorded similar vessels in the Temple of Seti. The Dogon tribe in Mali described amphibious beings descending from the sky in luminous ships. The Hopi legends speak of Kachinas— divine messengers from the stars. It's the same story retold across continents and centuries."

Rudi, voice low. "Then it's not just about Sumer. It's about the entire planet. They didn't guide one civilization—they shaped the foundations of human society."

Johan, carefully. "Which means the Anunnaki weren't experimenting with just one species. They may have been influencing multiple genetic lines. Different human prototypes created for different environments."

(Rudi steps back, processing the implications.)

Rudi, quietly. "So, humanity isn't the product of natural selection. We're a design?"

Johan, softly. "An engineered species. Adapted to help them rule Earth. But the question remains—why would they create us and then leave?"

Rudi, darkly. "Unless that was the point. They seeded the planet, supervised it until it flourished and then they left. In biblical terms: *'Blessed are the meek, for they shall inherit the Earth.'*"

Johan, scoffing. "Come on, Rudi, now you're pushing it. That's not what that phrase means."

Rudi, grinning. "Sure, it might be the wine talking" (*both men finally burst into laughter*) but what if we, as a society, have been misinterpreting the meaning all along—for lack of knowledge?"

Deciphering the Mathematical Sequences

The discovery that the ancient inscriptions contained intricate mathematical sequences—rather than simple phonetic text—marked another pivotal breakthrough in their research.

The Sumerians were renowned for their sexagesimal (base-60) system—an innovation that still underpins modern concepts of time and geometry. But the mathematical patterns embedded within these tablets revealed a complexity that far surpassed mere arithmetic or calendrical logic. They followed a deliberate, precise order—suggesting not simple records, but a form of coded language or encryption, designed for minds fluent in higher mathematics.

Even more astounding was the nature of these patterns: complex ratios, prime numbers, and geometric alignments that mirrored astronomical cycles. This pointed to a profound understanding not just of mathematics, but of celestial mechanics. The implication was staggering—were these sequences meant to be understood by beings already fluent in such advanced knowledge? Did the Sumerians inherit their mathematical genius from the Anunnaki themselves?

The sophistication of the data hinted at an intelligence operating on a level far beyond what early human societies should have possessed. As Johan continued decoding the structure within the inscriptions, he began to suspect the tablets weren't merely repositories of knowledge—but messages. Communications. Possibly even instructions, encoded in the universal language of numbers.

It was a revelation that shifted the scope of their work. The implications no longer belonged solely to history—they now touched the fabric of the cosmos itself.

A dimly lit underground research chamber. Pale shadows flickered across a vast table cluttered with clay tablets, astronomical charts, and scribbled equations. Johan and Rudi had been debating through the night. The wine was gone, replaced by steaming coffee and the hum of sleepless energy. Scattered papers and cuneiform fragments littered the space between them. The air was thick with discovery.

Rudi, holding up a tablet, eyes narrowed. "Now check this one out. This isn't just a star map. The patterns—look at the orbital sequences. These alignments aren't random. They follow the precession of the equinoxes. Whoever made this understood not just the Earth's cycles—but the long- term motion of the solar system itself."

Johan, tracing his finger across a sketched copy. "The precision is astounding. Thousands of years before the Babylonians began charting planets, the Sumerians were calculating axial tilt and orbital drift. That kind of accuracy implies consistent, long-term observation. But more importantly—it implies technology. Instruments. Tools we've never found."

Rudi, darkly. "Or tools they didn't want us to find."

(Johan steps to a shelf and retrieves a fragment etched with faint geometric patterns.)

Johan, quietly. "This piece; the symbols match the spacing between constellations recorded on the Planisphere. But the sequence—it repeats. Like a course correction."

Rudi, looking up. "A course correction?"

Johan, nodding. "Yes. These aren't just charts. They're navigational data. The adjustments suggest someone was actively steering—toward a destination."

Rudi, voice tightening. "Interstellar navigation?"

Johan, carefully. "Or interdimensional."

(A silence settles over the chamber, thick and heavy.)

Rudi, sharply. "That would explain the geometric consistency. The relationships between the constellations—they're not fixed to Earth's perspective alone. They're aiming for something else."

Johan, thoughtfully. "A moving reference point. A vessel in motion?"

Rudi, coldly. "Or a planet."

(Johan moves to a chalkboard filled with calculations, orbits, and star maps.)

Johan, gesturing. "These adjustments—precession shifts, parallax calculations, orbital eccentricities—they're not just tracking Earth. They're mapping a viewpoint from outside the solar system."

Rudi, following him. "Then that means . . ."

Johan, quietly. These charts weren't made for Earthbound observers. They were designed for someone returning to Earth."

(A beat of silence.)

Rudi, tightly. "If these are navigational charts, where's the destination?"

Johan, pointing to a spot on the chart. "Here. This sequence matches the Sirius system, as it appeared around 10,500 years ago. They calculated its orbital movements with precision—including Sirius B, a white dwarf invisible to the naked eye."

Rudi, voice sharpening. "How could they know that without telescopes?"

Johan, softly. "Unless they weren't observing from Earth. The Dogon tribe in Mali—they've described Sirius B for generations. According to their legends, the Nommo came from Sirius to teach them the secrets of the stars."

Rudi, nodding slowly. "And the Sumerians claimed the Anunnaki descended from the gates of heaven. What if those weren't metaphors? What if the 'gates' were literal?"

(Johan steps back, his gaze hardening.)

Johan, in a low voice. "These aren't just maps. They're coordinates."

Rudi, eyes widening. "You think they left us a way to follow them?"

Johan Rosen, carefully. "Or a way to return."

(Rudi sets the tablet down and steps away, processing the gravity of it all.)

Rudi, in a serious voice. "That would explain the architectural parallels across civilizations. The Egyptian pyramids, Mesopotamian ziggurats, Teotihuacan's temple complex. They're not just monuments. They're markers. A network."

Johan, turning toward him. "That's why every ancient site aligns with astronomical events. That's why ancient societies were obsessed with studying the stars. The question is—"

Both men say it at once:

"What were they tracking?"

The Hidden Connection

After much-needed rest and with sharpened minds, Johan and Rudi sat in the golden light of a new day, discussing the implications of their discoveries.

The idea that the Anunnaki—or some other advanced civilization—had left behind instructions for their return was both exhilarating and terrifying.

Johan leaned back, rubbing his temples. "If these texts are correct, they don't just point to a past visitation—they indicate a recurring cycle. The Earth Rebirth Theory might not be about natural disasters alone. It could mean an orchestrated event, a reset triggered by external forces."

Rudi's hands trembled slightly as he lit a cigarette. "And what if they're due to return? What if we're standing at the edge of another cycle?" The thought chilled him. "We need more information. If the Anunnaki—or whoever they were, left Earth, there had to be a reason. And if they intend to return, we need to understand their purpose."

Johan sifted through the ancient tablets spread before them. He was obsessed. Something was missing, he could feel it. A key that could tie everything together. Then one tablet in particular caught his attention.

It spoke of a celestial body—a rogue entity moving through the cosmic web in a precise yet elongated orbit. The texts named it Nibiru.

"Nibiru," Johan muttered, tracing his finger over the weathered surface. "The missing piece."

He looked up. "The Sumerians called Nibiru the twelfth planet—the home of the Anunnaki."

Rudi frowned, unconvinced. "But if Nibiru is real, how come modern astronomy hasn't found it?"

Johan paused, then began scribbling equations and charts based on the tablet. "Because it operates on a cycle we've never accounted for. The texts suggest an orbital period of about 3,600 years. It's not part of the inner solar system—it swings far out into deep space before returning."

Rudi inhaled deeply, the cigarette glowing in the quiet room. "A trajectory like that would have massive consequences when

it nears Earth." Johan nodded.

"Exactly. Gravitational disruptions, earthquakes, pole shifts, volcanic eruptions, even mass extinctions."

He turned to another section of the tablet, pointing to a spiral sequence of symbols.

"This could be a record of past cycles. Each return of Nibiru seems to coincide with cataclysmic events—the fall of civilizations, unexplained global disasters, abrupt shifts in power."

Rudi exhaled sharply. "It would explain a lot. The Great Flood, the collapse of the Indus Valley, even the destruction of Atlantis—if you believe in that."

Johan's eyes darkened. "And if the Anunnaki knew this cycle, maybe they planned around it. Maybe their departures and returns are synchronized with Nibiru's orbit. They leave before destruction—and return when Earth has stabilized."

Rudi tapped the manuscript thoughtfully. "But why return at all? What do they want?" Johan hesitated. "Control. Resources. Or maybe something deeper. If they engineered early human civilizations, maybe Earth is still part of their domain."

A heavy silence fell between them. Rudi stood abruptly and began pacing.

"If this is true, we need proof. Hard data. Astronomical evidence."

Johan leaned forward. "There have been reports—anomalous gravitational readings, strange perturbations in the orbits of outer solar system objects. Some astronomers think there's a massive unseen planet out there." Rudi nodded slowly. "Planet X." Johan sighed. "Yes. But what if Planet X and Nibiru are the same? The scientific community dismisses Nibiru as myth, but the ancient texts describe it with startling astronomical precision."

Rudi crushed his cigarette in the ashtray. "If it's real—and it's returning—how much time do we have?" Johan's expression turned grim. "It's hard to say. But if the cycle is accurate, we could be approaching another passage." Rudi's jaw clenched.

"And if it brings another catastrophe?" Johan's fingers curled around the manuscript's edge. "Then we need to be ready. We need to understand its effects—not just on gravity or climate—but on human consciousness itself. If Nibiru's return is part of a greater design, we need to know our place in it.

Nibiru could be the very reason ancient civilizations tracked the skies so meticulously. They weren't just mapping stars for myth or ritual, they were monitoring its orbit, trying to prepare themselves for what they knew would come. "Rudi nodded, the weight of responsibility setting into his bones.

"We must start immediately. We find the missing links. Track its orbit. Gather everything, we can." Johan stood, eyes locked on the ancient texts. "And we prepare—for whatever comes next."

CHAPTER 6

In the Grip of Time

Days turned into weeks as Johan and Rudi delved deeper into their research. They contacted trusted allies, smuggled more artifacts through secret channels, and pieced together fragmented accounts of lost histories. But time was running out.

World War II was escalating, and the Nazi regime was growing increasingly interested in occult and esoteric knowledge. Whispers reached Johan's ears that Himmler's Ahnenerbe was aggressively seeking artifacts of supposed supernatural significance. If they caught wind of what Johan and Rudi had uncovered, the consequences would be dire.

But someone had already caught wind of Dr. Rosen and Dr. Fisher's generation-long studies of the ancient world. This individual was not merely an observer—he was a scholar himself and the driving force behind why the German war machine had turned its focus toward searching for ancient and potentially powerful artifacts. He had embedded himself as a powerful financial backer, using his immense wealth and influence to steer the course of these expeditions from the shadows.

This man was Mr. Sloan, a multimillionaire with intentions completely different from those of the Rosen-Fisher team. While Dr. Rosen and Dr. Fisher were motivated by academic curiosity and the desire to preserve history, Sloan's motivations were rooted in power and domination. His ambitions aligned with those of the war-hungry German leadership—he sought not knowledge, but control. He wanted to harness the power of these ancient artifacts to bend the world to his will.

Sloan was acutely aware of Rudi's expeditions with the German military. He knew Rudi was after something significant, but he allowed him to proceed, calculating that he could benefit from Rudi's success by swooping in at the right moment to steal the discoveries for himself. Like a vulture circling over dying prey, Sloan would send soldiers to key archaeological sites under the guise of routine inspections. These "shake-downs" were nothing more than cover for his true objective—to scavenge the findings of other scientists and claim them as his own.

But Sloan's machines didn't stop there. He would often hold seminars on ancient civilizations at prestigious universities, not to educate but to recruit. He targeted impressionable young scholars, luring them with promises of prestige and adventure, only to mold them into agents for his own ends. These students would unknowingly serve as his eyes and ears across the globe, feeding him intelligence and helping him locate artifacts and information that would expand his growing influence.

Sloan was not simply a scholar or a financier—he was a predator. He moved within the academic world with practiced ease, masking his true nature behind a facade of intellectualism and benevolence. But behind that mask lay a mind driven by greed and domination, willing to exploit both ancient knowledge and human ambition to claim ultimate power.

The Nazi Obsession with the Occult

The Nazi regime's fascination with the occult is well-documented, particularly through the actions of Heinrich Himmler and the Ahnenerbe organization. Established in 1935, the Ahnenerbe—meaning "Ancestral Heritage"—was created as an SS institute to research the mythic origins of the so-called Aryan race. For Himmler, a devoted student of mysticism, the goal was not only ideological—it was spiritual. He believed the key to Nazi supremacy lay hidden in the forgotten past, buried in ancient ruins and encoded in symbols lost to time.

The Ahnenerbe's Quest for Supernatural Artifacts

Unlike traditional academic bodies, the Ahnenerbe operated more like a secret society than a research institute. Their missions stretched from the caves of France to the mountains of Tibet, driven by the belief that lost civilizations—perhaps ones tied to extraterrestrial or non-human influence—once held power beyond our comprehension.

Among their most coveted targets were relics like the Spear of Destiny, rumored to grant godlike power to its wielder, and the Holy Grail, said to hold secrets of immortality. But behind these headline-grabbing quests was a quieter, more alarming pursuit:

the search for ancient knowledge—mathematical, astronomical, and technological—that aligned disturbingly well with what Johan and Rudi had been uncovering in the old manuscripts.

A Collision of Agendas

Unknown to most, the Ahnenerbe's expeditions had stumbled across texts and tablets—many originating from Sumerian, Egyptian, and pre-Columbian sites—that echoed warnings of celestial cycles, catastrophic resets, and a planet known in ancient texts as Nibiru. What Johan and Rudi were discovering in secret bunkers, the Nazis were chasing under the guise of scientific exploration. The Anunnaki, described in ancient Mesopotamian texts as sky beings or gods, were now appearing in the confidential reports circulating through Ahnenerbe circles—though reframed through the lens of Nazi myth-making. To the Reich, they weren't just gods—they were ancestors. And if the myths were true, then the return of Nibiru wasn't just a cosmic event—it was a strategic opportunity to reclaim power from the stars.

The Shake-Down

One evening, as Johan worked late in the bunker, Karl burst into the room, his face pale with urgency. "Father! Men are outside—German officers. They're knocking on our front door."

Johan's blood ran cold.

Rudi, who had been reviewing maps at the far end of the chamber, stood abruptly. "It's begun."

Johan quickly extinguished the lanterns. "Karl, take Karin and hide in the tunnel passages. You remember the route? Then go to the safe house, we will meet there."

Karl nodded solemnly. He grabbed Karin's hand, and the

two children disappeared into the network of hidden corridors beneath the bunker.

Rudi looked at Johan. "We have to leave. Now."

Johan grabbed a satchel, stuffing it with the most vital manuscripts and the star map. "They can never get their hands on this."

A heavy pounding echoed through the bunker. The muffled voices of soldiers seeped through the thick stone walls.

Johan and Rudi locked eyes.

For centuries, their families had safeguarded knowledge that defied human history. And now, they could be hunted for it.

The pounding on the bunker door intensified.

"Mach die Tür auf!" the soldiers shouted, each brutal thud reverberating through the thick stone walls like the hammering of a war drum.

"Mach die verdammte Tür auf!" The screams grew more urgent.

Dust drifted through the air, shaken loose from the vaulted ceiling. The iron bolts groaned under the relentless assault. Outside, muffled German commands rose in volume—clipped, forceful, and sharp—slicing through the cold stillness like knives. Johan and Rudi exchanged a resolute glance; the unspoken weight of the moment etched into their faces. Fear hovered in the stale air, but neither gave it voice. They had come too far, sacrificed too much, to falter now.

What they guarded was more than ancient treasure. It was truth—dangerous, transformative truth. The brittle manuscripts and weathered artifacts in their care held knowledge that could unravel the carefully constructed narratives of human history. In the wrong hands, that truth would either be buried forever or weaponized.

Rudi's jaw clenched as another thunderous blow rocked the heavy door. The metal buckled slightly, groaning in protest.

"Tür auf! Los!"

Sweat glistened on Rudi's brow, despite the chill.

"They're not going to stop," he said grimly.

Johan's hand slid beneath his coat, brushing against the smooth leather binding of the ancient codex hidden beneath the fabric. Its weight grounded him—a quiet reminder of the purpose that had driven them to the brink.

He took a steady breath and met Rudi's eyes.

"Then we seal the hidden entrance to the tunnels and move."

A Desperate Escape

With the German officers closing in, Johan and Rudi knew they had no time to waste. Every second counted. Johan snatched the most vital artifacts from the table—fragile clay tablets inscribed with cuneiform, ancient scrolls, and the codex—slipping them carefully into a weathered canvas satchel. Rudi moved quickly beside him, packing fragments of pottery and metallic relics etched with symbols no modern scholar had yet deciphered.

A deafening crack split the air as another strike drove the iron door inward. The hinges shrieked in protest. Dust billowed through the dimly lit room, and a flashlight beam flickered through the widening gap beneath the door.

"This way!" Johan hissed.

He pulled aside a heavy stone panel at the far end of the room, revealing a hidden passage. The narrow tunnel behind it was known only to a select few; a secret passed down through generations.

Rudi slipped through first, crouching low as the shadows swallowed him. Johan followed, sealing the panel just as the front door gave way with a thunderous crash. Shouts erupted as German soldiers poured into the room.

The tunnels were damp and claustrophobic, the air thick with the scent of old earth. Water dripped from unseen cracks above, the sound hollow and rhythmic. Johan pulled a small flashlight from his coat, casting its beam along the rough, ancient stone walls.

"They're in the house," Rudi whispered.

"Alle Zimmer durchsuchen! Los!" a voice bellowed from above, distorted by the enclosed space. Footsteps pounded overhead—dozens of them—as soldiers stormed room by room.

Rudi cursed under his breath. "They're too close." "We need to split up," Johan said, breath ragged. "No." Rudi's eyes flashed. "We stick together."

Johan hesitated—the weight of the codex pressed heavily against his chest. If they were caught, everything would be lost. The knowledge they carried—the origins of civilization, the forgotten truth of the Anunnaki—would be erased.

"Okay, I'll lead them off. They can't find the secret tunnels, or they'll reach the libraries," Rudi said, his voice steady. "You take the journal and the artifacts. Get to the safe house. Protect the kids."

"You just said we should stick together; I'm not leaving you," Johan snapped.

"You must," Rudi said softly. He placed a firm hand on Johan's shoulder. "Go."

Johan's throat tightened. For a moment, they stood motionless, the weight of the choice between them like thunder in the silence. Then, with quiet resolve, Johan nodded.

Without another word, Rudi turned and sprinted down a side passage, his footsteps echoing into the darkness.

Johan sealed the entrance from the inside with a heavy slab of stone, then collapsed the inner wall against it. Now it was sealed—no one would ever find it.

He forced himself to move in the opposite direction, his breath quick and shallow.

Moments later, Johan heard the officers muffled shout:

"Da! Ich hör sie! Keiner entkommt, verstanden?!"

Rudi's plan had worked. The soldiers had taken the bait and were now chasing him away from the house.

Like a sly fox, Rudi doubled back through the trees, vanished into the terrain, and reentered the tunnels from another location.

Inside, Johan's only mission was survival.

The tunnel opened into a cavernous chamber—an ancient subterranean vault. He hesitated, drawn toward the archway ahead. His pulse quickened as he traced the symbols etched into the stone—marks left by the many hands that had helped construct these elaborate tunnels.

A stirring rose within him—something old and familiar. As if the stone itself was whispering his name.

He pressed on, the ancient journal clutched tightly in his hand. He could hear his pulse in his ears, breath ragged, footsteps echoing behind him. His only hope lay in the unknown ahead.

Then—suddenly—he heard it.

"Johan! Are you okay?!" Rudi's voice echoed through the stone, rough and strained.

Relief surged through him. Despite the fear clawing at his chest, they were reunited.

And the truth would survive another day.

In the safety of the distant safe house, they embraced the children—Karl and Karin—brave, shaken, but safe. They hugged tightly, laughter breaking through the tension. Joyful tears mixed with exhaustion as they clung to one another, jumping in place, overwhelmed with relief.

They had made it. For now.

The Guardians of Ancient Knowledge

Johan and Rudi were the guardians of ancient knowledge—a role passed down through countless generations of their families. Now, they stood as stewards of a legacy that reached far beyond written history: the profound inheritance of the Sky People. These celestial beings, revered in ancient Sumerian texts, were said to have descended from the heavens to impart wisdom and guidance to early human civilizations.

The artifacts and manuscripts in Johan and Rudi's possession held extraordinary insights into the Sky People's teachings— revealing their interactions with humanity, secrets of advanced technologies, and the cosmic cycles that shaped the rise and fall of civilizations over millennia.

But this legacy was not confined to one region. It was global—encoded across the world's most enigmatic ancient sites. A mysterious alignment between these locations suggested a vast, interconnected network of knowledge and power that transcended continents and epochs.

In the high Andes of Peru, *Machu Picchu* stands as a marvel of engineering. Its precisely cut stones, assembled without mortar, reflect techniques that remain unexplained to this day. The site's astronomical alignment and strategic placement atop a mountain ridge underscore the builder's deep understanding of celestial mechanics and Earth's energy lines.

Further south, Puma Punku in Bolivia defies conventional archaeological logic. Massive stone blocks—some weighing over 100 tons—are intricately carved with interlocking patterns and angles so precise that even modern tools would struggle to replicate them. Was this evidence of lost technology? Or something more?

In Baalbek, Lebanon, the ruins of the ancient Temple of Jupiter hold the legendary *Trilithon stones*—each weighing over 800 tons. The method by which these stones were transported and placed remains a mystery. Local legends speak of giants or celestial beings assisting in their construction, once again linking the site to the legacy of the Anunnaki.

In Egypt, the *Great Pyramid of Giza* remains a timeless enigma. Its perfect proportions, astronomical orientation, and the advanced mathematical knowledge encoded within suggest a sophistication that challenges mainstream historical narratives. Some believe it was more than a marvel of engineering—a machine, possibly a power source—designed according to principles inherited from the Anunnaki.

Göbekli Tepe, in modern-day Turkey, rewrote humanity's

timeline. Dating back to around 9600 BCE, it predates agriculture, cities, and written language. Its towering pillars, carved with animals and cosmic symbols, point to a deep spiritual and astronomical awareness—one that predates recorded history.

Across the Atlantic, the Mexican pyramids of Teotihuacan, including the Pyramid of the Sun and the Pyramid of the Moon, reflect profound knowledge of astronomy and geometry. Their alignment with celestial bodies and use of sacred geometry hint at a cosmic understanding likely inherited from an ancient, shared source.

The Maya pyramids of Central America—at sites like *Tikal* and *Palenque*—further this connection. Their intricate calendars and awareness of cosmic cycles suggest a lineage of knowledge passed down through the ages, perhaps originating from the same sky-born source.

Even Easter Island, with its haunting Moai statues and intricate polygonal walls, echoes this forgotten legacy. Carved from volcanic rock and set to face the horizon, these colossal figures are believed to embody ancestral wisdom. How they were transported and erected remains a mystery—another fragment of a global puzzle left unsolved.

These connections across ancient sites point to something larger: a shared memory, a forgotten global legacy. The architectural precision, astronomical alignment, and spiritual depth seen across these civilizations could not be coincidence. Johan and Rudi believed firmly that each pyramid had a unique function—not merely as temples or observatories, but as parts of a global system, perhaps even machines, interconnected and deeply purposeful. Each held its own mysteries—and possibly, keys to understanding the others.

Protecting this knowledge was never just about preserving the past. It was about safeguarding humanity's spiritual and technological inheritance. The wisdom of the Anunnaki was both a gift and a burden. In the wrong hands, it could be weaponized—used to control, dominate, and deceive.

Shielding these ancient truths from those who sought to exploit them became Johan and Rudi's sacred mission. For the legacy of the Anunnaki was not just the key to humanity's origins—it was the blueprint for its future.

A New Dawn

Johan and Rudi knew their journey was far from over. The world was engulfed in turmoil—World War II raged on. Yet amid the uncertainty, a glimmer of hope remained.

The knowledge they carried held the power to illuminate humanity's path, to unveil the mysteries of the past, and to guide future generations toward enlightenment.

With unwavering resolve, they pressed on—driven by the belief that their sacrifices would help usher in a new dawn of understanding and harmony.

The convergence of ancient wisdom and the chaos of World War II created a crucible in which Johan and Rudi's resolve was tested. Their steadfast commitment to preserving the legacy of the Anunnaki—even as Nazi occult pursuits encroached upon them—exemplified the enduring power of knowledge and the indomitable spirit of those who safeguard it. As they embarked on their perilous journey, they carried with them the hopes of countless generations, striving to ensure that the light of truth would prevail over the shadows of ignorance and tyranny.

The Return

Through the darkened tunnels leading out of the underground bunkers, Johan and Rudi fled with Karl and Karin close behind, their footsteps echoing off the cold stone walls. The damp chill of the underground passage clung to their skin as they pushed forward, driven by equal parts fear and resolve. The weight of their discovery bore down on them—not just the physical strain of the ancient manuscripts and artifacts strapped to their backs, but the crushing burden of the knowledge they carried. The truth they now possessed had the power to reshape human history—or destroy it.

As Johan and Rudi forcefully rolled off a huge slab of stone sealing the entrance, the tunnel opened into the frigid night. Biting mountain air filled their lungs as they emerged into the moonlit forest. The forest, with its natural camouflage and hidden trails, offered a fragile sense of security. But even as they rested, they knew that Nazi patrols and informants were never far behind. Every rustle of leaves or crack of a branch could signal approaching danger. Their reprieve would be brief—staying in one place too long would only make them easier target.

A thin mist curled through the trees, muffling the sound of the nearby river. Rudi turned back toward the entrance of the hidden passage—toward the underground library bunker that had safeguarded generations of truth-seekers and scholars. Within those walls lay not only history, but the answers to humanity's most profound questions. The idea of abandoning it felt like severing a vital artery.

Johan stepped toward him and grasped his shoulder firmly. Their eyes met beneath the pale glow of the moonlight. "We'll come back. They didn't find the hidden entrances to the tunnels or identify any of us," Johan said, his voice steady despite the chaos unraveling around them.

Rudi exhaled, his breath curling in the frosty air. His eyes darkened with doubt.

"Let's monitor it first—and if we can, we will," he whispered.

A howl from a distant hunting dog echoed through the forest, snapping them back to the present. There was no more time for reflection. Without another word, they turned and disappeared into the depths of the forest, the ancient manuscripts and artifacts pressed tightly against their bodies like sacred relics.

The Hidden Exodus

The final leg of their journey led them into the mountains, where jagged cliffs and shadowed forests formed a natural labyrinth—an ancient wilderness untouched and unforgiving. These secret escape routes were known only to the Rosen and Fisher families, and a handful of trusted allies whose bonds stretched back through generations. Their knowledge had been preserved in hushed voices, passed from parent to child through whispered instructions and cryptic maps hidden in false walls and family heirlooms.

Karl and Karin, the youngest heirs to this legacy, followed silently behind, their wide, solemn eyes reflecting the weight of what they were leaving behind—and the uncertainty of what lay ahead. Every step they took echoed with the stories they had been told since birth, of sacrifice, of escape, of survival.

"We're close," Johan murmured as they crested a rocky ridge, his voice barely louder than the wind. "Another mile through the valley and we'll reach the safe house. There, we can find out whether the underground tunnels and library bunkers have been compromised."

The group quickened their pace, weaving through the dense undergrowth, their movements silent but urgent. Time seemed to stretch and warp around them, the path narrowing as fear and hope battled in their chests. The weight of the satchel pressed heavily against Johan's chest—inside, documents, coordinates, and the last fragments of a threatened history.

Behind him, Karl's labored breathing grew louder, each inhale a struggle between exhaustion and resolve. Rudi, ever the silent guardian, kept pace with quiet determination, with Karin now cradled gently in his arms. Her small hand clutched his collar, her eyes half-closed but alert, as if sensing the fragility of this moment.

The Fischer Safe House

The Fischer family's safe house was more than just a refuge—it was a nerve center for resistance activity. Nestled deep within the rugged mountains, the remote cabin was fortified with essential supplies, communication equipment, and a network of trusted contacts ready to assist those fleeing Nazi persecution. The Fischer family had a long legacy of defiance against tyranny, dating back to the early days of Nazi expansion. Their home had become a sanctuary for resistance fighters, Jewish families, and Allied operatives seeking safe passage.

Reaching the safe house was a formidable challenge. The jagged cliffs and thick forests of the mountains provided natural cover but also posed serious hazards. The narrow trails were treacherous—often blocked by snow and prone to rockslides. Johan and Rudi had to rely on their intimate knowledge of the terrain, moving carefully to avoid detection. German patrols routinely swept the area, and any misstep could expose their location.

Karl and Karin, struggling to keep pace, followed closely behind as Johan and Rudi led the way. Rudi whispered directions in hushed tones, guiding them through narrow crevices and beneath fallen trees. The tension in the air was palpable—every snap of a branch or distant footstep sent a jolt of adrenaline through the group. They knew that if the Nazi search teams found anyone wondering through the woods, there would be questions they couldn't afford to answer—and the risk of generations of knowledge falling into the wrong hands was too great to bear.

A Glimmer of Hope

As dawn approached, the forest began to thin, revealing a faint path winding toward the Fischer family's cabin. Exhausted but resolute, the group pressed on, driven by the fragile hope that safety lay just beyond the next ridge. The distant glow of the rising sun filtered through the trees, casting soft beams of light through the misty air.

At last, Johan spotted the silhouette of the cabin through the fog. A thin wisp of smoke curled from the chimney—an agreed-upon signal that the house was safe. Relief mixed with exhaustion as they approached the heavy wooden door. Rudi rapped twice—a coded knock.

After a brief pause, the door creaked open to reveal Greta Fischer's cautious but familiar face.

"Quickly, inside," she whispered, ushering them into the warmth of the cabin.

Inside, the glow of the fire bathed their tired faces. Johan and Rudi collapsed onto the rough wooden floor, their breath ragged. Greta handed them steaming cups of hot broth as she listened intently to their hurried explanation. She nodded gravely.

"We'll talk more tomorrow. Rest tonight—you should save your strength."

Despite their exhaustion, sleep would not come easily. Outside, the war raged on, and the knowledge they carried remained a target. The Reich's agents would not stop searching.

But for now, they had found sanctuary—brief, fragile, but real.

Enough to breathe. Enough to plan. Enough to hope.

A New Theory Takes Shape

Now, at a new secret location beneath the current safe house, a dimly lit chamber buzzed with the intensity of scholarly debate.

Ancient manuscripts lay sprawled across the table, their cryptic symbols inviting endless interpretation. Johan and Rudi were deep in discussion, their voices a blend of excitement and frustration.

In the corner, Karl and Karin sat quietly, their wide eyes reflecting the warm glow of lantern light, captivated by the energy in the room.

Little Karl, now growing fast and showing the first signs of maturity, hesitated before raising his hand—a gesture he'd picked up from watching the adults.

Rudi paused mid-sentence, his eyes softening as he acknowledged the boy with a quiet nod.

"Yes, Karl?"

Karl glanced at his father. Johan offered an encouraging nod and a gentle, "If you must."

The boy's voice was steady, curiosity burning in his eyes. "The city on top of the mountains."

Johan and Rudi exchanged puzzled glances. "Yes . . .?"

"Could they have been built by space people?"

Johan sighed—a mix of exasperation and amusement. "Karl, not that again."

Undeterred, Karl pressed on. "But Papa, Rudi said—" "Mr. Fischer, remember?" Johan gently corrected.

Rudi interjected with a warm smile. "It's alright, Johan. After everything we've been through, I like when he calls me Rudi."

Encouraged, Karl continued. "Mr. Fischer said the heavy stones were taken from one mountain and moved to another, right? So, it sounds to me like they could make them fly."

Johan's expression shifted from mild annoyance to interest.

He leaned forward, intrigued.

"Or they found a way to eliminate gravity," he mused. Karl's eyes widened. "What do you mean, Papa?"

Johan gestured toward the table. "Pick up that fork, hold your hand palm-down, and open it."

Karl obeyed. The fork dropped to the floor with a clatter.

Johan nodded toward it. "That's gravity. If someone could eliminate it, the fork would float. And you could move it however you wanted."

Rudi chimed in, his brow furrowed. "But if we eliminate gravity, wouldn't *we*—and everything else—float too?"

Johan nodded thoughtfully. "Exactly. That would be the challenge—to isolate the effect. To target one object, or several, without affecting the environment around them."

The room shifted. The air itself seemed to hum with possibility. Karl beamed, glowing with pride. For the first time, he felt truly part of the conversation. His question had sparked something—not just dialogue, but discovery.

It was a moment that would define him—the first spark of a lifelong obsession to understand the very forces that bound the universe.

Karin, quiet and observant as ever, watched closely. She didn't want a future that mirrored her father's—away for months at a time, always chasing secrets. But the idea of making things *fly*—of understanding the unseen—that captivated her. She wanted that wonder, but without the sacrifice.

Theories of Ancient Levitation Techniques

The conversation between Johan, Rudi, and Karl touched on a subject that has long fascinated scholars and alternative researchers alike: how did ancient civilizations construct such monumental structures with seemingly limited technology? Several theories have been proposed:

Mechanical Advantage through Simple Machines

The most widely accepted explanation suggests that ancient builders relied on simple machines—levers, pulleys, and inclined planes—combined with large labor forces. The construction of the Egyptian pyramids, for instance, is often attributed to massive ramps and thousands of workers.

Rudi and Johan, however, often laughed quietly at the simplicity of this explanation. In their view, such theories underestimated the architectural precision and sheer scale involved in sites like Baalbek or Puma Punku.

Acoustic Levitation

A more fringe theory proposes that ancient civilizations used sound—generating specific frequencies to create levitation effects. Modern science has demonstrated acoustic levitation on small objects, suggesting that powerful resonances could, theoretically, counteract gravity.

However, no physical evidence currently supports the notion that this technique was used at any ancient construction site.

Magnetic Levitation

Some theorists have speculated that ancient builders harnessed Earth's magnetic fields or used magnetized materials to create repulsion and movement. Perhaps they manipulated natural geomagnetic hotspots, aligning structures with the Earth's energy grid.

While intriguing, this theory also lacks archaeological backing and remains speculative.

Extraterrestrial Assistance

Popular in pseudoscientific circles, this theory claims that ancient monuments were constructed with help from technologically advanced extraterrestrial visitors. Proponents argue that the level of engineering and astronomical precision found in structures like the Great Pyramid or Teotihuacan could not have been achieved by the known technologies of the time.

Though it captures the imagination of many, mainstream archaeologists reject this theory due to the absence of empirical evidence.

Regardless of the theory, one thing was clear to Johan and Rudi: the world's ancient sites shared something deeper—a universal language of mathematics, geometry, and celestial alignment. Whether through lost technologies, cosmic intervention, or a genius forgotten by time, the legacy they uncovered pointed to a forgotten era of profound knowledge and possibility.

And now, through Karl and Karin, that legacy was beginning to awaken once more.

The Distress Call

The hidden library bunker—once a sanctuary of knowledge and secrecy—was abruptly pierced by the shrill ring of the telephone. Johan's heart skipped as he lifted the receiver, sensing urgency before a word was spoken.

Greta's trembling voice came through the line.

"You must all hurry to the main house," she implored. "Elga has been in some kind of altercation with the German police."

Without hesitation, Johan, Rudi, and the children moved swiftly through the labyrinthine passages that connected the bunker to the main residence. The walls, lined with ancient tomes and relics, seemed to tighten around them as the weight of fear and uncertainty mounted.

They burst into the living room to find Elga—Rudi's cousin—

pale and visibly shaken. Upon seeing Rudi, she rushed into his embrace, her body trembling as she clung to him.

"It was horrible," she whispered, her voice cracking. "They were labeling Jewish-owned shops. When the owners protested, the police beat them—brutally. I couldn't just stand there. I grabbed one of the officers by the arm and begged him to stop. But more came. They arrested me. It wasn't until they checked my identification and saw I was a native German that they let me go."

Greta gently guided Elga to a chair near the fireplace and handed her a glass of water. The room fell into heavy silence. Shadows danced across their troubled faces as the fire crackled, the tension in the air palpable.

They all knew this was more than a single incident—it was a warning.

The Nazi regime's persecution of Jews was escalating rapidly, and the danger extended beyond the streets. For Johan, Rudi, and their families—already under threat for the ancient truths they protected—Elga's experience underscored just how narrow their margin for survival had become. They weren't only evading the Reich's grasp for forbidden knowledge; they were trying to stay ahead of a historical tidal wave threatening to engulf them.

Historical Context: The Nuremberg Laws and Rising Persecution

The incident Elga witnessed reflected a chilling pattern unfolding across Germany in the late 1930s. Anti-Jewish sentiment was no longer simmering—it was institutionalized, escalating toward catastrophe.

In the mid-1930s, the Nazi regime formalized its anti-Semitic ideology through laws designed to systematically marginalize

Jews. A pivotal moment came on September 15, 1935, with the enactment of the Nuremberg Laws. These included:

The Reich Citizenship Law, which stripped Jews of German citizenship, reducing them to mere subjects without political rights.

The Law for the Protection of German Blood and German Honour, which banned marriages and extramarital relations between Jews and non-Jewish Germans.

These laws entrenched racial discrimination into the fabric of German law and society, creating a legal foundation for further persecution.

Kristallnacht: The Breaking Point

The culmination of these policies erupted on November 9–10, 1938, in the state-orchestrated pogrom known as Kristallnacht— the *Night of Broken Glass*. Nazi paramilitary forces and civilians unleashed coordinated violence across Germany, Austria, and the Sudetenland:

- Over 1,000 synagogues were set on fire.
- Around 7,500 Jewish-owned businesses were looted and vandalized.
- Nearly 100 Jews were murdered.
- Approximately 30,000 Jewish men were arrested and deported to concentration camps.

The streets were littered with shattered glass—remnants of homes, shops, and sacred places destroyed—giving the event its name.

In the aftermath, Jewish families were devastated. Homes

were ransacked, businesses destroyed, and entire communities paralyzed by fear. To compound the trauma, the Nazi regime imposed a collective fine on the Jewish community, blaming them for the violence inflicted upon them. This calculated impoverishment was part of a broader agenda to force Jewish emigration and realize a *Judenfrei* (Jew-free) Germany.

A Family in the Crosshairs

For families like the Rosens and the Fischers, these events were no longer distant headlines or whispered rumors. They were lived reality.

Elga's experience served as a painful reminder: no one was truly safe—not even those of German lineage, not even those who remained silent.

Now, they faced an impossible equation: continue their work and risk discovery, or abandon their mission in order to survive another day.

Their only choices were escape, concealment, or resistance. And time was running out.

A Dangerous Revelation

If there was one thing threatening Johan and Rudi's plans, it was just that—trying not to get involved in the injustices spreading across the German streets. And how could they not? It took nerves of steel to turn a blind eye to the cruelty unfolding before their very eyes. Yet, any attempt to fight for justice would mean certain death. The civilians were outnumbered, outgunned, and at the mercy of the Nazi soldiers, who had no hesitation in using their weapons to instill fear and maintain control.

As the months passed, news arrived that artifacts, tablets, and manuscripts from excavation sites in Bolivia, Peru, and

Mexico were being delivered to Nazi headquarters. The influx of discoveries was so significant that SS officials were assigned to guard the storage facility—an airplane hangar turned high-security warehouse. Under the guidance of Mr. Sloan, it became clear that Hitler and his team of artifact hunters were onto something. This wasn't just about archaeology anymore; it was a pursuit of power—a search for answers hidden in the ancient past.

Johan knew he had to study them. He needed extensive clearance to access the facility, so he decided to sneak in. In a risky move, he blended in with a group of scientists. He didn't know who might recognize him, so he avoided eye contact—this opportunity was too valuable to waste.

Every entry and exit was closely monitored, his movements scrutinized. The weight of responsibility bore heavily upon him. Separating, photographing, and cataloging each artifact was meticulous work. While most pieces were fascinating in their own right, a few stood out above the rest—detailed stone sculptures resembling mathematical calendars, and a collection of exceptionally old clay tablets covered in cryptic inscriptions.

Johan's heart raced when he saw the symbols on the tablet. He recognized the style of writing immediately but needed confirmation. With measured composure, he copied several of the etched marks and symbols into his journal, careful not to draw attention to himself. This discovery had the potential to change everything.

That night, at the safe house, Johan sat with Karl and little Karin in their dimly lit study, poring over their newly extensive collection of notes, sketches, and past translations taken from the Nazis. Karl's sharp memory was their greatest asset, and tonight, it proved invaluable. The boy's hands trembled gently with excitement as he flipped through the pages of his father's journal.

"Papa, it's about the ancient manuscript, the one from Egypt, remember?" Karl asked, his voice barely above a whisper. He traced his finger along the journal's writings; his brow furrowed with concentration. "Look! The new notes from your journal—the symbols you wrote on it; they match the ones from Egypt's ancient manuscript."

Johan's breath caught in his throat. He leaned over, eyes widening as he compared the writings. The resemblance was undeniable.

"So, it is confirmed . . ." he murmured. "These civilizations supposedly had no way of contacting each other back then, but they did!"

"But of course they did," Rudi said, joining the conversation. "Our entire research seems to be leading to that conclusion."

The manuscript Karl referenced was ancient—far older than anything officially documented from Egypt's well-known dynasties. It had been safeguarded within the Rosen-Fischer family for generations, passed down as a relic of their ancestors' hidden knowledge. It bore three distinct scripts—and enigmatic symbols. The symbols remained undeciphered.

Johan adjusted his glasses and carefully lifted the ancient manuscript from its protective casing. The papyrus was weathered, its edges chipped from millennia of wear, yet the writings remained sharp, almost as if the hand that had written them had been guided by something beyond human skill.

Rudi's hands trembled as he carefully compared the symbols to a worn reference book, his breath quickening with each familiar mark. "This Sumerian-like symbols and the few symbols we were able to find in the ancient pyramids of Central and South America—they're almost identical to the symbols discovered on a temple wall in Eridu." His voice tightened as he traced a line in the book with a shaky finger. "Again, the message traces back to the cradle of civilization."

He flipped through the pages, eyes scanning furiously. "And now, when we cross-reference them with the symbols on the Egyptian manuscript . . ." He hesitated, glancing at the symbols etched into the brittle surface. "It's not random. It's structured—it seems to form a message. But how could civilizations so far apart, separated by millennia, have been speaking the same hidden language? Most importantly, how can we decipher the message?"

Johan stared at the ancient manuscript and Rudi's journal writings, his pulse quickening. "Which means that whatever civilization created these symbols must have influenced the civilizations of Sumer, Egypt, and the ancient pyramids of the Americas, but how? Are we looking at historical records of an advanced precursor civilization?"

Karl hesitated. "What if that civilization wasn't from this planet—the sky people, remember?"

The words hung in the air like a forbidden incantation. Johan shot his son a sharp look, but Karl didn't back down. Instead, he pulled up another document—a translated excerpt from an ancient Sumerian cylinder seal, transcribed by Johan himself.

"Listen to this, Papa. It's written in your journal," Karl said, reading aloud. "'Enki, the great benefactor, brought the wisdom of the stars to the people. He crafted them in the image of the gods, bestowing language and knowledge. But Enlil, fearing the corruption of divine order, sought to undo this gift and cleanse the world with his storm.'"

Johan inhaled deeply, closing his eyes for a brief moment. He had spent his life as an academic—a man of reason—a historian who prided himself on deciphering facts from myths. He knew their research on ancient civilizations and the sky people was leading to this conclusion. But to have evidence in front of him—this was something else entirely.

"You're finally confirming," Rudi said carefully, "that Enki and Enlil weren't symbolic figures at all but real beings?"

Karl's eyes gleamed with a mixture of excitement and trepidation, the spark of a young mind grappling with the weight of discovery. "Think about it. The stories across multiple cultures tell of gods descending from the heavens, imparting knowledge, and then mysteriously disappearing. These can't just be myths—they could be historical accounts of beings with technology so advanced that ancient humans could only comprehend them as gods."

Johan ran a finger over the symbols. The deeper he delved into the hidden records of the past, the more uneasy he became. This wasn't the first time he had encountered anomalies—artifacts that shouldn't exist, texts that hinted at impossible connections between civilizations that, by all logic, should never have crossed paths. But myth was becoming reality right in front of his eyes.

The ancient manuscript was different. It wasn't just an out-of-place relic. It was a bridge between worlds, between timelines, between what was known and what had been buried by time and secrecy.

A thought struck him. "If this was kept in our family for generations, then someone in our lineage knew. Someone understood what this was."

Karl nodded. "Which means someone wanted to protect it." Johan felt a chill crawl up his spine.

If their ancestors had safeguarded this knowledge, then surely others knew as well—organizations, societies operating in the shadows.

Perhaps some wanted the truth revealed.

But others might stop at nothing to weaponize it.

The Warning

A sharp knock on the study room door made them both jump.

Johan exchanged a wary glance with Karl before approaching cautiously. He paused, listening. Then slowly turned the knob.

Standing in the dimly lit hallway was a woman in a tailored coat, her piercing gray eyes scanning the room behind Johan before locking onto him. In her gloved hand, she held a weathered envelope, sealed with a strange sigil—a circular emblem of interwoven serpentine lines—an unmistakable mark that proved she was one of their allies.

"Dr. Rosen, Dr. Fischer," she said, her voice steady but urgent. "We need to talk. Now."

Johan's mouth went dry. Instinctively, he shifted to block Karl from view.

"Who are you?"

Without waiting for permission, the woman stepped inside. "My name is irrelevant. Elga let me in to deliver this message. What matters is what you've found."

Her gaze landed on the ancient manuscript on the wooden table. "That manuscript is part of something far greater than you realize. If you've started to decipher the symbols, you're already in danger."

Johan stiffened.

"Danger from whom? The Nazis? We're already aware of their interest."

She shook her head, glancing toward the window, her voice lowering.

"No. From those who have spent centuries making sure this knowledge never comes to light. A society older than the Reich. Their current leader is a man named Mr. Sloan."

Rudi pointed to the ancient manuscript. "Tell me—what do the symbols mean?"

The woman hesitated, then met Johan's gaze with grim resolve. "It's not just a record of the past." Her voice dropped to a whisper. "It's a set of instructions."

A heavy silence settled over the room.

Johan's mind raced. Instructions? From who? The ancient gods?

Or something else—something even more incomprehensible? Rudi swallowed hard.

"We have to know what it means. Before it's too late." The woman nodded.

"Then you have no time to waste."

Johan and Karl turned back to the manuscript. A realization struck Johan like lightning.

"We have a key," he whispered, his voice trembling with awe. The woman gave a rare, faint smile.

"You're right. It *is* a key. A key to unlock a secret knowledge and the precise coordinates of where to find it."

She stepped back toward the hallway.

"Now I must go. But consider yourselves warned." Her eyes lingered on Johan.

"Godspeed."

And with that, she vanished into the corridor, leaving behind more questions than answers.

CHAPTER 8

Theory Quest

The tension in the library bunker was palpable. The flickering glow of oil lamps cast long, shifting shadows against the stone walls, mirroring the uncertainty in the air. Johan and Rudi sat across from each other, surrounded by manuscripts, maps, and symbols too old for the world to remember.

Karl and little Karin sat off to the side, their eyes wide with curiosity, sensing—without fully understanding—the gravity of what was being said.

Days had bled into nights as Johan and Rudi tirelessly worked to translate the symbols from the ancient manuscript, cross-referencing every artifact and inscription they'd gathered from Egypt, South America, and now Antarctica.

"Rudi," Johan said, his voice a mix of awe and disbelief, "if your past findings in Antarctica are accurate, then everything we know about history is wrong. A pyramid—larger than those in Egypt—buried beneath the ice?"

Rudi nodded slowly. "And the sonar scans confirm it. Not just any pyramid, this one show precision engineering, possibly even more advanced than the Great Pyramid itself. And there are tunnels, they might lead to other structures. But there's more."

Johan leaned in, heart pounding. "Go on."

"There are markings on the outer layers of the pyramid. Similar to those on the manuscript. Similar symbols and writings we've seen in South America, Egypt, Eridu. It's all connected. These weren't isolated civilizations. They were part of a global network—maybe even a single civilization spanning thousands, possibly tens of thousands, of years."

The room fell into stunned silence.

Karl clutched his journal tightly. "Papa," he said softly, "if the symbols and writings are warnings could they be about time periods? Like, when the stars align, or a meteor shower returns? What if they knew when something bad was coming—and left the planet before it happened?"

Johan rubbed his temples. "It's starting to look that way".

Karin, who had been quietly observing, offered a thought that chilled the room.

"Maybe, they never left. Maybe they hid underground."

Rudi looked at Johan, eyes widening after Karin's comment beyond her age. "She makes a great point. The legends from South America, the beings who vanished into the Earth during cataclysms."

Johan nodded slowly, the implications setting in. "The Hollow Earth theory. Ancient tunnels. Continents connected.

The Descent into Shadows

Little Karin's comment weighed heavily on them. It opened new possibilities—and once again aligned with ancient tales of people living, or hiding, underground.

She looked proudly at Karl, and he met her gaze with a smile—a smile that told her everything: he was proud of her, too.

We're a team.

This wasn't just about decoding forgotten languages. It was about rewriting the entire human timeline.

"If they were so advanced," Johan asked, breaking the silence, "why did they hide?"

Rudi answered quietly. "A cataclysm. Or perhaps the return of something—like Planet X. Nibiru. Something they knew would come back. It's the only explanation for why they tracked the skies so obsessively. Maybe they weren't looking for answers, maybe they were waiting for a warning, a celestial warning."

Karin asked, "But why haven't we found them? Wouldn't there be stories?"

"There are," Johan said. "Scattered across cultures. Beings from beneath the Earth. The question is—were they myths or memories?"

Karl looked up. "If they had that kind of tech, maybe they didn't want to be found."

Again, silence. Not fear—*understanding.*

The Forgotten Truths

Then Johan returned with a stack of books and a gleam in his eye.

Agartha: The Hidden Kingdom

"Ever heard of Agartha?" Johan said, holding up a dusty tome. "It's said to be a hidden city beneath the Earth's crust. An advanced society, possibly remnants of the old world, with technology far beyond ours. Esoteric scholars have chased this legend for centuries. Imagine—entire civilizations beneath our feet, watching us."

The Nagas: Guardians of Ancient Wisdom

"Now this—Hindu mythology speaks of the Nagas. Serpent-like beings with immense power. They live in subterranean realms like Patala and Bhogavati. Guardians of ancient knowledge. They weren't just snakes—they were revered, almost god-like. And their cities? Said to be vast, glowing worlds beneath the Earth."

Derinkuyu: Evidence in Stone

"But it's not all myth. There's Derinkuyu, in Turkey—an actual underground city. It goes down 280 feet. Carved around the 8th century BCE. It could hold 20,000 people, livestock, everything. They had ventilation shafts, water wells, even escape routes. Real people. Real technology. They knew how to vanish beneath the surface."

The Hopi and the Ant People

Johan opened another book, eyes scanning.

"And here's the wildest part. The Hopi—Native American people—tell of the Ant People. When the First World ended in fire, the Ant People led survivors underground. When the Second World ended in ice, they did it again. Tall, thin beings. Elongated limbs. Big eyes. Sound familiar?"

Karl's eyes widened. "Like aliens?"

Johan nodded. "Or an ancient civilization mistaken for gods."

"The Hopi word for ant is *Anu*," he continued. "And their word for friend is *Naki. Anu-Naki.* The same name as the Sumerian gods who 'came from the sky.'"

Rudi leaned forward. "And the Hopi say we're in the Fourth World now, right? That we're heading toward the Fifth?"

"Exactly," Johan said. "And they say the Ant People will return when the shift begins. But only if we're ready—spiritually, ethically, ecologically. Their message is survival through humility and harmony."

He closed the book slowly. "Crazy, right?"

But no one laughed.

The Antarctic Excavation

"And do you want to hear more madness?" Rudi asked, unfolding a sheet of parchment with trembling fingers. Its edges were frayed, the ink slightly smudged—drawn in haste, but heavy with meaning.

He laid it flat on the wooden table, smoothing it gently. Across its surface were rough sketches, coordinates, and hastily drawn schematics. Despite the urgency behind the strokes, the detail was striking.

"This," Rudi began, pointing to the central sketch, "is the interior of the pyramid we've been exploring in Antarctica. The entrance is completely buried beneath the ice, but we discovered a small crevice that led into an antechamber."

Johan leaned in, studying the intricate lines.

"The passageways are carved at perfect, angular precision," Rudi continued. "They descend deep into the earth. The walls are so smooth they feel synthetic. Not like stone at all."

Johan's eyes moved to a secondary sketch—one that showed a tablet covered in glyphs.

"These symbols . . ." he murmured. "They match the ones on the South American artifacts."

Rudi nodded, his tone growing solemn.

"Exactly. We found several tablets inside—nearly identical in structure and language."

Johan's mind was already racing.

"And the Nazis? What do they plan to do with all this?" Rudi's expression darkened.

"They're keeping everything under tight security. SS officers guard the excavation site. They believe this place holds the key to ancient technologies—tools they think could shift the tide of the war. But they don't understand what they're playing with."

He paused, lowering his voice.

"There's something else, Johan. Something, *alive.*"

Johan blinked. "Alive?"

"We heard sounds—deep, resonant vibrations, like a low-frequency hum. Not the wind. Not the shifting ice. It came from *within* the pyramid. Constant. Purposeful. As if something in there is still *functioning.*"

Johan sat back, the implications crashing over him.

"If there's technology still active after thousands of years, then we're not just dealing with ruins. We're standing in the presence of something far more advanced than anything we can comprehend."

Rudi leaned forward, lowering his voice even more. "There's more. We weren't the first ones to enter." Johan's brow furrowed. "What do you mean?"

"Some of the entrances we found had been *cut*—with laser-like precision. Walls sliced through so cleanly that our engineers were speechless. No scorch marks. No tool residue. Just perfectly polished, smooth surfaces. No signs of struggle or decay. Whoever came before us had technology far superior to ours—and they left *nothing* behind. No clues. No tools. Just silence."

Rudi exhaled, his voice taut with both wonder and frustration. "We broke into a secret that someone else already unlocked. And whatever they found, they took it with them."

Expeditions to Antarctica

The Nazi Quest for the Ice Frontier

In the late 1930s, as geopolitical tensions escalated across Europe, Nazi Germany launched a significant and ambitious expedition to Antarctica. Led by Captain Alfred Ritscher, the mission took place from 1938 to 1939 and aimed to explore—and ultimately claim—a portion of the icy continent for the Third Reich. The result was the designation of a region known as New Swabia *(Neuschwabenland)*, named after the German region of Swabia.

The expedition was meticulously planned and well-resourced. The crew set sail aboard the *MS Schwabenland*, a vessel specially modified for polar exploration. Equipped with advanced aerial mapping instruments and Dornier Wal flying boats, the team carried out extensive aerial reconnaissance. Upon reaching the Antarctic coast, they surveyed large swaths of Queen Maud Land, covering over 600,000 square kilometers. To assert their territorial claim, they dropped aluminum swastika-inscribed markers across the landscape from the air.

But the mission, while officially scientific, would soon become the subject of persistent legend and global speculation.

The Shadow of Conspiracy

Though the Ritscher expedition was documented as a mapping operation, conspiracy theories have flourished for decades, suggesting that the Nazis had far more esoteric motives.

Some theorists claim that the Nazis were drawn to Antarctica not just for expansion, but because they believed it concealed remnants of an ancient, technologically advanced civilization. According to these accounts, the expedition allegedly uncovered massive pyramid-like structures buried beneath the ice—structures so geometrically precise and enormous in scale that natural explanation seemed implausible.

Other reports speak of vast subterranean tunnels and cavernous chambers, large enough to house aircraft or even entire military installations. The most persistent claim is the alleged creation of a secret Nazi base beneath the ice—known as Base 211, or in some accounts, Neu-Berlin. This base, theorized to lie deep below New Swabia, was said to be a final refuge for high-ranking Nazi officials and scientists at the end of World War II—some even speculating it was a secret escape route for Adolf Hitler himself.

Operation Highjump and the Postwar Mysteries

These theories gained further traction in 1947, when the United States Navy launched Operation Highjump, a massive expedition led by Admiral Richard E. Byrd. Officially, the mission aimed to test equipment and train personnel under polar conditions. However, rumors emerged that Byrd's fleet encountered unidentified flying objects—craft allegedly emerging from beneath the Antarctic ice and engaging in hostile maneuvers.

Byrd, in a post-expedition interview, reportedly warned of a technological threat originating from the polar region—an enemy capable of reaching from pole to pole in minutes. Though official records of his statement remain classified, the remarks have been cited repeatedly in alternative history circles.

Adding to the mystique were declassified Nazi documents revealing that Heinrich Himmler, head of the SS, had a profound interest in the region. The Ahnenerbe—an elite Nazi organization tasked with researching the occult and the origins of the Aryan race—is believed to have been involved in Antarctic operations. Some claim that experimental aircraft designs, including the Haunebu flying saucers, were secretly tested—or even perfected—beneath the ice.

Myth or Hidden Truth?

Despite the sensational nature of these claims, scattered fragments of evidence have kept the mystery alive:

- Satellite imagery has revealed unusually symmetrical formations beneath the ice in Queen Maud Land, prompting some to argue these are not merely natural peaks, but ancient pyramidal structures.

- Eyewitness accounts from postwar explorers and intelligence officers have described strange craft, unmarked installations, and restricted zones deep within the continent.

- Soviet and Allied intelligence reports have noted unusual electromagnetic interference and flight anomalies near suspected sites.

Skeptics argue that Antarctica's extreme climate naturally sculpts deceptive topographies, and that the so-called pyramids are likely nunataks—mountain peaks exposed by retreating glaciers. Others claim that Cold War secrecy and military operations created an atmosphere ripe for myth-making and disinformation.

Yet, the persistent silence surrounding Antarctic activities—combined with gaps in the historical record of the Ritscher expedition—continues to fuel speculation. If the Nazis did indeed uncover something extraordinary in Antarctica—be it ancient technology, hidden bases, or the remnants of a forgotten civilization—then the truth remains entombed beneath miles of ice, still waiting to be revealed.

The Key Translation

Over the next six months, Johan immersed himself in the painstaking work of deciphering the ancient tablets recovered from Rudi's expeditions. With Karl's sharp memory and precision, they cross-referenced inscriptions from the Antarctic pyramid, Egyptian manuscripts, South American relics, and Sumerian clay tablets. Slowly, painstakingly, the puzzle began to take shape.

The fragments—once isolated and indecipherable—now told a coherent story. Across continents and millennia, they spoke of a cycle of catastrophes: massive floods, volcanic eruptions, great fires, and prolonged darkness.

Survivors of these calamities, from each era, had left warnings—carved in stone, sealed in manuscripts, etched into temples. Messages for the future.

CHAPTER 9

Purity Reborn

Meanwhile, in the library bunker, the debate continued …

Rudi exhaled, voice low and grave.

"The Great Purification Cycle. The very event we're approaching now."

He tapped the ancient tablet in front of him.

"If these civilizations knew a recurring cosmic disaster was inevitable, then they must have planned for it. Somewhere, they left us clues on how to survive."

Johan nodded, his expression hardening.

"And we need to find them before the Nazis do. If they harness this knowledge, we're not just facing military dominance. We're looking at a force beyond anything humanity has ever seen."

The room went quiet. The air was heavy with truth.

A Conversation Across Time

The two men stood before the table, covered in scrolls, tablets, and worn books. Karl and Karin listened quietly nearby—young, but far from unaware.

Rudi broke the silence.

"Let's try to piece this together—from the top."

While flipping through a worn astronomy chart, Johan looked up thoughtfully. "The Great Year. A 25,920-year cycle tied to Earth's axial precession. Basically, the Earth wobbles slowly on its axis, which causes the stars and constellations to shift position over thousands of years."

Rudi, leaning over the table to examine a diagram, nodded. "Right. That wobble changes the position of the equinoxes over time. Ancient cultures couldn't have measured it with modern tools, but they knew. They tracked it."

Gesturing toward a blueprint of the Giza Plateau, Johan added, "Egyptians aligned the pyramids with Orion, Sirius, and other celestial markers. It wasn't just spiritual—it was mathematical, astronomical precision."

Rudi pointed toward a Sumerian star chart printout. "Same with the Sumerians. Their tablets chart the movement of stars and planets from 5,000 years ago. The Zodiac of Dendera? It's practically a map of the Great Year."

Johan reached for a copy of the Rig Veda and added with awe, "The Hindus nailed it too. Their Yuga Cycle mirrors the Great Year—Satya, Treta, Dvapara, and Kali Yuga. The Vedas describe human degeneration as part of a larger cosmic rhythm."

Rudi leaned back, folding his arms as he spoke. "And the Maya—5,125-year Long Count calendars. One-fifth of the Great Year. They saw the 2012 reset not as apocalypse, but as transition. A new cycle."

There was a pause, then Johan's voice grew lower. "But here's where it gets terrifying—those transitions? They always seem to bring destruction: floods, fires, quakes, cosmic impacts."

Rudi looked out the window, voice steady. "Every culture has its flood story. Gilgamesh. Noah. Utnapishtim. The Zep Tepi in Egypt—the First Time—civilization restarting after cataclysm."

Johan tapped his fingers against the desk, eyes narrowed. "So how did they know? How were they all saying the same thing across thousands of years?"

Rudi answered slowly, as if weighing the implications. "Maybe it was handed down—from a lost civilization that survived the last collapse. Or maybe, from the Anunnaki. The Sky People."

Johan walked to the shelves lined with site photos and artifacts. "Whatever the source, the monuments are the message. Pyramids. Stonehenge. Göbekli Tepe. They weren't just spiritual sites—they were time capsules. Aligned to the heavens, built to outlast these events."

He paused at a framed rendering of the Great Pyramid and spoke with conviction. "The Great Pyramid? It encodes pi, phi, the speed of light in meters, star alignments—it's a cosmic decoder. Its precision is beyond any ancient builder's tools."

Rudi stepped forward and laid out a set of diagrams. "And the Maya—Teotihuacan, Chichén Itzá—those structures track Venus cycles, eclipses, and equinoxes. And all tied to the Great Year."

Johan nodded, then pointed to an image of Göbekli Tepe. "But Göbekli Tepe—that's the wild card. It predates agriculture, cities—

everything. And some of the carvings represent constellations exactly as they were around 9600 BCE."

Rudi's expression turned grim. "Which is right when the last Ice Age ended."

"And it was deliberately buried," Johan added, his voice almost a whisper. "Someone knew the next reset was coming. They preserved it for us."

Rudi glanced down at a Sanskrit passage. "Same message in the Vedas—Kali Yuga, our current age of decay. Predicted thousands of years ago."

Johan walked past the bookshelf and gestured toward a set of ancient site photos. "Stonehenge, Carnac, Callanish—all precession markers. All warning signs."

The Forgotten Site

Rudi's eyes gleamed.

"You want a curveball? Adam's Calendar. South Africa. Mpumalanga. Locals call it *Enki's Calendar.*"

Johan raised a brow.

"Go on."

"It's a stone circle aligned to the solstices, equinoxes—and Orion's Belt. Some say it's 75,000 years old. And the legends say Enki built it. The same Enki who, in Sumerian myth, gave humanity knowledge."

Johan sat back, stunned.

"Then that site could be *the oldest astronomical observatory on Earth.*"

"And it's in perfect sync with the same cosmic framework. That means this knowledge spans from South Africa to Mesopotamia, Mesoamerica to India. The Great Year wasn't just known—it was encoded into human culture like a cosmic heartbeat."

As the fire crackled low and shadows stretched along the stone floor, Johan looked up from the ancient manuscript he'd been poring over for hours. "Which brings us back to the question that's haunted us from the beginning: Were they trying to warn us?"

Rudi set down the tablet fragment in his hand, his voice low but resolute. "I think so. I think they left us a pattern—a map through time. So that when the stars aligned again, someone would remember."

The room fell silent except for the creak of the old wooden beams above. Johan leaned back in his chair, staring out the window at the dark horizon. "And the cycle? It's starting again. We're in the tail end of the Kali Yuga. The signs are here—environmental collapse, war, spiritual decay."

Rudi's tone was steady, almost grim. "Which means the next shift isn't centuries away. It's imminent."

Turning back to the table filled with notes and sketches, Johan spoke with urgency. "If we can finish the translation in time—if we can find where they went, what they built—we might survive what's coming."

Rudi didn't move. He stared at the candlelight flickering over the tablet surface and finally spoke—barely above a whisper. "And if we don't . . ."

He left the sentence unfinished.

Johan and Rudi had come to understand that the ancient knowledge they uncovered was far more than historical curiosity—it was a survival manual. The Great Year did not simply chart the rise and fall of civilizations; it encoded the very rhythms of the cosmos, the hidden forces shaping human destiny.

Those who understood these rhythms held the key to predicting—and potentially surviving—the next great catastrophe. The architects of pyramids, temples, and megaliths had not merely left behind monuments. They had etched a warning into stone and starlight. They knew civilization itself was subject to the turning of the great cosmic wheel—creation, destruction, renewal.

Now, Johan and Rudi's mission was not just to preserve this knowledge, but to ensure that humanity would be ready when the cycle reached its next climax.

A Race Against Time

As World War II raged, the Nazi regime grew increasingly desperate—and increasingly obsessed. Their fascination with the occult, mythological origins, and lost civilizations became more than fringe interest. Organizations like the Ahnenerbe scoured the globe for relics and artifacts believed to hold supernatural power.

Johan and Rudi understood that time was slipping away. Their translations hinted at knowledge once possessed by ancient cultures—knowledge so advanced, so potentially volatile, that if weaponized, it could alter the course of the war or end the world.

With the combined work of Johan, Rudi, and the sharp minds of young Karl and Karin, they reached chilling conclusions.

A cataclysmic event was imminent.

All signs pointed to the return of Nibiru, the mysterious celestial body described in Sumerian texts—a rogue planet whose proximity could disturb Earth's delicate balance. Their calculations suggested that even a minimal shift in gravitational influence could trigger earthquakes, sea level surges, tsunamis, or awaken long-dormant volcanoes.

But it wasn't just physical.

The texts spoke of tests—trials that humanity faced with each cycle. Time and again, civilization failed. Survival came only through divine or external intervention: the biblical God saving Noah, or the Sumerian god Enki warning Ziusudra.

What was the true test? Was it spiritual?

Was it ecological?

Was it the ability to repent? Or to change?

And how—in a world spiraling toward war and darkness—could one possibly prepare for it?

The Last Goodbye

At the concealed entrance of the bunker, Johan and Rudi stood side by side, knowing this might be their final meeting.

Johan would stay behind, continuing the translations, diving deeper into the ancient symbology.

Rudi would lead a covert expedition to Antarctica, racing to reach the pyramid before the Nazis seized full control.

Their research pointed to a single, haunting conclusion: somewhere beneath the ice—deep within the structure—lay a key. A message, a tool, a warning something vital left behind by the ancients to help survive the next cycle.

They believed that unlocking it might make the difference between passing the test or perishing.

Rudi placed a hand on Johan's shoulder, eyes filled with resolve and silent dread.

"I am much older now, Johan we both are, I don't know how much they know. No matter what happens, make sure the knowledge survives. If we fail, the world must still know."

Johan nodded solemnly.

"And you—be careful. If those tunnels lead where we think they do, you're not just confronting history. You could be walking into something far older and far more dangerous."

CHAPTER 10

The Next Guardians

The passing years had not been kind to Johan and Rudi. The weight of their knowledge—the staggering truths they had unearthed, the discoveries that had shaken the very foundation of human history—had left scars, both visible and hidden. A lifetime spent in relentless pursuit of forbidden knowledge, forever glancing over their shoulders, had exacted a heavy toll. Their bodies had grown frail under the burden. Johan's once steady hands now trembled when he reached for a pen, his long, nimble fingers reduced to trembling shadows of their former grace. Rudi's once unyielding gait had slowed to a shuffle, his breath shallow and uneven, each step a quiet reminder of how far they had come—and how little time remained. The vibrant strength of their youth had faded, but their minds—sharp as blades honed by decades of discipline, paranoia, and fear—remained untouched by time's erosion.

Yet despite the toll, there was a quiet strength in knowing they had endured. The weight of their experiences had not crushed them; it had shaped them. Every scar was a testament to their survival, proof that even when the truth was too terrible to bear, they had not turned away. There had been victories, too—moments of light amid the darkness. The lives they had saved, the threats they had neutralized, the glimpses of hope they had preserved in a world that often teetered on the edge of chaos—these were the quiet rewards that had kept them moving forward when the nights were longest.

And now, they both knew their time was drawing to a close. The years had taken much from them, but not the awareness that the truths they carried were still too dangerous to leave behind unguarded. Yet instead of despair, they felt something else—a quiet sense of resolution. The fear that had haunted them in youth had faded with the years. They had made peace with the idea that some things would outlive them—and perhaps that was how it should be.

The End of the Second World War—A Brilliant Victory

The Second World War—the deadliest conflict in human history—finally came to a close in 1945. After six years of unprecedented destruction, the Allied forces emerged victorious, with the United States playing a decisive role in ending the tyranny of fascism.

Following the attack on Pearl Harbor in 1941, America transformed into a war machine. Industry, innovation, and manpower were mobilized with breathtaking speed. U.S. forces joined the Allied invasion of Normandy on D-Day, helping to liberate Western Europe from Nazi control, while Soviet forces pressed in from the East, crushing Hitler's regime from both sides.

In the Pacific, the U.S. fought brutal island-to-island campaigns, drawing closer to Japan with each battle—Guadalcanal, Iwo Jima, Okinawa. The war ended with shocking finality after the atomic bombings of Hiroshima and Nagasaki, forcing Japan's surrender on September 2, 1945.

The world was left scarred. Cities reduced to ash. Millions dead. But tyranny had been defeated. The United States emerged as a superpower, its courage, sacrifice, and industrial might instrumental in delivering a brilliant, hard-won victory.

For a moment, humanity exhaled.

The camps had been liberated. The weapons dismantled. The symbols of hate burned and scattered.

And yet—peace was a fragile illusion.

A Shadow Survives

Beneath the surface, rumors began to stir.

Whispers of a secret society—a faction that had survived the fall of the Reich. A name surfaced again and again in hushed tones: Mr. Sloan.

The enigmatic financier behind many of the Nazis' esoteric expeditions, Sloan had seemingly vanished during the final years of the war. But now, he was said to have reemerged—richer, more powerful, and more dangerous than ever before.

While the Reich had crumbled in the public eye, Sloan had slipped into the shadows. And with him, it was whispered, went the darkest secrets of Nazi research—and the stolen relics, tablets, and manuscripts that Johan and Rudi had fought so hard to keep hidden.

Now, those whispers grew louder.

Sloan was no longer acting through intermediaries. He was hunting personally. His reach extended into political circles, private foundations, and hidden laboratories. Entire excavation teams had gone missing in remote regions. Libraries were sacked. Witnesses silenced.

He wanted the ancient knowledge—the truth about the Great Year, the cosmic cycles, the warnings from the ancients. And he would stop at nothing to possess it.

The Quiet Before the Storm

Johan had learned to trust the silence less than the chaos. Danger didn't always wear a uniform or speak in marching orders. Sometimes it came dressed in suits, smiling over wine, cloaked in legitimacy.

He had seen empires fall and ideologies collapse—but ideas were harder to kill. Especially the kind that promised power beyond the natural world.

Now, with the war over and the ashes cooling, new wars were brewing—ones fought in the dark, where the prize wasn't territory or treasure, but truth itself.

Johan knew:

Their personal war had only just begun.

The Next Generation

Karl and Karin were no longer children. The wide-eyed innocence they once possessed had long since given way to quiet resolve. Shaped by the sacrifices of their fathers, they had stepped into the roles destiny had prepared for them. The knowledge passed down to them—the truths etched into brittle parchment and cold stone—had become both a gift and a burden. Neither Karl nor

Karin took it lightly. They knew that the weight of humanity's forgotten past, and perhaps its uncertain future, rested upon them. They lived it—running from false authority, guarding the truth like a sacred flame.

Karl had grown into a man of quiet strength. His dark hair, once untamed and falling over his forehead, was now cropped close. His eyes—deep brown like his father's—carried a guarded intensity, the kind forged by witnessing too much, too young. He had been trained not only in ancient knowledge, but in survival. He knew how to fight, how to decode, and how to disappear when necessary.

Karin possessed the same fierce intellect as her father, but there was an edge to her that Rudi had once seen in himself—a quiet ruthlessness shaped by years of navigating the shadows of power and conspiracy. Her long blonde hair was usually tied back, her sharp blue eyes missing nothing. She had a gift for reading people, for identifying their weaknesses—a talent that made her dangerous to anyone who underestimated her.

The Library Bunker

Johan sat in one of the old underground library bunkers, bathed in the dim, flickering glow of an oil lamp. These bunkers had been their sanctuaries for decades—sacred places where knowledge was hidden, preserved, and protected from the corruption of the outside world.

The rough stone walls were lined with shelves of ancient books, brittle parchments, and clay tablets etched with languages long forgotten. The air was cold and heavy, steeped in the scent of old paper, oil, and dust—the fragrance of forgotten time.

Wrapped in a thick wool blanket, Johan's thin frame seemed even smaller in the oversized chair. His breath fogged faintly in the chill. On his lap rested an aged leather journal—the one he had carried across continents, through war zones, and into the depths of mystery. It held the fragmented truths of the Anunnaki, Nibiru, and the Great Year—a prophecy carved across millennia.

Karl knelt beside him, gently adjusting the blanket around his father's shoulders. His hands—strong, steady, capable—were everything Johan's no longer were. But in Karl's eyes, Johan saw the same quiet intensity he had once glimpsed in his own reflection.

"You should rest," Karl said softly.

Johan offered a faint smile. "Not yet."

His voice was thin, but his gaze burned with clarity. "There's more work to do."

Karin stood near the shelves, her fingers trailing along the spines of books she had read—studied—a hundred times over. She turned toward them.

"We've already committed the key texts to memory. The translations are nearly complete."

"That's not enough, dear Karin," Johan said, his voice taut with quiet urgency. "Knowing the words isn't the same as understanding them."

Karin's brow furrowed. "You think Sloan has the missing pieces?"

Johan's eyes darkened. "If he does, he'll use them."

Karl's jaw clenched. "Then we take the fight to him."

Johan shook his head. "No. You survive. Protect the knowledge. That's the only fight that matters now."

A sudden noise echoed through the corridor—a faint scraping of stone against stone.

Karl's head snapped toward the entrance.

"It's probably nothing," Karin murmured, but her hand drifted instinctively toward the pistol holstered beneath her coat.

Johan didn't flinch. He had seen too much, lived through too many betrayals, to startle at shadows. And yet, he could feel it. The air had shifted. The weight of centuries pressed harder on his chest.

Karl rose, pulling a blade from his belt. "I'll check it out." He disappeared into the darkness of the corridor.

Karin crossed the room and knelt beside Johan, her hand resting gently over his. For a long moment, they said nothing.

"You've trained us well," she whispered.

Johan's hand tightened weakly over hers. Cold. But steady. "Be careful," he said.

"We always are."

Footsteps echoed faintly down the stone tunnel. Danger, ever-present, lingered in the background like the whisper of a storm on the horizon.

Johan looked down at the journal beneath his hand. He had carried it through the rise and fall of empires. But the knowledge it held, it was bigger than war. Bigger than any one life.

Because knowledge was power. And power was always dangerous.

Gentle Warning

Johan cleared his throat, his voice now more whisper than word. "Karl. Karin. It's time."

They turned toward him, sensing the weight of what was coming.

"Your fathers spent their lives ensuring that the truth would never be lost. Now, it falls to you."

Karl's jaw tightened. "You speak as though you're already gone, Papa."

Johan gave a weak smile. "I am an old man. The weight of

knowledge has been heavier than my body can bear. But you . . ." He looked between them. "You have what I no longer do—time."

Karin's voice cracked. "And what of my father? Shouldn't he have returned by now?"

Johan's eyes dimmed with memory. "I fear we may never see him again."

Karin placed a hand over his, her voice barely audible. "Why?"

He looked up, face grave. "His last message came days ago. Just short and to the point:

Not here. Must be elsewhere. Careful—they know. Keep K safe."

Johan's voice dropped even lower. "Sloan is watching. Tracking us. Rudi must have realized that. That's why he disappeared—to protect us, to protect you."

Karl's fists tightened. "Then I'll go after him."

"No," Johan said firmly. "If he warned us, it's because he doesn't want you walking into a trap. Rudi is clever. If there's a way back, he'll find it."

He paused, took a slow, measured breath. "But there's something more pressing. Something I've waited too long to tell you."

Karl and Karin leaned closer.

Johan placed his frail hands atop theirs, voice soft but unwavering.

"The Cycle is upon us again."

Karin froze. "You mean another Purification?"

Johan nodded. "The signs are here. Climate instability.

Quakes in places that should be quiet. Unrest among world powers. It's all happening again."

Karl's eyes searched his father's face. "So, what do we do?"

Johan's lips curled into the faintest smile. "You continue. You finish what we started."

He gathered his strength.

"Your father went to Antarctica because we believed an

important key was there. But his message tells us otherwise—*Not here.* Which means it's still out there. Hidden. Waiting."

Karin's mind spun. "The main underground archive . . ."

"Yes." Johan whispered. "Return to where we left off. There may still be clues we missed. The code must be completed." He looked at them both with a final clarity, a final fire.

"The knowledge you carry is more valuable than gold. More dangerous than any weapon. And it will be hunted. You must never stop running, never stop learning, never stop protecting it."

Silence wrapped around them like a shroud. The moment was sacred. Final.

And from it, a new mission was born.

The Torch Passed

Johan Rosen passed away in his sleep three nights later. It was a quiet departure. Peaceful. Expected, but no less painful.

Karl had known it was coming—he had seen the signs—and still, when it happened, a silence fell over him deeper than grief. The man who had guided him. Taught him. Fought beside him. His father. His mentor. His compass. Gone.

And in the stillness that followed, Karl felt the full weight of responsibility settle onto his shoulders. Not just for the knowledge.

But for the world.

At Johan's simple mountain burial, Karl stood beside Karin. Hand in hand.

The cold wind tore through the high ridge, flapping their long coats as they stared at the small, unmarked grave. The stone they had chosen was smooth and bare—no name, no dates. Just silence.

A resting place hidden from history.

Protected from those who would never understand.

Their fathers' legacies were too great to risk desecration. Too sacred to be turned into myth by those who would twist the truth into a weapon.

Karl clenched his jaw, swallowing the knot rising in his throat. "We continue," he said simply.

Karin nodded, her fingers brushing his as she whispered, "We must."

He turned to her then, *really* seeing her—

Not the girl he had grown up with, or the partner who had shared his study table and survival drills.

But the woman who had stood beside him in the fire.

Who had faced the same impossible truths.

Who had lost as much, learned as much, and carried just as heavy a burden.

Their eyes met.

For the first time—she didn't look away.

"You and I—I have your back," she said softly. "We were raised for this moment."

Karl exhaled. A breath he hadn't realized he'd been holding. "We were," he said.

"And I have yours."

And in that moment, the burden did not feel quite so heavy. Because they weren't alone.

They had each other.

And far beyond the mountaintop . . . the world was changing.

CHAPTER 11

Secret Archives

Karl and Karin wasted no time. Within days, they had returned to the underground archives, steeling themselves for what lay ahead.

This place wasn't just a library. It was a vault of ancient knowledge. A blueprint of the past—and perhaps a guide to what was still to come.

They immersed themselves for months in their fathers' work: journals, tablets, translated texts, and the now-fragile ancient manuscript. For the first time in their lives, they were without supervision—no older voice to direct them. It felt strange, almost surreal, but also, liberating.

Every day, they worked side by side—reading, translating, cross-referencing, decoding. They were the only people they trusted.

At night, they sparred, reviewing martial arts techniques—discipline forged into routine—before sharing a simple meal and retreating to their separate rooms.

And yet, there was something else. Unspoken.

Electric.

Sometimes, a simple touch of hands would draw a blush. A glance held too long. A laugh that lingered. But they stayed focused. They had a mission. And they would not fail it.

The Breakthrough

Then, one day—it happened.

"Look, Karl," Karin said, pointing at a tightly rolled set of aged manuscripts. "This was written by your grandfather."

Karl's eyes widened. He leaned closer, brushing her shoulder as they studied the delicate cuneiform inked across the parchment.

"Wait, let me see," Karl said, squinting. "It's a hidden note. I can't believe they missed this."

The Rosen family had long used cuneiform as a private cipher—a tradition spanning generations.

Karl began to translate slowly, carefully.

"It's my last name, followed by coordinates. Steps. Directions. It's a set of instructions." He looked up, stunned.

"It's leading somewhere. We just need the starting point."

They scoured the archive, eyes scanning every stone, every shelf, every groove.

Then Karin gasped, pointing to the wall.

"There. That stone—it has the letter 'R' carved into it. Like your family's crest."

Karl rushed to it, fingers tracing the weathered mark. "This could be it. The first step."

He followed the directions—left, right, through a corridor, then deeper still into the archive's dark, forgotten reaches. Finally, the path ended at a heavy stone wall.

Another room. Hidden.

Inside, the air was thick—heavy with age and meaning. The silence felt sacred. Scrolls lined the walls, ancient tomes untouched by time.

Karl frowned. "Now what?"

"We look for more," Karin said, her eyes scanning.

Across the far wall, Karl saw it—an 'F' etched into the stone.

His heart skipped.

"First it was my crest. Now yours."

Their eyes met. An electric realization surged between them. Karin whispered, "Maybe we were meant to find this. Together." She looked up—and froze.

"Karl, the ceiling!"

Etched faintly into the stone above, in ancient cuneiform: *As Above, So Below.*

Karl followed her gaze, then slowly looked down. "It has to be here."

Together, they lifted the hidden stone tiles, layer by layer—until Karl's hands struck something solid.

A hidden compartment.

Inside it: a manuscript bound in leather, older than anything they'd seen.

Karl handed it up to Karin and climbed out. She held it gently, reverently, before opening it.

The Hidden Power

"Listen to this," Karin said, voice awed. *"'Our recent findings reveal extensive underground structures beneath the Pyramids of Giza—possibly a vast hidden powerplant.'"*

Karl leaned in, eyes wide.

"A powerplant? That's exactly what Papa described under Antarctica."

Karin flipped the page.

"Five interconnected structures, linked by a network of corridors—suggesting complex subterranean design.'"

Karl shook his head in disbelief. "Five structures. This wasn't a burial site. It was a system."

"Eight vertical shafts," Karin continued, *"each 650 meters deep. Encircled by spiral staircases. The engineering is staggering."*

"And concealed," Karl added darkly. "Maybe the Egyptian authorities kept it hidden."

"Listen to this part—" Karin whispered.

"'Two massive chambers. Conduits possibly connected to a lost tributary of the Nile. Suggesting hydraulic or ritual function...'"

Karl leaned back, stunned. "Harnessing water energy maybe even resonance. The pyramids weren't monuments. They were machines."

"And then this—" Karin turned another page.

"'These findings reignite theories of the legendary Hall of Records, a repository of ancient knowledge hidden beneath Giza.'"

Karl's heart thundered. "The Hall of Records. Maps. Astronomy. Medicine. Lost technology. Could all of it be real?"

"If they could build this," Karin said, "they could've recorded everything they knew. They preserved it. Buried it—for a reason."

Karl whispered, "Then the pyramids aren't just wonders. They're mechanisms."

Karin closed the manuscript gently.

"What if the past isn't lost? What if it's just waiting to be found?"

She looked up, eyes sharp now.

"And Karl, what if this technology could be used? Not to heal. But to control? Or worse—to destroy?"

Karl's jaw tightened. "Then we can't let it fall into the wrong hands."

Karin's voice lowered. "And it all starts here. Beneath the sands of Giza."

The Next Mission

Karl's pulse raced.

Then we have our next destination," he said, steady.

Karin nodded, already unfolding a map tucked into the manuscript.

"Coordinates. Right here—in minute detail. Beneath the Pyramid of Khafre. This, Karl, this is it. If we had unrestricted access, it would take mere minutes to retrieve whatever lies there."

Karl exhaled slowly, eyes locked on the map.

"The Pyramid of Khafre," he echoed. *"Then we'll need a solid plan."*

What others would've called impossible, Karl and Karin saw as destiny. The answers waited beneath stone and sand, in vaults untouched for millennia.

The underground archive had spoken. The path was clear. And Karl and Karin were ready to walk it—together.

CHAPTER 12

The Key of Osiris

Karl and Karin stood beneath the blistering Egyptian sun, the Great Pyramid of Giza looming above them—a monument to ancient secrets, casting its eternal shadow across time.

The wind carried the sting of desert dust and the scent of history.

Karin adjusted her scarf, shielding herself from the heat. "You're sure about this?"

Karl's eyes gleamed. "The manuscripts were clear. Whatever's down there—it's been hidden for millennia. And we're the ones who are meant to find it."

Her gaze drifted toward the guards at the entrance—armed,

alert. The pyramids weren't just protected for preservation. They were being *watched*.

Then, a voice behind them. "Mr. Rosen."

They turned. A thin Egyptian man in a linen jacket stepped into view. Amir. Trusted, discreet.

"You have the payment?" he asked, low and fast.

Karl handed him a small pouch. Amir peeked inside. The glint of gold coins caught the light before he sealed it and nodded.

"The main guard is bought. He'll look away. You have fifteen minutes—then you're on your own."

Karl and Karin exchanged a look. "Fifteen's enough," Karl said.

Amir's eyes darkened. "Then may the gods favor you." He vanished into the crowd.

They approached the entrance. The guard gave a blank glance, then stepped aside—dusting his uniform as if bored.

Inside, the cool breath of the Khafre pyramid swallowed them whole. The air turned damp, heavy with stone and silence.

They moved quickly through the inner corridor until they reached a rusted gate—*off limits*. Locals knew it existed, but few ever spoke of what lay beyond.

The gold had done its job. The gate was unlocked.

Karl pushed it open—metal grinding, the sound echoing into the dark.

"Here we go," he whispered.

They descended. Shadows danced across the ancient limestone, flickering in the beam of Karl's flashlight as the passage narrowed around them. He swept the light across the walls, scanning the carvings etched into the stone.

He froze.

"Here—the entrance to the main chamber." They stepped inside.

The chamber pulsed with an eerie stillness. Massive, intricate. It didn't feel like a tomb—it felt like a machine.

Karin's eyes narrowed. "They hid this. Not to protect it, but to keep it for themselves."

Karl stepped toward the mechanism, hypnotized by its complexity.

"It's missing something," he said softly. "A component. It's been disabled."

She grabbed his arm. "Karl. Snap out of it. We're not here to study the machine—not now. Follow the map."

He blinked, then nodded. "Right. This way."

They followed the manuscript's path into a side corridor. A stone door, split down the middle.

"Look at this . . ." Karl murmured.

Karin's breath caught. "Could this be Marduk's hiding place? During the Pyramid Wars?"

Karl's voice dropped. "And if that's true, then this was where Ninurta broke in."

They bowed their heads as they stepped through the ruined threshold, as if asking permission from the past itself.

Karin moved beside him, eyes scanning the walls. "Cuneiform. Faint. But familiar . . ."

She touched a seam in the stone. It shifted. A hidden passage opened.

"Nice work," Karl said, his smirk brief. "We're not done yet," she replied.

They descended into the dark.

The Chamber Beneath

The passage spiraled downward. Symbols lined the walls— celestial alignments, Orion, Sirius, the Milky Way. The pyramids weren't just markers; they were maps.

At the bottom, the passage opened into a vast chamber.

A stone altar stood in the center, dusted in obsidian powder.

Newer cuneiform markings circled it like a seal.

Karl approached. "This is it," he whispered.

Embedded in the altar—a black stone. Obsidian. Smooth. Marked with symbols no modern scholar would recognize.

He reached out. As his fingers touched it, the room *shifted*.

A rumble echoed deep beneath the earth. Dust rained from above.

"Karl!" Karin shouted. The walls *shimmered*. The air *vibrated*. He yanked the stone free. And everything went still.

Karl held it in his hands—cold, heavy, carved with alien precision.

"The Key of Osiris," he whispered. He wrapped it carefully in linen, slid it into his satchel, and turned. "Let's go." They ran—parts of the chamber collapsing behind them. Stone crumbled. Dust roared. Up the spiral. Through the corridor. Back to the gate. And then—Click. A metallic snap. They froze.

At the entrance stood the guard. Rifle raised. Eyes cold. "I felt the tremors," he said. "Hand it over." Karl stepped forward. "You don't understand—"

"I don't care," the guard hissed. "My client's been waiting." His finger tightened on the trigger.

In one breathless moment, Karl lunged.

He knocked the rifle aside—the shot cracked, ricocheted. Karl twisted the guard's arm, slammed him down. The man screamed. Karl disarmed him in seconds, tossed the rifle aside, and stood.

"Stay down," he said.

Karin appeared beside him, already moving. "Let's go."

They emerged into the desert night. Moonlight lit the dunes like silver flame.

Karl adjusted his satchel, the Key pressing against his side.

"That was impressive," Karin said, a flicker of adrenaline still in her voice.

Karl gave a half-smile. "We're just getting started."

They vanished into the night—shadows trailing behind them as the pyramids watched in silence.

The Cut to Black

Later that night . . .

The guard made his report—breathless, panicked. He never saw the blade.

It slid clean between his ribs.

He gasped, blood bubbling from his lips. As he crumpled to the ground, a tall figure stepped from the shadows.

Gloved. Clean. Precise.

"As you wished," the voice said coldly. "No witnesses."

The figure paused over the dying man, then pulled a phone from his coat pocket.

"I'll find them," he murmured. "And I'll deliver the artifact."

A pause.

"No more mistakes, Mr. Sloan."

A World in Waiting

Karl and Karin made their way back home beneath cover of night, the desert winds still clinging to them. In their possession now— the Key of Osiris. A relic of myth, a tool of immense mystery, and perhaps, a final piece of a puzzle their fathers had spent their lives trying to solve.

It was a victory, but a costly one.

They had exposed themselves to Mr. Sloan—the man who had been waiting, watching, playing the long game. And though they had won the battle, the war was far from over.

Back in one of their underground study chambers, the cold stone walls pressed in with quiet intensity. Time seemed to pause around them. The Key of Osiris sat between them on the table—obsidian black, carved with unknowable symbols.

They had a new goal now.

Decipher the Anunnaki Code. Understand its purpose. And choose how—or if—they would use it.

Karin *(gazing intently at the symbols)* "Yes, and we're standing at the edge of it all. But we need time—time to piece it together. The sky people, Earth's cataclysmic cycles, the civilizations who studied the stars, Orion, the Pleiades . . . and now this—the Key of Osiris."

Karl *(eyes narrowing)* "And the long orbit of Nibiru. It keeps surfacing—Sumerian texts, Mayan glyphs, even hidden in Giza's architecture. It's like they all knew something—something about cycles of destruction and rebirth."

Karin *(turning a page carefully)* "But it is clear that the pyramids weren't just monuments! They were mechanisms—designed for protection or for communication? What if they were shut down for a reason?"

Karl *(thoughtful)* "Or what if the Anunnaki themselves deactivated them? Maybe they feared what would happen if their power fell into the wrong hands."

Karin *(softly)* "Do you remember when both our papas used to speak of the Anunnaki Pyramid Wars?"

Karl *(his eyes lighting up)* "Yes—the wars between the gods. Thoth—also known as Enki—and his son Marduk, also known as Ra. Our fathers always said the pyramids were the key to it all."

Karin *(leaning in)* "And now the Sumerian tablets are confirming it. There's a clear link between the Cult of Thoth and Enki. Thoth, the god of wisdom and magic. Enki, god of knowledge and creation. Both keepers of sacred knowledge."

Karl (*nodding*) "And Marduk's rise—it mirrors Ra's ascent in Egypt. Both took on solar aspects, both declared themselves supreme. Marduk fought Tiamat—the chaos dragon. Ra battled darkness in the underworld. The myths echo each other."

Ninurta: The Warlord of the Anunnaki

As the legend goes, the Anunnaki waged war for dominion over Earth and control of its resources, Marduk—son of Enki and a rising force among the gods—found himself in a precarious position. His ambitions to ascend above the elder gods had made him both a target and a threat.

During a pivotal moment of the Anunnaki conflict, Marduk vanished. Rumors whispered through the halls of Nibiru and across the Mesopotamian plains: he was hiding beneath the sands of Egypt, in a hidden chamber deep within the Pyramids— an ancient structure said to predate even the oldest dynasties, possibly built with extraterrestrial knowledge.

Within the pyramid, shielded by layers of stone and cosmic frequencies, Marduk entered a stasis-like state in a secret "Chamber of Renewal," guarded by loyal hybrids and cloaked from the prying eyes of his enemies. There, he waited—planning his return and the next phase of human evolution, one in which he would reign supreme.

Ninurta, son of Enlil, was the *supreme warrior* of the Anunnaki. He wielded the terrifying Sharur, a "talking mace" said to be both a weapon and an AI drone that could scout, strategize, and even communicate across dimensions.

When Marduk began his rise—staking his claim over Babylon and pushing for supremacy over Earth and Nibiru—Ninurta was sent to crush the rebellion. As loyalist factions formed behind Enlil, and others behind Marduk and Enki, the conflict escalated into a full-scale war—one fought in both the heavens (orbital platforms, perhaps?) and the Earth below.

The Pyramid Showdown

According to the ancient tablet's translations, Ninurta was the one who stormed the Pyramids during the height of the conflict. Not to destroy them—but to neutralize Marduk, who had turned the pyramid into a weaponized stronghold. Some say the inner chambers had been converted into a frequency generator or a command center.

But Ninurta didn't destroy the structure—he disarmed it. Mythologically, this is represented in Sumerian texts where he "removed the crystals" and took the "Black Stone of Destiny" (or DUG.GA) from the heart of the pyramid. It's said he repurposed or hid the artifact somewhere unknown.

Marduk was eventually trapped inside, not killed. The council of the Anunnaki couldn't agree on his execution. So they exiled him—some say in physical imprisonment, others say in dimensional stasis. Thus, Marduk became both a martyr and a time bomb.

Karin *(intense, adrenaline still in her voice)* "So these conflicts were real. We just found the Black Stone of Destiny—or as we know it, the Key of Osiris." (she continues) "The pyramids weren't tombs. They were machines. Weapons. Or tools. Tools to *control* the balance between chaos and order."

Karl *(resting his palm gently on a tablet inscribed with Sumerian cuneiform)* "That would explain everything—why they were hidden, why they were shut down. If the wrong force controlled them . . ."

Karin *(cuts in, voice low, haunted)* "They could destabilize the Earth. Or worse, reset it."

Karl *(eyes wide)* "What if the pyramids weren't just meant to observe the cycles of destruction—what if they were meant to regulate them? Or even prevent them?"

Karin *(whispering)* "And now we have confirmation . . ."

Karl *(leaning back, a shadow passing over his face)* "But are we meant to use them? Or simply understand them?"

Karin *(placing a hand over his)* "Maybe this is why we're here. Not just to inherit the knowledge—but to complete what they started. To protect the Earth from repeating the cycle."

Karl *(quietly)* "Or to break it entirely."

A silence settled between them—not of fear, but of awe.

Karin *(softly, her voice reverent)* "The Hall of Records; the knowledge of the gods; the cycles; the war, the mechanisms."

Karl *(closing the ancient text slowly)* "It's all connected. The pyramids weren't just marvels of engineering. They're messages, left in stone. And now we have the key."

He glanced at the black obsidian shard between them.

Karl "We must figure out whether it was meant to save us or to destroy us."

Karin *(whispering)* "And who, or what, might be waiting when we do."

CHAPTER 13

United Hearts

Karl and Karin stood at the precipice of a new dawn—their journey forged by the sacrifices of their ancestors, and strengthened by the love that had quietly, resolutely blossomed between them.

They had spent years deciphering messages hidden in ancient texts, chasing the echoes of lost civilizations, and preparing for the inevitable cycle of destruction and rebirth. Yet amidst the urgency of their mission, they had found something even more profound—a love that defied time, woven into the very fabric of their shared destiny.

Their bond wasn't born of fleeting passion, but of unwavering commitment. From the moment they had taken up their fathers' work, their hearts had aligned in purpose. They were two souls bound by knowledge, by trust, and by the silent understanding that no matter how heavy the burden, they would carry it together.

Their love was a quiet force—it required no grand declarations. It was there in every lingering glance, every shared discovery, every decision made with the other in mind.

But as fate wove them ever closer, they could no longer deny the intensity growing between them. Long nights spent poring over manuscripts by candlelight led to whispered conversations, fingers brushing on fragile pages, lingering a heartbeat longer than necessary. The weight of their mission pressed heavily on them—but in those quiet hours, their burden was lightened by the simple knowledge: *they were together.*

One evening, beneath a canopy of stars, their unspoken desires finally found a voice.

They had ventured into the valley, seeking solitude away from the ruins and relics. The night air was cool and carried the scent of jasmine. The sky stretched endlessly above them—a mirror to the depths of their emotions.

Karl turned to her, his eyes reflecting the constellations overhead.

"We've spent so much of our lives chasing the past, trying to secure the future. But right here, right now—all I want is this moment. With you."

Karin inhaled, her heart pounding. She had never known love like this—a force so deep, so pure, it felt eternal.

"Karl," she whispered, her voice trembling, *"we are bound by more than destiny. We are bound by love."*

Their first kiss was slow, reverent—a vow written not in words, but in the stillness between them. Time stood still as their souls entwined. For one fleeting, infinite moment, fear dissolved in warmth. It was a kiss that became their anchor.

What followed were countless stolen moments—hidden from the world, but more real than anything they had ever known.

Their love deepened as their mission did. They found comfort in each other's arms, their devotion shown not in dramatic gestures, but in the smallest things—the way Karl brushed a strand of hair from her face as she studied, or how Karin's fingers tightened around his when danger loomed too close.

It was in the heart of the ancient caves—a sacred place carved into the bones of the Earth—that they pledged themselves to one another. Alone, bound not by law, but by love.

The cave walls bore inscriptions of unions past—love stories etched into stone by those who had come before. In the flickering glow of torchlight, Karl and Karin spoke vows that had lived in their hearts long before this moment.

"You are my past, my present, and my future," Karl whispered, cradling her face. *"No force, no fate, no time will ever change that."*

Karin's eyes shone with tears.

"In this life, and beyond. I am yours. Forever."

The cave held their secret. Their vows echoed softly into the stone—and in that sacred silence, their love gave birth to something more.

Their passion was not reckless. It was reverent. A love that *created* rather than consumed.

And in that quiet sanctity, they surrendered to one another completely—their souls merging in an act as old as time, as profound as the stars above them.

It was there, in the stillness that followed, that life began again. A heartbeat. A whisper of something new. The continuation of a story written long before them.

As the dawn crept in, casting golden light across the cave floor, Karl held Karin close—his lips against her forehead.

"No matter what comes next, we'll face it together."

She smiled, her hand resting gently over her abdomen, where new life stirred.

"Together," she echoed.

Their love had already changed the future.

A Love Tested by Fire

Their love had endured countless trials—betrayal, deception, and the ever-looming shadow of those who sought to silence their truth. When their findings about the coming celestial event threatened to disrupt the world's fragile balance, they became targets.

A powerful faction, determined to suppress the knowledge, moved to eliminate them. And in a cruel twist of fate, they succeeded—at least, for a time.

Karin had been taken.

It happened in the dead of night, as they returned from a quiet stroll beneath the stars. Armed men descended, sent by Mr. Sloan—who not only wanted everything they knew, but also the Key of Osiris. His right-hand mercenary planned to use Karin as leverage, overwhelming them before Karl had a chance to react.

Karl fought with everything he had, but the numbers were too great. He was beaten down, left bloodied and broken, as Karin—bound and unconscious—was dragged into the darkness.

She was gone.

And all that remained in Karl was rage. And purpose.

But Karin was no mere victim.

As she regained consciousness, the cold bite of iron against her wrists and ankles told her she was restrained. But she did not panic. Panic was for the untrained, for those who lacked the will to fight back. She had spent years preparing for moments like these.

Her captors, smug in their numbers and weapons, assumed she would be an easy prize. They were wrong.

The moment an opportunity presented itself, Karin acted. The one closest to her made the fatal mistake of leaning in too close, gloating about her predicament. With a swift, powerful twist, she launched her bound hands upward, smashing his nose with a force that sent him reeling back. Blood sprayed across the dimly lit room as he collapsed to the ground, moaning in agony.

The second captor lunged at her, but she used his momentum against him. As he reached for her, she kicked her legs up, wrapping them around his neck and twisting sharply. The sickening crack of cartilage snapping was music to her ears as he dropped lifeless to the ground. But there was no time to revel in her victory. The third opponent, warier than the first two, hesitated only for a moment before attacking.

Karin anticipated his move. She used her bound hands to grab his wrist, twisted hard, and pulled him off balance. With a swift pivot, she drove her knee into his gut, then brought her elbow crashing down on the back of his neck. He crumpled to the floor, unconscious.

For a brief, shining moment, Karin believed she could take them all.

But then the others rushed in.

Three more assailants stormed the chamber, their eyes flashing with fury. Karin braced herself, but she was outnumbered. She fought with all her might, landing blows and dodging attacks, but the tide turned against her. A sharp pain exploded at the base of her skull—a coward's strike from behind. Darkness swallowed her once again.

Karl had not been idle.

When he discovered that Karin had been taken, something

inside him snapped. He was a scholar, a thinker, but beneath his intellect lay a warrior's heart. He tracked her captors through the treacherous terrain, studied their movements, and devised his assault with a strategist's mind and a fighter's resolve.

The underground compound where they had taken her was carved into ancient ruins they had once explored together. Karl approached with the patience of a predator. He moved like a shadow, striking down guards silently, his blows precise and devastating. His knowledge of pressure points made each encounter swift—one touch to the carotid artery, a jab to the solar plexus, a strike to the nerve clusters in the arms—each enemy fell before they could sound the alarm.

As he reached the chamber where Karin was held, his fury boiled over at the sight of her bruised but defiant form. Her eyes locked onto his, a silent understanding passing between them. She had fought. She had resisted. And now, he would finish what she started.

The kidnappers swarmed him. But Karl was ready.

The first opponent lunged with a knife. Karl sidestepped, grabbing the attacker's wrist and twisting until he heard bones snap. The weapon clattered to the floor, and with a swift strike to the throat, the man collapsed, choking on his own breath.

Another charged, fists swinging. Karl absorbed the first blow but retaliated with a devastating knee to the ribs, followed by a precise elbow strike that sent his opponent sprawling. The remaining men hesitated, exchanging uncertain glances.

Karl gave them no chance to regroup.

He moved like a storm, fists and feet striking with the force of controlled fury. Every movement was calculated—he was not just fighting; he was dismantling them, piece by piece. He struck pressure points in the arms and legs, rendering them useless.

They dropped one by one, their bodies betraying them under his expertly placed attacks.

Through the doorway, Karl's eyes flicked toward Karin. Her hands were tied behind her back, a strip of duct tape across her mouth. Next to her, Sloan watched with a cruel smirk, his arms crossed. Time was running out.

Karl's breath hitched as the arm clamped around his neck, crushing his windpipe. His pulse thundered in his ears. The missing man, Sloan's right-hand thug, had emerged from the shadows like a ghost—swift and deadly. His arm was thick, corded with muscle, and the pressure on Karl's throat tightened like a steel vice.

Karl's instincts kicked in immediately. He dropped his chin to protect his airway, but the man's grip was relentless. His vision blurred at the edges as oxygen deprivation began to take hold. He stumbled backward, feeling the brute's body pressing against him, heavy and solid.

Breathe. Center yourself. Remember your training.

Karl adjusted his stance, his feet shifting on the dirt floor. He stopped struggling—flow with the force, not against it—just as his Jiu-Jitsu instructor had taught him. If he kept fighting directly, he'd burn out. Instead, Karl sagged slightly, relaxing his body, making it seem like he was losing strength.

The thug adjusted his grip to tighten the chokehold—that was Karl's opening.

In a sudden, explosive movement, Karl tucked his chin hard to his chest and twisted his body, turning into the hold rather than away from it. He trapped the attacker's arm with both hands, pulling it downward while his hips shot forward, breaking the angle of the choke.

The thug grunted in surprise. Karl stepped his left leg behind the man's right leg, then twisted his hips sharply—a textbook *osoto gari* throw. The man's weight shifted, and Karl drove him backward. The thug's feet left the ground. He crashed hard onto his back with a sickening thud.

Karl didn't hesitate. He dropped his knee onto the man's chest, pinning him down. The attacker bucked, trying to free his arm—but Karl anticipated it. He slid into position, his legs locking around the man's arm in a tight triangle.

Karl leaned back, hyperextending the arm—the man screamed as the joint strained. A second later, Karl shifted his hips and snapped the arm at the elbow with a sharp crack. The scream turned into a guttural moan.

Without missing a beat, Karl transitioned to a rear-naked choke. His forearm snaked under the man's chin, pressing into the carotid arteries. His other hand locked over his wrist, and Karl squeezed.

The man's thrashing slowed. His arms clawed weakly at Karl's grip, then fell limp. A few seconds later, Karl felt his body go completely slack. Out cold.

Karl stood, his breath ragged, his muscles burning. He turned toward the doorway. Sloan's smirk had vanished. The tall man reached into his jacket—for a gun.

"Now it's your turn," Karl said, his voice dark and steady. Karl moved before Sloan could draw.

Karl circled him, eyes locked on Sloan's predatory stance, reading every subtle shift in weight, every flicker of tension in his muscles. He was waiting for the perfect moment.

Sloan's hand moved toward his gun in a flash, but Karl was already ahead of him. His eyes narrowed, reading the intent in Sloan's muscles before they even moved. The gun barely cleared the holster before Karl's foot snapped upward—a sharp front circular kick that sent the weapon spiraling through the air, clattering to the ground several feet away.

Sloan's eyes widened in shock—just in time to catch the blur of Karl's leg whipping through the air. A classic *Bruce Lee* move: dragon whips its tail.

The spinning roundhouse connected with a sickening crack against Sloan's jaw. He hit the ground hard, spitting blood as the world around him tilted and swam.

Karl's chest heaved, but his eyes stayed cold. He watched as Sloan forced himself up, shaky but furious. Blood dripped from the corner of his mouth as he wiped it away with the back of his hand. Then Sloan lunged—a beast of a punch hurtling toward Karl's face with bone-breaking force.

Karl slid sideways, turning the attack into empty air. His body moved like water, fluid and precise. Sloan's momentum betrayed him, dragging him forward—and that's when Karl's knee rocketed upward into his gut.

Sloan folded with a strangled gasp, his breath punched from his lungs. He dropped to his knees, coughing violently. Karl wasted no time. He stepped over Sloan's back, twisted him down, and mounted him in a perfect full mount position. Sloan's arms were pinned beneath Karl's legs, leaving him defenseless.

Karl's breath came in ragged bursts. His eyes burned with cold fury as his knuckles curled. Then the storm broke.

"Don't *ever* lay your hands on her again!" Karl roared between strikes, his voice echoing through the empty space.

"Don't you ever lay your hands on her again—do you hear me?!" he shouted, continuing the ground-and-pound, fists slamming with controlled fury.

"You touch her again, and I swear to God—I'll kill you!"

Sloan's face was a bloody ruin beneath Karl's fists, his breath hitching in ragged gasps. He coughed, raising a trembling hand in surrender. "P-please . . ." he choked out, his voice barely a whisper. "I'll leave you alone. I swear . . ."

Karl stood over him, his chest heaving, his pulse hammering in his ears. His fist hovered midair, knuckles taut and ready to deliver the final blow. He could end it right now. End him right now. But he hesitated.

Sloan rolled over, his back exposed—a fatal mistake. Karl moved in a flash, fast as a lightning strike. He slid his arm under Sloan's chin, locking in a rear naked choke with perfect technique. Sloan's body thrashed and twisted with eyes wide open trying to prevent what was about to happen but Karl tightened his grip, squeezing with merciless precision.

"Night-night, you scumbag." Karl growled through gritted teeth.

Sloan's struggles slowed, then stopped. His body sagged, going limp in Karl's arms. Karl released him, letting his unconscious form slump to the ground. He stood over Sloan's motionless body, his breath slowing, his heart still pounding like war drums.

It was over.

But the question lingered, gnawing at the edges of Karl's mind: Should I have killed him? Would mercy come back to haunt him? Or had sparing him been the right choice?

Only time would tell.

Karl turned to Karin, who had already begun freeing herself from the ropes. Relief surged through him as he rushed to her side, his hands gently cupping her bruised face. His eyes, dark with worry, searched for any sign of pain.

"Are you okay? Did they hurt you?" His voice was low, strained with the weight of fear and adrenaline still thrumming through his veins.

Karin managed to crack a faint smile, her eyes soft despite the exhaustion etched into her face. "No," she whispered, her voice weak but steady. "And thank you for coming to the rescue."

Karl's throat tightened, his jaw flexing as the adrenaline began to fade, leaving behind raw emotion. His hand brushed over her cheek, his thumb tracing the outline of a bruise. "If anything ever happens to you . . ." His voice trembled. "I don't know if I could—"

"Shhh . . ." Karin hushed him softly, placing a finger over his lips before guiding his head toward hers. Their foreheads touched, the warmth of her skin grounding him, steadying the storm inside him.

"You fought well," he murmured, his voice rough with emotion. "So did you," she replied, her voice clear and steady despite the ordeal she'd just endured. Her hand rested on the back of his neck, her touch light but anchoring.

Karl closed his eyes for a brief moment, letting the tension slip away. With a final glance at the scattered bodies of their fallen enemies, he slipped his arm around Karin's waist, holding her close.

"Come on," he said softly. "Let's get out of here."

Side by side, they moved through the darkened corridor, their silhouettes merging into one as they disappeared into the night. Behind them, the echoes of battle faded into silence—but the bond between them, forged in fire and blood, had never been stronger.

A Love That Shaped the Future

Their escape was not merely a victory—it was a testament to their love. A love that had withstood fire and blood, a love that had refused to be extinguished. It was in that moment, as they stood under the open sky once more, that they knew their purpose was greater than ever.

Karl and Karin were no longer just seekers of knowledge.

They were warriors of truth, protectors of the legacy that would shape the future. And together, they would ensure that the world did not fall into darkness.

The night air was thick with the scent of damp earth and pine, a stark contrast to the acrid smoke and blood they had left behind. Their breaths came in ragged gasps, their bodies aching with exhaustion, but neither of them would falter now. Not after everything they had endured.

Karin turned to Karl, her piercing blue eyes reflecting the faint moonlight above. "We can't stop here. They'll be looking for us."

Karl nodded, his jaw set in determination. "We need to find shelter, regroup, and plan our next move. There are still secrets we haven't uncovered, and if we don't act fast, they'll bury the truth forever."

Their enemies were relentless, powerful forces that thrived on deception and control. The very knowledge Karl and Karin had uncovered was enough to topple empires, to shatter the chains that bound millions. But that knowledge came at a cost, and now they were hunted.

They moved quickly through the dense forest, their hands brushing against rough bark and tangled undergrowth as they navigated the shadows. Every rustling leaf, every distant howl of the wind sent a fresh jolt of paranoia through their veins. They had seen too much, lost too much to be careless now.

After what felt like hours, they stumbled upon an old, abandoned cabin nestled between the trees. The wooden structure was worn by time, its windows shattered, but it would provide them the temporary refuge they needed.

Karl pushed the door open with a creak, his muscles tensed for an ambush, but the cabin was empty. He exhaled in relief and gestured for Karin to follow. "We can rest here for a few hours. Come morning, we'll head north."

"We'll find out," he said finally. "But for now, we need to focus on surviving."

As exhaustion threatened to pull them into unconsciousness, they held onto each other, drawing strength from the only certainty left in their world: their love and their unwavering mission. The battle was far from over, and the darkness had not yet won.

With Mr. Sloan and his team beaten to a pulp, he vanished into the shadows, disappearing for a long time. Perhaps his promise to leave them alone had been nothing more than a lie—a desperate ploy to buy time and regroup. Karl and Karin both knew better than to trust the word of a man like Sloan. If anything, his retreat likely meant he was biding his time, growing stronger, preparing for a return.

Karl and Karin took the opportunity to regroup as well. They gathered the essential artifacts and manuscripts they needed, securing the last missing pieces of their research. Then, they disappeared into a secret location—a hidden refuge where no one could reach them. Finally, they had the chance to work undisturbed, to study the ancient texts and piece together the puzzle that had haunted humanity for millennia.

But research wasn't the only thing on their minds. For the first time since their journey began, Karl and Karin allowed themselves to breathe—to let down their guard and exist outside the weight of their mission. In the quiet of their sanctuary, they found each other—not as partners on a mission, but as something deeper.

Their connection, forged through fire and danger, became something electric—something undeniable. They couldn't keep their hands off each other. What began as stolen glances and lingering touches escalated into a fusion of bodies and souls, a merging of energy in complete, effortless synergy. For the first time, they allowed themselves to put each other ahead of the mission—above the duty, the danger, the fear of the unknown. In the protective bubble of their hideout, they became one, losing themselves in each other with a passion that left them breathless.

But peace was never meant to last.

It started as whispers beneath the earth—deep, unnatural tremors in places where no earthquakes should have been possible. Then came the tsunamis—massive walls of water triggered by volcanic eruptions beneath the ocean floor. Something was stirring beneath the crust of the Earth, something ancient and powerful enough to disrupt the very gravitational balance of the planet.

Karl stood at the window, his hand pressed against the cold glass as the distant sound of rolling thunder and the smell of coming rain filled the air. Behind him, Karin sat by candlelight, scanning an ancient text, her expression dark with realization.

"It's happening," she said softly.

Karl turned to her, his jaw tightening. "It's time."

The brief respite they had carved for themselves was over. The signs were too clear to ignore. The Earth itself was rebelling—reacting to forces they had yet to understand.

Karl crossed the room, his hand brushing against Karin's shoulder. She met his gaze, her eyes steady despite the weight of what lay ahead.

"We knew this was coming," she said.

Karl nodded. "Then we prepare for it."

Side by side, they stepped back into the storm. The mission was no longer just about knowledge—it was about survival.

CHAPTER 14

Awakening Light

From the moment he took his first breath, Jake was unlike any child before him—a product of true love and devotion between his parents, Karl and Karin. Even as an infant, he possessed an uncanny awareness. His piercing brown eyes held an intelligence far beyond his years. While other babies cried, Jake remained unnervingly calm, observing the world around him with an intensity that unsettled even the most seasoned doctors. Nurses whispered about the baby who never broke his gaze, who seemed to comprehend the world with a wisdom that defied his newborn form.

As he grew, it became clear that Jake had inherited more than just his parents' intelligence. He possessed an extraordinary ability to see beyond the surface of things, to uncover truths hidden in plain sight. By the age of two, he was forming full, complex sentences, engaging his parents in conversations that left even adults astounded. By four, he was dismantling and reassembling electronic devices without instruction, instinctively understanding the mechanics behind them. His mind was a machine of unparalleled precision, absorbing knowledge at a rate that baffled everyone around him.

Unlike his parents, who had grown up in the aftermath of war, Jake was raised in a time of peace. He had the opportunity to experience a relatively normal childhood—going to school, making friends, and exploring the world. But while other children were learning to read and write, Jake was already solving complex equations and grasping linguistic structures with an almost supernatural ease.

By the age of six, he was deciphering ancient texts that had taken scholars lifetimes to interpret. His hunger for knowledge was insatiable; he devoured books at a speed that astounded educators. He mastered languages, physics, and philosophy with an elegance that suggested not just intelligence but something deeper—a connection to knowledge itself. Yet alongside his intellectual pursuits, Jake displayed a remarkable physical aptitude.

But socializing was a different challenge altogether. Jake loved playing sports and enjoyed running around with other kids, but the moment he tried to share his thoughts—his theories about ancient civilizations or the mysteries of the universe—he was met with confusion and ridicule. When he spoke about the Anunnaki, the other kids would wrinkle their noses.

"Anuna-who?" they would ask, laughing.

At first, Jake couldn't comprehend why the other children

didn't see the significance of his discoveries. It was as if their minds were closed—conditioned to think within the narrow framework of what they were taught in school. When he mentioned that Columbus didn't discover America because there were already thriving civilizations on the continent, the teacher would glare at him with thinly veiled frustration.

"The land was always there," Jake would say, raising his hand during class. "The people who lived there had built societies long before Columbus arrived. He didn't discover it—he altered its course in history."

"Young man," the teacher would reply curtly, "sit down."

Jake sat, but his mind boiled with frustration. Why did everyone cling so stubbornly to a version of history that was incomplete—that was wrong?

He soon realized that people resisted certain truths—even when faced with evidence. They clung to familiar narratives, even if they were false.

Oblivion, after all, was bliss.

Still, he didn't let the rejection discourage him. He understood now: he was different. He had been born for something greater—and not everyone would see the world the way he did.

Karl and Karin were not ordinary parents. They were scholars and warriors—descendants of an ancient lineage devoted to understanding the celestial cycles that shaped human history. They recognized their son's potential early on and trained him not only in academic pursuits but in physical mastery as well. From a young age, Jake was immersed in both Kick-boxing and Jiu-Jitsu, developing a level of precision and foresight that seemed almost preternatural. By fifteen, he was defeating adult sparring partners with a combination of agility, strength, and an uncanny ability to predict his opponent's next move.

Despite his gifts, Jake remained humble. He was still just

a boy, but he carried the weight of something far greater than himself—a quiet gravity that set him apart from others his age. His parents had always known he was special, but it wasn't until they witnessed the full scope of his genius that they truly understood his purpose.

Over the following years, Karl and Karin dedicated themselves to preparing Jake for what lay ahead. They traveled the world, seeking lost knowledge and hidden truths. In the mountains of Tibet, Jake trained with monks who taught him to harness his energy, to meditate so deeply that he could slow his heartbeat to near stasis. In the deserts of Egypt, he explored the hidden chambers beneath the Sphinx, deciphering messages left behind by ancient civilizations. In the jungles of South America, he learned from shamans who taught him to connect with the Earth's energies in ways that defied scientific explanation.

It was a stormy night when Jake, a teenager, approached his parents with a revelation that shook them to their core. Rain lashed against the windows, and the low rumble of thunder seemed to echo the gravity of his words. He had spent weeks analyzing ancient star maps left behind by the Anunnaki— cryptic charts that countless scholars had tried and failed to decipher.

"I've found the pattern," Jake said, his voice steady despite the storm raging outside. His eyes—sharp and unnervingly calm— reflected the dim light of the room.

"The cycle isn't just a series of natural disasters," he explained. "It's a cosmic alignment—a shift in energy that resets civilization itself. This isn't random. It's part of a larger design. The cause isn't just the gravitational pull of celestial bodies—it could be triggered by a recurring shift in Earth's magnetic polarity or even a direct meteor impact."

He paused, letting the weight of his words settle. His parents stared at him, a mixture of awe and fear etched into their faces.

"I've been studying both your parents' work—my grandparents—and your own research," Jake said, his voice steady as he spoke to his parents. "The ancient manuscript, the symbols, the Key of Osiris, it's all connected."

"The similarities are undeniable. And if we don't decipher the Anunnaki code now, humanity won't survive this one."

Karl and Karin exchanged a silent, knowing glance. Their son—their greatest creation—was the key to everything they had worked for. Their family's ancient texts had always spoken of a child born under a rare alignment, one who could interpret the celestial warning left behind by the predecessors of humanity. They had never imagined that child would be their own flesh and blood.

By eighteen, Jake had become more than a prodigy. He had become a leader. Underground movements began to form, drawn to the truth he presented. Scientists, ex-military officials, and spiritual leaders all sought his guidance, recognizing that the boy who had once been an anomaly was now humanity's best hope.

As Jake grew older, he came to understand that differences among people were not weaknesses but strengths. He found solace in friends who shared his passion for martial arts, music, philosophy, and technology. But even among those closest to him, he struggled to find people who could comprehend the full scale of the truths he had uncovered.

The signs of impending disaster were growing clearer. The Earth's magnetic field was weakening. Birds were flying in erratic patterns, unable to rely on their natural instincts. Dormant volcanoes were becoming active. Yet the media and governments still dismissed the warnings as natural phenomena. The ignorance was maddening—but Jake knew how fragile humanity's future was.

And he knew that if he didn't act soon, humanity might not survive what was coming.

After Meticulous Planning

Jake had now started college, determined to pursue a master's degree in computer science. He understood that technology would be one of his greatest allies. The rapid advancements in artificial intelligence fascinated him—he saw AI not just as a tool, but as a potential key to decoding the complex patterns of the cosmos and uncovering the hidden mechanisms behind the approaching celestial alignment.

By then, nearly every prestigious university in the world had heard of Jake—his brilliance, his unparalleled mind, and his extraordinary academic record. Institutions lined up to offer him full scholarships, but Jake chose Oxford. Its proximity to the Oxford Museum was the deciding factor. Scholars there were working to translate newly discovered Sumerian tablets—tablets Jake believed might hold crucial information about the Anunnaki and the coming cosmic event.

But Jake wasn't content with merely attending Oxford. He struck deals with other universities across the globe, arranging research exchanges and specialized seminars. His goal was not just to gain knowledge but to build a team—a network of experts with highly specialized skills. He knew he couldn't face the coming challenge alone. He needed the best minds in the world, and he was finding them—one by one—in all continents.

But time was running out.

The signs were becoming impossible to ignore—earthquakes striking in places with no known fault lines, weather patterns shifting unpredictably, and species vanishing overnight without a trace. Migratory birds were flying off course, crashing into cities, or failing to find their way home. Dormant volcanoes were awakening, and the oceans were rising at an alarming rate. Humanity, however, remained blissfully unaware, going about its daily routine as though nothing was happening.

Even the world's governments—those secretly monitoring celestial events—dismissed the mounting evidence. Political leaders called it "climate change," "natural cycles," or "statistical anomalies." But Jake knew better. He had studied the patterns; he had seen the correlations in the ancient star maps and decoded the messages left behind by the ancients. The window to act was closing fast.

And then came the breakthrough.

An ancient artifact—one Karl and Karin had spent their lives searching for—surfaced at the Iraq Museum. It was called the Knowledge Stone.

Said to be the last remnant of wisdom left behind by the Anunnaki, it was a cipher containing the final calculations necessary to understand and prepare for the alignment. Scholars had long dismissed it as legend—a myth. In the Sumerian tablets, the Knowledge Stone was called *Me* (pronounced "may").

What are the *Me*? The Me are divine decrees or fundamental principles that govern civilization and all aspects of the universe. In the Sumerian myth *Inanna and Enki*, the goddess Inanna steals the Me from Enki, the god of wisdom and the freshwater deep.

The artifact made little sense on its own—a series of symbols and coordinates etched into black obsidian. But Jake recognized the pattern almost instantly. The symbols matched the underlying code he had seen in the star charts and in another artifact closely guarded by his parents: the Key of Osiris. It was as if the missing piece of the puzzle had been placed in his path at the moment humanity needed it most.

Jake knew it wasn't a coincidence. The artifact had been hidden for centuries, buried by those who either feared its power or misunderstood its significance. And now, as the world teetered on the brink of catastrophe, the key to saving it had reappeared—again at the cradle of civilization.

In secret, the curators of the Iraq Museum allowed Jake to take the Knowledge Stone, along with other critically important artifacts found at the same site, to complete his studies. They feared another attack.

The destruction of artifacts at the Iraq Museum occurred during two significant periods:

Looting During the Iraq War: In April 2003, following the U.S.-led invasion of Iraq, the National Museum in Baghdad was extensively looted. Taking advantage of the security vacuum after the fall of Baghdad, looters plundered the museum, resulting in the loss of approximately 15,000 artifacts, including invaluable items such as the diorite statue of King Entemena of Lagash and nearly 5,000 cylinder seals. This looting was part of a broader pattern of cultural heritage destruction and theft that plagued Iraq during this time.

Destruction by ISIS: In February 2015, ISIS released a video showing militants destroying artifacts in the Mosul Museum. Using hammers and drills, they demolished statues and relics, claiming these objects promoted idolatry, which contradicted their interpretation of Islamic teachings. This act was part of ISIS's broader campaign to erase cultural and religious heritage sites they considered heretical.

These events represent profound losses to Iraq's rich cultural history and have drawn international condemnation.

Jake knew there was no time to celebrate the findings. The

alignment was drawing closer, and the frequency of natural disasters was increasing. Earth's magnetic field was weakening, and the planet's core was becoming unstable. Jake had seen the calculations—he knew what was coming. Without intervention, civilization itself could be erased.

CHAPTER 15

Genesis of Hope

The signs had been there for years—whispers buried in scientific journals, theories concealed beneath political agendas, and warnings dismissed in favor of short-term economic gain. Yet, the Rosen-Fischer lineage had paid attention. For generations, they had gathered knowledge, prepared for the worst, and waited for the moment when their foresight would shift from precaution to necessity.

With Jake now out of college and his full team assembled, he was leading the charge. The Rosen-Fischer lineage was moving faster and more decisively than ever before. Jake was a force of nature—brilliant, relentless, and unyielding in his pursuit of salvation. His mind worked at a pace that left even the most seasoned scholars breathless.

He refined their calculations with pinpoint accuracy, identifying the precise remaining locations where underground sanctuaries could still be built—with a precision that felt almost supernatural.

Under his guidance, hidden communities began to take shape—safe havens constructed in the most stable and geologically unaffected regions on Earth. Through meticulous analysis, the team of scientists identified planetary "safe zones," and Jake ensured these sanctuaries were more than mere shelters.

They were fortresses.

Jake and his team designed energy systems capable of sustaining life for centuries, drawing power from geothermal vents and magnetic fields. Entire ecosystems were cultivated underground—artificial sunlight nurtured gardens and crops, while advanced purification systems provided an endless supply of clean water. He developed methods of preserving knowledge—not only in physical archives but in advanced holographic matrices encoded with human history, art, and science. He even created genetic preservation chambers—vaults designed to safeguard the biological blueprint of humanity, should the surface become uninhabitable.

The structures were engineered to withstand far more than natural disasters. They were shielded against radiation, seismic shifts, and atmospheric collapse. Some sanctuaries were buried beneath kilometers of stone; others were concealed by electromagnetic barriers, rendering them invisible to scanning technologies. Jake left nothing to chance.

And proud they were.

Karl and Karin stood side by side in the observation chamber of one of the deepest sanctuaries, their hands entwined as they watched their son lead a group of scientists through the vast underground city. The soft hum of machinery echoed through the chamber, mingling with the quiet murmur of voices below.

Jake moved among the scientists with quiet authority, his presence steadying the frightened and reassuring the uncertain. His gaze was sharp and focused, his posture confident yet calm. He radiated the quiet strength of a leader who knew exactly what needed to be done—not out of ego or ambition, but because he understood the weight of responsibility.

Karl's heart swelled with pride and relief. He had passed down everything he could—the hard-won wisdom of the past, the strength to endure, and the courage to fight. But Jake had become more than Karl had ever imagined. He was a man forged by fire— not just brilliant, but compassionate. A leader not by force, but by trust.

Karin's eyes shimmered with tears.

"He's ready," she whispered.

Karl's hand tightened around hers.

"Yes," he said softly. "He's everything we hoped for."

As they embraced in a warm, tight hug, they both realized they had spent their lives fighting for this moment—running from the darkness, uncovering forbidden truths, and defying the forces that had tried to erase the legacy of human history.

The battles had left scars, both visible and hidden. But they had endured.

And now, standing at the threshold of a new beginning, they knew their mission was complete.

Jake would lead them forward.

He would rebuild.

He would protect.

Karl and Karin had given him the gift of knowledge, but it was love that had shaped him—true, unwavering, selfless love. It was the quiet strength behind every decision he made, the reason he had refused to give up when the odds were insurmountable. Love had given him purpose—and now it would give humanity a future. As Jake passed, Karl placed a steady hand on his shoulder.

Their eyes met—father and son—with a quiet understanding that needed no words.

"You've done well," Karl said.

Jake smiled faintly. "Thanks to you and Mom for putting me on the right path. But it's not over yet."

Karl nodded. "No. But you're ready."

Jake's smile lingered for a moment before he turned and walked away, his steps purposeful as he disappeared into the heart of the underground city.

Karin leaned her head against Karl's shoulder. They stood together in the flickering light of the subterranean world, knowing that their role was shifting. They would always be part of Jake's life—not only as his beloved parents but as a source of guidance and wisdom when he needed it. But it was time to step aside and let him lead the charge.

Those who truly understood the gravity of what was happening to the planet were finally coming together. Differences of color, religion, and politics were fading beneath the greater urgency of survival. It was time to put humanity's divisions aside and unite under the one force that had the power to heal and rebuild—love.

Because love—true, unwavering, selfless love—is the most powerful force of all.

And in that love, humanity would find its future.

Jake ran his fingers over the intricate symbols etched into the Key of Osiris, feeling the grooves in the black obsidian as if they might whisper their secrets to him. He then carefully compared them to the Knowledge Stone—like placing two tuning forks of the same frequency side by side until they vibrated in unison, automatic synchronicity—and he could feel it. Sense its energy.

It was early morning, but the underground research chamber pulsed with golden lamplight, bathing the ancient artifact on the table. The air smelled of old paper and coffee—the scent of countless late nights spent chasing the truth.

He glanced up from the black obsidian to the bulletin board on the wall. It was cluttered with maps, photographs of ruins, printouts of myths, and pages of scientific articles. Red strings connected pushpins from one clue to another: a map of the world marked with sites like Göbekli Tepe, Giza, Stonehenge, and a red circle drawn in the middle of the Atlantic Ocean with a question mark. In the center of the board, written in bold black marker, were the words: "The First Clue."

Jake exhaled slowly. This was it—the culmination of years of work passed down to him by his parents. *Mom, Dad*, he thought, *I'm so close now*. The burden of responsibility weighed on his shoulders, but it also steeled his resolve. He remembered being a child, falling asleep to his mother's soft voice telling him about lost cities beneath the waves, about heroes who preserved knowledge through a great flood. He remembered his father's study, overflowing with books on geology, archaeology, and astronomy, all trying to answer a question that haunted them: *What happened 12,000 years ago? And will it happen again?*

Across the table, Dr. John Weber adjusted his spectacles and peered at the black obsidian. Tall and lean with silver hair, John's steady hands betrayed a slight tremor of excitement as he held a magnifying glass over the artifact. Beside him stood Dr. Shirley Weber, his wife and lifelong research partner. Shirley's brown hair was pulled into a loose bun, and she had a pen clenched between her teeth as she studied a notepad filled with transcribed cuneiform symbols from the tablets, deciphered Mayan and Göbekli Tepe symbols, and was now comparing them to the black obsidian. John and Shirley had dedicated their entire lives to uncovering this mystery, and they had been dear friends of Jake's parents. In fact, Jake had come to regard them as family—wise elders who had guided him.

Shirley removed the pen from her mouth and broke the silence. "The inscription on this black obsidian and the Knowledge Stone. It still astounds me. We've confirmed it's a form of early Sumerian cuneiform mixed with symbols found at the pyramid in Antarctica, as well as the Mexican and Peruvian pyramids," she said quietly, tracing a line of wedge-shaped characters on a rubbing of the black obsidian and Knowledge Stone surfaces. "Civilizations separated by millennia, yet here their languages are together on two different artifacts that seem to complete each other."

John nodded, tapping a reference book. "It corroborates what your parents believed," he said, glancing at Jake. "All these ancient myths and sites—from Sumerian flood stories to the carvings at Göbekli Tepe—are pieces of a much older memory. A memory of a catastrophic event." He turned to a map pinned on the board, where someone had scrawled "Younger Dryas Impact—10,900 BC?" with arrows pointing to regions of abrupt climate change.

Jake swallowed the lump in his throat. His parents, Dr. Karl and Dr. Karin, were close friends of Dr. Henry Chen and Dr. Mei Lin, who had died in a remote desert five years ago under mysterious circumstances while following one of these clues. They had passed on their research, which ended up in Jake's hands: crates of notebooks, encrypted hard drives of data, and a letter. In that letter, they urged them to continue the quest—to find the truth that could save humanity from repeating a cycle of destruction.

Jake had been reading and re-reading that letter every night. *"We have only pieces of the puzzle, Karl and Karin, and we are being followed, you can find our work at our agreed location"* they wrote. *"But you must see it completed. For all of us."*

He was shaken from his thoughts as a new voice echoed from the stairwell entrance to the chamber. Dr. Rebecca Nikas, a young archaeologist and Jake's long-time friend—her father was a renowned Greek archaeologist and her mother a Scottish history major—a key member of the team—she descended the steps carrying a tray with three steaming mugs.

"I figured we could all use some caffeine," she said with a warm smile, handing coffee to Jake, John, and Shirley.

Rebecca had joined them a few months ago after publishing a groundbreaking paper on Pleistocene extinctions. She was sharp, curious, tall, had straight auburn hair—and just as invested in solving this mystery, especially after Jake confided in her about the finding of the Key of Osiris and the Knowledge Stone.

"Ah, wonderful. Thank you, Rebecca," Jake said, accepting the mug and exchanging a warm smile. He took a careful sip and thought to himself, *Wow, Rebecca sure looks gorgeous!* before returning his focus to the artifact.

Jake looked around at the team assembled. Aside from John, Shirley, and Rebecca, there was also Miguel Sanchez, a geologist and sonar specialist, currently asleep in his bunk after spending the night rechecking ocean floor maps, Yumi Takahashi a Biophysicist and Software Architect specialized in Systems Engineering and Dr. Naomi Okoye, an engineer who had been analyzing the technological schematics they discovered. Naomi was due to arrive later that morning. They all believed in him, and in this mission. For a moment, Jake felt the magnitude of it— they were carrying the torch lit by his family and by others before them, going back generations. It was humbling.

He cleared his throat. "Alright," Jake began, addressing his dream-team, his voice echoing softly off the stone walls, "let's go over this step by step. What do we know now, and what's missing?" Shirley flipped open her leather-bound notebook. "From the beginning: We have long suspected that there was a global cataclysm around 12,000 years ago—the end of the last Ice Age, a period known as the Younger Dryas. Your father and I gathered evidence from various disciplines: geology, ancient mythology, archaeology. Up to now, we've established several key points."

She ticked off on her fingers, launching into a familiar summary they had discussed many times, but now they finally had concrete leads to confirm each part. "First, something sudden and devastating occurred approximately 12,800 years ago. There is geological evidence of a catastrophic event—the Younger Dryas Impact Hypothesis suggests a cosmic impact struck Earth around 10,900 BC, causing massive fires and a dramatic climate shift. Proponents of this theory have found microscopic diamonds, high levels of platinum, and other impact markers in sediment layers from that time."

As she spoke, Rebecca moved to the board and pinned up a satellite image of Greenland's ice with an annotation about a "platinum anomaly," and another printout showing a layer of dark sediment labeled "Younger Dryas black mat."

Jake nodded. "Right. There were those studies of a 'black mat' layer across multiple continents, indicating widespread fires and soot deposition," he added. He had practically memorized his parents' research papers. "And extinction spikes—North America lost dozens of megafauna species, like the mammoths, around that time."

John interjected; his eyes bright. "Then we have the archaeological evidence. Göbekli Tepe in Turkey—built not long after the proposed impact—has carvings that appear to commemorate a comet strike. Pillar 43, the so-called Vulture Stone, seems to show symbols matching constellations and a falling fiery object. Researchers interpreted it as a date stamp for 10,950 BC, right when the Younger Dryas event happened." John reached behind him to a shelf and pulled down a laminated high-resolution photograph of the Vulture Stone.

Rebecca took the photo and laid it on the table for all to see. The pillar's surface was carved with strange animals—a vulture with outstretched wings, a scorpion, and a headless human figure. "The headless man here might symbolize human suffering or death," Rebecca pointed out, tracing it. "And these animals correspond to star patterns. They concluded it was effectively a record of the sky at the time of the disaster, possibly tracking the Taurid meteor stream, which could have been the source of the comet fragments".

John carefully positioned a magnifying light over the photo. The ancient carving came into stark relief under the lamp: the vulture, clutching what looked like a circular object, the scorpion poised below. There were abstract symbols too—ones that looked like H-shapes and a sun-like disk.

"It gives me chills every time," Jake said quietly, leaning over to look. He recalled how excited his mother had been when the Göbekli Tepe findings were first published. She had called him late at night from halfway around the world just to exclaim that the ancients knew—they witnessed something and tried to preserve the memory.

Shirley tapped a particular section of the pillar image. "See these three crescents and circle near the top? If they indeed align with the sun and moon symbols, it's like they're marking the heavens at a specific moment. It's astonishing—a Neolithic site potentially recording an event in the sky with such importance that they deified it in stone."

Rebecca gently slid another image beside it—a printout of an academic article abstract. "And that site's very existence—11,000 years old, right after the cataclysm—implies organized civilization rebounded or survived. It's as if someone was waiting for the skies to clear, then immediately started building an observatory-temple. Perhaps to monitor the heavens, to warn future generations." She read a line from the paper softly, almost to herself: *"We find compelling evidence that the famous 'Vulture Stone' is a date stamp for 10,950 BC ± 250 yrs, corresponding closely to the proposed Younger Dryas event and that a key function of Göbekli Tepe was to observe meteor showers and record cometary encounters."*

Jake ran a hand through his hair, thinking. "So, they carved what they saw: a broken comet, destruction. Perhaps the survivors at Göbekli Tepe tried to ensure we would remember the danger from the sky." He then gestured to the map where a red line had been drawn through various locations. "And what about these alignments my parents noted? The ancient architectural alignments around the world—we shouldn't forget those."

Shirley followed his gaze and smiled knowingly. This was her specialty. "Indeed. Your father was very keen on this." She went to the board and pointed at images of the Great Pyramid of Giza, Machu Picchu, and an aerial shot of the Nazca Lines in Peru, all connected by a red string of yarn. "It used to sound like a wild theory, but we've measured and checked: Many ancient sacred sites align on a single great circle around the Earth. Giza, Machu Picchu, Nazca, Easter Island—all are positioned with only a minuscule error, as if deliberately set on a global ring."

Rebecca's eyebrows rose. She had studied this before, but seeing the visual web John and Shirley had assembled made it tangible. "Within a tenth of a degree, wasn't it? The margin of error is so small it's hard to call that a coincidence."

"Exactly," Shirley affirmed. She took a pushpin and tapped on an image of a globe with a great circle drawn through the sites. "It's as if an advanced civilization—or a network of knowledgeable survivors—placed markers around the world. Markers that might encode something."

John chimed in, warming to the topic. "Perhaps a message or a warning, hidden in plain sight. The ancients encoded their knowledge in myths and in the very layout of their monuments. Take the Great Pyramid," he continued, moving to a diagram pinned up just below the pyramid photo. It was covered in notes and numbers. "Its dimensions contain astonishing mathematical correlations. If you multiply the height of the Great Pyramid by 43,200, you get the polar radius of the Earth; multiply its base perimeter by 43,200, you get the Earth's equatorial circumference." He tapped the numbers he had written: *Height 481 ft x 43,200 = ~3,938 miles (Earth's radius)*. "This number 43,200 isn't random—it's derived from the rate of the Earth's axial precession (our planet's wobble). They scaled the Earth itself into the pyramid. How on Earth did they know that?" John's eyes shone as he posed the rhetorical question.

Rebecca let out a low whistle. "I remember when I first heard that statistic. I double-checked it because I couldn't believe it. But it's accurate within a very small margin. Either it's an unbelievable coincidence or they knew the size and shape of the planet."

"They definitely knew," Shirley nodded. "And who are *they*? Not the dynastic Egyptians, at least not originally. The knowledge was inherited. We suspect these are remnants of a much older civilization—possibly what legends refer to as Atlantis or something akin to it, like the Anunnaki—who encoded what they could before moving on."

CHAPTER 16

Atlantis Rising

The word *Atlantis* hung in the air for a moment. For so long, it had been taboo among serious scholars—dismissed as fantasy. Yet here, in this room filled with evidence, *Atlantis* had become a possibility too compelling to ignore, demanding not just belief, but investigation. It was shorthand for the advanced lost civilization they had spent years tracking.

Jake felt a familiar pang in his chest. The name had inspired his parents—and earned them ridicule from colleagues in equal measure. But they had been right to persevere.

The Moment of Becoming

Jake stepped up to a large table strewn with papers, tools, and ancient artifacts. At its center sat a sleek laptop and a compact projector, both wired into a live analytical feed focused on the Key of Osiris and the enigmatic Knowledge Stone—two relics that had baffled historians for decades.

Just then, Miguel Sanchez, the team's sonar expert, entered the lab with practiced care, carrying the two priceless artifacts. He was guiding them toward the central testing station for the next round of analysis.

As he crossed the threshold, every speaker in the room emitted a sharp, high-pitched tone—an unsettling, piercing sound. Miguel flinched and turned toward Yumi Takahashi, the team's data analyst, who had just yanked off her headphones. Her face was contorted in pain.

"Did you hear that?" he asked, concerned.

"Yes! Loud and clear—ouch!" she said, rubbing her ears. "What was that?"

"I don't know," Miguel replied, his brow furrowed. "But it started right as I came in with the artifacts. The speakers chirped like they got hit with an energy discharge—maybe some kind of interference between the objects and the speakers' magnetic field."

He gently placed the artifacts on the lab table and began setting up the camera equipment. He remembered Jake's earlier instruction vividly: *"Make sure to register every second."* Those words echoed now in Miguel's mind—and suddenly, their urgency made perfect sense.

Yumi—eyes wide, adrenaline surging—exclaimed, "That was a huge clue!" Without another word, she bolted out of the room.

"Yumi, wait!" Miguel called after her, confused. *Weird time for a bathroom break, he thought.*

But moments later, Yumi returned—not with a personal story, but with two heavy magnet blocks cradled in her arms.

"Okay," she said, her eyes gleaming with curiosity and excitement. "Let's test this."

She began moving the magnets slowly around the artifacts, watching for any sign of interaction. Nothing.

"How about placing the magnets on the table with polarities reversed, and the artifacts in between?" Miguel suggested, pacing a little as his mind raced.

Yumi nodded and carefully repositioned the magnets as instructed. Suddenly—one of the artifacts shifted slightly, as if nudged by an invisible force.

"Did you see that? Or am I going nuts?" she asked, voice rising in disbelief.

Miguel's eyes widened. "Are the cameras rolling?" he asked urgently.

"They're on," Yumi confirmed.

"You're definitely not going nuts—it *moved!*"

They quickly adjusted the camera angles and distances, experimenting with different configurations. After a dozen tries, they finally discovered the sweet spot. The artifacts rotated gently, pulled toward the center of the table, and clicked together with a soft, magnetic snap.

The ancient symbols etched into the surfaces of the artifacts began to glow faintly, intertwining like threads in a loom. As they merged, the glowing inscriptions formed the same enigmatic symbols found in the ancient Egyptian manuscript that had eluded decipherment for generations. Slowly, a swirling holographic projection emerged—at first dim and unstable, flickering like a distant radio signal straining to lock onto its frequency, as if time itself were trying to remember.

Miguel stared, awestruck. "I can't believe my eyes. Do we have more magnets?"

Yumi dashed out again and returned moments later with two additional blocks. As she added them to the layout, the projection grew more defined but still shimmered with an elusive, misty quality.

"Help me rotate the table," she said. Together, they aligned the magnets to correspond with the cardinal directions—north, south, east, and west.

Instantly, the projection stabilized. A luminous image hovered in the air, spinning with impossible precision, its colors and symbols shifting in mesmerizing patterns. It was a fully coherent, three-dimensional recording—an ancient message encoded and hidden for millennia.

They had done it. They had activated the hidden mechanism of the Key of Osiris and the Knowledge Stone—using a magnetically induced field resonating in harmony with Earth's natural frequency.

It was brief, but breathtaking. A message from a lost civilization.

And they had captured every second on video.

Miguel and Yumi had just finished speaking, their voices still hanging in the air like the echo of a distant explosion. What they described—what they *witnessed* in the lab—didn't just defy logic. It shattered it.

No one moved.

A heavy silence fell over the room.

The team stood frozen, each caught in their own storm of disbelief, struggling to process a truth that felt impossibly vast, almost mythic in scale. It wasn't just science they were confronting—it was something older, deeper, and far beyond anything they had prepared for.

Rebecca's eyes darted between them, searching for a crack in their story—some hint of exaggeration, of misremembering—but there was none. Miguel's knuckles were still white from clenching his fists. Yumi's voice, though steady, had trembled beneath the weight of what she'd seen.

Jake stepped forward, slowly. "You're sure?"

"We also have what the hologram showed us," Miguel said later, patting the laptop like a loyal dog. On screen: a ghostly image of swirling blue light.

"That gave us a direct message from the past," Yumi added. "Or as close as we're ever going to get."

At the mention of the hologram, John and Shirley stepped closer, their expressions turning grave.

Rebecca dimmed the lights. "Shall we run it?" she asked. Without waiting, she clicked play.

The projector hummed. Above the artifacts, light particles gathered and danced. A 3D holographic scene shimmered into being.

Jake was in pure ecstasy at the sight of the merging symbols—transforming seamlessly into the exact glyphs found in the ancient Egyptian manuscript. His eyes widened with wonder, his voice rising with unrestrained excitement.

"That's it! *That's it!*" he exclaimed, almost breathless. "Finally—after all these years!"

His hands trembled slightly as he stepped closer to the projection, unable to look away. The decades of research, dead ends, and late nights had all led to this single, electrifying moment of revelation.

A deep voice echoed through the room, speaking in an

unknown tongue—yet somehow, its meaning pierced directly into their minds. It bypassed language entirely, resonating on a level deeper than words, as if the message had been encoded for the soul.

A tall, robed figure appeared within the projection, standing in a grand marble hall illuminated by ethereal light. He held a ceremonial staff, its head adorned with a swirling symbol of stars. His face was solemn, weathered by time and burden. Behind him stretched a vast night sky—unfamiliar constellations twinkling across the darkness, and a brilliant comet with a long, glowing tail arcing overhead.

The comet split.

Fiery fragments rained down toward Earth. One slammed into a frozen polar region, erupting in a blinding flash of light. Another plunged into the sea, sending towering tsunamis racing across vast oceans. The ghostly images showed ancient people fleeing in terror, their cities drowned, their cries lost to time.

"Umu darâ . . . nam-tar . . ." Jake whispered, his voice trembling as he recognized the words in Sumerian. *"The Celestial Warning . . ."*

The Earth dimmed, veiled in thick ash. The sky turned gray. Then—another vision. A breathtaking ocean-side city appeared, radiant with towering spires and gleaming marble streets.
Atlantis.

They watched in horror as monstrous storms descended upon it. Lightning slashed the skies. Walls of water roared through the streets, toppling towers and flooding temples. In moments, the magnificent city was swallowed by the sea, leaving only memory.

Jake felt tears sting his eyes. He clenched his jaw, overcome.

Beside him, Shirley wept quietly, her hands clasped tightly at her chest.

The robed figure's voice softened. The scene changed once more.

Now: survivors. Small bands of people, silhouetted by firelight, gathered together. Some built ships to cross unknown waters. Others climbed jagged mountains, seeking refuge. In their hands, they carried glowing fragments—artifacts. The same ones now sitting on the lab table.

The vision shifted again.

At its climax, the robed man raised his staff high. Behind him, a massive structure materialized—an enormous, metallic pyramid fused with a circular, ringed gateway pulsing with energy. Lines of cuneiform numbers scrolled down its surface like a prophetic news ticker.

Then, a voice—this time unmistakably in English—cut through the air with clarity and purpose:

"Exodus Protocol."

The phrase reverberated throughout the lab, clearly an automated overlay triggered by the artifacts themselves. It wanted them to understand.

And then—darkness. The projection faded.

Silence fell across the room, thick and absolute.

Jake finally exhaled, his voice raw. "Miguel, Yumi, incredible work."

Rebecca let out a shaky breath, eyes wide. "That machine they *built* something. Something meant to survive."

She whispered it again, more reverently this time, as if speaking the name of a lost god:

"Exodus Protocol."

From the stairwell, Naomi Okoye's voice chimed in, calm and confident. "And based on the schematics encoded in that projection, that machine shares design similarities with the hidden devices under pyramids around the world."

Naomi descended the stairs, laptop under her arm. She had clearly come rushing the moment she heard the projector hum.

Jake greeted her with a smile. "Perfect timing."

Naomi brought up the machine's image—ghostly and indistinct, but visible. "It's massive. Likely several stories tall. From what I can tell, it generates immense energy. It could be a portal, a dimensional gate, or a planetary stabilizer. We can't be sure. But the energy output is off the charts."

John rubbed his chin. "Teleportation?"

"Or stasis," Shirley suggested. "A way to keep people alive until the world stabilized again."

Rebecca added, "Whatever it was—it was their plan to survive."

He looked at his team. "The Exodus Protocol was real. And part of it might still exist. But the question is: *where?*"

Naomi zoomed into a map of the Atlantic Ocean. "We may have found it."

A red X glowed near the Azores—300 kilometers to the southwest. When the cuneiform numbers scrolled down like a news ticker during the 3D message, they were automatically decoded by AI, revealing the coordinates. Buried in math, star alignments, and cuneiform inscriptions, everything pointed here.

John leaned closer. "That's in the middle of the Atlantic. Near where people have claimed to see underwater ruins."

Jake's heart pounded. "It could be the capital city. Or a major outpost."

Shirley touched a framed photo of Karl and Karin on a ship deck, holding a sonar printout. The same region.

"They suspected something there too," she said softly. "But never had exact coordinates."

Jake swallowed hard. *We're almost there*, he thought.

Naomi continued, "This plateau is 150 meters deep—within

reach of ROVs and trained divers. If that Exodus machine is anywhere, it's there."

Rebecca nodded. "We have to go. Before anyone else gets there."

Jake met John's eyes. They both knew who she meant.

Dr. Sebastian Falk. And his shadowy benefactor—Mr. Sloan.

Falk had mocked their research publicly, while stealing it privately. His backer was rumored to belong to a secret group determined to control knowledge of any cyclical cataclysm.

"I haven't shared this until now," Jake said, voice steady, "but I believe we're being watched. My parents' colleagues died under strange circumstances. And now my parents have gone dark. Mr. Sloan once made my father a promise to stay away. He knew it was a mistake not to finish it then."

Shirley gasped. John clenched his fists. "Do you have proof?" "Not solid," Jake admitted. "But too many signs point to sabotage."

Naomi added, "Dr. Falk has been creeping where he doesn't belong. He was caught near Dr. Weber's laptop during the last conference."

Rebecca nodded. "A former colleague hinted that a private group has classified entire sites—and keeps tech out of public knowledge."

Jake exhaled. "Mr. Sloan is real. And he may already be on the move."

Shirley straightened. "Then we must move faster. Cautiously. But the truth must come out."

John placed a hand on Jake's shoulder. "We're with you."

Jake looked at each of them—his team, his allies. Every face met his with fire in their eyes.

The race to Atlantis had begun.

Destination: Atlantis

"Alright then," he said, steady and clear. "We have a location. We have evidence and a plan forming. Let's prepare for an expedition to the Atlantic site immediately. We'll arrange for a research vessel, submersible equipment, diving gear—whatever it takes. Naomi, I'll need you to secure the ROVs and maybe a small sub if possible. Miguel and Yumi should double-check the sonar maps for any hazards in that area. Rebecca, you compile all our historical and myth references that might help interpret what we find there—especially anything about that Exodus machine or Atlantean architecture. John and Shirley, let's reach out to our contacts who can help quietly fund and equip this trip on short notice. I have a feeling we should keep this off the official channels as much as possible."

Everyone sprang into action at Jake's words. The quiet scholar was now leading them with calm authority. He inherited that from his parents too—the ability to captain an expedition.

Shirley went to boot up another computer, already drafting emails to a trusted old Navy friend who now captained a research vessel. John flipped open a satellite phone, preparing to make some calls. Naomi and Rebecca huddled over the map, discussing logistics and what tech to bring. The room, moments ago reverently silent in the wake of the hologram, was now buzzing with urgent energy.

As the flurry of preparation began, Jake stepped away to the edge of the room where a faded world map hung. His eyes traced from Turkey (site of Göbekli Tepe) to Egypt (Giza), to the Yucatán (asteroid that took the dinosaurs, an earlier cataclysm), and finally to the Atlantic, where a red X now marked their next destination. So much history, so many cycles of destruction and rebirth, converged on this quest.

On a shelf by the map sat a framed photograph of his parents—

the same one Shirley had touched. Jake picked it up gently. Karl and Karin were younger there, laughing and radiant on that deck in the sun. He spoke to them in his mind: We have it. Your puzzle—our puzzle—the pieces are being found. We are on the verge of finding what you were looking for.

For a brief moment, he felt a warmth, as if a hand rested on his shoulder—imaginary, yet comforting. He closed his eyes and let out a breath. "We'll finish this," he whispered. "I promise."

When he opened his eyes, he found Rebecca standing beside him, offering him a small, encouraging smile. She had the printouts he'd asked for: one was a translation of the Sumerian flood myth from the *Eridu Genesis,* where the god Enki warns Ziusudra of the coming deluge. Another was a summary of the Hopi legends of the Four Worlds, where the previous world was destroyed by flood and only those who listened to the warnings—sheltering in hollow reeds—survived. Rebecca had been cross-referencing myths, and she knew Jake wanted to see the patterns.

"These are the stories from opposite sides of the world telling the same tale," she said as he took the pages. "Different words, same message: a great flood, a warning, a few survivors in a vessel. It's uncanny."

Jake quickly skimmed the familiar lines. He had read them before, but now, in light of the hologram, they stood out in sharp relief. "It's not just a coincidence," he murmured.

"It's memory. Human memory of what happened, passed down through generations in the form of myth."

Rebecca nodded vigorously. "Yes. And think of how many cultures have such a story—the Mesopotamians, the Hopi, the Maya, the Greeks with Deucalion's flood, the Indians with Manu, even the Norse have a flood after the Age of Ice. The cycle of destruction and rebirth is a recurring theme."

John put an arm around Shirley. "We'll need to consider that what happened before could happen again. That might be why the ancients left these clues for us. Not just to find their city, but to learn something crucial to protect our future."

This led to a more philosophical discussion as the team continued preparations. There was resolve in everyone's eyes now: they weren't just going to find Atlantis for the sake of history—they were going to arm the present with knowledge to safeguard the future.

Twilight Looms

While Jake and his team raced to prepare for their journey, far across the Atlantic in a wood-paneled boardroom in London, another gathering took place.

Here, the atmosphere was hushed and the lights dim. A projector cast a faint blue glow on the faces of a few men in tailored suits sitting around a polished mahogany table. On the screen was a satellite image of the Canary Islands port, and in the corner of that image was the profile of a research vessel: the *Elysium*.

Dr. Sebastian Falk steepled his fingers and leaned forward, his sharp features illuminated by the screen. His thin lips curled into a slight smirk as he watched live footage of crates being loaded onto *Elysium*'s deck. The feed came from a high-altitude drone that Falk's benefactors had dispatched. They were nothing if not thorough.

"So, it's confirmed: Karl's little protégé is heading out to sea," came a voice from the darkness. The speaker remained out of the projector's light—a man well known to both Falk and the Rosen-Fisher family: none other than Mr. Sloan.

Sloan, after his near-death beating many years ago—spared only by the generosity of Jake's father, Karl—had stayed under the radar, acquiring crucial information and building up his army of mercenaries. Or, as he liked to arrogantly call them: The Aureus Society—an enigmatic and immensely wealthy organization that had both funded and guided Falk's efforts for years. Falk had never met the Society's inner circle; Sloan was the main conduit, his ordinary name belying the cold authority in his tone.

Today, an older, stronger, and smarter man, his moves were even more calculated—but always at the cost of others, in this case, Dr. Falk.

Falk adjusted his gold cufflink and spoke with casual confidence. "Yes. Jake and his team are mobilizing quickly. They must have solved the location of the machine. Does he even know about the others? They're likely bound for the coordinates we've been trying to pinpoint ourselves." He tapped a laser pointer on the map, indicating a red X in the mid-Atlantic. "Here."

Sloan leaned into the light just enough to reveal calculating gray eyes. "The Azores Plateau. We suspected it as much.

Falk continues "Your hunch about the Key of Osiris and Knowledge Stone was correct. It appears Jake did have them, after all."

Sloan suppressed a flash of irritation. Of course he was correct; he often is. It frustrated him to no end that Karl's son had inherited the very artifacts he had been trying to obtain for years. Sloan had spent decades cultivating an image as a skeptic of these fringe theories, all while secretly collecting artifacts and data for Aureus. He did it for the grants, yes, and for the eventual glory—but also because he truly believed ordinary people couldn't handle the full truth. Chaos would ensue; only a select few should hold such knowledge and use it to shepherd humanity.

"So, the little brat has the keys and now a solid fix on the map," Sloan sneered. He couldn't help it—his disdain for Jake ran deep. Jake's parents had outmaneuvered him many times, publishing findings Sloan had been on the verge of stealing. He had resented how Karl and Karin were respected for what he deemed pseudo-science. Not to mention the final battle between him and Jake's father—when Sloan took a major beating and was left for dead. And now their upstart son was on the cusp of the greatest discovery of all time.

Falk squared his shoulders. "No matter. He's doing us a favor by finding the exact spot. We'll simply take over from there. Once he leads us to the site, we'll intervene and secure everything."

Sloan's eyes glinted. "Intervene, yes. But remember, subtlety. The Society wants the artifacts and what lies beneath that ocean, but we prefer to operate in the shadows. No international incidents."

Falk bristled. Subtlety. He knew what that meant: make them disappear quietly. "Understood. I have a plan in motion. A second vessel, *Argos*, under a private flag, has been stationed in the Cape Verde Islands on standby. It's crewed by contractors loyal to me. They can reach the target coordinates as fast as *Elysium*, if not faster."

He clicked to the next slide. It showed an imposing black yacht equipped with a helipad and a submersible crane. "The *Argos* is armed with an advanced ROV and a minisub. And a few 'specialists' from our Mediterranean salvage operations." By specialists, he meant mercenaries trained in underwater combat, courtesy of Aureus' deep pockets. "We'll shadow Jake's ship at a distance. Once they begin their dive, my team will move in, confiscate the artifacts and data, and ensure no witnesses remain to tell tales."

His voice was calm, clinical as he described essentially murdering his rivals. To Falk, it was just a necessary calculation. He had no personal bloodlust; in fact, he had never dirtied his own hands—it was all done by his recruits. Plus, he had orchestrated plenty of accidents before. He had been in touch with the men who sabotaged Mr. and Mrs. Chen's jeep in the desert five years ago—an unfortunate blown tire on a steep ravine road was all it took. He had scarcely lost a wink of sleep over it.

Sloan tapped a finger on the table. "We must be certain to retrieve the Key of Osiris and the Knowledge Stone intact, as well as any records or technology from the site. And Doctor—" Sloan fixed Falk with a hard stare—"see that the Exodus device, if it exists, does not fall into uncontrolled hands. The Council is particularly interested in that. The idea of teleportation or whatever it may be. It cannot become public or be wielded by those outside our oversight."

Falk nodded. "Of course. If it's functional, we'll secure it or disable it. As a measure, if we fail, I'll destroy it to prevent anyone else from using it. Our aims align, Mr. Sloan. Like you, I have no intention of letting a bunch of academics unleash unknown powers upon the world."

There was a pause. Sloan regarded Falk for a moment, and Falk sensed perhaps a hint of skepticism in the man's expression. Despite years of service, Falk always felt the Society kept him at arm's length—a useful tool but not truly one of them. The thought rankled, but he forced a gracious smile.

"Good. Now, tell me about Jake's team," Sloan said. "What are their strengths? Any potential complications?"

Falk had done his homework.

He brought up the profiles on the screen—grainy images flickering to life: Jake, John, Shirley, Rebecca, Naomi, Yumi, and Miguel.

He spoke with the clinical precision of someone cataloging threats.

"Jake—son of Karl and Karin, as expected. Not to be underestimated. He's inherited both his parents' intellect and shows clear leadership. The others follow him for a reason."

He tapped the next file.

"Dr. John Weber—archaeologist and experienced systems strategist. Decades of fieldwork under his belt. His wife, Dr. Shirley Weber—historian and linguist, with a background in computer science. They're older, but sharp. Resourceful. Not to be ignored."

Another swipe.

"Dr. Rebecca Nikas—younger, highly intelligent, a skilled archaeologist with a mastery in linguistics. Adaptive. Could handle unexpected variables well."

He paused, narrowing his eyes at the next file.

"Naomi Okoye—engineer. Technically gifted and fast. If she figures out the advanced systems, she could be a real problem."

Another tap.

"Yumi Takahashi—exceptional mind. Software architect and systems engineer with a degree in biophysics. Brilliant. Fast under pressure. Definitely a threat in a control-room environment."

And finally:

"Miguel Sanchez—geologist, retired Navy SEALs, highly experienced in field logistics. Physically capable. Agile, tough. If it comes to a fight, he's the one to watch."

Falk leaned back slightly, considering the lineup on screen.

"Together, they're more than competent—and they're loyal to each other. That makes them dangerous."

He sighed as he flicked through their images. In truth, he had little personal malice toward most of them; they were collateral. Only Jake truly irked him, as if the boy's very existence was stealing away from his own world recognition.

"They have expertise in many areas," Falk continued, "but they are academics, not soldiers. I doubt they'll offer significant resistance if confronted forcefully, especially underwater or in a remote setting. The key will be catching them off-guard. Possibly we can sabotage their communications or equipment first."

Sloan interjected, "We prefer minimal direct engagement. If sabotage can do the job—sink their ship, cut off their oxygen— do so. Frame it as an accident if possible. But if confrontation is unavoidable, ensure you have overwhelming advantage. No messy fights, no escapes."

Falk offered a thin smile. "I have it covered. I've arranged for a little surprise to delay them as well. A storm is forecast near their route—nothing we control, of course, but we can exploit it." He gestured to a weather chart. "And I've placed a man in the Canaries port to slip a tracer onto their ship's hull. We'll know their exact position at all times."

Sloan nodded approvingly. "Excellent. And Doctor—do remember our priorities. The knowledge above all. Lives are expendable; data is not. If Jake somehow has records beyond what we think—retrieve them or wipe them out."

Falk's eyes glinted behind his glasses. "Understood. By the end of this, the Aureus Society will have everything: the artifacts, the understanding of the pyramid machines, and all of Jake's research. And the world will remain blissfully ignorant."

As he said the last words, Falk felt a mixture of triumph and an odd pang of guilt. He quelled the latter quickly. He was doing humanity a service, he told himself. People panicked over far less; if they learned a cosmic disaster might recur or that ancient super-machines existed under the pyramids, civilization could destabilize.

Far better for a competent elite to handle it, quietly prepare, perhaps use the technology to safeguard a select few when needed. That was the Society's vision, and Falk had bought into it. Knowledge is power, and power is safest in a few hands—especially his own.

Sloan stood, signaling the meeting's end. "We will expect updates as the operation proceeds. Don't fail, Doctor Falk." The mild tone of those words did nothing to mask the threat beneath them.

Falk stood as well and gave a curt bow of his head. "I won't." As Sloan exited, flanked by two silent aides, Falk remained in the boardroom, looking at the frozen profiles of Jake and his friends on the screen.

He walked up to the projected image of Jake's face. The young man had an open, earnest look in the photo (it was likely from some conference or university website, Falk thought). Falk almost pitied him—Jake had no idea what was coming.

"You should have chosen the lecture halls, Jake boy," Falk whispered to the image. "Playing with ancient knowledge is far beyond your grasp, you'll only get yourself and your companions killed."

He tapped a key on his laptop, sending a coded signal to his team. It was time for him to depart as well; his private jet was waiting to fly him to Cape Verde, where he would board the Argos. From there, he would oversee the interception personally. He didn't intend to let anyone else take credit for discovering Atlantis. As he shut down the projector, the boardroom plunged into near-darkness. Only a single desk lamp remained, shining on a dossier labeled *Project Exodus—Confidential*. Falk closed the dossier, tucked it under his arm, and strode out with purpose.

In the silence that followed, the London rain pattered against the windows. The stage was set and the players in motion. Across thousands of miles of ocean, Jake's ship would soon set sail into a brewing storm, unaware that a darker storm—the Aureus Society—was gathering to meet them.

Voyage into the Unknown

Two days later, the *Elysium* cut through the Atlantic waves under a steel-gray sky. The research vessel was sturdy and utilitarian, 80 meters of reinforced hull fitted with cranes, a helipad, and state-of-the-art navigation equipment. As it left the last traces of the Canary Islands behind, its prow pointed toward the open ocean and the adventure ahead, Jake felt a mix of exhilaration and trepidation.

It was late afternoon. Jake stood on the starboard deck, one hand on the cold rail as the wind whipped at his face. The sea stretched out in every direction, a shifting expanse of blues and silvers. In the west, the sun struggled to pierce a bank of dark clouds—a storm front that had been building since morning, trailing them. Captain O'Connor had assured them it was nothing the *Elysium* couldn't handle, but Jake couldn't shake a sense of foreboding as he watched distant lightning flicker in those clouds.

He turned as Rebecca approached. She zipped up her windbreaker and leaned on the railing next to him. "Thought you might want something warm," she said, handing him a stainless steel mug. The rich scent of hot tea wafted up. Jake accepted it gratefully.

"Thanks," he said, taking a sip. It was sweet and spiced, just what he needed.

Rebecca gazed out at the horizon. "Hard to believe, isn't it? We're actually on our way to Atlantis," she mused, her voice half-laughing at the absurdity and half-awed. "I mean, I grew up reading stories of lost cities and now. I'm on the team that might find the greatest one of all."

Jake smiled.

"If someone had told me a year ago I'd be leading this expedition, I'd have laughed too."

His eyes followed a pod of dolphins arcing playfully in the *Elysium*'s wake. Even nature seemed to hint at optimism—though the looming storm on the horizon told a different story.

"What about you?" he asked, turning slightly. "What got you into all this? When we first met, you said your research had a purpose. You mentioned a colleague at the British Museum who hinted at a secret group. That sounds like quite a story."

Rebecca shrugged, tucking a loose strand of hair behind her ear. "It's nothing as dramatic as what we're doing now. I was always drawn to the unexplained pieces of history. The empty gaps, the anomalies. At university, I wrote my thesis on the Piri Reis map— you know, that medieval map that seems to show Antarctica's coast without ice. People called it fringe, but I argued it was based on ancient source maps possibly from a lost seafaring culture. My advisor nearly had a fit," she smirked. "I guess I never really fit in the mainstream.

"Then I met your mother at a conference last year. Her presentation on comparative flood myths was truly inspiring— thoughtful, layered, and filled with insights I hadn't considered. We spoke afterwards, and she encouraged me to never lose that spark of curiosity. I told her about the cup of coffee you and I shared, sometime ago, and she smiled. She gave me a brief update about you—said you were assembling a team for something big.

She also mentioned, almost in passing, that sometimes you still brought up my name."

They both let that moment sink in, shying away from eye contact and looking down, blushing with half smiles.

She continued: "You have a pretty cool mom, she has amazing energy, always positive."

Rebecca's eyes glistened as she recalled Jake's mother's kindness. Jake felt a pang but managed to smile. "She has that effect on people. And she saw potential in you, clearly."

Rebecca continued, "So when she told me you were continuing your parents' research, I had to be part of it. It felt like everything I cared about was coming together—the myths, the science, the chance to actually find something that could rewrite history."

They shared a companionable silence, sipping tea, letting the wind fill it. Overhead, a few gulls followed the ship hopefully. The water had turned choppier; *Elysium*'s bow rose and fell rhythmically over growing swells.

From the deck speakers came Captain O'Connor's lilting Irish accent: "All hands, prepare for rough weather. Secure loose equipment and brace for a squall in the next hour." On cue, a distant rumble of thunder underscored his announcement.

Rebecca pulled her jacket tighter. "I'd better go help Naomi tie down those sample crates," she said, nodding toward a set of heavy boxes on the aft deck that were sliding slightly with each roll of the ship.

Jake nodded. "I'll join you in a minute." He lingered a moment after she left, finishing his tea and committing this scene to memory: the endless ocean, the taste of salt in the air, the excitement coursing through him despite the chill. They were truly underway.

He glanced upward at the foremast, where their array of antennae and satellite dishes stood. Unbeknownst to the others, earlier that day Jake had found a strange device magnetically attached near the base of the mast—a small waterproof cylinder with an LED that blinked intermittently. It wasn't standard equipment. Miguel, who had some electronics know-how, suspected it was a tracker. "Miguel, keep an eye out. If anyone comes, let's be prepared," Jake said with serious intent.

Jake had quietly removed it and stowed it in a metal box (to stop transmissions) without alarming the group. He didn't want them to start the expedition paranoid, but he made a mental note: someone is tracking us. Likely Mr. Sloan. It only affirmed their need for vigilance.

Jake left the rail and helped secure the deck. He and Miguel double-checked the submarine winch and the ROV housing, making sure all was battened down. The crew moved efficiently, clearly experienced with sudden weather. Captain O'Connor himself came down to assist, a stout man with weathered features and steady eyes that missed nothing.

By nightfall, the storm struck in earnest. The *Elysium* pitched and groaned against 20-foot waves. Rain pelted the deck in sheets, and the wind howled through the superstructure. Inside the mess hall, which doubled as a common room, Jake's team gathered, strapped into bolted-down chairs around a table with raised edges to catch sliding items.

Plates and silverware rattled. A particularly large wave hit, making the ship shudder; Rebecca's cup of soup sloshed and nearly spilled. Miguel instinctively reached out to steady a model of the *Elysium* that was perched on a shelf.

"This is a nasty one," Miguel said, knuckles white where he gripped the edge of the table. A native of coastal Spain, he was used to storms, but even he looked nervous. "Captain says it came out of nowhere, intensifying much faster than expected."

John, wiping his glasses dry for the tenth time, chuckled low.

"It would appear Poseidon is testing our resolve." He tried to make light, but everyone was tense.

Shirley patted John's hand. "Reminds me of that squall we endured off Bimini back in 1987, doesn't it John?" she said, raising her voice to cut through the thrum of rain on the hull. She turned to the others. "We were following up on some underwater stone formations—this was when Karl and Karin were newly married, Jake was just a toddler then. A hurricane nearly ran our small boat aground. We actually had to dump some equipment to lighten the load and make it to port. Lost a good camera and some scuba gear to the sea that day."

John nodded, smiling at the memory. "We huddled in a leaky cabin playing poker with a soggy deck of cards, if I recall correctly. Your father kept trying to use chocolate coins as betting chips, which of course melted everywhere..." He broke into a laugh and the others chuckled with him. Jake pictured it: his young parents and the Webers on a tiny boat, defying a hurricane in the name of discovery.

"My mother loves storms," Jake said softly. "She always said the rain reminded her that even the sky has emotions—fury, tears— but that after it unleashes them, calm returns." He found himself sharing an intimate recollection, drawn out by the camaraderie. "When I was little, during thunderstorms she'd wrap me in a blanket on our porch and we'd watch the lightning. She'd tell me each storm has a purpose, and that fear can be overcome by understanding."

Naomi smiled. "She sounds like a wonderful person."

"Well, she is," Shirley agreed, reaching across to squeeze Jake's shoulder. "And she'll be so proud of you for this."

Jake felt warmth rise in his chest, a mix of pride and longing. "I hope so. I feel like they're with us, in a way." He pulled out a waterproof field journal from his pocket and carefully opened it to reveal a laminated letter tucked inside—his mother's letter to him. "This is from her. I keep it close." He hadn't shared it with anyone yet, but in that moment, he wanted them to know.

By the dim glow of the red emergency light (turned on to preserve night vision on deck), he read a portion aloud:

My dearest Jake, if you are reading this, it means we could not join you for reasons unexpected. We have given our lives to this search, believing it of vital importance to humanity. Now we pass that torch to you, our beloved son. Do not be afraid of the truth. Seek it with courage and integrity. The puzzle pieces will fall into place in your hands. And when they do, you must act for the good of all. We have faith in you.

Love, Mom and Dad

The room was silent except for the roar of the storm outside. Rebecca wiped a tear. John and Shirley looked down, blinking rapidly. Naomi exhaled, "Your parents knew the importance of this day. They prepared you for it, Jake."

He folded the letter back gently. "I read those words every night. They keep me going." He cleared his throat, feeling a bit self-conscious for having bared his heart like that. But the others regarded him with such kindness that he didn't regret it.

Miguel offered a lopsided grin. "And you've got us with you too, *Jefe*. We're all in this together."

Yumi finally breaks her silence and pounds on the table: "Let's do this!"

"Together," Jake affirmed smiling.

They all salute each other with handshakes and high fives as their ship rides the storm.

Captain O'Connor's voice crackled over the intercom. "Apologies for the rough ride, folks. Forecast shows another two hours of this squall, then we should see some easing. Hold tight, *Elysium* is a tough lass."

Relief spread through everyone. They were exhausted from bracing themselves physically and mentally for hours. One by one, the group retired to their bunks to rest while they could.

Jake stayed up a while longer, insisting on taking a watch on the bridge. The captain welcomed the company, and together they scrutinized the radar for any blips. For a time, the screen was clear except for typical static and distant freighter traffic far from their course. But just before Jake turned in for the night, he noticed a faint echo that appeared briefly at the very edge of their radar range behind them. It vanished with the next sweep.

He narrowed his eyes. "Captain, could that have been an artifact from the storm, or another vessel trailing us about 20 kilometers back?"

Captain O'Connor frowned, adjusting a knob. "Hard to say. The seas are still rough; could be a false return. No transponder signal detected." By maritime law, ships over a certain size should broadcast an Automatic Identification System (AIS) signal. Whoever was back there had it off. "We'll keep an eye out," he assured.

Jake left the bridge quietly, his unease growing. There was something out there, he was almost certain. Falk or not, they would not face it unprepared.

Before he finally crawled into his bunk, he stopped by the small armory locker and withdrew one of the flare guns and a flare grenade. He hoped it would never come to needing weapons, but a flare could serve as a distress signal or a surprise deterrent if necessary. He hid it in a waterproof pouch among his diving gear.

Lying in the narrow bunk, lulled by the now much gentler rocking of the ship, Jake's mind churned despite his fatigue. They were drawing closer to the great mystery. In roughly 18 hours, by current ETA, they would be above the site that could be Atlantis. His heart quickened with anticipation at the thought of descending into those depths and being the first people in millennia to see what lay there.

He stared at the ceiling, where a faint leak from the storm dripped a rhythmic pattern, and let his thoughts drift. In a semi-dream state, he imagined the city as it might have been: golden spires and wide canals, humming with the energy of the Exodus machine at its heart. He saw people gazing up in terror at a darkening sky as comets rained fire. And then, he imagined an Atlantean leader—perhaps the same robed man from the hologram—ushering survivors into a portal of light.

We will find it, he vowed silently. *And we will learn how to prevent it from happening again.*

With that promise echoing in his mind, Jake finally surrendered to sleep, as the *Elysium* steamed onward into the calm night, bearing them faithfully toward the coordinates that had haunted human dreams for ages.

The Sunken City

By the following afternoon, the storm had long passed. The sky was a brilliant blue, and sunlight danced on gentle waves as *Elysium* arrived at the target coordinates. Excitement on board was palpable. John, Shirley, and Rebecca crowded around the sonar station in the ship's lab while Miguel, Yumi and Naomi prepared the submersible on deck. Jake moved between both groups, monitoring every detail.

"Slowing to one knot," Captain O'Connor's voice came from the bridge over the intercom. The engines throbbed softly as *Elysium* glided into position.

Inside the lab, the high-resolution side-scan sonar was already deployed, its sensor sweeping the seafloor 150 meters below. A monitor showed a real-time bathymetric map rendering in false-color relief.

At first, the seabed appeared as expected: a broad plateau rising from deeper plains, strewn with sediment dunes shaped by currents. Then, as the ship moved eastward, the sonar image began to reveal anomalous shapes: right angles, straight lines, unnaturally smooth surfaces.

"Look there," Rebecca said, voice quivering with anticipation. She pointed to a series of rectangular forms emerging on the sonar map. They were arranged in a grid-like pattern. "Those could be building foundations or walls."

Shirley leaned in, adjusting her bifocals. "It certainly isn't just geology. Nature seldom makes perfect rectangles that size. That's structure." She glanced at John, and he reached over to pat her hand in silent shared triumph.

John toggled the 3D view. As the sonar completed a pass, an outline of what looked like a vast complex came into focus. A long, linear feature extended for nearly a hundred meters—possibly a collapsed colonnade or roadway. Adjacent to it were blocky masses that could only be ruined buildings. One structure, near the center of the cluster, rose higher than the rest, its outline forming a rough square of about 200 meters on a side with a gap or courtyard in the middle. From this central structure a broad avenue seemed to run southward.

"That must be the citadel or temple area," John murmured, tracing it on the screen with a trembling finger. "It matches Plato's description surprisingly well—a central plain with structures and a great temple."

Indeed, Plato's account described concentric rings of city and a central island with a temple to Poseidon. The sonar wasn't detailed enough to show rings, but what lay beneath them certainly looked like a city's remains.

Jake entered, already clad in a neoprene dive suit rolled down to his waist, and caught the last bit. He absorbed the sonar image—his heart pounding as recognition dawned. They had found it. The silhouette of a lost city hidden in the depths. His voice was barely above a whisper: "Atlantis."

No one contradicted him. It was undeniable now that something artificial lay below.

Captain O'Connor joined them briefly, arms crossed, grinning. "Congratulations, folks. Whatever name we give it, there's a damn city down there. We've anchored just off the southern edge of it. Depth is 120 meters at our position. Shall we commence dive operations?"

"Yes," Jake said, snapping into action mode. "Naomi, Miguel and I will take the sub down. Rebecca, Yumi, you operate the ROV from here to scout ahead of us and film. John, Shirley, coordinate observations topside and guide us using sonar. We'll keep an open comm channel."

They all moved with crisp efficiency, excitement overcoming any fatigue from the previous night.

The submersible Neptune was a three-person research sub, a spherical acrylic hull encased in a metal frame with thrusters. It looked like a giant glass bubble—perfect for panoramic views. Miguel, being certified in sub piloting, climbed into the pilot seat. Jake and Naomi squeezed in behind him, their knees almost touching in the compact space.

Jake carried with him a specialized waterproof tablet loaded with translation software and reference databases—ready to record and interpret any inscriptions. At his belt was also the flare gun he had stashed, which in an underwater emergency might be of limited use, but he felt better having something. Naomi had a tool kit for sampling and basic repairs, and a waterproof case containing scientific instruments like a spectrometer and Geiger counter (they wanted to check for any unusual radiation or magnetism near the machine site).

Once inside, they latched the dome. Through the clear sphere, Jake could see John, Shirley, and Rebecca waving from the deck. He gave a thumbs-up. Over the sub's internal radio, Captain O'Connor's voice came: "Neptune, comm check."

"Neptune here, reading you five by five," Miguel responded, flipping the array of switches that brought the sub to life. The hum of batteries and the gentle hiss of oxygen flow filled the small cabin.

"Lowering you down. Good luck down there," Captain said. A crane arm lifted the sub and swung it out over the water. With a splash, Neptune descended, tethered briefly by a cable until Miguel signaled all systems go. Then the crane released.

They began to sink beneath the surface, water enveloping the plexiglass viewports. Sunlight filtered down in shimmering beams that gradually dimmed to a green-blue twilight as they went deeper. Small fish darted by, startled by the sub's presence.

On Neptune's dashboard, a depth gauge ticked: 50m, 70m, 100m. The outlines of *Elysium*'s hull above grew faint and then vanished. Jake felt a flutter of nerves—they were truly entering another world now, one of eternal darkness broken only by their lights.

At 120 meters, Miguel leveled out. "We're above the seabed, maybe 20 meters up," he said. He turned on the forward floodlights. Powerful LEDs cut through the gloom, illuminating a sector of the ocean floor in cold white light.

"Rebecca, how's the ROV feed?" Naomi asked over the comm. Back on the ship, Rebecca had deployed their ROV (Remotely Operated Vehicle), a torpedo-shaped robotic camera with propellers and a claw arm. It was tethered to *Elysium* by a fiber-optic cable for live video and control.

"ROV is in the water and descending. You should see its lights about 30 meters to your north," Rebecca's voice crackled in their earpieces. "I'm going to sweep south toward that main structure we saw."

"Roger that. We have it on sonar," John added. "Neptune, suggest you approach from the south side of the complex first—there was an open plaza-like area there which might be easier to navigate."

"Copy," said Miguel, gently pushing the sub's thruster lever.

Neptune glided forward.

Jake pressed his face to the dome. As they slowly advanced, the first objects came into view out of the darkness: stone blocks, each the size of a car, lying in jumbled piles. Some were half-buried in silt. He realized they were at the edge of a collapsed outer wall or building.

He caught a glimpse of something on one of the blocks as they passed—a carving? "Hold on, swing the light left," Jake told Miguel. The pilot obliged.

On the face of a fallen monolith, eroded but unmistakable, were carved symbols: concentric circles and radiating lines. Part of it flaked away as Neptune's current disturbed the silt, but Jake's heart jumped. It looked very much like a stylized sun or star with rays—much like the iconography of sun-gods around the ancient world.

He hit the record on his tablet's camera through the dome. "We're seeing definite engravings on stones. Possibly an artistic motif. Looks like a sunburst or wheel."

John's excited voice came: "Indeed? Get as many shots as you can. That motif might recur on more intact surfaces deeper in."

They pressed on. The sub navigated over what appeared to be a paved road—rectangular slabs neatly laid, some still aligned in rows. It widened into the open plaza area John had mentioned. Here, fewer large blocks cluttered the ground, suggesting this was an empty space in the city's layout.

And then, beyond the plaza, Neptune's lights fell upon the great structure.

A collective gasp sounded in the sub's cabin. Rising out of the dark water was a broad staircase flanked by broken obelisks. The staircase led up to a massive platform or plinth. Atop it was the vestiges of pillars arranged in a rectangle—likely a temple's foundation. Many columns had fallen and lay diagonally against each other; a few still stood, reaching up like lonely giants toward the surface far above.

The scale was breathtaking. Even in ruin, the structure exuded grandeur. The top of the platform might have been 10 or 15 meters above the seafloor. Neptune's depth gauge read 135m—the base was a depression a bit deeper than the outskirts. "Neptune, we see it on your video," came Shirley's hushed voice. She was on the ship watching the sub's live feed that Neptune was transmitting acoustically. "It's like the Parthenon under the sea. How beautiful." Even through the comm static, one could hear her tearing up.

Jake felt tears prick his own eyes from the sheer emotion of it, thought of his parents came to mind—"Mom, Dad, I wish you could be looking at this." To see something built so long ago, now silent and sunken, was overwhelming. Yet, amid the wonder, he remembered their mission. They needed to find the machine, the evidence of the Exodus Protocol.

"We should look for an entrance or chamber," Naomi said, ever practical, though her voice trembled. "Perhaps the device is inside or below the temple."

Miguel circled Neptune slowly around the perimeter of the temple platform, maintaining a respectful distance to avoid accidentally bumping any unstable columns.

On one side of the temple base, they found a gaping hole—as if part of the wall had been blasted out from inside. Rubble spilled from it down the steps. The opening was large enough for the sub to possibly slip through, but that would be risky in tight quarters. Safer to send the ROV.

"Rebecca, do you see the breach on the temple's west side? Can you guide the ROV in there?" Jake asked.

"Affirmative, I see it," Rebecca answered. From above, she maneuvered the ROV toward the temple. The sub's occupants saw its twin lights appear and hover at the breach.

"I'm sending it in," she said. On *Elysium*, her eyes were glued to the ROV's camera feed as it went through the broken wall and into darkness. She turned on the ROV's stronger floodlamp.

Inside, a corridor appeared, surprisingly intact. The beam revealed walls adorned with continuous bands of carvings, untouched by currents here, and a floor that seemed to be tiled with black and white stone in geometric patterns. It looked eerily preserved.

"Oh my," Rebecca muttered. "I'm in some kind of hallway. There are inscriptions everywhere. I'm recording everything."

In Neptune, Jake watched the feed relayed from *Elysium*.

The carvings on the inner walls were clearly visible: rows of symbols unlike any script in current use. Some looked vaguely like cuneiform mixed with hieroglyphs, exactly as they saw on the black obsidian stone. Others were pictorial: one panel showed figures of people standing under a sky of stars, another depicted a bright object (a comet?) streaking downward, another had wavy lines that might represent floods or water.

"It's telling the story," Jake whispered, transfixed. "The story of the cataclysm tracking over the years, perhaps . . ."

He yearned to go in person to see those walls, but he knew rashness could be deadly. He'd let the ROV safely reconnoiter first.

Rebecca guided the ROV further down the corridor. It turned a corner and entered a wider chamber, perhaps an antechamber of the temple's inner sanctum.

"There's some collapse here, but I can navigate," she said. On the video feed, chunks of ceiling littered the room, but enough space remained for the ROV to wiggle through. As it did, the feed crackled momentarily—likely the dense stone walls weakening the signal.

The picture returned to clarity as the ROV emerged into what looked like the central hall of the temple. Everyone on the ship and in the sub held their breath.

In the ROV's light, they saw the hall was circular and large— maybe 30 meters across. Around its perimeter stood statues or rather, what remained of them. Several tall humanoid figures carved of stone, worn featureless by water, but one could still see they once had intricate robes and hats or helmets. Some had arms outstretched.

One statue near the center caught the light: it was different, appearing metallic rather than stone.

Rebecca piloted closer to it. The team's excitement spiked—

metal does not usually fare well underwater for millennia, unless it was extraordinary material like gold or an alloy.

"Focus on that metal statue," Naomi said eagerly.

The ROV camera centered on it. The figure was humanoid but stylized, perhaps twice as tall as a person. It stood on a pedestal that was part of a machine-like apparatus: behind it was a large ring structure, about 5 meters in diameter, tilted at a slight angle and attached to a base. The metal figure actually seemed to be integrated into the ring—its hands were raised, touching the ring's inner edge as if holding it up or perhaps controlling it.

Jake's heart rate skyrocketed. "That's it! It looks like the device from the hologram!" He recognized the ring structure—it was like the one shown in the hologram that the robed man activated. Even though this was long inert and partly crusted with marine life, the shape was unmistakable.

Naomi was practically bouncing in her seat in the sub. "I can't believe it's still standing. It must be made of some corrosion-resistant metal. We might be looking at an alloy or metal not used in known ancient times."

Rebecca carefully rotated the ROV's view to survey the whole apparatus. The ring was mounted on a blocky base with what looked like broken pylons or consoles around it. The statue merged into the ring might represent a deity or guardian of the device— perhaps Poseidon or some Atlantean engineer immortalized. At the statue's feet lay what appeared to be shattered glass or crystal—maybe the remains of panels or a power source.

"Radiation check?" came John's voice. They had discussed the possibility that an ancient power source could emit radiation.

Naomi pointed a handheld Geiger counter at the viewing dome, as the sub by now had drifted near the temple exterior. The counter clicked at background levels only. "No significant radiation detected here from outside. When we go in, we should check again, but it seems safe so far."

The comm line from the ROV fizzled again as Rebecca tried to get closer. "Signal's cutting in and out, possibly interference from the structure," she reported. The dense stone or maybe electromagnetic fields from the device (if any remained) could interfere.

CHAPTER 18

Gatecrashers

Suddenly, Miguel stiffened, listening to a different channel on his headset—the dedicated sonar/alert channel. He spoke urgently: "Captain, I'm picking up something on sonar—a new contact."

On *Elysium*, the bridge crew had indeed spotted a sudden blip moving toward them fast, just 5 kilometers out. Captain O'Connor responded briskly, "Confirmed, Neptune. We have an unidentif–"

His transmission was cut off by static. In Neptune, the comm to the ship hissed and fell silent. Miguel tapped the console. "We lost contact with *Elysium*."

At the same time, through the murk outside Neptune's dome, Jake saw two streaks of light: bioluminescent trails? No—

headlights. Two of them, coming from behind, then splitting to flank Neptune. Another submersible—or divers with scooters—were upon them.

Without warning, a heavy bang rattled Neptune as something collided with its frame. The sub pitched to starboard. Naomi cried out as she was thrown against the dome. Jake braced his arms against the seat.

Out of the corner of his eye, through the plexiglass, Jake saw a dark shape—another mini-sub much smaller than Neptune, or some kind of unmanned underwater drone—scrape past them. It had intentionally rammed them.

"Hang on!" Miguel shouted, stabilizing Neptune and turning on its side thrusters to hold position. He switched on the external camera to see behind. The feed showed two sleek vehicles—one was indeed a small two-man submersible painted matte black, the other looked like an ROV but larger and weaponized with a manipulator arm. Both were not from *Elysium,* that was certain.

From the black sub, a spotlight beam now stabbed toward Neptune's dome, dazzling them. Over the common open frequency, a voice came through, crackling but intelligible:

"Attention, this is Dr. Sebastian Falk. By authority of the International Heritage Commission, you are ordered to cease exploration and surrender all materials."

The sheer gall left Jake momentarily speechless. Falk's tone was icy and commanding, though a little distorted underwater.

Jake recovered and thumbed his mic. "Falk! You have no authority here. This is our find. *You're* the one interfering illegally." He kept his voice level, but anger surged. That Falk would dare to claim an 'International Heritage' mandate was preposterous—he was abusing terms to confuse or justify his actions.

In Neptune's cabin lights, Naomi's face had gone pale. Miguel grit his teeth, hands hovering over the controls—unsure whether to attempt escape or hold ground. They were unarmed except for the flare gun with Jake, which in an underwater sub-to-sub scenario was useless.

Falk's voice crackled again, colder. "Jake, I anticipated your intransigence. Very well. I will take what I need by force. This knowledge is too important to be left to amateurs and glory-hunters. You should have walked away."

Immediately the smaller drone-like vehicle moved in front of Neptune. It had some kind of device on its front—a tubular object. There was a sudden burst of air bubbles and a muffled thud—it was firing something!

A sharp clang reverberated—an underwater projectile slammed into Neptune's port side. The lights flickered as Miguel fought the controls to keep yaw steady. A tiny spider-web crack appeared in the outer layer of the acrylic dome—not a breach, but a bad sign. If the dome shattered at this depth, they'd be crushed.

"We need to retreat, now!" Naomi said, fear edging her voice. Miguel didn't hesitate; he hit full reverse on the thrusters.

Neptune began to back away from the temple, kicking up clouds of silt.

"Jake, this is bad," Miguel muttered privately on the sub's internal intercom. "We can't outfight them."

Jake's mind raced. If they retreated blindly, Falk could chase them down easily or shoot again. But if they maneuvered among the ruins, maybe the terrain could even the odds. Plus they needed that data from inside the temple.

"Go toward the temple structure, into the plaza," Jake ordered.

Miguel, trusting Jake, steered Neptune directly into the plaza they had just left. The two hostile craft gave chase—the black sub and its armed drone darted after them like sharks.

On *Elysium*, pandemonium had broken out when communications were lost. John and Shirley shouted into the radios, trying multiple frequencies. They watched on sonar as Neptune's transponder moved erratically with two unknowns around it. The deck crew saw a silhouette of a strange vessel near the surface momentarily—likely Falk's support ship—before it submerged to hide. Captain O'Connor cursed, "Pirates or whoever, they've jammed us. We can't even reach the coast guard."

Rebecca was still staring at the ROV feed from inside the temple hall, which now was static—the cable must've been cut or the ROV knocked offline in the fray. She felt helpless, fear gnawing at her for her friends below. "We have to help them," she pleaded to the captain.

O'Connor had already loaded two of the ship's crew into the inflatable fast-boat. "I'm sending men to see if we can snag their support ship or at least cut any lines. But underwater, it's up to your friends. We'll do what we can."

Back underwater, Neptune zigzagged over the ruins. Miguel dared not go too fast in case of colliding with debris. The hostile mini-sub was more agile, zipping around to Neptune's flank and trying to herd them into the open. The drone took another shot—this time a spear-like harpoon grazed Neptune's aft, tangling in a propeller. The sub lurched as one of its thrusters jammed, forcing Miguel to compensate with the others.

"Prop 3 is fouled—I can't get full thrust!" he called.

A voice burst in on their comm—different from Falk's, likely one of his mercenaries: "Stop your engines and we'll spare your lives. Resist and you die now."

Jake looked at Naomi and Miguel. Surrender? In that moment, surrender likely meant Falk would take it all, their data, maybe kill them anyway. And nothing would stop him from taking or destroying the evidence of the cycle. No—they had come too far. He unclipped the flare gun from his belt. An idea sparked. "Miguel, when I say, cut all lights and give me one second of fullballast release—enough to jolt us."

Miguel shot him a quizzical glance but nodded sharply.

Jake switched to external loudspeaker—an option Neptune had to communicate with divers. "Alright! We'll power down, don't shoot," he said, trying to sound defeated.

The pursuing sub eased its pressure slightly, drifting closer, and the drone paused weapon firing but remained poised.

Jake quickly slid open Neptune's top airlock—a small portal for emergencies or diver exit. Water did not flood in yet—there was a pressure barrier since Neptune's interior was pressurized at atmospheric level and sealed; opening fully would flood them, but he could pop a device out without decompressing the cabin.

He loaded the flare grenade (essentially a magnesium pyrotechnic) into the adapted line thrower tube of the flare gun. A standard flare wouldn't ignite underwater, but this one was a naval emergency flare rated to burn even submerged by a powerful chemical reaction.

"Now!" Jake yelled.

Miguel killed Neptune's exterior lights, plunging them into darkness. Simultaneously he hit the ballast purge for a one-second burst. The sub jerked and dropped a meter suddenly, as if losing control.

In the sudden, chaotic darkness, Jake reached past the cabin's defensive mechanism and fired the flare gun toward the pursuing drone and sub, like a torpedo. The flare grenade shot out and, struck near the drone's nose.

A blinding flash erupted underwater—a sphere of searing white-magnesium light that illuminated the ruins like an underwater sun. For a moment, day returned to the depths. The drone's camera sensors were surely overwhelmed; even

Neptune's cabin was flooded with harsh light despite their internal darkness.

The mercenary piloting the drone cursed as his vision went white. The flare also produced a cloud of bubbles and smoke. It threw off their pursuers' targeting.

Miguel immediately gunned Neptune's remaining thrusters, using the distraction. The sub surged forward and upward, aiming to put the bulk of the temple platform between them and the attackers. Through the flare's fading glow, the silhouette of the great ring device loomed above them in the temple hall, but Miguel skimmed Neptune just over the plaza floor, ducking behind a fallen column.

The enemy drone fired wildly—a projectile whistled past Neptune, missing by a wide margin. The black sub, trying not to crash, veered off, scraping the temple staircase and snapping off an ancient pillar in its haste.

Naomi whooped, "It's working! They're disoriented."

But the advantage would be brief. They needed to either disable the attackers or force them to retreat. Another idea came to Jake—risky but maybe their best bet: the machine.

"Get us into the temple hall—right to the device!" he urged.

Miguel, trusting Jake, steered Neptune directly into the gaping wall breach from which the ROV had gone. It was a tight squeeze for the sub, which was larger than the ROV, but the collapse had widened the entry enough. Metal screeched as Neptune's frame rubbed stone, but then they were inside the corridor.

The sub's lights back on now lit the interior brilliantly, revealing the carved walls and intact mosaic floor. They slid into the circular chamber with the statues and device. The water here was calmer, less silt—the ROV had cleared much of it.

Neptune settled just in front of the great ring. Up close, Jake marveled at its construction: It was made of a dull gray metal with faint engravings all along its circumference. In the center of the ring, there was now only empty water—whatever portal effect or door had been there was long gone. The statue integrated with it was of a robed man, eyes once likely inset with gems now empty sockets.

Falk's sub and drone were regaining composure and they weren't far behind—Neptune's sonar showed them approaching the breach.

Jake had one wild plan: The device likely had never been powered on in eons, but perhaps it still had some reactive elements. If he could trigger anything—an electromagnetic pulse, a vibration—it might scare or impede the attackers. Alternatively, the structure could be unstable; a shock might bring it down on their heads (and unfortunately Neptune too if not careful).

No time to deliberate deeply. Jake toggled Neptune's manipulator arm controls. A mechanical claw on the sub's front extended. He grabbed one of the fallen chunks of crystalline material at the statue's feet—it looked like a broken piece of some core. Perhaps highly energetic once, now inert? Or maybe not entirely?

He thrust that chunk into the center of the ring and then used the manipulator to strike the base of the ring apparatus, hoping to jolt something.

There was a dull gong sound through the water. For a second, nothing happened. Then Neptune's interior lights flickered. Naomi gasped, looking at her instrument panel. "Some kind of magnetic surge. Did you see that?"

Before Jake could reply, a low rumble began. The statue's eyes flickered with a faint light—or was it a reflection from Neptune's own lamps? Hard to tell, but an eerie glow suffused the ring, a pale blue shimmering along the inner circumference. The water inside the ring began to churn as if a small vortex had been born.

On the ship, John and Shirley saw on sonar a sudden spike of acoustic noise from the temple location.

In the temple hall, the sound rose—Neptune's hydrophones picked up what could only be described as a deep humming chant, almost like the echo of long-silent machinery awakening for a final gasp.

Falk's sub had just poked its nose and lights through the breach when this occurred. The pilot of the drone paused, uncertain. Over Falk's sub comm, they heard him bark, "What are they doing?!"

Suddenly, a bolt of energy—akin to a lightning strike but underwater—arced from the ring to one of the collapsed metallic pylons. It was brief and small, but enough to send shockwaves of bubbles and a thud through the water. Neptune rocked gently, but the brunt aimed outward.

The black sub in the corridor was caught in that shock. Its systems flickered; inside, Falk and his mercenary co-pilot felt their hair stand on end as electricity coursed through their hull. The sub's mechanical arm twitched uncontrollably and the engine sputtered.

The drone, tethered to the sub by a command link, also went haywire, its thrusters spinning it in an uncontrolled circle.

"Mayday– systems failing!" cried Falk's co-pilot.

Falk, panicked and enraged, shouted, "Retreat! Pull back!"

The black sub reversed clumsily out of the breach, scraping more debris as it did. The drone, still spinning, crashed into the corridor wall and got wedged in fallen blocks.

In Neptune, Jake watched as their adversaries retreated, astonished that the device had responded at all. The blue glow subsided now, and the humming faded, leaving the hall dark and silent once more. A few pieces of stone from the ceiling drifted down—the structure might have been destabilized slightly, but it still held.

Miguel didn't wait for a second chance; he propelled Neptune out of the temple as well (through a different gap in the roof that the energy discharge had conveniently opened a bit). They emerged into open water to see the black sub ascending and fleeing northward, trailing sparks.

"Yeah, you better run," Naomi murmured, half in disbelief.

Jake dared a last look down at the temple from above. The great ring was now dark again. Whatever he had awoken, it seemed to have settled—perhaps permanently extinguished by that effort. But it had served its purpose now.

"Jake, Naomi, Miguel—come in!" It was John's voice, loud and joyous in their headsets as the jamming finally cleared. "We see the hostile sub retreating. Are you alright?"

"We're okay!" Jake replied. "We had to get creative, but we're alright. The device reacted to a stimulus. We'll explain later. How's Rebecca and the ship?"

Rebecca's voice cut in, relieved and excited. "I'm here! My ROV is probably toast but who cares—you guys are safe. The intruders are bugging out. Captain O'Connor is giving chase at the surface but they're fast. Doesn't matter. We did it, Jake!"

In Neptune, all three shared a moment of laughter and adrenaline-fueled relief. They had fended off the danger.

But Jake's eyes turned back to the ruins below, and his laughter quickly turned to a somber smile. "We still have a mission," he said. "We need whatever information we can get from down here, let's photograph and video everything, grab whatever you believe are clues for the next step, obviously this was just the first part of something much bigger."

The villain vanquished (for now), they could work calmly. Neptune returned to hover inside the temple hall. The statues stood silently as they likely had for millennia. Jake guided the sub's lights around to capture every inch of carvings on the walls.

Naomi deployed a small robotic probe from Neptune (like a mini-ROV) to pick up the broken crystal chunk Jake had inserted in the device—perhaps it was a power cell or memory storage that could be studied.

They spent another hour diligently recording. Now with Falk gone, Jake even dared to exit the sub in dive gear (Neptune had an airlock for such purpose). He trusted Captain and crew above were keeping watch for any return of hostiles. Wearing an atmospheric diving suit (like a hard suit that can operate at depth), he stepped onto the temple floor—becoming perhaps the first human to walk there since the Ice Age.

With a handheld high-resolution camera, he moved along the walls, videoing the story-panels in detail. He placed small marker buoys near significant script sections for Neptune's instruments to precisely map their positions.

One panel depicted what clearly was a map of the world with certain points marked, the number 3 as written in cuneiform on top of what resembled Greece on the map—likely where survivors went or where other facilities were. He pointed it out to the camera: "This could be showing refuge sites or something, maybe other colonies or vaults, or maybe another one of these devices."

"Another panel showed figures carrying long cylindrical objects toward Vimana-looking ships—or was it a portal? Hard to say. The style was remarkably similar to Sumerian and Egyptian art, but distinct, as if they were the root and those later styles were branches."

At last, Jake stood directly before the great ring device. In his bulky suit, he reached out and gently touched the metal. It felt smooth and cold. On its base was a plaque of sorts—lines of Atlantean script.

He focused his helmet camera on it. "This looks like an inscription, maybe instructions or a dedication." The characters glinted where his suit light hit them. He traced them carefully with one gauntleted finger, mentally noting each pattern.

Though underwater and muffled, he felt a resonance—as if the metal faintly vibrated with latent power. Perhaps it was just his imagination. The Exodus Portal—what secrets had it held? He wondered if any of those who stepped through it had survived somewhere.

He offered a silent thanks to the creators of this place, these long-lost engineers and sages. *We found you*, he thought, *and we will remember.*

Returning to Neptune, he and Naomi collected a few small artifacts that were loose: a fragment of an inscribed ceramic tablet, a rusted but interesting gear-like object perhaps from the mechanism, and a stone scarab-like amulet that Naomi found near a fallen priest statue (likely dropped in the ancient chaos).

Their cargo full of invaluable relics and data, Neptune ascended at last.

When they breached the surface, late afternoon sun greeted them. The storm-tossed night felt like a bad dream in the warm light.

The crew of *Elysium* whooped and cheered as the crane lifted Neptune back onto the deck. The moment the hatch opened, Jake was helped out by crew and immediately enveloped in a tight hug by Rebecca (still in her wetsuit from earlier ROV handling). John pumped Miguel's hand vigorously, and Shirley actually planted a kiss on Naomi's cheek, making the younger engineer blush and laugh.

Captain O'Connor kept a professional distance, but Jake walked over and shook his hand with heartfelt gratitude. "Captain, we owe you for sticking with us."

He tipped his cap. "I've seen some things in my time, but this takes the cake. Thank you for letting me be a part of it—and glad we sent those bastards running. They scooted once the sub surfaced; my crew couldn't catch them, but we got the drone they abandoned. Might be some tech in it for you to analyze as a bonus." He winked.

Indeed, on deck was the black drone, dented and missing a harpoon, but largely intact, hauled up by the inflatable crew. Miguel eyed it with interest. "I'll be happy to pick that apart later."

CHAPTER 19

Data Hunt

They wasted no time securing the precious artifacts and data cards in secure cases. While the ship's crew began preparations to get underway (in case Falk returned with reinforcements—better to be moving), the core team gathered in the lab to conduct a preliminary analysis of what they had recorded.

Even before formal translation, the pictograms told a clear story. Using high-resolution stills, John and Shirley began translating parts of the script by cross-referencing the symbols found on the artifacts.

It took several hours into the night, but gradually, they deciphered key passages. One long inscription along the base of the device read (once transliterated and translated with some help from both Sumerian and proto-Greek comparisons):

In the year of the great serpent in the sky, when fire rained upon our lands, the Council of Twelve enacted the Exodus Protocol. By the decree of Poseidon, Lord of Waves, and Ninurta, Keeper of the Celestial Arks, we carried the sacred knowledge and seeds of our people through the gate to safety.

Shirley read that aloud, each word trembling on her tongue as meaning coalesced. They looked at each other in wonder—names from different mythologies used side by side: Poseidon (Greek sea god) and Ninurta (a Mesopotamian/Anunnaki god associated with war and the pyramids). It was as if confirming that these legends stemmed from a common source: this Atlantean Council.

"Carried through the gate to safety."

Miguel sat back, whistling softly. "So, some of them escaped somewhere using this. Another place? Another dimension?"

"Or perhaps to high ground elsewhere on Earth—a far colony," Rebecca suggested. "If it was a portal, maybe to somewhere like the Andes or Himalayas, wherever was safe." She pointed to the world map panel they had recorded. There were markings on mountains.

They translated more:

Another section detailed how the "Star of Doom split the sky" and "the ocean swallowed the lands"—clearly referencing the comet impact and ensuing flood. There were numbers too—counts of survivors, perhaps, and a chronology.

One crucial line they discovered near the map showed a cycle. It spoke of "a cycle of the great sun, 12,000 years in turning, when the heavens unleash fury."

Jake's hands shook as he highlighted that part. "Twelve-thousand-year cycle . . ." he muttered. He looked up at the others crowded around the screen. "They're outright telling us the destruction comes in cycles, just as we thought. Likely referencing precessional or astronomical cycles. The Younger Dryas event was ~12,800 years ago—and now we're essentially at that interval again."

Naomi, who had been quiet, spoke up softly. "I ran some numbers while you were translating. There's a known cycle related to cometary orbits—the Taurid meteor stream we've mentioned. Some astronomers suspect it has a heavy bombardment cycle roughly every 12–13 millennia. Also, possibly linked to the sun's grand activity cycles. It could align with this. The ancients must have observed or recorded at least two such events to predict a cycle—maybe an even earlier catastrophe we don't know of."

So it's not just the influence of Nibiru's return—there are other variables, likely triggered by its proximity. Its gravitational pull could be disrupting the meteor belt, sending fragments toward Earth," Jake said, his voice edged with frustration.

Rebecca shivered.

"There's a legend—a fire that ended the 'Age of the Gods' around 24,000 years ago. Mostly esoteric lore. But it's possible they had records that stretch back that far."

"So, the take-home message," John said gravely, "is that the Atlanteans are warning us. They intended for someone to find this and know: the cycle will repeat, and they moved the heart of their machine to a different location. They obviously hoped future generations would be prepared—or perhaps they hoped to break the cycle with their machine. But they still suffered the fall."

"And check this writing out: 'Beware, there are those who want you to fail the test,'" Jake said.

"Who wants who to fail?" Rebecca asked, followed by, "What test?" from Yumi.

Shirley put her hand over a section of text she had been working on and drew a sharp breath. "Oh dear."

Everyone turned to her.

She pointed at a final set of symbols at the end of one wall inscription, which she had tentatively translated. "It gives what looks like a date or time reference for when the cycle returns. It's broken off, but I see here something like: 'when the constellation of the Lion is on the eastern horizon at spring and the great star returns.'"

They all realized what that meant. The constellation of Leo on the eastern horizon at spring describes an age—the Age of Leo. That was roughly 12,000 years ago last time (around 10,800 BC). It's due again, in fact, it cycles every ~26,000 years, but the Age of Leo specifically will next occur after the full precessional cycle. However, that phrasing might metaphorically point to now, since Leo is rising before dawn in our current epoch's transition. Or possibly "the great star returns" referred to the comet coming back.

Naomi interjected more concretely: "The great star could be a comet—maybe the returning fragment of whatever hit them. Possibly the text implies that when certain conditions, like Leo's prominence, occur, the comet returns. Alternatively, maybe they timed it from their own destruction: 'in X years it returns.' Did we find a number X?"

Shirley shook her head sadly. "The number is broken off. But all context indicates soon. Possibly now. They likely intended the far future—which is our present."

A heavy silence fell.

Jake inhaled deeply. "Look, we all knew this was happening. We have plenty of underground sanctuary cities built for this very moment. We must find the new location where the Atlanteans transported the key to this whole thing. They mentioned a test— and those who don't want us to pass it. If we don't pass, there will be no sanctuary city on the planet that will survive the long-term effects of Earth's destruction. We must pass whatever this test is. If the cost of failing is destruction, what would be the reward for passing it?"

He looked at each member of his team. Just days ago, they had been chasing a puzzle for academic and personal fulfillment. Now they held the fate of humanity's future knowledge in their hands. "But we can no longer face this planetary crisis alone. Let's keep what we've found about the machines to ourselves until we know it won't be misused by the likes of Falk and Sloan. But the erratic signs are here—they can no longer deny them. The question is: how do we unite the world for a common cause?" Jake finished his heartfelt speech.

"We publish it, of course," Miguel said. "Loudly. Everywhere." "But who will believe us at first?" Rebecca countered. "We have proof though—video, artifacts. That will help. But some will call it a hoax. And even if believed, what then? Mass panic? Or the world uniting to build shelters or deflection systems?"

John put an arm around Shirley. "We'll need to coordinate with astronomers and world leaders. This evidence is strong— you can literally see the astral mathematical equations. And the dating can be corroborated by geological finds—we can tie it with the Younger Dryas clearly. Perhaps governments have quietly suspected something—the tracking by the Aureus Society suggests some do."

Shirley nodded. "If we handle it carefully, we can present it as: an incredible archaeological discovery and a call to investigate potential cosmic threats. Maybe that way, it's taken seriously. We don't want to scream doomsday without concrete current data or we'll be dismissed as cranks."

"But what would be the correlation between the Younger Dryas and Nibiru's return? Maybe when the planet starts its approach, it disrupts large objects from the asteroid belt? We need the eyes of the world tracking this; much like the ancients did—all eyes tracking the stars," Jake emphasized.

Shirley tapped her keyboard. "I'm already contacting some colleagues at NASA, SpaceX, and ESA under the radar—sending them snippets of the translated text, asking for their thoughts on comet periodicity and current tracking on Planet X. I better not mention its name as Nibiru to avoid the closed-minded comments. Perhaps they can confirm if any known near-Earth object correlates with our timeframe."

Jake rubbed his temples. He was exhausted, but his mind would not rest. Sloan and those like him would surely try to interfere, but now they had the truth securely documented and multiple copies of the data stored (they had already duplicated all video and translations to multiple drives and distributed them among the team).

He walked out onto the moonlit deck. The others followed, one by one, drawn by the night air and the need to decompress after the intense day.

The *Elysium* was heading back eastward under a calm sky. Stars glittered overhead in their eternal vigil. Jake found the constellation of Leo—low in the west now as the night advanced— its brightest star, Regulus, twinkling. Somewhere out there, perhaps, lurked the "great star"—the next visitor in the cycle, still invisible.

He closed his eyes and breathed in the salt air, centering himself. When his eyes opened, they were full of determination. There was much to do, but humanity had a chance—a chance to break the cycle, to prepare an Exodus of its own if needed, or to prevent the catastrophe altogether.

Rebecca joined him at the rail. "Beautiful, isn't it? Hard to imagine those stars could spell our doom," she said softly.

"Or our salvation," Jake replied. "They guided us here, after all. The stars and the ancients."

He pulled out his mother's letter again, wanting to read it under the starlight. As he unfolded it, something slipped from between the pages—a small photograph he hadn't seen in a while. It was a picture of him as a boy on his parents' boat, Karl holding him on his shoulders and Karin laughing up at them. All three squinting in bright sun, carefree.

He realized that photo had been taken not far from this very spot—his parents had sailed the Atlantic searching for clues all those years ago. He showed Rebecca the picture and told her so. She smiled. "They're here with you now, you know. And I think—I hope—they know that you succeeded."

Jake felt a warmth and nodded. He whispered toward the sea, "We did it, Mom and Dad. We found what you entrusted us to find—the celestial warning. And now we'll decipher the code to protect everyone."

John clinked a mug (filled with emergency whiskey from the captain's stores) against a metal rail to get everyone's attention. "Team, come gather for a second!"

They stood in a loose circle on the deck, the moonlight painting them in silver.

John raised his mug.

"To the bravest and finest group of people I've ever had the honor of working with. We accomplished this mission—together."

"Hear, hear," everyone murmured, raising whatever they had (even bottles of water or soda—Naomi had a wrench she jokingly lifted as a 'toast').

"And," Jake continued, "to all those who came before—the souls of Atlantis, who managed to speak to us across twelve millennia. We hear you."

They drank or sipped quietly, each lost a moment in thoughts of the past and future.

The Real Work Begins

Finally, Jake spoke, his voice firm. "Tomorrow, once we reach land, the real work begins—sharing this knowledge and convincing the world. There may be those who try to stop us, but now we hold irrefutable proof." He looked around at his friends—no, his family now. "I can't promise it will be easy. But we carry a responsibility as heavy as that ring device—to ensure the cycle of destruction becomes a cycle of survival."

Shirley put her hand over Jake's on the rail. "We will. That's what the Exodus Protocol was ultimately about—survival. Continuity. We are part of that continuity."

Rebecca gazed at the sky. "Even the Hopi speak of previous worlds destroyed—one by fire and one by flood—and that we live in the Fourth World now. They said if we don't live rightly, this world could end too. Maybe that's true, but now we know about the celestial warning. It's almost poetic—we, the distant descendants, get to be the ark-builders this time, armed with ancient knowledge and modern science." She grinned suddenly. "I just wish I could see the look on the academic establishment's face when we publish all this!"

They chuckled. The tension broke further. Miguel started fantasizing about how they'd exhibit the artifacts in the British Museum (after ensuring global action for safety, of course).

Naomi teased that she'd patent whatever she learned from the metal alloy.

Jake watched them banter, pride swelling. In his mind, he pictured an Atlantean elder—perhaps that robed figure—nodding in approval. The relay race of knowledge had passed the baton, and they would run with it.

As the night deepened, one by one they drifted to their bunks, finally catching some well-earned rest. Jake and Rebecca stayed a few minutes longer on deck. They looked to the east, where the first hint of dawn was glowing. Venus, the morning star, shone brilliantly—a beacon of hope.

He closed his eyes and let the cool air wash over him. When he opened them again, he saw a shooting star streak across the brightening sky—a silent flourish across the heavens.

"Did you see that? It was so beautiful; maybe a sign?" Rebecca asked with a vibrant smile. She moved closer to Jake and slipped her hand into his.

Excitement gave way to quiet stillness as their eyes met, this time with a different intent. They were looking into each other's souls, drawn together by a quiet, natural force—like magnets.

They faced each other, then fell into a tight embrace, holding on as if the world depended on it. When they finally pulled apart, their eyes locked. Flushed and breathless, they shared their first kiss.

They lingered in that moment, the warmth of their bodies melting into each other, filling their hearts with indescribable joy. Maybe it was just a meteorite burning up—nothing unusual.

But to Jake and Rebecca, that streak of light felt like a promise kept. A message from Atlantis, from his parents, a sign from the universe itself: Now you know. Now do something with it.

Jake smiled into the rising sun; his fingers laced with Rebecca's. He whispered, "We'll be ready."

The clue to solve the puzzle had been found, its truth being brought to light. And as Jake and his team turned toward the future, they carried with them the wisdom of the ancients and the determination to change the course of the world's story—ensuring that this time, when the heavens threatened, humanity would unite, prepared and unafraid. The cycle of destruction would meet the strength of knowledge and the will to survive, and from that confrontation, a new story would be born: one of hope, resilience, and life enduring against the odds.

CHAPTER 20

Inseparable

Late at night, Jake paced beneath the flickering lamplight of the study, the weight of centuries pressing down on his weary shoulders. Bookshelves lined one wall, crammed with leather-bound volumes on archaeology and astronomy; their spines glinted faintly where the lamplight touched. The air was thick with the scent of old paper, mixed with the bitter trace of coffee grounds from an earlier brew.

On the corner of the table, a half-eaten loaf of bread and a cluster of olives lay untouched—forgotten sustenance in the frenzy of discovery. Through the open window of the secluded villa, the Aegean Sea shimmered under a moonless sky, mirroring the cosmic mysteries they were trying to unravel. A chorus of cicadas pulsed through the warm night air, a rhythmic backdrop to the charged silence within. Neither of them noticed the sound; their attention was fixed entirely on the clues spread before them.

Since the Atlantis expedition, Jake and Rebecca had become inseparable.

Jake often thought about the deep respect and loyalty his parents had shared—and for the first time, he felt certain that Rebecca was someone with whom he could build that same kind of bond.

Rebecca sat hunched over a faded parchment, her reading glasses perched on her nose. Her auburn hair fell in silky strands around her face, framing green eyes that peered over the rims with a quiet intensity. Shadows pooled beneath her delicate features, etched with both determination and the sun-soaked imprint of years spent in the field.

In her hand, she held a ruler against a worn world map pinned to the table. The map was scarred with pushpins at sites of ancient significance: Göbekli Tepe, Giza, Teotihuacan, Stonehenge, Easter Island, Nan Madol, and more. Pencil lines connected the pins, forming a grand geometric web that spanned the globe. Rebecca's tight, precise script surrounded the markings with annotations—fragments of a larger truth hidden beneath centuries of myth and silence.

Jake watched her, his pulse quickening. They were on the edge of something vast—something that could rewrite history.

"We're missing something," Jake murmured, breaking the silence. He ran a hand through his short, dark hair and stopped pacing to lean over the table. His eyes, sharp but bloodshot from sleepless nights, scanned the notes covered in equations, ancient symbols, and dates. "We have all the pieces, but the pattern is still incomplete."

Rebecca didn't immediately reply. She shifted her gaze from

the map to a thick journal open to a page of star diagrams. The journal was her own field diary, filled with sketches of ruins and constellations, and margins full of cross-references to myths. She tapped a pencil on the table thoughtfully.

"Each site corresponds to an astronomical alignment or event," she said quietly, more to herself than to Jake. Her voice was gravelly from a long day of discussing theories; it carried the accent of a woman who had lived in many countries—a faint Greek lilt coloring her British-educated cadence.

Jake exhaled slowly and nodded. This was the crux of it—the reason they had zigzagged across continents chasing the whispers of dead civilizations.

"Göbekli Tepe lined up with the stars over ten thousand years ago," he said, touching a pin in southeastern Turkey on the map. "The Pyramids of Giza mirror Orion's Belt." His finger moved to Egypt. "Teotihuacan's layout encodes the sun and the calendar."

He listed them, each name a reverent invocation. "Stonehenge; summer solstice sunrise. Easter Island . . . moai facing the horizon, as if awaiting something." He paused, eyes drawn to the far reaches of the Pacific on the map. "And Nan Madol—built on volcanic prismatic basalt, for purposes we still can barely fathom." "But there is a pattern here, you see it too, right?" Jake asked to look for confirmation.

Rebecca looked up over her glasses. The lamplight caught the intensity in her eyes. "Not just any pattern," she said. "A warning. A message." She rose slowly, the chair scraping on the stone floor. Despite the late hour and her tired body, renewed energy animated her as she walked around the table to stand beside Jake. Together they faced the map like generals surveying a battlefield.

For a moment, the couple were silent. The only sounds were the distant chirp of night insects and the rustle of parchment under the rotating fan above. Jake's mind swirled with everything they had learned in the past weeks.

He glanced proudly at Rebecca, recalling how they met.

A few years earlier—Oxford University

A younger Jake sat in a crowded lecture hall, notebook in hand. On the dais at the front stood Rebecca Nikas, then an outsider to the British academic establishment. The hall buzzed with low murmurs; many professors and students had come out of curiosity or skepticism to hear the eccentric young archaeologist's claims.

Rebecca clicked to the next slide in her presentation—a photograph of the Pyramids of Giza under starry skies. "These structures, and many like them around the world, share alignments that cannot be mere coincidence," she asserted passionately. "They point to knowledge of astronomy far beyond what we credit ancient civilizations for. And taken together, they may form a global pattern."

A distinguished professor in the front row snorted. "Are you suggesting, Dr. Nikas, some form of prehistoric international scientific community?" he interjected, sarcasm dripping. Laughter rippled through a few of the attendees.

Rebecca didn't flinch. "In a manner of speaking, yes—either a shared legacy of a lost civilization or a concerted effort by ancient cultures to encode warnings and knowledge." She changed the slide to show Göbekli Tepe's pillars. The image of Pillar 43, with its mysterious vulture and orb carvings, filled the screen. "This site in Turkey, Göbekli Tepe, dates to roughly 9600 BC—before farming, before writing—yet it stands as a constructed monument of astonishing complexity. Why? We see carvings here that might correspond to constellations, a record of a date around 10,950 BC, perhaps marking a cataclysm."

That drew some whispers.

Jake, seated in the middle row, leaned forward, his heart pounding in his chest. His breath quickened, and his eyes widened as the words sank in. He could barely believe what he was hearing. Here was someone—a peer—standing before the class and discussing the connection between ancient sites, celestial alignments, and catastrophic events. These were the very ideas Jake had been desperate to exchange with someone for as long as he could remember. It was as if the universe had finally answered his silent call.

And it wasn't just the subject matter that captivated him—it was Rebecca.

She stood confidently at the front of the lecture hall, the soft glow of the projector illuminating her face. Her auburn hair framed sharp, intelligent green eyes that darted across the room as she spoke. There was a quiet intensity to her, a precision in her tone that suggested she wasn't just repeating theories—she had lived in these ideas, studied them, connected them in a way most people would never dare to.

Jake was hooked.

As Rebecca's voice filled the room, Jake's hand flew across his notebook, scribbling furiously to keep up with the flood of information:

Orion = Giza alignment?
Göbekli Tepe = comet impact 10,950 BC?
Ancient civilization global network??

Each idea sparked a fire in his mind. His thoughts were racing, linking her words to the knowledge his parents had passed down to him—the ancient star maps, the Sumerian tablets, and the coded patterns left by the Anunnaki. He remembered his father's hushed bedtime talks about a great flood and the forgotten civilizations that had vanished beneath the waves. His father had spoken of humanity's lost history as if it were a sacred truth, buried beneath layers of myth and manipulation.

And now, here was Rebecca—standing there, confirming it.

Validating it.

She spoke with the certainty of someone who had seen the patterns herself, someone who had pieced together the puzzle from fragments scattered across time. Jake's pulse quickened. He had spent his life feeling like an outsider, burdened with truths that others either mocked or dismissed outright. But Rebecca wasn't just speculating—she understood. She was speaking his language.

Jake's mind spiraled through the possibilities. Why did most people struggle with these concepts? If Göbekli Tepe truly marked the aftermath of a comet impact, that would align with the sudden global temperature drop during the Younger Dryas period—something the mainstream scientific community had long struggled to explain. And if the Pyramids of Giza were aligned with Orion's Belt not just symbolically but as part of a larger astronomical map, then the implications were staggering. It would suggest that ancient civilizations possessed a level of astronomical understanding that modern science was only beginning to grasp. Wouldn't that be a positive finding?

Rebecca was connecting the dots in real time, revealing a hidden narrative of human history that Jake had always known existed but could never fully prove. Until now.

He leaned forward further, nearly falling out of his seat.

Rebecca paused, her gaze sweeping across the room. Her eyes briefly met Jake's.

She hesitated. Just for a moment. But Jake saw it—a flicker of recognition.

It was as if she knew that he understood. As if she could sense that he was following her thoughts beyond the surface level—that he saw the deeper structure beneath the history she was presenting.

Jake's scribbling slowed as his mind shifted from frantic excitement to razor-sharp focus. Rebecca was onto something big—something even larger than she might have realized. He could see the connections forming, the pattern hidden beneath the chaos.

He realized with a sudden jolt of clarity: She might be the person he had been searching for.

After years of feeling like an outsider, like the only one who could see the hidden design beneath the fabric of history, Jake finally felt that connection—the sense that someone else could see it too. Rebecca wasn't just another brilliant mind. She might be a key. A missing piece.

Jake's mind raced with questions. Did Rebecca have access to the same ancient texts his parents had studied? Had she uncovered something new, something Jake had missed? And more importantly—if she had already come this far on her own, what could they accomplish together?

Rebecca's lecture was ending, and she was ready to answer anyone's questions, but Jake barely noticed. His notebook was filled with notes, the ink smudged where his hand had pressed too hard in his excitement. The room buzzed with quiet chatter as students gathered their things. Jake was gathering his thoughts—what an amazing woman. But not everyone shared his excitement.

A gray-haired archaeologist stood up abruptly. "This is preposterous. You are cherry-picking archaeoastronomy to weave a fantasy of an 'Atlantean' civilization," he barked. "There is no evidence of any advanced precursor culture; these alignments can and do happen by chance. Stonehenge aligning to the solstice is ritual, not science. We do not need aliens or Atlantis to explain human ingenuity!"

Rebecca opened her mouth to respond, but another professor added loudly, "And invoking the Anunnaki? These discredited theories have no place in serious discourse!"

More laughter, some of it derisive. Jake's cheeks burned on Rebecca's behalf. He could see Rebecca's jaw tighten as she tried to maintain composure.

Calmly, Rebecca addressed the room, "I am not saying aliens built the pyramids, Professor. I am saying our ancestors were smarter and more organized than we think, and perhaps they had reason—like a collective trauma—to invest so heavily in these monuments. The flood myths, the astronomical alignments, the sudden appearance of sites like Göbekli Tepe—these are clues, if we are willing to treat them as such."

The gray-haired archaeologist waved a hand dismissively. "Clues to a story in your head! Your so-called pattern is an illusion." He gathered his notes, clearly done listening. "I won't waste more time." With that, he stalked out of the lecture hall. A few others followed, shaking their heads.

A flush crept up Rebecca's neck. The moderator tried to rein in the meeting, but the Q&A had devolved into a few snide remarks and much of the audience disregarding the speaker. Through it all, Jake stayed glued to his seat, eyes never leaving Rebecca Nikas, who, despite the ridicule, continued answering questions politely until the end.

His heart raced as Rebecca turned and walked toward the lecture hall exit. He stood frozen for a moment before following her, his mind burning with questions and the thrilling sense that, finally, the pieces were beginning to align.

As the crowd dispersed, Jake approached the lectern. Rebecca was packing up her slide transparencies and notes, her shoulders slumped ever so slightly—the only sign that the drubbing had gotten to her.

"Dr. Nikas?" Jake blurted, almost tripping on the projector's cord in his eagerness.

Rebecca looked up, expecting another critic, but instead met the bright, earnest eyes of a young gentleman practically vibrating with energy. "Yes?"

"That was incredible," Jake said, his voice low but fervent. "I mean, I'm sorry they were so rude, but I believe there's something to your ideas. Actually, I—I've noticed some of those connections myself." He realized he was babbling and shut his mouth, his face reddening.

To his relief, Rebecca broke into a warm smile. "Have you now? What's your name?"

"Jake Rosen-Fisher. I'm a long-time D.Phil. student in Archaeology."

Rebecca extended her hand, her grip firm. "A pleasure, Jake. Thank you for hearing me out. It seems you might be in the minority today." She chuckled, a mixture of gratitude and self-deprecation.

They were still holding hands when Rebecca's pen slipped from her grasp. Jake instinctively knelt to pick it up at the same time as Rebecca, and their heads collided with a soft thud.

"Oh! Sorry!" they both said in unison, rubbing their foreheads. A beat of silence passed before they broke into laughter, the sound light and easy. For a moment, they just sat there, grinning at each other like two rare souls who had just stumbled upon something extraordinary. Hearts racing and minds buzzing with curiosity, they were eager to discover more—about each other and the inspirations that had brought them to this moment.

Jake found himself speaking rapidly, words spilling out: "When you mentioned Göbekli Tepe and that possible comet—I read about the layer of charcoal and the sudden cooling event. And my father used to talk about the Flood story and ancient gods giving warnings. Your talk tied so many loose threads I've been puzzling over. I just wanted to say you're not alone in thinking there's more to these ancient sites."

Rebecca's eyes twinkled with renewed enthusiasm. She glanced around to ensure they were relatively alone, then said conspiratorially, "It's always a comfort to find an open mind. The academic world—" she nodded toward the doors through which the skeptics had fled—"can be rather rigid. But truth often lurks at the fringes of accepted knowledge."

Jake nodded vigorously. "If there's any way I could assist your research, maybe we could work together or learn more as a team I'd be honored." He could hardly believe his own boldness, but something told him this was a crossroads moment.

Rebecca studied the young man before her—the intensity in Jake's expression, the sincere excitement. It reminded her of herself. "Be careful what you offer, Jake. I may very well take you up on that." She began to stack her papers, then paused. "I'll be in Oxford for a few days. Perhaps we could grab coffee tomorrow and chat? I'd like to hear what threads you've been following."

Jake agreed so fast it made Rebecca laugh. They exchanged contact information.

As Jake walked out into the cool Oxford evening, clutching his notes, he felt a surge of purpose. The stars above seemed to shine with new meaning. His feet felt light, as though he were walking on the moon, and he found himself smiling spontaneously, as if high on life. That night, he barely slept, his mind racing with anticipation for the journey about to begin.

For the next two days, Jake and Rebecca met whenever their busy schedules allowed. It felt natural—they were clearly tuned to the same frequency. Eyes fixed on each other, they spoke about their research and plans for the future. Jake invited Rebecca to be part of his future team, but she had already committed to other plans and needed to finish what she had started.

Despite their travels keeping them apart, Rebecca and Jake stayed in touch—both knowing they wanted to be friends forever.

City of the Ancients

Jake blinked away the memory. Here he was, a few years later, side by side with Rebecca Nikas, on the brink of solving a mystery that spanned millennia. He had kept his promise to help—and more than that, he had become an integral part of both the quest and her life, just as she had become part of his.

He cleared his throat and pulled a stack of files closer. "Let's go through them one more time," he said, determination overriding exhaustion. "Site by site. What do we know, and what does it point to?"

Rebecca offered a thin smile. "One more time," she agreed softly, understanding that Jake needed the repetition as much to organize thoughts as to fend off despair. She sat back down, and Jake took the seat opposite her, bracing himself for a deep dive into humanity's most ancient mysteries.

Jake took a deep breath, his voice steady but tinged with urgency as he continued:

"My parents achieved what many thought was impossible—a major breakthrough that changed everything we knew about our world and its ancient history. Their discovery began with the unearthing of a powerful and enigmatic artifact known as the Key of Osiris. This relic was not simply found in a museum or stumbled upon in the desert; it was painstakingly recovered from the hidden chambers buried deep beneath the monumental structures that lie under the pyramid of Khafre in the Giza Plateau of Egypt. These subterranean passages, untouched for thousands of years, held secrets far older than any civilization we know. It was there, amidst dust, darkness, and echoing silence, that they first glimpsed the machinery of something far beyond human understanding.

Years passed, and the trail seemed to grow cold, until fate brought forth the resurfacing of another critical artifact—the Me, or rather, what I represent: the Knowledge Stone. This ancient databank of forgotten truths and lost civilizations re-emerged under mysterious circumstances at the National Museum of Iraq, nestled among centuries of looted and recovered antiquities. It was hidden in plain sight, disguised as a relic, but in truth, it is a sentient archive of encoded wisdom, possibly even non-human in origin.

Together, the Key of Osiris and the Knowledge Stone formed a kind of celestial compass—each containing encrypted fragments of information, symbols, coordinates, and prophetic visions that, when pieced together, revealed the exact location of our next destination: the fabled, long-lost city of Atlantis.

Once we reached the sunken ruins—buried beneath layers of myth, water, and time—we encountered something that both shocked and confirmed our deepest theories. Within the heart of Atlantis, amid the shattered structures and alien geometry, we found a machine. Not just any machine, but a dormant, ancient mechanism nearly identical in design and function to the one my parents had uncovered beneath Khafre's pyramid. It was clear now: these machines were not isolated anomalies. They were part of a planetary network, an interlinked system left behind by an intelligence so advanced it defies comprehension.

However, not all discoveries bring hope. The holographic records preserved within the Atlantean databanks revealed a sobering truth: Atlantis had failed. Whatever test or trial these ancient civilizations were subjected to, Atlantis did not succeed. As a result, the city was obliterated—whether by natural cataclysm or self-destruction, the data was unclear. But before its annihilation, in a final act of preservation, the key—perhaps the last and most vital piece of this intergenerational puzzle—was moved. It was hidden in a new, secret location to safeguard it from the destruction that consumed Atlantis.

And now, that responsibility falls to us. We must find this location, and the next possible clue before the cycle begins anew. Time is no longer on our side. Earth is already exhibiting early signs of upheaval—massive tectonic shifts, volatile climate surges, magnetic disturbances, and catastrophic waves that threaten to tear apart entire coastlines. These aren't coincidences; they're warnings.

We are running out of time. If we fail to act—if we delay even a moment longer—the consequences may be irreversible, not just for us, but for all life on this planet."

Rebecca leaned in, her voice calm but laced with intensity, as if piecing together a cosmic riddle in real time.

"According to your family's extensive research—the volumes of journals, decoded symbols, and oral accounts passed down through generations—there's one common denominator that binds all these ancient and seemingly unrelated sites together. It's not just architecture, not just advanced mathematics or astronomical alignments. It's something far older. Something not entirely human. Across every culture, from the temples of Mesoamerica to the ziggurats of Mesopotamia and the subterranean vaults beneath Egypt, one name—or rather, one identity—continually resurfaces: the Sky People. Known to the Sumerians as the Anunnaki."

She paused, her eyes scanning the holographic display in front of them, where overlapping timelines and planetary diagrams flickered like digital constellations.

"These beings weren't just observers—they were involved. Every major leap in human evolution, every golden age of knowledge, was followed by a fall. A collapse. A flood. A fire. A disappearance. Over and over again, as if we were stuck in some kind of celestial loop. That's the correlation I'm trying to draw here—the connection between the test and the repeated destruction of civilizations. It's not random. It's not accidental. It's systemic. A pattern. A cycle."

Her expression turned solemn, voice quieting as she added, "It almost sounds like textbook mythology: good versus evil, light versus darkness or, in Sumerian terms, Enki versus Enlil. When you put those two figures into the equation of humanity's story, everything starts falling into place with unsettling clarity. Enlil, the severe, the wrathful—depicted as the one who desires humanity's end, who triggers the floods and cataclysms to wipe the slate clean. And Enki—the benefactor, the rebel among gods— who intervenes time and time again to preserve humanity, to give us another chance. But the question that's been haunting me is ...why?"

Rebecca's eyes met Jake's. "What if this isn't a conflict? What if it's a game? And what if we—every civilization that's ever risen and fallen—we're just the pieces on their board?"

Jake's jaw clenched, and he nodded slowly, the weight of her words sinking in. His reply came with a grim resonance, shaped by years of studying ancient warnings no one else dared to believe.

"Brilliant Rebecca! That's just it," he said. "The test—mentioned over and over in the ancient writings and glyphs—it's not a metaphor. It's literal. And that test, I think that is the game. A game not of chance, but of evolution. Adapt or perish. Evolve or be erased. There's no 'save point' in this game, no backup plan. If you fail, you start over. From nothing. Zero. As if everything we've built, everything we've become, is disposable in their eyes."

He stood and pointed to a celestial chart projected above them. "And there are variables—cosmic variables. The writings spoke of a planet, one with an incredibly elongated orbit, existing at the far edge of our solar system. Some call it Nibiru, others call it Planet X. Whatever its true name, its presence could disturb the gravitational balance of our solar system. Its passing could cause seismic instability, reverse Earth's magnetic poles, even trigger a crustal displacement event. Global upheaval—mass extinction—reset." He shivered involuntarily, as if the implications were physically cold.

"This is nightmare fuel. But it's real. And it's happening again. The signs are already here—volcanic activity, climate chaos, electromagnetic anomalies. The clock is ticking, faster than we can track. We *must* stop the cycle this time. We must end the test." His voice cracked slightly under the pressure of the unknown. "But where do we look next? That's the question that's driving me insane. If Atlantis was destroyed to hide the next clue—where did they send it? Where did *Enki* send it?"

This debate had become a familiar refrain between them—an ongoing intellectual dance that hovered between curiosity and obsession. Time and time again, their conversations circled back to the same haunting question: how much of what we consider the brilliance of ancient civilizations, their architecture, their astronomical precision, their encoded myths—was the product of purely homegrown human genius, and how much, if any, might have been inherited? Perhaps from an older, forgotten super-civilization or even from visitors that came from the stars.

It was a question that had haunted thinkers and fringe scholars alike for centuries. But for Rebecca, a seasoned academic trained to navigate the razor's edge between radical theory and respectability, the line was especially delicate. In public lectures, journals, and conferences, she carefully walked the line, leaning toward the established view: that the ingenuity of ancient peoples had simply been underestimated by modern arrogance. But behind closed doors, in the dim glow of ancient star charts and over mugs of late-night coffee, she allowed herself to entertain a different possibility—one that thrilled and terrified her in equal measure. "The Sumerian texts speak of gods who came from the heavens," she said now, her voice low and steady, as though simply speaking the words aloud could summon forbidden knowledge. "They weren't metaphorical in their descriptions. They were explicit—sky chariots, beings of immense stature and knowledge, arriving from beyond. And then there are the Egyptians. They didn't claim to invent their wisdom. They openly credited it to Thoth, the god of wisdom, writing, astronomy. And then there's Zep Tepi—'The First Time.' A period in their history when, according to their own inscriptions, gods walked the Earth as rulers, and the world was different. Not myth—memory."

She paused, her fingers idly tracing the worn edge of an old map strewn across the table between them. It was filled with notations, circles and lines connecting sacred sites across the globe, like some ancient conspiracy hiding in plain sight.

"Maybe," she said, almost whispering, "those gods weren't gods in the divine sense, but beings—entities—who came before. Guardians of some kind. Or watchers. And maybe, just maybe, when the last great cataclysm came, they didn't all die. Maybe some of them stayed behind, or left messages. Lessons. Clues encoded in myth, in architecture, in the stars. And maybe the survivors—those who remembered—carried that knowledge with them across continents and centuries. A spark passed down through oral tradition, buried in the symbols and rituals we've barely begun to decode."

Rebecca rubbed her chin thoughtfully, her eyes scanning the lines and symbols they had mapped out over the years. "It's possible. More than possible. Think about it—an ancient network of observers. Not an empire, not a single culture, but a distributed web of knowledge. Each site a node, each monument a data point, each legend a clue. And not just regionally. Globally. A planetary system of sacred geography, spanning from Stonehenge in England to the pyramids of Giza, from the Nazca lines to Angkor Wat, from Göbekli Tepe to the submerged structures near Yonaguni."

She reached out and pointed to the map, drawing invisible lines between these points, her movements slow and reverent. "They weren't isolated marvels. They were connected. Aligned. By mathematics, by astronomy, by intention. Whoever—or whatever—was behind this had a plan. A message. We just haven't learned how to read it yet."

Jake watched her, knowing full well this was more than theory for her. It was belief—not blind, but informed, tempered by evidence and gut instinct. He could see it in her eyes: the fire of someone standing on the edge of a precipice, looking out over truths too vast to fully grasp, and choosing to keep walking forward anyway.

Jake leaned over the cluttered table, his finger tracing an arc across the worn map spread between them. His voice dropped into that thoughtful tone Rebecca had come to associate with one thing: a breakthrough.

"There's something that's been percolating in the back of my mind," he said slowly. "We've talked about floods. About cataclysms. But zoom out for a second—look at the bigger picture. It's not just one culture telling these stories. The idea of a Great Flood, it's *everywhere*. You can't escape it."

Rebecca's eyes lit up with recognition, her scholar's mind already leaping ahead. "It *is* astonishing, isn't it? The consistency, the eerie parallels. In Mesopotamia, you have the tales of *Atrahasis* and *Utnapishtim*—both warned, both survivors of a divine deluge. Then there's the Biblical account of Noah in the Near East. In Greece, *Deucalion and Pyrrha*, the flood unleashed by Zeus to purge a corrupted humanity. In India, *Manu*, saved by the avatar of Vishnu, a fish who warns him of what's coming. The Maya, the Aztecs—they speak of cycles of creation and destruction, of floods erasing entire worlds. Even the Polynesians—on remote islands separated by vast oceans—have deluge legends passed down through chants and oral histories."

Jake raised a finger as if marking a crucial point on an invisible chalkboard. "Nearly every culture. Every corner of the planet. It's as if all of our ancestors, scattered across time and geography, preserved some deep, ancestral memory of drowning lands of survival in boats or clinging to mountaintops. Like they all *went through it*—and passed the story down, each in their own way."

He leaned back, eyes clouded with thought. "Anthropologists have catalogued hundreds of flood myths. Sure, some might be independently conceived. But many—maybe most—could be distorted echoes of real events. The end of the Ice Age, for example. Rapid sea level rise. Massive glacier melts. Sudden, violent climate shifts. Entire coastlines swallowed in generations. If you were there, if you *survived*, it would feel like the gods were drowning the world."

Rebecca's voice dropped as she picked up the thread, her tone more somber now. "And the Sumerian flood story, if we look closely, it's more than just myth. It's a *debate*. The gods don't all agree. Enlil is the one who demands humanity be destroyed—says we're too noisy, too unruly. A failed experiment. But Enki—also called Ea—defies the others. He warns one man. Tells him to build a vessel. Tells him how to survive." She glanced at Jake. "Sound familiar?"

He gave her a half-smile, part amusement, part awe. "The Anunnaki—if we use that term for their pantheon—they had a schism. Some wanted to preserve us. Others wanted to wipe the board clean and start over."

He sat forward, energized now, as if a current had passed between them. "And that theme—of a merciful figure giving a warning versus a wrathful one causing destruction—it shows up *everywhere*, not just in flood myths. *Prometheus*, in Greek myth, warned Deucalion. *Vishnu* warned Manu. Even in Native American lore, there are stories of spirit animals or sky beings who warn humans of the coming disaster. So really, this idea of Enki versus Enlil—it's not just a mythological dichotomy. It's an *archetype*. A universal pattern: one faction trying to save humanity, another willing to let us perish."

Rebecca nodded, her expression now tinged with gravity. "Which, let's be honest, is exactly what we're seeing now—*in the present day*. If the pattern holds, then there are modern-day Enkiites—those trying to use the knowledge of the past to help us. And there are those who would exploit it. Or use it to cull, to control. Enlil's inheritors, operating in shadows."

Jake felt a chill creep up his spine. "We've *seen* it. The attack in Atlantis. That wasn't random. That was orchestrated. Human agents, yes—but acting on behalf of something deeper. Something ancient. Secret orders. Hidden agendas. The kind of power that's survived the fall of empires."

Rebecca's voice softened, almost conspiratorial. "If the Anunnaki were real—and I'm no longer ruling that out—then maybe they weren't gods in the way we think of them. Maybe they were an earlier race. Maybe they were *us*, before a reset. Or maybe, something else entirely. Beings with technology advanced enough to manipulate climate, tectonics, even global magnetic fields. If that's true, then the Flood wasn't just a reaction to nature—it was an *induced event*. And Enki, the rebel, went behind the council's back to give us a chance."

Jake's eyes returned to the map, his gaze settling on a specific spot—Greece. The myths, the monuments, the alignments; it was all converging.

"If that's the case," he said slowly, "then the next piece we're looking for—the next artifact, the key to the mechanism—it's not just symbolic. It could be literal. A device left by Enki. A machine capable of either *triggering or halting* global catastrophe. And he left breadcrumbs—not just in structures or symbols, but in myths. In the collective memory of humanity. Hoping that one day, we'd become advanced enough to recognize the signs and follow the trail."

Rebecca reached out suddenly and grasped Jake's shoulder, her fingers tightening with a force that surprised even her. Her eyes were wide, gleaming with intensity—no longer the calm, calculating scholar, but a woman standing at the edge of revelation.

"I believe exactly that," she said, her voice low but fervent. "We're closer than we've ever been. Maybe closer than anyone has been in thousands of years. The ancients left breadcrumbs—clues buried in myth, stone, and memory—and we've followed them across continents, through temples, tombs, and sunken ruins. And now, after everything, it culminates in Atlantis. Or rather—*what came after.*"

Her hand moved swiftly to the table, unrolling a worn parchment they had recovered from the Atlantean chamber—the one scorched around the edges, ink faded but unmistakable. A crude yet precise map, and etched at the top in unmistakable cuneiform script: the number 3—an anomaly when placed over a map of Greece.

Rebecca's breath caught as her mind shifted into overdrive. She could see it all again—her studies, her years pouring over fragmented texts and forbidden translations, threads of forgotten mythologies that wove together into something terrifying and beautiful. Her thoughts returned to one of the most potent myths of all: *The Titanomachy.*

The so-called "Battle of the Titans." A cosmic war waged in a time before time, when the fabric of the world itself trembled under the weight of celestial fury. A war not of metaphor, but of memory—dim recollections passed down as myth, distorted by centuries of retelling.

She had long theorized what many dismissed as heresy: that the *Titans*, the *Nephilim* of Genesis, and the *Anunnaki* of Sumerian lore were not separate myths, not distinct pantheons— but shattered reflections of a singular origin. Ancient rulers of the Earth, perhaps even of the stars. Cast down. Demonized. Forgotten, but never truly gone.

CHAPTER 21

Titanomachy

nd now, the path led them straight to *Delphi*.

Her voice dropped to a whisper, thick with awe and gravity. "The Titanomachy, it wasn't just a clash of gods. It was a war for dominion over *Earth*. The Titans, led by Cronus, ruled from Mount Othrys. They weren't just mythological metaphors. They were real. Powerful. And they fell to the Olympians—Zeus and his kin—after ten brutal years of war. Mountains split open. Oceans rose. The sky roared with fire. The planet itself was reshaped by the violence of beings beyond comprehension."

She could see it all in her mind's eye: a battlefield the size of continents, scorched and torn by forces that dwarfed human scale. Hyperion, the Titan of Light, clashing with Helios—his descendant, his usurper—in a cataclysm of solar fire. Krios, wrapped in storms, lashing out against Poseidon, the seas boiling under their fury. Atlas, unbreakable, finally brought to his knees—doomed to bear the weight of the heavens as penance.

Even Prometheus and Epimetheus, enigmatic brothers caught between loyalty and foresight, had played their roles in the war. Prometheus, ever the rebel, siding with the Olympians—perhaps out of a desire to preserve humanity itself.

But the most terrifying figure of all had been Typhon.

Typhon—the final weapon of the Titans. A creature of chaos, a storm incarnate. A hundred serpentine heads, eyes that bled fire, and a roar that shook the stars. He rose in defiance, the Titans' last hope, and nearly succeeded. Even Zeus faltered before him. Their final battle wasn't myth—it was apocalypse. Volcanoes erupted. Rivers changed their course. The skies blackened. The world teetered on the brink. In the end, Zeus triumphed—but only just—and cast Typhon beneath Mount Etna, where legend claimed his rage still simmered, reshaping the world through tectonic fury.

A shiver ran down Rebecca's spine. Every culture told versions of this story. Giants who fell from grace. Beings of immense power cast down. The Nephilim, offspring of divine beings and mortals, described in ancient Hebrew texts. The Anunnaki, the celestial architects who came from the stars and shaped humanity. Different names. Same echoes. What if they *were* the same? What if these weren't just stories, but encoded memories?

And now Delphi—long considered sacred, the *navel of the world,* the very point where the divine and mortal realms converged— was calling to them.

"It all fits," she murmured. "Delphi wasn't just a spiritual center. It wasn't just where oracles spoke in riddles. It was a *conduit.* A nexus. What if the sanctuary there—the Temple of

Apollo—was built over something far older? Something that the ancients buried? A device, a vault, a control mechanism left behind by Enki. Hidden in plain sight beneath layers of myth and stone."

Her finger stabbed the map with conviction, landing squarely on the circle they'd drawn in central Greece. "Delphi. It's the only place all the clues point to now."

Jake stared at the spot, his pulse quickening. Delphi. The cradle of prophecy. Where the Pythia once channeled gods beneath clouds of gas and sacred geometry. They had suspected for weeks, but now, the certainty in Rebecca's voice was infectious.

If what she said was true—if Delphi housed the next piece of the puzzle, the ancient mechanism meant either to prevent or unleash catastrophe—then this was it. The final stretch. The last stand against a cycle older than memory.

Outside, the winds howled through the olive groves that clung to the hills around their villa. The world was unraveling—earthquakes, magnetic anomalies, strange lights in the skies. Governments denied, distracted, delayed. But the signs were everywhere, and the countdown had already begun.

Inside, amid open scrolls, blinking monitors, and a growing sense of urgency, Jake and Rebecca stood shoulder to shoulder, poised to follow the last trail left by a forgotten war. A war that never truly ended.

And it would end—or begin again—at *Delphi*.

Jake cleared his throat, his voice steady as he leaned over the map spread across their makeshift war table. He tapped a red circle drawn in central Greece.

"Delphi," he said. "*Omphalos.* The center of the world, according to the Greeks. If the ancients were hiding something critical—something powerful—this would be the place. A convergence of prophecy, myth, and buried knowledge."

Rebecca nodded with conviction. "It lines up. The Greeks believed Delphi was the spot where Zeus's two eagles met after flying from opposite ends of the world—marking the Earth's navel. That's why they placed the Omphalos stone there, the symbolic center. And then there's the Oracle—the Pythia—who sat above that mysterious chasm, inhaling vapors and speaking in riddles."

Her voice dropped. "We always assumed it was just geology—hallucinogenic gases from beneath the earth. But what if that wasn't it at all? What if the fumes were a *side effect*—something emitted by a hidden device? A mechanism still active, lying dormant all this time?"

A chill ran through Jake. The idea sounded wild, but after what they'd seen in Atlantis, wild no longer meant impossible.

"In Atlantis, we found their machine buried beneath the ruins," he said. "Ancient, complex—like nothing modern tech can explain. And the map we recovered there; it had a number scrawled in cuneiform: 3—right over a sketch of Greece. They were pointing us here. Delphi isn't just symbolic—it's *next*."

Rebecca gave a breathless nod, her thoughts racing. "The Pythia might have been reacting to more than just gas. If there was a machine beneath the temple—something designed to transmit subtle signals—she may have unknowingly been interfacing with it. Delivering messages from a system no one remembered existed."

Jake's brow furrowed, gears turning fast. "And then there's the destruction of Atlantis—not just legend anymore. We *saw* the ruins. We've walked those chambers, found the knowledge caches. Plato's account wasn't fantasy. He said Atlantis fell in a single day and night of catastrophe—floods, earthquakes, total collapse."

"And he got that story from Egyptian priests at Sais," Rebecca added. "Which makes it even older. And that timeline? Roughly

9600 BC—the end of the Ice Age, when sea levels rose and the climate destabilized.

Just then, a low buzz cut through the silence—Jake's encrypted phone. He glanced at the screen, and his jaw tightened.

"It's our contact in Athens," he said. *"Message reads: Unknown parties active in Delphi region. Watch yourselves."*

Rebecca inhaled sharply. "So they know, or at least suspect enough to get dangerously close."

"They may not know the exact location," Jake said, "but if they're in the region, it's only a matter of time. We have to move." He swept his eyes across the room one last time. Their research sanctuary—filled with decades of collective study, ancient texts, field notes, fragments of truth painstakingly pieced together. But they had everything they needed now.

It was time to act.

Rebecca folded the annotated map carefully, her fingers steady. Jake packed quickly: Rebecca's leather journal, key printouts, climbing rope, flashlights, and the Glock pistol—still the only real protection they had.

Outside, the wind howled through the trees like a distant warning. Inside, two scholars-turned-seekers stood at the threshold of a myth no longer confined to myth.

Delphi wasn't just a destination. It was the next test.

CHAPTER 22

Mysteries of Delphi

Outside, the night was thick and moonless, a vast black canvas stretched above them. Overhead, the Milky Way spilled like a river of stars across the heavens, as if the universe itself were offering guidance—or bearing witness.

They moved quietly, loading their carefully chosen gear into the trunk of their rental—a nondescript gray sedan chosen precisely because it blended in. No markings. No attention. Just another pair of travelers on Greek roads under cover of darkness.

Jake slid behind the wheel, checking the mirrors with practiced calm. Rebecca, in the passenger seat, clutched one last document: a translated fragment of an Orphic hymn devoted to

Apollo. She scanned the lines one more time, eyes darting over ancient words filled with layered meanings.

"Born in Delos . . . slew the Python at Delphi . . ." she murmured, almost to herself. The words tasted strange in her mouth tonight—less like myth, more like prophecy.

Then, with a soft sigh, she folded the paper and placed it in her satchel. She was too restless to read now. The time for study had passed.

As Jake started the engine, the sound was almost jarring in the night's stillness. They pulled away from the villa, the tires crunching softly on gravel. Behind them, the scent of olive groves lingered in the air, mingling with the briny perfume of the Aegean Sea. That place had been a sanctuary. Now it was just another waypoint in a rapidly unraveling world.

They drove in silence for a time, the headlights carving long, shifting tunnels through the dark. The road twisted and narrowed, flanked by tall, silent cypress trees that stood like sentinels on either side. The world outside was quiet—unnaturally so.

Both of them were deep in thought, mentally running through possibilities, backup plans, worst-case scenarios. Rebecca's mind drifted to seismic triggers and buried mechanisms. Jake's raced ahead to Delphi—to what might lie beneath the ruins, and who else might already be there. Mercenaries. Rival factions. Booby-trapped chambers. Ancient technologies no modern mind could predict.

A thousand variables. And one unshakable constant: the stakes were total.

To cut the tension, Jake reached forward and clicked on the radio, tuning to a local station. Static filled the cabin, then resolved into a scratchy Greek broadcast.

"... αναφορές για ακραία καιρικά φαινόμενα συνεχίζονται ..." said the news anchor.

Rebecca listened, translating softly. "Reports of unusual weather patterns continue. Just today, hail the size of apples fell on northern China. Meanwhile, a severe drought in South Africa worsens, fueling humanitarian crises. Scientists warn that extreme weather is becoming more frequent . . ."

The broadcast continued: *"In other news, a 5.8 magnitude earthquake struck coastal Peru this evening, causing panic but minimal damage. Seismologists are puzzled by a recent uptick in mid-range quakes occurring in atypical regions. The United Nations is set to convene an emergency climate summit as global temperatures hit new records. Tensions rise as major powers exchange accusations over control of natural resources . . ."*

The car remained silent, but the mood inside shifted. The voice on the radio was clinical, dispassionate—a calm litany of accelerating collapse.

Jake turned it off when the signal began to dissolve into static. The silence that followed was heavier now, pulsing with implication.

He looked at Rebecca. She met his gaze, her eyes reflecting the weight of everything unspoken.

Then he pulled the car gently off to the side of the narrow road and stopped. For a beat, neither of them moved. Then Jake reached across the center console and brushed a strand of Rebecca's hair from her face, tucking it gently behind her ear.

Their eyes locked.

And then, without a word, they leaned into each other—the kiss slow, deliberate, a moment suspended between two storms. It wasn't desperate, nor hurried. It was grounding. Their lips touched softly, and in that instant, the world faded. No temples, no ancient machines, no collapsing timelines.

Just *life*.

Just that raw, ineffable energy that surges when two souls

connect—the energy that says we are still here, we are still human, and that the feeling of love in our hearts is stronger than ever.

It was the truest defiance against the chaos to come.

"This is why we have to succeed," Jake said softly, his hand gently brushing through Rebecca's hair as the car rumbled through the dark. His voice was barely more than a whisper, but it carried the full weight of their mission. "People are already struggling . . . surviving on the edge. A cataclysm on top of all this . . ."

". . . could push civilization past the breaking point," Rebecca finished for him, her gaze locked on the winding road ahead. Her voice was calm, but beneath the surface, she radiated urgency. "But if we can stop it, maybe, we buy enough time for humanity to get its act together."

Jake nodded slowly, his jaw tight as he gripped the steering wheel a little harder. Outside, the road twisted through silence and shadow. They passed no one, save for the occasional lonely truck or distant bus—ghost lights fading behind them. Civilization was somewhere out there, restless and unaware, sleepwalking toward the edge of a precipice.

At the very least, he thought, stopping the end of the world would give humanity a fighting chance to fix the mess it had made. One battle at a time.

They drove on through the black hours of the night.

By the time they turned off the main road toward Delphi, the stars were beginning to dim. A pale gray haze on the eastern horizon signaled the approach of dawn. The narrow mountain road wound upward in tight bends, threading through pine forests and rocky outcrops. The air thinned as they climbed, growing crisp and sharp with altitude and tension.

Mount Parnassus loomed above them—ancient, watchful.

Jake eased the car off the dirt track into a thicket of trees, pulling into a natural hollow about a mile from the archaeological zone. He killed the headlights and shut off the engine. The silence that followed was absolute.

"This is close enough," Jake said, his voice low but resolute. "We go on foot from here."

They retrieved their gear from the trunk in practiced silence. Jake checked the Glock, sliding it into the holster at his hip with a quiet click. Rebecca slung on her pack and picked up a sturdy wooden walking stick she'd brought—part hiking aid, part potential weapon.

No more theories. No more maps. This was the part where things could go sideways.

They began hiking, slipping into the shadowed terrain—scrub brush, boulders, the occasional twisted olive tree. The sky above was lightening by degrees, casting the landscape into soft indigo hues. Ahead, the outlines of ancient Delphi began to emerge like ghosts from the stone: broken walls, half-standing columns, scattered relics of a sacred past.

The Temple of Apollo rose from the slope like a dream of order amid ruin, its few remaining columns silhouetted against the first light of dawn.

They had chosen their approach carefully. Skirting a ridgeline to the northwest, they bypassed the official tourist entrance and came in high, above the sanctuary. The air carried the faint scent of dust, pine, and ancient stone.

They paused behind a dense cluster of oak trees that overlooked the heart of the site. From their vantage point, they saw the sacred terraces unfolding below: the temple platform, the stone tiers of the theater carved into the hillside, and, farther down, the ancient stadium. To their right, nestled in a natural cleft, the Castalian Spring shimmered faintly—the waters where pilgrims once purified themselves before hearing the Oracle.

Jake raised a compact pair of binoculars and scanned the area.

In the growing dawn, he spotted one figure—a man in a security uniform, walking near the museum building with a flashlight. He appeared relaxed, unaware of anything out of the ordinary.

"Only one guard," Jake whispered. "Far enough not to bother us if we're quiet."

Rebecca nodded. They slipped down a narrow goat path, weaving between brush and loose rock until they reached the perimeter fence. A low chain blocked the way. They climbed over quickly and quietly, landing on sacred ground.

Now they were inside the sanctuary of Delphi—the very heart of it.

To their left, the massive polygonal stones of the ancient retaining wall towered above them. Each block fit so precisely against the next that not even a blade of grass grew between them. These walls had seen the rise and fall of empires. And now, two more figures passed silently beneath them, chasing whispers from a forgotten war.

They moved low and fast, ducking behind fragments of ancient friezes and toppled drums of marble columns. The wind stirred faintly, rustling through the ruins, and birds began to call from the trees below.

Jake's foot scraped loose a shard of marble, and it skittered across the stones with a sharp clatter. Both of them froze, hearts pounding.

Somewhere in the village below, a dog barked. They held still for a long breath.

No shouts. No footsteps.

After another tense second, they resumed.

Jake's pulse was hammering in his ears. This was the most dangerous stretch—exposed among the ruins. If the rival faction had arrived ahead of them, this could turn violent fast. He mentally traced the layout of the site, recalling details from old excavation reports and his own past visit.

"The replica Omphalos stone is near the temple ruins," he whispered. "But more importantly, the Greeks dug a tunnel under the temple in the 19th century looking for the Oracle's chamber. They only found a small grotto but modern scans hinted at deeper caverns below."

Rebecca pointed toward the crumbling base of the temple. "There was an opening near the *adyton*—the inner sanctum—where they found that fissure with the fumes. It's probably covered now, maybe by a grate or slab, but that's our best entry point."

They crept forward, threading carefully between ancient stone. The Temple of Apollo loomed ahead, broken but defiant. Its columns cast long shadows across the flagstones. Somewhere beneath it, they hoped, was the mechanism. The relic. The truth.

The breeze stirred again. Light crept across the land. And Delphi, the navel of the Earth, was waking.

The Temple of Delphi

They found it—just as the old excavation reports had hinted.

Near the rear of the crumbled temple platform, where the *adyton* once stood—the inner sanctum where the Oracle of Apollo had sat upon her tripod—a portion of the floor looked markedly different. The stones were newer, mismatched, clearly reconstructed. And embedded at the center, just as they'd hoped, was a square metal grate, about three feet across on each side, bolted tight to the floor.

Rebecca dropped to her knees beside it, her fingers brushing lightly over the cool iron. She leaned in, peering into the darkness below.

A faint, acrid scent drifted upward—a trace of something ancient, almost volcanic.

"Sulphur," she whispered. "This is it. The fissure. The place where the Oracle sat. Where the visions came."

Jake knelt beside her, peering down into the abyss. A wave of goosebumps spread across his arms. The dark hole beneath the grate seemed to *breathe*—not in sound, but in atmosphere, like it was alive with latent power. Waiting.

He reached into his pack and retrieved a multitool, flipping out the wrench attachment. He tried the bolts. They were old—decades, maybe even over a century—and crusted with rust. But not tamper-proof. Whoever sealed this place had assumed no one would come back with a reason.

Jake began working methodically, his hands steady but fast. One bolt loosened. Then another. Each twist felt like unsealing a part of history no one had touched in ages.

Minutes passed. The quiet scraping of metal on metal was amplified in the still morning air. The final bolt groaned, a long metallic squeal that echoed faintly off the ancient stone.

Jake grimaced. He froze. That noise had carried.

And just then—like fate punctuating the moment—a beam of light cut through the ruins, sweeping across a nearby Doric column barely thirty yards away.

Rebecca's breath caught in her throat. Jake grabbed her hand.

A security guard.

The flashlight danced lazily, its glow illuminating fragments of ancient treasuries and scattered marble. The man was humming to himself, casually pacing his route, unaware that history was unfolding in the shadows just ahead of him.

Jake and Rebecca moved fast and fluidly, muscle memory and adrenaline taking over. They ducked behind a section of fallen architrave—a massive carved beam that had once supported the temple's roof. Now it offered them sanctuary.

They pressed close, face to face, chest to chest, hearts hammering in synchronized rhythm like twin war-drums. They could hear each other's breath, hot and shallow. Neither dared speak. They didn't need to. Their eyes locked, communicating in silent agreement—stay still, don't move, wait for the moment to pass.

The flashlight beam swept a few more feet paused, then moved on.

The guard meandered past, completely unaware. His footsteps faded into the distance, his humming becoming a soft echo swallowed by time and stone.

Still pressed together, Jake and Rebecca didn't move for several heartbeats more. Then, slowly, they exhaled—the breath they didn't realize they'd both been holding.

They stayed in the embrace for a moment longer, not from fear, but because it anchored them. Amid all the danger, the myth, the magnitude of what lay beneath, this—*this*—was real. A heartbeat. A human connection in the face of the unknown.

"Too close," Jake murmured, his lips brushing her forehead. "We have to get below," Rebecca said, her voice quiet but urgent. "Now."

Jake nodded, and they slid back toward the grate. The final bolt was off.

Together, they lifted the heavy iron square just enough to slide it aside. A rush of stale air rose from below—warm, mineral-rich, laced with the scent of deep earth and forgotten fire.

The opening yawned like a mouth beneath the temple—dark, ancient, and waiting.

Beneath the yawning opening lay a steep vertical drop of

approximately fifteen feet—a descent not perilous, but certainly not something one would want to tackle unprepared. Time and decay had not been kind to the shaft, but an iron ladder, dark with rust and likely installed decades prior by long-gone archaeologists or preservation teams, remained affixed along the northern interior wall. It clung there with stubborn tenacity, its bolts corroded but still holding firm against the weight of years and dust.

Jake tightened the straps on their pack with practiced efficiency, making sure it sat high and snug on their back. Every movement was silent, purposeful. Without a word, and after exchanging a glance with Rebecca—one that conveyed both cautious anticipation and the electric thrill of discovery—they turned and gripped the ladder. The metal felt cold and slightly slick beneath their gloves. Slowly, silently, Jake descended first, one hand wrapped around the flashlight clipped to their vest, the narrow beam slicing through the darkness like a needle of light.

Rebecca followed a moment later, wincing as she tested her weight on the upper rungs. The strain pulled at the old injury in her right shoulder, sending a brief flare of discomfort through her frame. She clenched her jaw, exhaled through her nose, and pressed on, step by deliberate step. Despite the ache, she moved with confidence. She had climbed far worse.

The base of the shaft opened into a small, irregularly shaped subterranean chamber. The space beneath the temple felt ancient and untouched, like a pocket of forgotten time. The beams of their flashlights played across coarse, uneven rock walls and a floor of packed earth littered with minute fragments of stone and mineral deposits. Dust motes shimmered in the beams, disturbed by their breath and presence.

A faint, almost imperceptible shimmer of movement caught

their eyes—a wisp of translucent vapor curling lazily from a hairline fissure in the wall to their left. It danced as if alive, coiling into the air before vanishing. Rebecca leaned in slightly, squinting. "There," she murmured, gesturing toward the vapor with her light. "The pneuma. Just like the accounts described."

Indeed, it was the famed breath of the earth—the ancient oracle's breath. In classical antiquity, it was believed that gases like ethylene, seeping from the deep places of the earth through natural cracks and vents, could induce altered states of consciousness. Priests and priestesses, seated above such fissures, would fall into trances and speak prophecy. This was no myth—the geological reality was here before them.

Rebecca panned her flashlight slowly, methodically scanning every crevice. Her beam settled on a mound of collapsed debris at the far end of the chamber. Behind it, partially obscured by stone and time, was something unexpected—a narrow aperture, a slit in the wall just wide enough for a human form to squeeze through.

Jake joined her, eyebrows raised.

"That's not in any of the published plans," he said softly. "I've reviewed all of them."

Rebecca nodded slowly. "Perhaps seismic activity opened it further. Maybe it was always there, just hidden. Whatever the cause, it wasn't known."

The two approached it cautiously. Beyond the narrow opening was a tunnel that sloped downward, descending deeper into the earth at an angle that felt almost purposeful. The air was colder here, damp and rich with the scent of minerals, moss, and something more difficult to name—something ancient.

The walls of the tunnel bore signs of both nature and intervention. Rough-hewn rock gave way here and there to unmistakable tool marks—grooves and cuts made by human hands, long, long ago. The passage narrowed in places, forcing them to crouch as they moved, flashlights bobbing ahead of them. The stone beneath their boots was slick with condensation.

"This must lead to the lower chambers," Rebecca whispered, her voice trembling with restrained excitement. The weight of centuries pressed in all around them, but so did the exhilaration of standing on the edge of the unknown.

Jake took the lead again, navigating the passage with deliberate care. Each step echoed faintly. The air grew warmer the deeper they went. And then, without warning, the tunnel widened abruptly.

They emerged into a large cavern—roughly circular in shape, perhaps thirty feet across and with a domed ceiling rising fifteen feet above their heads. Their flashlight beams danced across the surfaces, revealing an interplay of natural beauty and artificial construction. Stalactites clung to the outer rim of the ceiling, glittering like teeth in the gloom. But their attention was immediately drawn to the structure at the heart of the space.

It was unmistakably artificial.

A raised platform, waist-high, sat in the center of the chamber—its form rectangular and precise, its material a seamless fusion of worked stone and ancient metal. It resembled, in some ways, a sarcophagus or altar, but more than that, it evoked the impression of a console, or perhaps a sealed container built with an intent long lost to time.

Jake froze at the sight. Their breath caught in their throat, eyes wide.

Inscriptions covered its surface—not merely in one language, but in many. Lines of cuneiform flowed into Greek letters, which in turn bordered what appeared to be Egyptian hieroglyphs, their worn carvings meticulously etched with purpose. These were messages—warnings, instructions, invocations perhaps—

layered across the ages by cultures that had each encountered this machine, and felt the need to mark it.

Rebecca stepped forward slowly, reverently, her hand outstretched.

"Atop the structure, look," she whispered.

A dome—hemispherical and dark with tarnish—rose from the top of the device, made of what looked like oxidized bronze or aged copper. Mounted above it was a crystalline prism, transparent and faceted.

The device, impossibly, was humming.

Very faint, barely audible, but real. A vibration beneath the air. The kind of sensation that made the hairs on one's neck rise. Jake's mind raced. The warmth in the chamber. The residual gases. Could this machine be drawing power from geothermal sources? Had it remained alive, dormant, waiting?

Rebecca lowered her hand to the carvings, tracing a line along one of the etched scripts.

"This is it," she murmured, almost breathless. "By Zeus or perhaps by Enki. We've found it."

Jake moved around the perimeter of the structure, scanning the chamber. In the corners, obscured by shadow and dust, he spotted odd shapes—coils of metallic piping, crystalline nodules embedded into the rock, conduits perhaps, or sensory nodes. The entire space was more than a tomb—it was a system.

"This machine's unlike the others," he said, speaking half to himself. "It's not enormous. Not some monstrous engine of myth. It's main system is compact; intricate. Almost fragile."

Rebecca nodded thoughtfully. "Maybe it wasn't built for spectacle. Maybe it was built for something more focused. More precise."

Jake ran a hand along the edge of the platform. "It looks

intact," he said quietly, a mix of awe and fear in his voice. "Look around. We need to find something—clues, artifacts, anything that tells us how to activate or understand this."

Rebecca pulled a small digital camera from her satchel, her fingers trembling slightly. She began documenting everything, snapping photo after photo. "If this is meant to function," she said, "there should be a core, or a lever, or sockets. Some kind of interface."

And then they saw them.

Three circular indentations on the upper surface of the device. Around each there were more etchings, denser and more intricate. They looked like receptacles—placeholders for something that had once been there.

"They're empty," Jake said, dismay creeping into his voice. "Someone got here before us. We were too late."

Rebecca stared at the vacant sockets, heart sinking.

"Looks like the activation pieces, whatever they were, they're gone," Jake said bitterly, fists clenched. "Now what?"

CHAPTER 23

No Easy Road

Before Jake could even open his mouth to speak, a voice echoed ominously from the shadowed tunnel behind them—a voice dripping with arrogance and control.

"Step away from it, please, gentleman."

Both Jake and Rebecca whirled around, their flashlight beams slashing across the dark like blades of light—until they stopped, fixed on a figure stepping into view. The breath caught in Rebecca's throat. Her fingers tightened reflexively around the flashlight, knuckles pale.

Standing there with calculated ease was Dr. Sebastian Falk, flanked on either side by two men dressed head to toe in black tactical gear. Their faces were obscured by visors and shadow, but the matte gleam of their rifles, raised and ready, was clear enough. Falk, ever the image of cool menace, wore a light tactical vest over dark clothing, his lean frame held with the effortless confidence of someone who believed in their own invincibility. A pistol rested in one hand, low but ready.

He looked every bit the man Rebecca remembered from her university days—hair slicked back with unnatural precision, eyes gleaming with cruel intelligence, and that damn smug smirk playing at the corners of his mouth like a wolf who's just cornered its prey.

Jake instinctively stepped in front of Rebecca, shielding her with his body. His pulse thundered in his ears. He didn't need to ask who it was—he *felt* the danger rolling off Falk like heat from a fire.

"Dr. Rosen-Fisher," Falk said smoothly, his voice laced with a faint, cultivated German accent that somehow made the words more menacing. "So, we meet again."

The tone was light, even conversational—but the glint in his eye, razor-sharp and calculating, betrayed the true weight of the moment.

"Don't flatter yourselves," he continued, taking a slow step into the cavern, the crunch of gravel beneath his boots the only other sound. "This isn't chance. This isn't fate. This is the product of careful orchestration—every move calculated, every shadow followed. You've been most helpful."

He gave a mockingly slow clap, the sound echoing hollowly in the stone chamber.

"In Atlantis, you slipped from our grasp," Falk said, tilting his head slightly, as if reminiscing. "You were clever. Resourceful. But even then, I knew—you were only leading us to the next piece."

He gave a slow, measured smile.

"The first and second mechanisms would have remained

hidden without you. Without your family's obsessive fieldwork. Your brilliant little breadcrumbs."

And then, with a lazy gesture toward the glowing machine: "Here we are. At the cusp of the third."

Rebecca's skin prickled as the two armed men fanned out, forming a triangle with Falk at its apex, rifles rising to shoulder height. Trained. Steady. Merciless.

Falk's smile flattened into something colder. "Now, the satchel bag. If you would, Dr. Rosen-Fisher. Slowly."

Jake's jaw clenched. He glanced over his shoulder at Rebecca.

She gave the slightest of nods.

With restrained fury, Jake shrugged off his satchel bag and tossed it toward Falk with a heavy thud. Inside it, he knew, was more than simple notes. It held months of analysis, years of field knowledge—mathematical equations, cosmic event correlations, ancient linguistic references—the very key to unlocking the machine's full functionality. And now it was falling into the wrong hands.

He knew Falk hadn't just been chasing relics. Falk wanted *dominion*—the mechanisms were pieces on a board, but his endgame had always been global power.

Falk's men rifled through the pack quickly. "Here it is," one of them said gruffly, pulling out a leather-bound journal and tossing it to Falk, who caught it with the ease of someone accustomed to receiving tribute.

Falk flipped through the pages with maddening calm, eyes scanning the symbols, the sketches, the annotations. He made a pleased sound low in his throat.

"The Atlantean data, the stellar alignments, the ancient symbols, the Anunnaki scripts," he murmured. "You really did your homework, didn't you? We were hunting the same truth in Atlantis, after all, only I was willing to take shortcuts."

Rebecca's heart hammered. Seeing Falk here confirmed everything she'd feared. He hadn't given up. He had only grown more dangerous.

"You're too late," she said sharply, edging a step sideways behind one of the stone columns. "It's over."

Falk's laughter was light but edged with madness. "Over?" He motioned toward the humming mechanism, its glow now subtly pulsating. "No, Dr. Nikas. It's only just beginning."

Another figure moved in the tunnel behind Falk—a shadow blending with the wall. More guards. More guns. Their escape route was already compromised.

Jake's hand was still near his waistband, near the concealed Glock. But drawing it now would be suicide. They'd be gunned down before the first shot.

So he spoke. "You're going to use this thing to what—destroy the world? Sacrifice billions of lives just to prove a point? Why?" His voice cracked, a mix of fury and disbelief.

Falk's expression darkened. "Why?" He repeated softly, almost sadly. "Because the world is rotting, Jake. Decadent. Diseased. The people have failed themselves. A cleansing is overdue. Call it a purge, a realignment, divine judgment—I don't care. What matters is that a new golden age rises from the ashes. And I will rule it."

Rebecca's lip curled. "Spare me the rehearsal of Enlil's lines, Falk. You know you're not part of the Anunnaki pantheon, you're just a greed, miserable son of a bitch!"

Falk's polite smile twisted into a sneer. "Believe what you will. My men and I are the only ones prepared to do what is necessary. Mr. Sloan has no idea that I can align this machine to obey my every command. I will rule the world—not him! And you, Rebecca, you would hand this power to the feckless masses and watch them squander it."

"A voice crackled suddenly in Falk's earpiece: *"Falcon, we have company above. Locals and guards—perimeter breach. Scuffle at the east approach."*

Falk pressed the earpiece. "Contain it. I need only minutes."

Outside, the ancient Delphi site was in chaos. A small group of guards had stumbled upon Falk's men while opening the site at dawn. In the panic, one of the mercenaries had detonated an explosive at the museum entrance, sending debris flying and triggering panic among nearby tourists. Sirens could already be heard outside in the distance.

But Falk was unfazed.

From a pouch on his vest, he produced three obsidian objects. They were palm-sized, gleaming black, each one carved with strange, luminous symbols. Jake's stomach dropped. He knew immediately what they were: the activation keys. Carved from volcanic glass and likely stolen from sacred sites around the world, these were the key pieces.

Falk, seeing Jake's recognition, smirked. "Ah, you see. We too did our homework. While you chased alignments, we acquired the activation artifacts, and now I need your alignments to place the black obsidians in their proper slots."

He placed each stone into the slots on the mechanism's top. With a click and a pulse of light, the machine responded. Its humming deepened, reverberating like a giant cat purring beneath the earth. A light began to emanate from the inscriptions, crawling across the surface like molten metal.

Rebecca and Jake locked eyes. There was no stopping it now.

The mechanism's prism lit up, casting a ghostly, shifting map of constellations into the air. The cave was bathed in celestial light.

A map began to form—dynamic, alive. Stars shifted into position, aligning over a region. Coordinates sharpened. The pattern locked onto a new location.

"Iraq," Rebecca whispered. "The fourth mechanism . . ."

Jake nodded grimly. But his focus wasn't on the stars. His eyes scanned the glowing symbols now racing across the device's base—cuneiform warnings pulsing with faint red light. He recognized the phrase instantly.

"Fail to align . . . Test must be taken. *Beta Protocol initiated.*"

He froze. *Beta Protocol.* He translated the following lines in his mind.

This wasn't full activation. It was a fallback—a secondary trial. A failsafe. The machine had detected incorrect input. Falk had activated something, yes—but not what he thought.

Jake met Rebecca's eyes and gave a subtle nod: *bad.*

Then, without hesitation, he reached for his gun. Not to shoot—not yet. But to prepare. He had seconds.

The mechanism let out a sudden whir, then a grinding, shifting sound like tectonic plates sliding into place.

And the prism flared.

The cavern filled with cascading light and trembling energy.

The floor rumbled beneath their feet.

Falk stepped back, stunned but still grinning. "Behold," he shouted above the noise, "the stars themselves acknowledge our power!"

But Jake knew better. This was not power.

This was a warning.

Never a Dull Moment

Seizing the distraction, Jake acted. In one swift motion, he drew his Glock and fired at the nearest mercenary. The gunshot boomed in the enclosed space. The man cried out, dropping his rifle as a bullet tore through his thigh.

The second merc swung his weapon toward Jake, but Rebecca

was already moving—she lunged and rammed her heavy walking stick into the man's midsection. The rifle discharged into the ceiling as the man fell back, winded, and she knocked him out with a hit to the head.

Falk, furious, turned his pistol on Jake. "You fool—!" He squeezed the trigger.

Rebecca, however, running toward Jake, let out a warrior's scream followed by a long "Nooooo!" She threw her body in front of Jake's, arms open in protection. The bullet meant for Jake struck Rebecca high in the left shoulder. She gasped, collapsing to her knees and then slowly to the floor.

"Rebecca!" Jake roared in anger, emptying his magazine at Falk. But Falk was already diving for cover behind the mechanism. Bullets sparked off the metal casing and shattered a chunk of the cavern wall.

One slug hit the second mercenary—who was struggling back up—causing him to howl and retreat toward the tunnel.

For a heartbeat, silence fell, except for the humming of the machine. Jake darted to Rebecca's side. Blood was oozing from a through-and-through wound near her upper arm. She was pale but conscious, teeth gritted in pain.

Falk rose from behind the mechanism, fury contorting his face. In the flickering light, he looked almost demonic. "Enough of this!" he shouted. He slammed his hand onto the mechanism's dome and began to intone something—words in Sumerian, or maybe Akkadian—a command? The projected star map above flared, focusing on a particular constellation, Scorpio? Or Sagittarius?

Jake realized with dread that Falk might be initiating something. The ground trembled. A deep rumble echoed from somewhere far below. Dust trickled from the ceiling.

The machine bore a very intricate sacred geometric symbol that was becoming less and less defined as the symbols disappeared from its core. *It is a countdown! The countdown has been initiated. Beta Protocol must be bad for all of us near the machine*, Jake thought.

Thinking fast, he reached for the one thing he had left—the multitool. He flicked out a sturdy screwdriver bit.

Rebecca, dazed, saw Jake's intent and mustered her strength. "Do it . . . try to destroy it . . ." she rasped.

Jake sprang up and lunged at the mechanism, doubting if the sturdy screwdriver bit would be enough to cause damage to the machine.

But Falk intercepted him, charging Jake in the middle section of his body and bringing him to the ground. Jake, without missing a beat, shifted his hips and rolled with the momentum, reversing the position and straddling Falk's torso in full mount. He rained down vicious elbows and punches—each strike precise and punishing—starting the ground and pound with relentless fury.

Suddenly, two mercenaries lunged in from behind, grabbing at his arms and shoulders, trying to pull him off. One wrapped an arm around Jake's neck, the other aimed to lock down his legs. But Jake regained his posture with a sharp twist of his body, tucking his chin to avoid the choke. He exploded upward in a powerful bridge, forcing both attackers off balance.

Rolling to his knees, he snatched the arm of the mercenary still clinging to him and executed a smooth Jiu-Jitsu sweep, flipping the man onto his back. Before the other could react, Jake struck with a quick teep kick to the gut, staggering him. He followed up with a brutal liver hook, then a swift head kick that sent the mercenary crashing to the ground, unconscious.

The first attacker tried to scramble up, but Jake was already on him—slipping behind and cinching in a rear-naked choke. Within seconds, the mercenary's struggles ceased.

Breathing heavily but focused, Jake rose to his feet, blood

on his knuckles, eyes locked on Falk—who was now recovering, propping himself up on one arm, dazed but furious.

Jake wiped the sweat from his brow and advanced, his fists tightening.

"Your turn," he growled.

The two mercenaries—ruthless, well-trained, and until recently relentless—were now out of commission, at least temporarily. Their bodies lay motionless on the grated floor, either unconscious or too wounded to rejoin the fight. That left only two men standing amid the chaos, the dim flickering lights, and the echoing alarms of the compromised facility: Jake, bloodied but still determined, and Falk, his longtime nemesis, ever calculating and ruthless to the bone. The air between them seemed to vibrate with tension, thick with history and unresolved rage.

Falk, sensing the final confrontation had come, turned sharply and caught sight of Jake charging toward him. Without hesitation, he raised his weapon—a heavy-caliber pistol with custom engravings—and squeezed the trigger, firing with the wild desperation of a cornered animal. The first shot missed, ricocheting off a nearby console in a shower of sparks. The second shot found its mark, barely—a grazing hit that tore across Jake's left side. A white-hot ribbon of pain bloomed along his ribcage, burning through flesh and fabric alike. He clenched his jaw, grunting but refusing to slow. The adrenaline flooding his system dulled the agony and propelled him forward like a freight train.

With a burst of energy, Jake leapt. He vaulted cleanly over the raised platform, landing with calculated force directly atop Falk. They collided with a violent crash, two forces of will locked in primal struggle. They grappled viciously, limbs tangled in a brutal contest for dominance. Jake, acting on instinct and training, struck out and managed to knock Falk's pistol from his grip. The gun clattered loudly against the floor and skidded out of reach.

But Falk was no pushover. Years of mercenary work had hardened his body into a weapon, and he fought like a man who knew this was his last stand. With unexpected strength, he rammed a sharp elbow into Jake's chest, targeting the very spot where the bullet had grazed him. The impact knocked the wind from Jake's lungs and sent him stumbling backward.

For a heartbeat, both men were separated, breathing heavily, eyeing each other like wild animals sizing up their prey. Jake recovered first. With a grunt of effort, he stood tall, brushing dust and sweat from his tattered clothing. His eyes, cold and sharp, met Falk's with fierce determination.

"When will you ever learn?" Falk muttered, almost to himself, almost like a mantra.

CHAPTER 24

The Wrath of Zeus

Falk's lip curled into a mocking sneer. He reached down to his belt and retrieved something small—innocuous-looking at first. But with a practiced flick of his wrist, the object extended with a sudden flourish, emitting a high-pitched series of interlocking metallic clicks. It was a collapsible weapon—now fully extended into a slender, deadly cane-sword. The blade glinted under the mechanism glowing pattern, revealing a fine edge, likely forged from heat-treated steel, tempered to perfection. Its pointed tip looked more surgical than medieval.

"Let's dance," Falk growled with manic glee, brandishing the weapon with the flair of a showman and the precision of a killer.

Then he charged.

Falk moved fast—unnaturally fast—his strikes almost too quick to follow. The sword sliced through the air with high-pitched whistles, each swing meant to end the fight in one clean, brutal stroke. His movements were erratic but strangely rhythmic, like a madman possessed by muscle memory. The weapon's edge carved glittering arcs in the low light, deadly and deliberate.

Jake, however, wasn't caught off guard. He shifted into a fluid stance, relying on years of martial arts training, channeling the teachings of Jeet Kune Do. He moved not just with speed, but with intuition—as if he could read Falk's mind, anticipating the path of the next swing before it even started. Ducking under one strike, sidestepping the next, he finally closed the gap between them.

With perfect timing, Jake latched onto Falk's sword-wielding wrist. In the same motion, he executed a textbook counter: a sharp, precise elbow strike to Falk's face, delivered with brutal efficiency. The blow connected with a meaty *crack*, and Falk's head snapped back. His body went slack for a moment—just long enough.

Jake didn't hesitate. He shifted his stance, leveraged his balance, and hurled Falk across the room in a practiced throw. Falk's body sailed through the air and crashed into the cold metal floor with a jarring thud, his custom weapon flying from his grasp in the opposite direction.

For a second, Falk believed he had a chance. He hit the ground hard but rolled, instinctively turning toward where his pistol had landed. It wasn't far. A short crawl, maybe. Salvation was almost within reach.

But Jake was faster.

Seeing the glint of intent in Falk's eyes, Jake pivoted and sprinted—not for the gun, but for the fallen sword. His hand wrapped around its cool steel hilt just as Falk began to rise.

Without a moment's pause, Jake turned and rushed toward

the large device at the center of the chamber—the prism. A strange and mysterious construct, it was now fully active, rotating on its multi-axis gimbal, glowing ominously with pulsing energy.

Falk now has the gun and starts to position himself to take aim at Jake.

With the weapon raised high, Jake leapt once more and stabbed the blade upward, aiming directly for the rotating mount. The blade met resistance but did not stop—it pierced the sensitive mechanism with a harsh, jarring *clank*. Sparks burst from the contact point. The entire machine shuddered.

The jolt of power came without warning.

A shockwave of invisible force burst outward from the mechanism the moment Jake's blade pierced its heart. The energy wasn't just light or sound—it was something *deeper*, something ancient and intelligent. It hit Jake square in the chest, as if the machine itself had retaliated, unwilling to die quietly.

The impact flung him across the chamber like a rag doll caught in a hurricane. He smashed into the far wall with a hollow thud, his limbs splayed, his breath stolen. For a moment—just a sliver of time—his vision vanished. The world disappeared.

In its place was blue.

A deep, endless blue, like the color of the sea a thousand feet beneath the surface, where light barely dares to reach. It wasn't just a color—it was a feeling. Vastness. Silence. Surrender. Then the blue lightened, softening to a serene sky-blue hue, as though the sea had become the heavens, as though something—*someone*—was gently guiding him back.

And then, suddenly, his vision returned. Harsh light. Smoke.

The jagged shadows of the broken chamber.

He gasped, lungs heaving, ears ringing like a thousand bells tolling at once. He couldn't hear Rebecca's desperate attempts to see if he was okay. He couldn't even hear himself. Only the high-pitched whine of overloaded senses. It was like being struck by lightning—and yet, he was alive.

Somehow, impossibly, the machine had spared him.

He didn't know why. Maybe it *knew*. Maybe that ancient intelligence—buried within wires, crystal, and stone—had sensed his intent. Maybe it had understood that he wasn't trying to conquer it, or wield its power like Falk had. He was ending it. Sacrificing it. For the greater good.

And in that final moment, the machine chose mercy.

Then, with a hideous grinding noise, the prism froze mid-rotation. The gimbal jammed, unable to adjust or continue. The entire room trembled as the machine reacted violently to the sudden obstruction.

Red warning lights flared across every panel and surface. A chorus of mechanical beeps and distorted alarms erupted from hidden speakers or sonic features. Symbols began to flash on nearby screens—cuneiform writings, ancient and unreadable, followed by a stark, digital message in blinking crimson letters:

ABORTING . . . TRANSFERRING DATA.
ABORTING . . . TRANSFERRING DATA.

The phrase repeated, echoing through the chamber like a final gasp.

And in that moment, everything changed.

Falk's eyes widened, a flash of confusion and disbelief flickering across his features. He hadn't expected that move—hadn't calculated for the unpredictable, the desperate. Not from Jake.

"What have you done?!" he roared, voice cracking with both fury and fear, his eyes darting to the now-jammed mechanism.

Jake staggered backward, chest heaving, blood from his side

soaking into the tattered remains of his shirt. He found temporary safety behind a column, struggling to stay upright. His entire body was trembling—not just from exertion, but from the magnitude of what had just happened. Falk, ignoring him now, lunged toward the device, his boots clanging against the stone floor in a frenzied dash.

The projected star map overhead flickered violently, its celestial patterns spasming out of sync. No longer a map, it now looked like a broken constellation bleeding static into the chamber. The once-deep rumble of the mechanism—the low, haunting resonance of ancient power—devolved into a chaotic, erratic vibration, like a trapped beast gnashing against its cage.

Across the room, Rebecca struggled to stay conscious, her back pressed against a cold pillar for support. Blood from a shoulder wound had soaked into her jacket, and her face was pale with pain and exhaustion. Still, she raised her voice, laced with urgency and dread. "It's malfunctioning," she warned, each word a battle. "Step away. It might—"

She never finished.

A thunderous *crack* sliced through the chamber like a whip. One of the three black obsidian stones embedded at the top of the mechanism split in two, the fracture spreading like spiderwebs through its core. It emitted a sharp, unnatural shriek as if the stone itself was screaming. The device gave a violent jolt, as though the entire structure had hiccupped in time.

Falk's face twisted in panic. He reached for the three obsidian artifacts, hands trembling. Perhaps he thought he could still shut it down, still salvage whatever forbidden ritual he had hoped to complete. But his fingers found only vibrating stone and searing heat.

Too late.

With a blinding flash, a bolt of what looked like lightning arced from the crystal prism directly to Falk. It struck him like the wrath of Zeus.

The sound was unholy, like the universe tearing open.

The energy enveloped him, blue-white and blinding. Falk's body convulsed, lifted off the ground as the energy tore through him, burning from the inside out. For a split second, his skeleton was visible, illuminated in stark, ghastly relief beneath his skin. He never screamed—there was no time. The power surged through him like divine judgment, and then hurled him like a ragdoll across the chamber.

He slammed into the cavern wall with bone-shattering force, the impact echoing like a death knell. His crumpled body slid to the ground and did not move. Smoke curled from his limbs, tendrils of vapor rising from the now-lifeless form.

Jake instinctively shielded his face from the blinding after-glow. The mechanism's brilliance began to fade, its lights dimming to a flickering, sputtering glow. The violent humming ceased entirely, replaced only by the dying whine of fried circuits and the soft hiss of leaking gases. The scent of scorched ozone and molten metal filled the room, acrid and heavy, like the aftermath of a lightning storm in a graveyard.

For a long, fragile moment, the chamber held its breath.

The only sounds were the labored, ragged breathing of the survivors. The two remaining mercenaries, now stripped of their bravado, huddled at the far end of the chamber. One was crawling toward his fallen comrade, his motions hesitant and fearful. Neither looked ready for another fight—they had seen the unthinkable. And they were ready to run. To escape. To carry word of this disaster to their superior: the shadowy and powerful Mr. Sloan.

But Falk was gone. Not merely defeated—obliterated by the very force he had tried to control. Consumed by his own hubris, vaporized by the wrath of an ancient technology that defied understanding. All that remained of him was a scorched mark on the wall and the scent of ashes.

Jake should have chased down the mercenaries, should have finished the job before they could report back. But his mind wasn't on them anymore.

It was on Rebecca.

She had collapsed into a seated position, her strength fading fast, her head leaning back against the stone pillar as though she might slip away at any moment. Jake rushed to her, ignoring the pain in his side. He knelt beside her, his hand pressing against her bleeding shoulder. The wound was bad, but survivable. He tore a strip from his own shirt, wrapping it tightly as a makeshift bandage.

"We did it . . ." he said breathlessly, as if saying it aloud would make it feel real. "We stopped it."

Rebecca opened her eyes slowly. Her expression was soft, distant, but a glimmer of pride touched her lips. "It seems Enki won this round," she whispered. Then she coughed—a dry, painful sound—but still managed a half-smile.

From above, distant voices rang out—shouts in Greek. The sound of boots. Local law enforcement had been drawn by the gunfire and the explosion. The ancient temple, once a forgotten ruin, was now a crime scene. Or a battlefield. Or something far stranger.

Dawn was breaking. The golden light spilled through the cracks in the ceiling like a promise, illuminating dust motes that danced in the morning air.

Jake knew they had to leave—now. If they stayed, the questions would come fast, and the answers were too strange for any official report. Worse still, there were others who might try to silence them if word of the device got out.

He helped Rebecca to her feet, careful and gentle. She winced, but nodded. She could move—with his help. He reached down and retrieved Falk's pistol from where it had fallen. Then, carefully, he approached the still-glowing remains of the mechanism. Two of the obsidian stones remained intact, pulsing with faint inner light. Jake plucked them from the mount and tucked them into his satchel. Whatever this device had been, he wasn't going to leave its pieces behind for someone else to abuse.

The mercenaries were already gone. Vanished into the shadows like rats fleeing a sinking ship.

"Did you see that 3D map when the mechanism was on?" he asked Rebecca. "I think I know where the fourth location might be—Middle East, surrounding areas. Iraq would make sense."

"How about Turkey to regroup?" Rebecca suggested. "It might be safer ground to continue our studies and collect more clues."

Jake and Rebecca took a moment to breathe, to steady themselves. Then they turned and made for the ladder that led up into the ruins above.

"Okay. Let's get out of here."

Outside, police vehicles screeched to a halt. The guard, disheveled and half-crazed, babbled wildly to the officers about intruders and explosions and lights from the depths of the earth.

Jake and Rebecca didn't wait. They slipped out the back, moving swiftly through the trees to where their car was hidden among the dense foliage. Rebecca leaned on him, every step a strain. Jake's side ached like fire, but he pushed through the pain. There was no time for weakness.

Within minutes, they were on the road, heading down the back side of Mount Parnassus. Behind them, Delphi faded into the morning haze—a quiet little town now hiding the wreckage of something that should never have been awakened.

In the passenger seat, Rebecca reclined, pale but conscious, pressing a cloth to her wounded shoulder. The bullet had gone clean through, missing bone and artery. She would recover. Jake glanced at her, his heart aching with a cocktail of emotions—relief, guilt, love, awe.

He realized then that he was shaking—not from fear, but from the weight of what had just happened. They had stopped it. Whatever "it" was.

He reached over, brushing her cheek with trembling fingers. "Thank you for saving me from that shot," he murmured, voice low, raw. "But what were you thinking? I can't lose you. I need—I love you."

Rebecca's eyes filled with tears, one rolling down her cheek as she whispered, "And I can't lose you. I love you. I always have."

For a moment, the car might as well have floated. Everything else fell away. The pain, the mission, the world. All that remained was the connection between them—anchored in something older than even the ancient device they had just destroyed.

Jake blinked, refocusing on the winding road ahead. "We did it together," he said. Then, after a pause, he added, "And we had help."

He thought of all the strange coincidences, the lucky escapes, the invisible hands that had nudged them forward. Maybe it had been fate. Or destiny. Or maybe those long-dead priests of Göbekli Tepe, long-forgotten, had left behind more than ruins. Perhaps their final prayers had just been answered—across millennia.

By the time they reached the coast, the sky was fully lit. They ditched the car in a sleepy fishing village and caught a ride heading east, leaving behind the smoldering ruins and ancient secrets buried beneath Delphi.

But they weren't running. They were moving forward.

Because the code wasn't fully deciphered. The stars still had stories to tell. And somewhere—perhaps in Iraq—the fourth location waited.

And so did the next chapter of their story.

CHAPTER 25

Göbekli Tepe Bound

The early morning sun cast long shadows of the T-shaped pillars across the dusty ground. Jake walked slowly around Enclosure D of Göbekli Tepe, tracing the same ring of stones they had studied for years—one of the places where their search for truth had, in a sense, begun. Now it felt like coming full circle, with the pillars standing right in front of them.

In the quiet, Jake approached Pillar 18—the one with the leaping fox carving—and placed a hand on it, the limestone felt warm, already holding the heat of the new day. A few yards away, Rebecca stood speaking in low tones with the site director.

They had come to Turkey under the pretense of routine research. Officially, Rebecca and Jake were on sabbatical after a particularly harrowing stretch of fieldwork. Unofficially, they were laying low—deciding their next steps.

A gentle breeze stirred the dry grass around the ancient stones. Jake closed his eyes and let the atmosphere seep in. He felt at peace here. This site—born millennia ago from trauma—now radiated quiet serenity. Perhaps because its purpose had finally been fulfilled.

Rebecca finished her conversation and strolled over, her arm still in a sling. It was mostly for show now—the wound was healing well, though the stiffness lingered.

Nadine followed close behind, a well-worn notebook tucked under her arm.

Nadine—Turkish-born, raised in America, a combat army sharpshooter, and a technological powerhouse—had flown in quietly from the U.S. at their request. She was one of the few people they trusted implicitly, and she had been eager to join the team after completing her last mission.

She moved with the quiet confidence of someone who had nothing left to prove. Every step, every glance, was efficient and assured. Her presence was grounding—steady, like the hum of well-tuned machinery running flawlessly in the background.

"Everything set?" Jake asked.

Nadine pushed a stray lock of hair beneath her headscarf. The sun was already fierce.

"Our friends will handle the rest," Nadine said.

Jake recapped, "We're calling it The Celestial Warning. All the information from our research will be dispersed across separate vaults. And the data has been triple-encrypted and entrusted to people we can rely on."

Rebecca nodded. They had agreed to catalogue all the information in hard drives and give them to different guardians around the world—ensuring that no single faction could reassemble them. As for the knowledge they had gathered—the photos of the mechanism, the translations of its inscriptions, the sensor readings Jake had taken during the brief activation—they would keep that under lock and key. Maybe one day, if humanity truly united for good, it could be studied safely. Until then, it was too dangerous to release.

Nadine smiled faintly. "You two realize you basically saved the world and no one will ever know, right?"

Jake chuckled. "The world not ending is reward enough." Rebecca placed a hand on his shoulder. "My sentiment exactly.

Though, I admit, part of me wouldn't mind a little recognition from those pompous fools at Oxford." She winked.

Jake laughed. It felt good—cleansing, like shedding an old skin. They had been through hell and come out alive.

As they walked toward the exit, work crews were beginning to arrive, laying tarps over parts of the site to shield them from the sun. Jake slowed and turned back one last time.

He reached into his pocket and pulled out a small object: the amulet his father had given him as a child—a tiny bronze pendant of the Babylonian god Ea (Enki) riding a fish. He had carried it through every step of this journey.

Approaching Pillar 18, he found a niche in the stone and carefully placed the amulet inside.

"Thank you," he whispered—not to the stone, but to whatever forces had guided them. Enki, the spirit of humanity's ancestors, sheer luck—he wasn't sure.

As he opened his eyes, the word "Eridu" surfaced in his mind, like it had been placed there by the hand of God or Enki himself.

Jake smiled and realized. "Of course."

He rejoined Rebecca and Nadine, and together they walked down the dusty path to the site's exit, where a jeep was waiting to take them to Sanliurfa.

To Past, Present, and Future

Before climbing into the jeep, Nadine paused beside the driver's side door, her expression suddenly turning playful. From the inner pocket of her weather-worn jacket, she produced a small silver flask, the metal catching and scattering the morning sun like a signal flare from a calmer world.

"A little celebratory raki," she declared, lifting it slightly with a mischievous smile. "For those who nearly died saving humanity from a mythological hard reset."

She tossed it gently to Rebecca, who caught it with her good hand, raising an eyebrow.

"We *rarely* drink," Rebecca said, half-grinning as she uncapped the flask. The scent hit her—sharp, aniseed-sweet, familiar. "But I guess today qualifies."

The three of them stood in a loose triangle beneath the open, cloudless sky. The dry Turkish wind danced through the tall grass around them, carrying with it the faint scent of dust and wild thyme. The morning sun was already warming the backs of their necks, painting the horizon in a haze of golden-white light. Their faces were flushed—not just from heat, or exhaustion, but from something deeper: *relief.* That high, rare oxygen of having survived what felt like another major trial.

Rebecca raised the flask first, her voice quiet but clear.

"To the past—which taught us."

Nadine—ever composed, but with eyes that now carried a glint of something earned—accepted it next. She gave a short nod of acknowledgment before adding:

"To the present—which we protect."

She took a slow, reverent sip and handed the flask to Jake.

His free hand grabbing a hold of Rebecca's as he took it—a touch brief but charged with all the unspoken words between them. He looked at her and smiled, soft and real. The kind of smile you only learn how to make after nearly dying for something bigger than yourself.

"And to the future," he said, holding the flask a little higher. "May we make it brighter."

The raki hit hard—fire on his tongue, burning down to his chest, warming a space that had felt cold for far too long. He exhaled slowly as he passed the flask back, its lingering heat like a seal—a ritual complete.

The jeep's engine coughed, then purred to life.

They climbed in. Nadine slid into the driver's seat, adjusting the mirror with mechanical calm. Rebecca nestled beside Jake in the back, carefully cradling her bandaged shoulder. The rough road ahead stretched across the arid landscape like a scar—but also like a path. A beginning.

As the jeep jolted forward, tires crunching over loose gravel and kicking up a dusty plume behind them, Jake leaned back into the cracked leather seat. Through the rear window, the ancient hills of Göbekli Tepe shimmered in the morning haze—their silhouettes growing smaller, then fading completely, swallowed by sunlight and time.

The taste of the raki lingered, bitter but grounding. A sharp, burning reminder of how close they'd come—not just to dying, but to losing everything.

Jake exhaled without tension.

Beside him, Rebecca was already scribbling furiously into her leather-bound journal, the cover stained by rain, sweat, and a hundred expeditions. Her writing was fast, instinctive—capturing details while they were still warm. Jake didn't have to ask what she was recording. He knew her rhythm, her method. She was catching memory before it drifted into myth.

Up front, Nadine hummed along to a Turkish folk tune playing softly on the radio. Her phone was buzzing in her lap—encrypted messages from their allies and informants. She glanced at it briefly, thumbed out a reply. Their unseen network was still active, still watching. Silent guardians. Unsung heroes.

Jake closed his eyes for a moment, head tilted back.

The sky above the windshield stretched wide and impossibly blue—somewhere up there, the ancient stars were realigning. Not according to forgotten scripts carved in stone, or the whims of vanished gods—but perhaps, now, by the hands of those determined to forge a better path.

A new era was coming. Not dictated by machines buried beneath temples or obsidian keys passed through bloodied hands—but by choice.

Human choice.

Jake opened his eyes, as he felt something rare. Something fragile, but unmistakable.

Hope.

They had deciphered another warning—a message buried beneath thousands of years of silence. It wasn't inscribed in any single language, but woven through symbols, architecture, myth, and math—a riddle scattered across civilizations like breadcrumbs through the dark. Every clue had demanded sacrifice. Every revelation had come at a cost. And still, they pressed on.

This piece—unearthed, barely understood, nearly fatal—had not been a prophecy of doom.

It had been a *map*.

A map to salvation. A design. A choice.

The ancients, whoever they were—priest-scientists, stargazers, something older—had not intended to frighten their descendants. They had intended to *prepare* them.

Jake stood on a craggy ledge, the Turkish landscape unfurling beneath him like a painting touched by fire and gold. The sun had begun its slow descent behind the distant hills, casting the world in hues of ochre and rust. Below, fields of wheat and olive trees swayed in the breeze like waves on a forgotten sea.

His boots crunched against the gravel as he stepped forward. From up here, everything looked timeless—as if this moment could stretch into forever. The wind brushed past him, warm and dry, whispering across his skin like a voice from the deep past.

Beside him, Rebecca stood quietly, her presence calm and grounding. Her braid was wind-tossed, a few strands catching the dying light like strands of copper. She held herself with quiet strength, her arms crossed gently, her weight balanced in that familiar way—steady, centered. Battle-worn and brilliant.

Her faint smile didn't reach her eyes, not quite. It wasn't relief.

It wasn't joy.

It was *resolve.*

"We have so much work to do," she said softly, as if speaking to the wind, or the generations yet to come.

Jake turned his head to look at her. He studied the curve of her cheek, the sunburn fading on her neck, the strength beneath the softness. He thought of everything they'd survived—Falk's madness, Sloan's reach, the betrayals, the nights lost under foreign stars. He thought of the ancient voices that had guided them. Of the map etched in light.

"I know," he said simply, his smile crooked, his eyes tired but alight. "But we're not running anymore. We're getting ready for it, to face it."

A silence stretched between them—full, but not empty. The wind shifted again, bringing the distant sounds of goat bells and a radio playing somewhere in the valley. It felt like the world exhaling.

Rebecca glanced at him, then back at the horizon. "To face what exactly."

Jake nodded. "A trial. A test of worth."

The stars would rise soon, one by one, and begin their endless dance across the sky. The same sky the ancients watched, millennia ago, when they set this plan in motion.

Jake reached out and gently touched Rebecca's hand.

Behind them, Nadine leaned casually against the hood of the dust-covered jeep, her sharp eyes glued to the glowing screen of her phone. A continuous stream of encrypted messages flowed past—bursts of coded text, coordinates, satellite pings, short status updates from their far-flung network. Allies. Scientists. Field agents. Keepers of the silence.

Most of the messages were fragmentary—quiet victories, redacted findings, whispers of distant tremors—both literal and political. Warnings layered in caution, but also resolve. The world was still perilous. Still frayed. Still broken.

Nadine didn't look up when she spoke. "The stars are aligning."

Her tone was deceptively calm—the kind that precedes storms.

"Literally," she added. "Our astrophysicists say the shift's accelerating. Whatever's coming, it's picking up speed."

Rebecca turned her head, brow furrowing. "How long do we have?"

Nadine finally glanced up, her expression tight. "Months, maybe. Could be years or tomorrow morning." She let out a breath and locked the phone. "Too many variables. Not enough constants."

Jake rubbed the back of his neck, his mind already working through worst-case scenarios. He stared into the horizon, the shape of something unspoken hovering behind his eyes.

"It could be Nibiru," he muttered, mostly to himself—but the others heard. "Maybe it's still beyond our visibility threshold, but even its movement, however slight, could throw off our entire solar system's balance. We're already seeing the ripple effects—abnormal tides, increasing tectonic activity, volatile solar surges. It's a chain reaction. Earth responds like a chain reaction. Volcanoes, earthquakes, tsunamis . . .''

He shook his head, voice hardening.

"We *must* find the next location. We must be ready—for *whatever* it decides to throw at us."

Silence settled over them, heavy with knowing.

They had deciphered enough now to understand: the celestial warning had not been about despair. It had been a call to *action*. A blueprint buried in dust and myth, designed to help the world survive its next reckoning.

But that blueprint was incomplete.

"We just need time," Rebecca said softly, almost like a prayer. "Time to process it all."

Jake nodded, his jaw tight. "I know—and time's ticking. But we can't do this on the run. First, we prepare. Then, we plan. And most importantly, we recover."

They had been running on fumes—chased by secrets, haunted by shadows, hunted by enemies who wanted knowledge weaponized instead of preserved. They had bled for truths no one else dared to believe in. The toll had been steep.

Now, even just for a moment, they needed to *breathe*.

The sun was beginning to dip low in the sky, casting long amber shadows across the rolling Turkish hills. The rocky earth turned a burnished bronze, the olive trees swaying gently in the warm wind. Above, the heavens shifted from brilliant gold to velvet violet. The first stars blinked into being, delicate and eternal.

Somewhere far in the distance, cicadas buzzed. Closer still, Nadine and her team began packing up the site.

But Jake's thoughts wandered—to everything they still hadn't solved. The climate was spinning out of balance. Fires, floods, megastorms. The magnetic field was showing signs of inversion—satellites behaving erratically, compasses twitching. Humanity might be a few short years from watching GPS vanish and global communications collapse.

And then there was Sloan's Order.

Falk may have died, consumed by the machine he sought to control—but Sloan had not. His followers had splintered, regrouped in the dark. Recent chatter suggested they were still active, still waiting. Falk's death had made a martyr of him. Sloan would want blood. And he wouldn't make the same mistakes twice.

Jake knew vengeance would come. But not today.

He turned toward Rebecca. She stood with her face tilted toward the sun's fading warmth, her eyes half-closed, her body silhouetted against the twilight. Her hair caught the dying light like a copper flame. She looked tired. Beautiful. *Unbreakable.*

Jake's chest tightened with quiet gratitude. They had earned this silence. Earned this breath.

"We'll figure it out," Rebecca murmured, without opening her eyes—as if reading his thoughts. "We always do", she added.

Jake smiled faintly and reached for her hand. Her fingers curled around his instinctively, and he felt the quiet rhythm of her heartbeat against his palm—strong, alive, *real.*

"Let's go somewhere untouched," he said. "Somewhere the world hasn't changed yet. Somewhere still quiet enough to think and finish piecing this together. We need perspective. And peace."

Rebecca opened her eyes and looked at him, truly looked.

Then she smiled.

"That sounds like a plan."

Jake closed his eyes for a moment. The last warmth of the sun kissed his face. The dust still swirled around their boots, as if reluctant to let them go.

Whatever came next—be it the wrath of the heavens, the return of ancient enemies, or the unmaking of the Earth's very crust—they would face it.

Together.

CHAPTER 26

Sanctuary

The last few months had passed like a dream—soft-edged, salt-sweet, and golden.

Jake and Rebecca had given themselves the rare gift of *pause.*

After years of decoding prophecies, disarming ancient machines, and outrunning shadows from both the past and future, they had needed time—not just to recover physically, but to rediscover themselves outside of danger. The warm waters off the coast of Northern Brazil had become their sanctuary. Days were spent sailing between quiet coves where no satellites tracked them, where the only patterns they studied were the tides and the stars.

At night, they would lie on the deck of their small rented

catamaran, shoulder to shoulder, wrapped in worn blankets, gazing up at constellations older than language. For the first time in what felt like a lifetime, Jake had stopped scanning every horizon for threat. His grip on the present—once clenched like a fist—had relaxed. They *breathed* again.

But the past, as always, had a way of whispering to them.

It started with a half-joked comment from a local fisherman in Salvador. A strange rock, he said. With old markings. "Up near Rio," he had told them, "a mountain with a face, carved by gods or aliens, depending on who you ask."

Jake had blinked at the name.

Pedra da Gávea

The monolith had hovered in fringe research circles for years—mostly dismissed as pseudoscience. But rumors of its markings had persisted. And more recently, whispers of those markings being *not Phoenician*, as once believed, but *Sumerian*.

That changed everything.

They sailed south slowly, tracing Brazil's vast, gorgeous coastline. By the time they reached Rio de Janeiro, the city rose like a mirage—the curve of Sugarloaf Mountain, the sprawl of favelas, and there in the distance, rising above the forest like a watchful sentinel, Pedra da Gávea.

The mountain loomed 842 meters high, its weathered granite flanks streaked with age and shadow. It looked less like a natural formation and more like something *meant* to be seen—a monument. And on the western face, unmistakable even from afar, the contours of a *face*. Eyes. A nose. A mouth. Time-worn, but *intentional*.

Some called it erosion.

Jake wasn't so sure.

The climb was grueling. Dense Atlantic forest clung to the slopes, roots gripping stone, insects humming in the thick air. But when they finally reached the ledge where the markings were said to be, both of them fell into silence.

There they were—faint but present. Not just cracks or wear marks. Symbols.

Etched, aligned, rhythmic.

Rebecca traced one with her fingers, brushing away lichen. Her journal was already open, a pen tucked behind her ear. Jake stood beside her, flipping through printed references of Sumerian and Phoenician inscriptions.

The resemblance was *unsettling*.

Some of the markings mirrored known Sumerian cuneiform—the wedge-shaped impressions too deliberate to ignore. But others were hybrid, transitional, like linguistic drift frozen in stone. As if the writer had been adapting or merging tongues.

They documented everything. Photographs. Measurements. Angle of erosion. Comparison sketches.

Mainstream archaeology was clear—the markings were nothing more than pareidolia and wishful thinking. But Jake had seen enough *coincidences* in his life to know that sometimes, the impossible was just the unexplained waiting for context.

What truly shook him wasn't the inscriptions—it was the intent he felt. The presence of design.

It looked like a head—very ancient, very weathered. As if this mountain had been used. As if the face was meant to be a signal, seen from the sea.

And the markings? Not just a record, but a message—one of warning, or remembrance.

Just then, Rebecca's tablet chimed. A message from Shirley.

Rebecca had reached out earlier, asking her to dig deeper into the subject.

"Jake, check this out," she said, turning the screen toward him. "It just came in from Shirley."

The message read:

Some believe the carvings on Pedra da Gávea are ancient Phoenician inscriptions, possibly linking the site to seafarers from the time of King Solomon (circa 10th century BCE). A supposed inscription was translated by fringe theorists as: 'Tyre, Phoenicia, Badezir, Firstborn of Jethbaal.' Badezir was a real king of Tyre and the son of Ithobaal (Jethbaal), who ruled after Hiram I—a known ally of Solomon (see 1 Kings:5).

"We're staring at a missing chapter of human history," Rebecca said one evening as they watched the sun fall behind Pedra da Gávea. Her voice was hushed, reverent.

"I can only imagine the people who wrote this, standing here like we are now looking at this view, thousands of years ago," Jake murmured.

Theories piled atop theories. Could the mechanisms—the ones hidden in Greece, Egypt, Atlantis—be part of a global network? Could Pedra da Gávea have once been a waypoint? A beacon? Or a lock?

Rebecca stands atop Pedra da Gávea, the wind tousling her hair as she gazes out across the breathtaking panorama of Rio de Janeiro. The late afternoon sun casts a golden hue across the landscape, painting the sky in soft oranges and pinks, while clouds drift lazily below her—yes, *below*. At over 800 meters high, Pedra da Gávea rises like a giant, ancient sentinel above the forested city, giving Rebecca the sense that she's walking on the edge of the sky.

To her east, across the verdant expanse of Tijuca Forest, the unmistakable figure of the Christ the Redeemer statue emerges— arms stretched wide in eternal embrace atop the Corcovado Mountain. From this distance, Christ appears both monumental and ethereal, as though suspended between heaven and earth.

The light catches the white soapstone, causing it to shimmer subtly against the backdrop of the blue sky and rolling mountains. It looks as if he's watching over the city and perhaps even over Rebecca herself.

Below, the city unfurls like a vibrant tapestry—Leblon and Ipanema beaches curve gently along the Atlantic coastline, where the ocean glitters like shattered glass. Tiny figures can be seen dotting the shorelines. The urban grid of Rio weaves through hills and bays, with favelas clinging to the slopes and modern high-rises basking in the sun.

To the south, the Cagarras Islands sit like scattered stones on the sea, and to the north, the unmistakable hump of Sugarloaf Mountain pierces the sky. Planes silently cruise into Santos Dumont Airport, tracing slow arcs over Guanabara Bay, and the sound of distant traffic hums faintly—barely a whisper compared to the pulse of the wind up here.

Rebecca lingered at the edge of the cliff, where the world dropped away into clouds and stone. The air was thinner up here—laced with salt, wind, and the subtle perfume of distant rain. She stood perfectly still, her breath slow, her eyes wide with wonder.

Below, the city of Rio sprawled like a living mosaic—colors shifting in the late-afternoon light, the sea glinting like hammered silver.

Clouds curled around her boots like waves of smoke, and the sky felt impossibly close. Up here, between earth and sky, she felt something ancient stirring. Something *benevolent.*

The moment was still. Almost sacred.

The wind toyed gently with her hair as she took a deep breath, allowing herself to feel small—in the best possible way. Not insignificant, but *connected.* Part of a larger rhythm.

Then Jake's voice, soft and reverent, broke the quiet. "What a blessed place."

She blinked, slowly turning her head to look at him. He had stepped up beside her without her noticing, his expression just as awe-struck, his presence grounding.

Rebecca's lips parted, her voice low and breathy, the words almost a sigh.

"Indeed..."

The simple exchange held weight. Not theological, not scientific—but *human*. Two explorers, having stared down the abyss of apocalypse, now standing at the edge of the world, reminded that life could be *beautiful* too.

Jake reached out, gently brushing his fingers along hers. Not a grab—just a connection. An anchor. And together, they watched the last rays of sun pierce through the clouds and turn the city below into a golden dreamscape.

But Peace Was Fleeting

It began subtly.

A tremor here. A small quake there. Nothing alarming at first— nothing that couldn't be explained away by tectonic fault lines or seasonal pressure shifts. Scientists appeared on television with composed expressions and soothing words. "Perfectly normal," they said. "No need for concern."

But the tremors didn't stop. They *intensified*.

Reports from every corner of the globe flooded the networks: microquakes in regions with no fault lines, animals fleeing forests before the shaking began, compasses twitching without cause. Then the volcanoes awoke—not just one, but many. Dormant giants, quiet for thousands of years, were suddenly belching smoke and fire into skies that hadn't known such fury in centuries.

Coastlines crumbled. Tsunamis surged without warning,

slamming into cities with apocalyptic force. Rivers reversed flow. Birds fell from the sky.

And then the satellites started *failing*.

GPS anomalies, data corruption, entire communications blackouts in some areas. The Earth's magnetic field—the invisible armor shielding the planet from solar radiation—was shifting. Not in millennia, as scientists had once theorized, but now. In *real time.*

Jake sat at his desk, shoulders hunched, watching the chaos unfold on his laptop screen. The videos played in silence: plumes of black smoke rising over Jakarta, Manhattan constant floods, panic on major cities, people mass evacuations.

The anchors didn't bother to hide their panic anymore. The truth was out—and the planet was unraveling.

Rebecca stepped quietly into the doorway, holding two cups of coffee. She set one beside him and leaned on the frame, her gaze locked on his face.

"What's wrong?" she asked, though she already knew.

Jake didn't look up. "The world's coming apart," he said flatly. "The earthquakes are accelerating. And now the poles—magnetic north is drifting faster than ever recorded. Scientists are calling it 'unexpected.' But we know better."

Rebecca's eyes narrowed. "It's not supposed to happen this fast.

"No," Jake muttered, rubbing his temples. "But it *is.*"

She crossed the room and sat beside him, letting their shoulders touch. That single point of contact—warm, grounding— reminded him they were still here. Still fighting.

"If the Anunnaki ever return," Jake said, his voice low, "what will they think of us? They left this planet in our care—and what have we done with it? We're destroying it. We keep trying to save the world, only to ruin it ourselves.

Maybe that's why humanity fails over and over again.

Maybe that's why we're always forced to begin all over again . . ."

Rebecca completed his thought, her voice trembling with the weight of everything they'd both been holding back.

"We have to stop not only the planetary cycle of destruction," she said, "but change humanity's selfish, vicious circle—polluting the air, deforestation, killing wildlife, destroying the oceans and rivers. What is *wrong* with us?"

Her voice cracked as she stood, unable to sit still anymore. "Every other living species on this planet contributes to its ecosystem. *Every single one.* We're the only species that doesn't. We don't live in harmony—we *disrupt* it. We bring destruction to everything we touch . . ."

She turned toward the window, her arms wrapped tightly around herself.

"What's the disconnect here?" she whispered. "Maybe we truly don't belong here. Maybe what's happening—all of this—is the Earth shaking off the parasites . . ."

She turned back to Jake, her eyes glistening, her breath shaky. "Us."

Her voice broke completely on that last word, and then the tears came. No more holding it in. It had finally caught up with her—all of it. The contrast was too much to bear: the memory of paradisiacal sights, places like Rio where the world still shimmered with beauty and life, now colliding with the possibility that it could all be gone, swallowed up by fire and sea.

Jake rose without a word and pulled her into his arms. She didn't resist. Her sobs were quiet but full, and he held her, feeling the tremble of her grief as if it were his own.

Jake reached for her, pulling her into a fierce embrace. She didn't resist.

Jake held her in a tight, comforting embrace, her breath hitched once, then she buried her face against his chest, letting herself feel it.

"We won't sit still," he said softly but firmly. "We'll figure this out. Generations have studied this phenomenon. Our lives crossing paths—everything we've done up to this point—maybe it's fate. Maybe destiny."

He pulled back just enough to meet her eyes.

"Whatever we call this force we feel in our gut, pushing us forward, we need to trust it. Tap deeper into it. We need to look at things from a new perspective—get above it, outside it, beyond the noise. A different angle might show us what we've been missing."

Rebecca was silent for a moment, her eyes locked on the chaotic satellite images flashing across the screen. Then she said it—not as a suggestion, but as a decision long in the making.

"Maybe it's time to go up to the space lab."

Jake's head snapped toward her. "What?"

"They've offered us the opportunity before," she continued, her voice measured, but firm. "Back when things were still manageable. We said no—we weren't ready then. But now we need the view from above. A different perspective. We can't just study the planet anymore—we need to *watch* it. In real time.

Track the anomalies. Map the magnetic drift. Observe the global tremors, atmospheric patterns, solar interference—all of it."

Jake leaned back slowly in his chair, eyes narrowing. He didn't reject the idea—but he didn't embrace it, either. Not yet.

"The station is in low orbit," he said after a pause. "It's not like we can book a commercial flight anymore. Launch protocols are fractured. Ground crews are scattered. Airspace is locked down or overwhelmed by emergency responses. Getting there won't just be hard—it'll be damn near impossible."

Rebecca nodded. "I know. But not *unreachable*. There are private launch pads. Experimental programs. Backup access systems we helped design. You know as well as I do that when governments failed to act, some of our allies made *sure* we'd have a backup plan."

Jake stared at her. He remembered.

Back-channel conversations with aerospace engineers. Meetings in windowless rooms with climate scientists and rogue physicists. Emergency orbital platforms funded by tech magnates who feared this exact scenario. They were all whispers—contingency plans—but now, those whispers might be the only way forward.

He rubbed the back of his neck. "Even if we get a green light, it's going to take time. Coordination. A launch crew. Fuel. Orbital trajectory calculations. There's a narrow window."

Rebecca leaned in, her voice low. "We've never been closer to the truth. And the ground is falling apart beneath our feet. We can't afford to guess anymore. We need answers—and the data coming off that station could be the key to *everything*. The anomalies. The pole shift. The seismic chain reaction. Maybe even the *next machine*."

Jake exhaled through his nose. "If we go up, there's no guarantee we'll come back."

She met his eyes. "There's no guarantee we stay alive down *here*, either."

A long silence passed between them—not of disagreement, but of understanding. The kind of silence that follows when both people realize they've already made the same decision in their hearts.

Finally, Jake nodded.

"Alright. Let's reach out to Dr. Cordero. If anyone can pull strings and prep a launch window, it's him."

Rebecca stood and picked up her coffee, now cold.

"Excellent, we're past the tipping point," she said quietly. "We need to go higher if we're going to survive what's coming."

As Jake typed the first encrypted message to their old contact in Patagonia—a physicist with deep connections to the orbital science programs—he felt the weight settle over him. This wasn't just the next step.

It was the last safe vantage point before the storm truly broke.

CHAPTER 27

The Space Lab

Two weeks later, the shuttle launch was quiet and unannounced.

No fanfare.

No televised countdown.

No roaring crowds or waving flags.

The world below had no room for spectacle anymore. Its governments were fractured, its people distracted by the daily tremors of a dying planet. Civilization was unraveling—thread by thread—and there was no time left for ceremonial rites or public hope.

The launchpad stood beneath a dull gray sky, heat rising off the tarmac in shimmering waves. What had once been a place of exploration and ambition now looked like a relic itself—battered, patched, functional. The skeleton crew that prepared the shuttle worked with quiet efficiency. Tired engineers. Disillusioned technicians. Men and women who no longer believed in miracles, but who still chose to serve something greater than fear.

At the base of the ramp, Jake's team stood assembled—one by one stepping into the open, the dust of past battles still clinging to their boots.

Rebecca, calm and steady as ever, her eyes sharp with resolve.

John, the systems strategist, already calibrating the flight plan in his mind.

Shirley, scanning the perimeter with a soldier's awareness, fingers twitching near her gear.

Naomi, organizing communication protocols, double-checking encrypted uplinks.

Yumi, the quiet biophysicist, clutching her tablet like a shield, her mind three steps ahead.

Miguel, Navy SEAL veteran and field logistics expert—solid, silent, loyal.

And Nadine—the newest addition—wore the expression of a sharpshooter: hard, focused, unshakable. After flying jets in the army, she became a space shuttle pilot for private aerospace companies, making her the most experienced and reliable pilot among them.

They stood in a loose circle beneath the gantry, framed by the low whine of wind and the distant hum of fueling lines. For a brief moment, no one moved.

Then Miguel broke the silence.

"What up, fam?"

They saluted one another—not with formality, but with unspoken reverence.

A series of nods. Loud, laughing hugs. Firm handshakes.

Miguel and Nadine, with their military background, connected immediately. It wasn't just the way they spoke in clipped, efficient phrases or how they instinctively checked entrances and exits upon entering a room—it was something deeper. A shared language of experience. Of warzones, impossible choices, and the unspoken burden of surviving things others couldn't imagine.

"You Army?" Miguel asked.

"Air Force. Special Tactics," she replied. "You?"

"Marine Recon. Retired, kind of." A small grin ghosted across his lips. "Still can't stand civilians who stack gear wrong."

Nadine cracked a smile—brief, but real. "Yeah. Like watching a toddler play with grenades."

Jake noticed the interaction, nodding to both. "Glad to see the two of you getting along."

"We speak the same language," Miguel said. These were not strangers on a shared assignment.

They were family—forged in fire, failure, and faith. Every one of them had lost something.

Every one of them had been changed by what they'd seen: the machines, the ancient warnings, the sky slowly turning against them.

But here, in this single breath of stillness, they were together again.

United by one truth:

There was no turning back. They had their assignments. They knew their roles.

No one needed to ask why they were here.

They all carried the same truth behind their eyes—the same awareness pulsing through their blood like a quiet drumbeat.

This was about more than survival. It was about redemption.

Reclamation.

And the chance—however small—to tip the balance back toward life.

Rebecca stepped closer to Jake as the engines cycled into standby. Her voice was soft, but unshakable.

"We finish this. Together." Jake nodded, jaw set. "Together."

The gantry lights flickered green.

A low hum vibrated through the steel grating beneath their boots, signaling the final go-ahead.

The hatch began to open with a hiss of pressurized air, revealing the shadowed interior of the shuttle.

One by one, they moved up the ramp—slow, deliberate steps echoing inside their helmets. The air smelled of coolant and machinery, sterile and sharp.

Each crewmember gave a final glance back toward the Earth-bound platform, where technicians watched with unreadable expressions behind thick glass.

Inside, the cockpit buzzed with low electronic chatter. Jake ducked under the curved doorway, the bulk of his suit brushing the frame, and took his place.

He fastened the harness, the straps biting into his shoulders as he leaned back. His fingers curled around the worn edges of the armrests, grooves formed by generations of nervous grips.

The sky waited.

So did the silence between stars.

Engines rumbled awake, shaking the cabin with the promise of flight. A voice crackled over the comms—"T-minus ten and counting."

Jake exhaled, steadying his breath as the countdown ticked toward inevitability.

Then came ignition.

The shuttle surged upward, a thunderous push against gravity.

Jake sat motionless, pressed into his seat by invisible weight, his body one with the trembling frame.

Outside the narrow window, the sky shifted—from brilliant blue, to deep indigo, and finally to black as they broke through the stratosphere.

Stars emerged, cold and unmoving, scattered across the void.

Minutes passed. The engines fell silent, replaced by the muted calm of orbit.

Earth curved below in a silent sweep of clouds and continents. The Space Lab appeared ahead—a glint of metal against the darkness, slowly rotating, waiting.

Guidance thrusters fired in short bursts as the shuttle adjusted course.

"Approaching docking corridor," the pilot announced.

The lab's outer ring grew larger in the viewport, its antennae bristling like insect limbs, solar panels unfurled like wings. Jake leaned forward, heart tapping a steady rhythm.

It was time.

Time to step into the next chapter of human reach.

The receding curve of the Earth was stunning—fragile and impossibly small against the yawning emptiness of space. His breath fogged the glass as he leaned closer, staring down at the swirling oceans and sprawling landmasses glinting beneath the planet's thin, protective veil.

It was beautiful. And it was changing.

Across from him, Rebecca sat still, her slender frame secured by the harness. Her hair was tied back in a loose braid, a few strands escaping to frame her face. Her eyes were sharp and focused, the reflection of the Earth shimmering in her gaze. There was tension in her jaw, but her expression remained calm—steady, as always.

Behind them, Nadine manned the operations console, her head bent over a tablet. Lines of data scrolled rapidly across the screen as the station's remote systems came online. Her dark eyes flicked across the readouts, fingers dancing with practiced precision. Her lips were pressed into a thin, unreadable line.

"We're coming up on the station," she said, her voice clipped and professional.

Jake's heart thudded in his chest as the station appeared through the forward viewport—a dark silhouette against the endless sea of stars.

It was massive. A sprawling network of interconnected modules, docking arms, and long spindled corridors. Lights flickered along the structure's hull as the external systems reactivated, the station waking from years of dormancy.

Jake's stomach tightened as the shuttle's guidance systems engaged. A low hum reverberated through the cabin as the magnetic locks aligned. The station drifted closer, swallowing the shuttle's field of vision until there was nothing but cold metal and shadow beyond the window.

Rebecca reached across the narrow gap between their seats and took his hand. Her fingers were cool, her grip strong and grounding.

"Here we go," she said softly.

Jake exhaled slowly, his gaze shifting toward her. "Ready?" Rebecca smiled faintly. "Always."

A soft jolt ran through the cabin as the shuttle made contact with the docking bay. A metallic hiss followed—the sound of pressurization and magnetic seals engaging.

"Docking complete," Nadine said. Her voice was steady, but Jake could see the tension in her posture—the tightness around her mouth, the slight tremor in her hands. "External atmosphere stabilized. We have a green light."

Jake watched as the station's lights flickered to life. Pale white beams traced along the docking bay, illuminating the polished metal of the hull and the dark recesses of the maintenance corridors. A faint hum of power filled the air—the quiet, steady heartbeat of the station awakening after years of dormancy.

They were alone now—cut off from the noise and chaos below.

Floating above the storm.

Jake's hand tightened around Rebecca's. He could feel his pulse thudding beneath his skin, matching the rhythmic vibration of the station's power grid.

Nadine unstrapped herself from her seat and floated toward the airlock. She pressed her palm to the console, and the inner doors slid open with a quiet hiss. Beyond them stretched the hollow corridors of the station—dark and cold, the flicker of emergency lights casting fractured shadows along the metal walls. "I'll initiate the core sequence," Nadine said. "Give me fifteen minutes to stabilize the primary systems."

Rebecca nodded, her expression calm. But Jake saw the tension beneath the surface—the flicker of unease in her eyes as Nadine disappeared down the corridor.

Jake lingered at the edge of the airlock, staring into the dark. The station was enormous—larger than he had expected. The walls were lined with faded insignias from the agencies that had once built it. A relic of a time when nations could still cooperate, when humanity had still believed in the possibility of a future among the stars.

That future had fractured.

"Jake."

Rebecca's voice pulled him back.

Jake turned toward her. She was floating a few feet away, her hands resting lightly against the wall. The dim lighting softened the edges of her face, casting shadows beneath her eyes.

"We should suit up," she said.

Jake hesitated. His gaze drifted toward the window—toward

the Earth turning far below them. It seemed so small from up here. Fragile. Breakable.

A part of him wondered if they were already too late. "What if we are already too late?" he asked quietly.

Rebecca's expression didn't change. She pushed away from the wall, her hands catching the edges of his harness as she steadied herself in the low gravity.

"Then we do what we always do," she said. Jake met her gaze. "And what's that?" "We keep fighting."

Jake's hand found hers. Their fingers tangled together. He could feel the slight tremor beneath her skin—a quiet echo of his own fear.

Rebecca's mouth curled into a small, defiant smile. "We're not out of options yet," she said.

Jake inhaled slowly, steadying himself. The station's systems were still coming online—the rhythmic hum of the engines growing louder as the atmosphere equalized. Beyond the hull, the cold silence of space stretched on forever.

He squeezed Rebecca's hand. "Okay," he said. "Let's get to work."

Rebecca's smile widened. "That's the spirit."

Jake followed her through the airlock as the inner doors sealed behind them.

Somewhere behind the station's walls, Nadine's footsteps echoed faintly through the steel corridors. The station was vast and cold, but it was awake—alive in a way that Jake hadn't expected.

He felt that flicker of hope returning. The world below was falling apart—but up here, above the storm, they had a chance to set things right.

They weren't too late. Not yet.

The World Faces Despair

Jake stared down at the Earth through the cold glass of the viewing window. From this vantage point—high above the broken planet—the truth was undeniable.

The window of time was closing. Fast.

If there had been a final mechanism, it hadn't been activated in time. No backup plan. No last-minute rescue. No one else was coming. It was up to them now—to figure something out, and quickly.

The Great Purification Cycle had returned, sweeping across the planet with relentless force. Entire cities teetered on the edge of extinction. The scars of catastrophe were visible even from orbit—vast swathes of land fractured by tectonic upheaval, coastlines swallowed by rising seas, metropolises reduced to smoking craters beneath a canopy of ash and storm clouds.

The bunkers were holding—for now. Millions had fled underground, buried beneath reinforced layers of rock and steel. But even that safety felt like a countdown. Jake knew better than to mistake survival for salvation. The planet below was changing—violently, irrevocably. The contours of the Earth itself were shifting, morphing into something unfamiliar. Something new.

From this height, Earth looked heartbreakingly small. Fragile. A trembling marble wrapped in a gossamer veil of white and blue. A planet in the throes of rebirth—or collapse.

The space station floated silently above it all, a lone sentinel keeping watch over a dying world. Its curved hull reflected the dim glow of the distant sun—a flicker of silver against the vast, black canvas of space.

Once abandoned and left to drift, the station had slept for years, its systems reduced to standby. But now, it was humanity's last platform. The final staging ground for one last effort. One final hope to break the cycle.

Jake stood still at the viewport, his reflection faint—a pale ghost in the glass. His breath misted the surface with each slow exhale.

He had come a long way to reach this place, far beyond anything he'd once believed possible. The path that led here had been carved through impossible choices, broken alliances, and sacrifices that still whispered through his dreams.

But he had made it. Not by luck.

Not by fate.

By necessity.

"It's worse than we thought," Rebecca said, her voice breaking the silence.

Jake didn't turn toward her. His eyes remained fixed on the planet below.

"I know."

She floated toward him, her tethered boots brushing softly against the metal floor. The pale glow of the station's console screens lit her face—soft light outlining the worry etched into her features, the tension held in her jaw and eyes.

"We knew this was coming," she said quietly, almost to herself.

Jake exhaled in frustration, slow and tight. "But knowing didn't make a difference."

Rebecca reached out and touched his shoulder. Even through the layers of his suit, he could feel the warmth of her hand—grounding, real.

"It might," she said.

Jake's gaze swept across the room, meeting each of their eyes in turn. There was fear there—but also determination. A quiet, burning resilience.

As if something had possessed him—an instinct rising from deep within—Jake stood and began addressing his team:

"We have one mission," he said, his voice steady. "We must find the next machine."

The hum of the station's life support systems filled the silence between his words, a mechanical heartbeat echoing through the stillness.

"When we were leaving the ruins of Göbekli Tepe, the name *Eridu* came to me," Jake continued. His voice was quiet but steady, carrying the weight of something that had been buried for too long.

"I didn't say anything at the time because, honestly, I didn't want anyone thinking I was going crazy." He gave a dry, humorless laugh. "But then again, crazy is the new norm now, isn't it? We *found Atlantis*, for goodness' sake!"

He started to pace, his energy rising with the memories. "And that's not even the wildest part. I got *zapped* by the machine in Delphi. Lost my vision for a few seconds. Everything went black—completely gone—and then suddenly, this burst of electric blue. I can't explain it, but for those few seconds, I felt connected to it. To the machine. Like it was *aware* of me.

It knew my intentions. It knew it was dying—and it spared me." He stopped pacing, eyes distant now.

"So when we took that trip to Göbekli Tepe, and I was touching one of the pillars—just a simple, thankful gesture—the word *Eridu* appeared in my mind. Not spoken, not imagined. Just there. Clear as day.

And I kept asking myself: *Why Eridu*? What did it mean? What was the connection?"

Jake stepped forward, his movements calm but electric with purpose. He reached for the central console and activated the display. A low hum filled the room as the lights dimmed and a holographic projection flickered into life, illuminating the observation bay with a spectral glow.

A globe slowly spun before them—not just Earth, but Earth *overlaid* with something else.

Dozens of glowing points emerged across the planet's surface, each representing a location—ancient sites, ruins, temples. As the rotation continued, geometric lines connected them: triangles, spirals, intersecting circles and ley lines. It wasn't random. It was patterned, as if the Earth itself had been etched with sacred mathematics.

Sacred geometry.

A blueprint hidden in plain sight.

Jake stared at it, transfixed. The golden nodes pulsed gently like a living heartbeat.

"Ah…" he said softly, more to himself than the others, "where to begin, when tracing the footsteps of the sacred across the Earth?"

He turned toward Rebecca and Nadine, his voice growing stronger, steadier, now resonant with the clarity of someone who had finally cracked open the code.

"From the pyramids of Giza, to Puma Punku in Bolivia. From Teotihuacan to Tikal, to the forgotten ziggurats buried beneath the sands of Iraq and the highlands of Iran—these weren't built at random. These weren't just spiritual or ceremonial sites. They're markers. Anchors."

He turned back to the hologram, expanding the image to reveal the tectonic boundaries—the cracks in the Earth's skin. The sacred sites lit up along the edges like pressure valves.

"These places—they *align* with major fault lines, seismic nodes, zones of instability," he said, his voice rising with urgency. "And that's not a coincidence. The ancients knew. They understood the mechanism."

Rebecca's brow furrowed. "You mean the planetary system."

Jake nodded. "The *Earth* was the mechanism. Or at least, a

part of it. They built their temples—these sacred geometries—to harmonize with its cycles. To stabilize it. *Harness it.*"

He zoomed in further, the globe shifting to highlight the Mesopotamian basin.

"And when you start to correlate these locations with the stories of the Anunnaki—the keepers, the engineers, the 'gods' who walked the Earth—the pattern sharpens. And then you follow that thread back through the fog of myth and legend until you arrive at the beginning."

The hologram zoomed in again—this time on the ruins of Eridu, now mostly lost beneath layers of sediment, sand, and forgotten war.

"Eridu," he said, voice dropping to a reverent whisper. "The first city. The *cradle*. Where the gods were said to have first touched down."

Rebecca stepped closer, watching as glowing glyphs began to scroll around the floating projection—fragments of Sumerian text, translated side-by-side in real-time.

"Enki," she murmured.

Jake turned to her and nodded. "Enki was worshipped in the temple of E-abzu, right here. The god of water, creation, wisdom—and mercy. His counterpart, Enlil, was the god of air, authority, judgment. Enlil's temple was at Ekur, in Nippur. That place was about law, control, obedience."

He paused, letting the weight of it land.

"If we're looking for a mechanism to *punish* humanity, it's at Enlil's temple," he said. "But if we're looking for a mechanism to *save* it—to stabilize the Earth, to halt the magnetic collapse, the quakes, the floods . . ."

His finger hovered over the glowing point that marked Eridu. "It's here," he said. "Salvation—as the ancient tablets say—comes from Enki."

Yumi stared at the screen, visibly shaken by the scale of what they were seeing.

"You're saying the ancients built a planetary network of sites to work with Earth's energy?" she asked. "And now that it's destabilizing, we're unraveling because *that network's gone offline?*"

Jake nodded solemnly. "And Eridu is the key to rebooting it. Or at least, to understanding what went wrong."

Rebecca looked from the globe to Jake. "Then that's where we go next."

A deep silence settled between them, broken only by the soft pulsing of the holographic Earth, as if the planet itself was waiting; hoping.

Jake nodded slowly, his gaze fixed on the slowly spinning globe hovering in the center of the room. "Yes," he said. "But there's more."

He reached toward the console, fingers gliding over the control interface. The projection expanded—the Earth shrinking in scale as celestial coordinates bloomed outward. Orbit lines, planetary bodies, data fields in motion. Then, at the outermost edge, past Neptune's ghostly arc, a fourth point flickered into view.

A dark, silent marker. Nibiru.

The room dimmed as the projection glowed cold and blue. Jake's expression darkened. "The calculations are consistent. Its trajectory, its proximity, it's real. And it's moving faster than expected. Nibiru's growing gravitational influence is already disrupting Earth's field. It's what's driving the polarity shift, the earthquakes, the volcanic unrest."

He zoomed in—fault lines pulsing red. Tectonic plates flickering like exposed nerves. The Earth was stressed. *Fractured.*

"If it gets any closer," he said, "it could destabilize the crust entirely. Oceans will rise. Continents will break. And if that happens…"

"There won't be a planet left," John finished quietly.

The silence that followed wasn't empty—it was *heavy*. The kind of silence that descends in a church or a tomb.

Jake's jaw clenched. "If we don't find the next mechanism—if we don't *activate* it before Nibiru reaches the tipping point—this cycle doesn't just end in disaster. It ends permanently."

Shirley's gaze sharpened, slicing through the tension. "And you think the mechanism—Enki's—is still intact?"

Jake met her eyes. "We're going to find out."

A low, rising hum echoed through the station as the core power systems surged to full capacity, the data streams updating in real-time.

Jake turned, his voice cutting through the room with command. "All hands-on deck. Begin full-spectrum scans. Every ancient site, every seismic node, every known and hidden temple—scan for subterranean anomalies, electromagnetic pulses, anything unnatural."

The team moved fast.

Drones in orbit repositioned with precision. Deep-penetration satellites triangulated patterns across desert, jungle, and ice. On the command deck, dozens of screens lit up like neurons firing in a storm of data.

Nadine was in charge of scanning the Eridu Temple, though the satellites hadn't yet reached optimal alignment for that sector. "In the meantime, double-check everything," Jake said. "Then triple-check it. This isn't guesswork. If we're wrong, we might not get another shot." Time dragged on.

Tension thickened like fog, heavy and silent. Scan after scan.

False positives. Blank returns. Hints of buried ruins that dissolved into geological noise. Every lead collapsed into nothing.

And then—

"We have a location," Nadine said, her voice tight with controlled excitement.

The room snapped to stillness.

She stood, her tablet hovering in front of her, eyes locked on the data.

"Confirmed seismic activity, irregular magnetic resonance, and a deep artificial structure—matching Sumerian architectural signatures. Jake, you were right. It's coming from the ruins of E-Abzu. From beneath Enki's temple."

The projection zoomed in—coordinates burning into the map like a brand.

Miguel exhaled slowly. "Whatever's down there, it's big."

Jake stepped closer, his face unreadable. "Enki hid the machine from both humanity *and* Enlil. Buried it where no one would think to look—at the source."

"If it's still operational . . ." Rebecca began.

"It could stop the cycle," Nadine finished.

"We could only hope so . . ." Jake added quietly.

The words hung in the air like a prophecy. Beyond the glass, Earth turned—vast, wounded, still beautiful. Smoke curled from volcanoes. Storm systems spiraled like living beings. The magnetic field shimmered and shook, fraying like a threadbare cloak.

Rebecca's lips twitched into a faint, fearless smile. "We've faced worse odds."

Jake mirrored her with a warm smile. "I always loved your cheerful outlook."

Rebecca stepped closer, brushing her hand gently against his. A subtle gesture, but powerful—the bond between them forged in fire, tempered by loss, and sealed by purpose.

"So?" she asked softly.

Jake took a breath—the kind you take before jumping into deep water.

"We go back," he said. "We find the machine. And this time, we finish what the ancients started."

Rebecca's eyes gleamed. "Let's get to work."

The room moved again. Systems reoriented. Data synced to field gear. Emergency codes were transmitted to allies on the ground. A shuttle route calculated.

Jake turned toward the viewing window one last time. Earth was breaking—but not yet broken.

They still had a chance.

And they weren't leaving without a fight.

Mesopotamia, The Birth of Civilization

The descent from the space lab was anything but smooth.

Jake braced himself against the seat as the shuttle hit another pocket of turbulence, the metal frame groaning under the stress. Thick clouds churned outside the narrow windows, boiling masses of dark gray and white, streaked with the electric glow of distant lightning.

The shuttle shuddered violently as it punched through the atmosphere, the friction of reentry causing the outer hull to vibrate with a low, bone-deep hum. The harness across Jake's chest bit into his ribs as he gritted his teeth, his knuckles white where they gripped the edge of the console.

"We're coming in too fast," Nadine said from the cockpit, her voice sharp and focused. Sweat glistened on her forehead as her hands worked the controls with practiced precision. "Atmospheric drag is heavier than expected. Adjusting trajectory."

Rebecca sat to Jake's right, her hands gripping the armrests. She was calm, her eyes narrowed as she stared toward the cockpit display. The dim light from the instrument panels reflected in her gaze, turning her expression into a mask of quiet focus.

"We need a landing site," Jake said, his voice tight. "Somewhere close."

John's hands flew over the controls. "I've got three possible sites—two in the Persian Gulf, one in the Mesopotamian Basin."

"The Basin's too exposed," Nadine said.

"Agreed," Jake said. "And the Gulf's too risky. We need to stay off radar."

"Iraq," John said, his eyes narrowing as he brought up a topographical display. "There's a stretch of uninhabited desert just inside the border. Neutral territory—no major military installations within a hundred-mile radius."

Nadine's gaze sharpened. "Coordinates?"

"Uploading now," John said.

The shuttle lurched as another blast of turbulence rattled the hull. Warning lights flickered across the control panel as the autopilot adjusted for the shifting wind patterns.

Nadine's fingers worked rapidly over the console. "Adjusting angle of approach. Jake, I'm going to have to burn hard to stabilize the descent."

Jake nodded. "Do it."

The shuttle's thrusters roared to life, and the cabin vibrated with a deep, resonant growl. Jake felt the pressure increase as the ship corrected its trajectory. His ears popped as the atmosphere thickened around them, the blackness of space giving way to the murky gray of storm-laden skies.

Rebecca's hand closed over his. Jake glanced toward her. Her grip was steady despite the violent shaking of the ship.

"We've survived worse," she said, her mouth curling into a small, fierce smile.

Jake's gaze softened. "True."

Nadine's voice cut through the noise. "One minute to final approach."

The shuttle dropped through the cloud cover, and the landscape below came into focus—a stretch of barren desert, sunbleached sand and jagged rock extending to the horizon. A flash of dark green to the west marked the faint remnants of vegetation near a dry riverbed.

"There," Jake said, pointing toward the rocky outcropping. "Set us down there."

"Got it," Nadine said.

The shuttle banked hard, the thrusters firing as the landing gear deployed. Dust and sand kicked up into a swirling storm as the ship descended, the powerful engines sending out shockwaves that trembled through the earth.

Jake's stomach lurched as the landing struts made contact. A violent shudder passed through the frame as the shuttle skidded several meters across the rough terrain before grinding to a halt.

"Touchdown," Nadine announced, releasing a shaky breath. "Systems stable. No hull damage."

Jake unbuckled his harness and rose from his seat. His legs felt leaden beneath him as the artificial gravity disengaged. He steadied himself against the bulkhead and turned toward Rebecca.

"You good?"

Rebecca nodded. "Let's move."

Jake hit the release on the cabin door. With a hiss of depressurization, the outer hatch slid open, and a wave of dry desert heat poured into the cabin. The air tasted sharp and metallic, laced with the scent of ozone and sand.

Jake stepped onto the ramp and squinted against the brightness of the sun. The desert stretched out before them—an endless expanse of bone-white sand and broken rock. The distant mountains shimmered beneath the heat distortion, their jagged peaks slicing into the sky.

Rebecca and Nadine followed Jake down the ramp, while John, Shirley, Naomi, Yumi, and Miguel gathered the supplies needed for the foot trip.

Nadine already had her tablet in hand, the screen glowing softly with a grid of directional markers. Her eyes flicked over the data as she walked, focused and composed—every step calculated. "We're three kilometers from the coordinates," Nadine said. "The scanner's picking up residual electromagnetic activity beneath the surface."

Rebecca's gaze darkened. "It's there."

Jake's hand rested on the holster at his side. He scanned the horizon, noting the absence of life—no birds, no insects, not even the rustle of wind across the sand. The silence was absolute.

Jake turned toward his team.

"We move fast," he said. "Minimal exposure. We get in, secure the site, and study the mechanism."

Naomi's mouth curled into a wry smile. "Simple plan." Jake's gaze sharpened. "Let's only hope it stays that way."

Rebecca's hand brushed his arm as she passed him, her eyes gleaming with quiet confidence.

"After you, captain," she said.

Jake allowed himself a small smile before adjusting his tactical vest. His gaze swept once more across the barren horizon.

They were running against the clock now—and the margin for error was gone.

"Let's move," Jake said.

The team moved out across the sand, their footsteps vanishing into the wind. The heat shimmered across the horizon, casting distorted shapes across the broken landscape.

Three kilometers.

And beneath the sand, something ancient was waiting. The machine.

The key to breaking the cycle. Or triggering the final end.

Jake's jaw tightened as the desert stretched out before them. There was no turning back now.

But their landing had caught someone's attention . . .

The oppressive heat of the Mesopotamian desert pressed down like a living weight, smothering the expedition team as they advanced toward the ancient ruins of Eridu. What had once been a cradle of civilization now lay buried beneath millennia of sand and silence. The wind whispered through broken stones, stirring memories older than language.

The air was thick with history—a blend of dust, sun-scorched earth, and something deeper, something watching.

Shirley adjusted her headscarf, eyes scanning the endless dunes. Her voice cut through the shimmering air.

"Stay alert. This area's been contested. Factions pass through here all the time. We might not be alone."

As if summoned by her words, a distant rumble rolled beneath their boots—not seismic, but mechanical.

The team dropped instinctively, dust swirling around them. Over the rise of a nearby dune, a convoy of armored vehicles emerged, kicking up plumes of sand. Their matte exteriors were scarred by conflict, their insignias painted in blood-red and black—unmistakably rogue militia. Mercenaries. Possibly aligned with Sloan's shattered network.

"Defensive positions!" Jake barked, already drawing his side-arm.

He and Rebecca moved in perfect synchronicity, falling into cover and providing immediate suppressing fire. Their coordinated bursts of precision shots kept the advancing militia pinned long enough for Yumi and Naomi to sprint for shelter—Naomi dragging their field terminal under one arm, Yumi shielding vital equipment with her body.

Miguel, positioned closer to the ridge, spotted movement just ahead—a lone figure crouched low, transmitting coordinates. A terrain scout. Eyes hidden behind dust goggles, fingers working fast over a short-range transmitter.

Miguel charged without hesitation.

The scout turned too late.

His hand moved for the pistol at his side, but Miguel was already in motion—reading the moment like a seasoned tactician.

With surgical precision, Miguel twisted his hips and launched a rising inside-out kick, the heel of his boot crashing into the scout's wrist just as he drew his weapon. The gun spun skyward, clattering to the ground several feet away.

What followed wasn't a fight. It was a lesson.

A brutal, controlled storm of fists and fury.

Miguel struck with the economy of someone who didn't waste energy—elbows, punches, knees—each hit calculated, each movement a response to the scout's faltering rhythm.

The scout barely got off a grunt before he went down—hard. His gear cracked.

His comms unit shattered.

And his voice—the one meant to call in coordinates—fell silent before he could utter a word.

Miguel stood over him, breathing steady, eyes sharp. The message was clear.

No one's locking on our team today.

The skirmish ignited

Gunfire tore across the dunes. Bullets snapped through the air like angry hornets. Sand exploded around them as the militia unleashed suppressive fire, trying to flank from both sides.

Naomi tried to reposition—she was exposed. As she ran, a shot rang out.

She was hit.

"Naomi!" Yumi screamed, as Naomi tumbled down the sand dune, her body limp against the slope.

For a moment, the group was disoriented—panic threatening to scatter them. Instinct screamed to break cover, to run to her, to help. But that was exactly what the militia wanted: draw them out, isolate them.

They were gaining the upper hand.

Jake turned to Rebecca, eyes blazing. He reached for his weapon.

"I won't let this end like this," he growled. "Miguel, John—let's circle them!"

But Nadine was already moving. Calm. Silent. Deadly.

She took to higher ground without a word. The wind whipped across the ridge as she steadied her breath, her eyes scanning targets with the precision of a hawk.

One by one, she picked them off—militia riflemen, vehicle drivers, front-line scouts.

Each shot was clean. Efficient. A whisper of justice. The tide was turning.

Amidst the chaos, something shifted.

A sound rose—not human, not mechanical. A low, harmonic chant that pulsed through the sand beneath their boots. It vibrated in their chests. It resonated in their teeth.

It didn't come from the militia. It came from below.

Jake's eyes went wide. "Do you feel that?"

Rebecca nodded grimly, still firing. "Yes! What could this be?"

It wasn't imagination. The ground felt charged. The air, electric. Whatever slept beneath Eridu was no longer content to dream. The ancient forces woven into these ruins had sensed their presence—not of bullets, but of intent.

The militia must have felt it too. Superstitions came to mind. Panic set in. Coordination broke. Within minutes, their numbers crumbled. Vehicles turned. Retreat signals shouted. They vanished into the horizon like dust caught in a windstorm.

The desert fell quiet.

The only sound was the soft echo of the chant, still lingering like a Tibetan singing bowl.

The team emerged from cover—breathing hard, dust-caked, eyes wide but unbroken.

"Everyone alright?" Rebecca called out, sweeping the line. Grunts, nods, murmured affirmations followed.

Shirley checked Naomi's shoulder—a scrape, nothing too deep. Miguel exhaled slowly, rolling his bruised knuckles. Nadine reloaded with clinical calm.

The team pulled into a group hug, Nadine at the center.

Arms wrapped tightly around her from all sides—a collective embrace of gratitude, relief, and admiration. No one said a word at first. They didn't need to.

Nadine had been the key. Her bravery, her precision, her insight—she had saved the mission. Saved *them*.

For a few precious seconds, they simply held her close, the warmth of shared survival pulsing between them like a heartbeat.

They were still here. Together.

"We need to keep moving," Jake said, urgency hardening his

voice. He looked ahead—the edge of Eridu was just visible now, jagged ruins rising from the sand like half-buried bones. "We've already been seen. The longer we wait, the worse it gets."

He stepped forward, leading them into the heart of the ruins. Rebecca followed, her hand resting on the hilt of her weapon, eyes still scanning the sand like it might speak again.

Because it might.

The chant had stopped.

But the earth remembered them now. And Eridu was awake.

CHAPTER 28

E-Abzu

E ridu—the cradle of civilization, nestled in the southern reaches of ancient Mesopotamia.

Mesopotamia, meaning "land between the rivers," referred to the fertile plain flanked by the Tigris to the east and the Euphrates to the west—a land first chosen by the Anunnaki upon their arrival on *KI*, Earth.

Here, in this arid yet sacred ground, mudbrick ziggurats once rose from the desert floor, tier upon tier, their stepped silhouettes kissing the sky. They stood as enduring symbols of humanity's reach toward the divine, rising above the flat, sunbaked plains like ancient stairways to the heavens.

The air shimmered with heat, a wavering mirage that danced

over cracked stone and crumbled ruins. The scent of clay, dust, and salt lingered in every breeze that drifted in from the southern marshes, carrying whispers of a time when gods walked among men.

At the very heart of Eridu stood the E-Abzu—the sacred temple of Enki, god of wisdom, fresh water, and creation. It was a place where the boundary between mortal and divine blurred, where ritual, myth, and mystery converged. Here, beneath the temple's shadowed corridors and cool stone halls, the waters of the abzu—the primordial deep—were said to flow, connecting Earth to the hidden realms below.

This was not merely a city. It was a threshold. A beginning.

A memory etched into the bones of the Earth.

Inside the ruins of the temple, time was slipping through their fingers.

Whatever Enki had hidden, it wasn't obvious. Dust swirled in shafts of sunlight breaking through the cracks in the ancient ceiling. Fragments of Sumerian glory lay buried beneath the sand and stone, obscured by centuries of decay—and secrets.

The team was tired, sweating, and increasingly frustrated. Hours had passed. They had mapped every visible chamber, run sensor scans, and pored over carvings for a hint of how to access the underground complex.

Still, *nothing.*

"If there's something down here," Rebecca said, brushing her hand across a worn pillar, "it's well hidden."

"We must find a way through," John snapped, the pressure mounting in his voice. "Every minute counts."

The group fanned out again, scanning every corner, every stone. Jake stood stubbornly at the central altar, the massive offering table rising like a monolith in the middle of the temple floor.

"I've tried it already, *Jefe*!" Miguel called from across the room. "That thing's solid. Doesn't move."

Still, Jake knelt beside it, something nagging at him—a gut instinct that wouldn't let go.

That's when Naomi approached, cradling her sling-bound arm. Her voice was casual but laced with curiosity. "Guys, did anyone actually *look* at these inscriptions on the base?"

Jake's head snapped around. "What?"

He rushed over, dropping to his knees beside her. Sure enough—half-buried in sand, worn by time—markings were etched along the base. Symbols. Words.

He grabbed a brush from his pack and began sweeping carefully, revealing line after line beneath the dust.

"This has to be it!" he said, eyes wide with excitement. "Naomi, you probably just found our next clue!"

Across the room, Miguel let out a cheer and scooped Naomi into his arms, spinning her around with pure joy.

"Put me down! Put me down—my arm hurts!" Naomi hissed, swatting his shoulder with her good hand.

"Are you *crazy*? We're trying *not* to attract attention, re-member?"

"Guys, over here!" Jake called out, voice rising with urgency. "Help me clear the rest of the altar base!"

The team crowded in. With delicate hands, they cleaned off the sand-caked inscriptions until they had a full sentence—or maybe an encoded phrase.

"I can't make sense of this," Jake muttered, eyes scanning the script. "Shirley—punch this into the AI cuneiform translator."

Shirley pulled up the program on her tablet, input the symbols, and watched as the translation appeared on the screen:

Frequency: ~7.83 Hz (fundamental frequency)

Jake's breath caught. "That's exactly what I thought it said" Before he could say more, Rebecca stepped in. "In holistic circles, 7.83 Hz is referred to as the Earth's heart beat. The Schumann Resonance. The frequency of harmony."

Yumi nodded, picking up the thread. "It's just below human hearing. But if scaled up, it corresponds to a low B or A#. It's a baseline. A harmonic root. And of course, there are octaves."

Jake's eyes lit up. "There's more," he said, running his hands along the altar's edge. "These markings here—they align with the northwest wall, but there are echoes pointing to the other walls too. Go! Check them! Look for *anything* unusual."

The team scattered, combing the chamber.

Nadine, standing near a partially collapsed wall, called out. "Over here! This wall—it's not structural. It's decorative. A *facade*."

As they cleared rubble, an ornate architectural piece emerged— stone framed, symmetrical, and strange. In its center stood what looked like a metallic tuning fork, fused with the structure.

"It's incredible," Nadine whispered. "This is a resonant chamber. The wall's a conductor."

"Check the other walls!" Jake called. "They might be the same!"

They were.

Behind hidden panels on each of the four walls—concealed beneath layers of ancient carvings and time-worn debris—four identical structures slowly revealed themselves. One stood on each cardinal point, their arrangement forming a perfect acoustic square around the central altar. The stonework was precise, unnervingly so, as if shaped not merely by human hands but by some greater intelligence attuned to harmony and resonance.

"I get it . . ." Jake stood abruptly, eyes wide with revelation. "They're receivers. Tuned to the Earth's frequency. Like a symphonic circuit."

He turned to the others, scanning the group with urgency. "Does anyone have a device that can generate low-frequency tones?"

Nadine raised her hand. "Military comm unit—satellite-linked. I can patch in any signal. I've also got access to a tonal frequency generator app."

"Perfect," Jake said, nodding. "Dial in 7.83 Hz—the Schumann resonance. Amplify the output, then place it next to one of the tuning structures. If I'm right, they'll resonate in harmony."

Nadine got to work immediately, her fingers flying across the device's interface. Within seconds, the chamber began to vibrate with a barely perceptible hum—a deep, low-frequency tone that hovered just at the edge of hearing.

She placed the comm device beside the first structure. And then . . .

It started to vibrate.

Slowly at first—a faint tremble, like a heartbeat awakening. Then, with growing intensity. One by one, the other three structures joined in, each picking up the frequency, harmonizing like tuning forks picking up each other's frequency.

The sound filled the space. Not loud, but profound—a resonance that felt *alive*.

Then the altar began to tremble.

The vibration deepened, not in pitch but in power—a presence more than a sound. It pulsed through their bodies like a current, like warmth, like some ancient memory rising from the Earth itself. It was as if the planet were singing through their bones.

The altar shimmered at the edges, growing translucent. It no longer looked solid. It was phasing—vibrating so rapidly it appeared motionless, like a hummingbird's wings frozen mid-flight.

Then, without a sound, it lifted.

Jake stepped forward, breath caught in awe. He placed his hands on the stone—and gently pushed.

The massive slab floated effortlessly, shifting as if weightless, moving with the ease of a balloon caught on a breeze.

And beneath it . . .

A dark, circular shaft. Stone stairs, hand-carved, spiraling down into the unknown depths below.

"This is just incredible," Jake whispered. Then louder, to the team: "We've found the entrance!"

The group gathered around, peering into the darkness yawning below.

"I'll stay behind," Miguel offered. "Guard the entrance."

"No," Jake said, shaking his head. "We go together. If anything happens down there, we're stronger as one."

"I second that," John added firmly.

"Together we stand, divided we fall," said Shirley, checking the clip on her sidearm.

And just like that, one by one, they began their descent. Into the unknown.

Into the heart of Enki's sanctuary.

Where time, sound, and spirit converged. And where destiny waited in the deep.

CHAPTER 29

What Lies Beneath

Its architecture was a fusion of the organic and the mechanical—a structure that defied time, combining the artistry of forgotten civilizations with a precision that suggested a technology beyond human understanding.

Massive pillars lined the perimeter of the chamber, rising like the ribs of some enormous creature. The stone was dark and smooth, etched with complex patterns—spirals, intersecting lines, and constellations that shimmered faintly beneath the dim blue light drifting through the air. The walls were carved with geometric designs—symbols of stars, waves, and celestial orbits—ancient yet precise, their symmetry untouched by erosion or the passage of time.

The ceiling, barely visible through the haze of flickering light, arched into a vaulted dome of carved stone and inlaid crystal. Faint points of white light glittered across its surface—an artificial night sky, a perfect celestial map mirroring the heavens above.

The floor was constructed of polished basalt, smooth beneath their feet. Thin veins of metallic light threaded through the stone in concentric rings, radiating outward from the temple's center. The light pulsed in slow, rhythmic waves—a heartbeat that seemed to vibrate through the floor itself.

And at the heart of the temple stood the machine.

It was colossal—a towering construct of metal and crystal, rising from the floor like the trunk of an ancient tree. Dark metallic plates spiraled around its core, interlocking in patterns that mirrored the carvings on the surrounding walls. Luminescent blue-white light pulsed through conduits branching from the structure, flowing into the stone beneath and disappearing into the walls.

The design was symmetrical yet alien—both artifact and engine. Crystal rods and dark metal spines curved outward from the central core, forming radial arms that resembled both natural fractals and the gravitational rings of planetary systems. The light within the core pulsed gently—not with the rigidity of machinery, but with something closer to breath. To life.

Surrounding the machine were concentric rings of raised platforms, each inscribed with intricate symbols and ancient markings. Jake stepped closer, heart pounding, as his eyes traced the patterns—and recognition struck him like a bolt.

These were the same symbols found in the ancient Egyptian manuscript his family had protected for generations. Now, at last, it all made sense.

The designs weren't random. The glyphs mirrored those etched into the surrounding walls and ceiling—a tapestry of cosmic knowledge: star charts, harmonic frequency patterns, lunar phases, and the elliptical paths of planets. It was a cosmic blueprint, encoded in stone.

Between the platforms ran narrow channels of glowing light, weaving delicate streams of energy that pulsed like liquid starlight through the stone. The lines weren't just decorative—they were alive, flowing with purpose, as if the very architecture was a living conduit between Earth and the cosmos.

The outer edges of the chamber were framed by tall monoliths—seamless pillars of dark stone, carved with spiraling waves and interlocking rings. Jake had seen those patterns before—in Sumerian reliefs, in fragments recovered from Atlantean ruins. Some monoliths had partially collapsed, their broken edges revealing hollow interiors filled with crystalline filaments and dark, metallic veins.

But the temple walls were more than stone. Beneath the surface, pulses of light moved through invisible conduits—flowing patterns of energy, like veins beneath the skin of a living body. The stone seemed to hum—not with sound, but with resonance. With frequency.

Thin beams of white light fell from above, illuminating the chamber in soft, focused halos. Dust drifted lazily through the beams, glowing in the temple's ambient light. The air was cold and thin—but under the chill was a charge. A low vibration that made the hairs on the back of Jake's neck rise.

There was a scent in the air—ancient and subtle. The mineral tang of damp stone, mixed with the metallic sharpness of ionized air. The temperature dropped noticeably near the core; the closer they moved to the heart of the temple, the colder it became.

Beyond the main chamber, through arched passageways barely visible in the shadow, lay corridors and stairways—a labyrinth of deeper levels carved into the rock below. Faint points of light flickered in the distance, echoes of the temple's long-dormant systems waiting to be reawakened.

Embedded within the walls were vertical recesses containing strange metallic structures—rods, plates, and crystalline lattices, dormant mechanisms that pulsed faintly with light. Others remained dark and inert. The arrangement suggested layers of design—interconnected systems built across millennia, each fitting into a greater whole.

There was no decay. No sign of weathering. The materials here were too perfect, too advanced, to erode.

This was no ruin.

The Temple was waiting.

At the base of the central machine, thin rivulets of light traced patterns across the floor—symbols that matched glyphs found in the temples of ancient Sumer and relics from early Mesopotamia. They resembled star maps—planetary alignments, orbital geometries, and gravitational fields.

The light shifted gently, adjusting in subtle pulses—responding to something unseen. To Earth's gravitational pull. To the phases of the moon. To the approach of *Nibiru.*

The temple was *breathing.*

Jake watched the shifting patterns beneath his feet. He could feel it—a hum in the stone, just beneath his boots. It wasn't random. The temple was reacting.

Compensating. It was *alive.*

The silence within the chamber was profound—not empty, but *expectant.* Every breath, every step, felt absorbed into the stone, like the temple was listening.

A vibration passed through the floor—subtle but distinct. The light beneath Jake's hand shifted, orbiting slowly like planets around an invisible sun.

This wasn't human technology. It was something older.

The Sumerians had called Enki the god of wisdom and creation—the giver of knowledge, the mediator of gods. But myths only scratched the surface.

The Temple was no sanctuary. It was a mechanism.

A machine built to preserve planetary balance—to maintain harmony between the Earth's core, its magnetic field, and the gravitational pull of the stars.

And now . . .

It was waking up.

The walls bore the unmistakable traces of an intelligence that had shaped them—not human intelligence, but something older. Something forgotten.

Rebecca's voice crackled through the comms, slightly distorted by the magnetic interference surrounding them.

"Look at the architecture" Her voice was low, filled with awe. "This predates Sumer. The precision, the scale. This very spot we're standing on is most likely the origin of all human civilization."

Jake swept his flashlight across the carvings. The pale beam caught the edges of spiraling patterns etched deep into the stone. Despite the ruinous state of the city, the designs shimmered faintly beneath the dust—as though some residual energy still clung to them.

"This place isn't just ancient," Rebecca continued, her breath hitching. "It's foundational."

Jake's gaze darkened. "Now that we know Enki and Enlil were real and their conflict was real" He trailed off, his pulse quickening. "Then what else from mythology was real?"

"Probably all of it," Yumi replied flatly.

Myths had always been humanity's way of explaining the past—simplifying the unknowable into stories of gods and monsters. But what if those myths were more than just stories? What if they were distorted memories—fragmented truths buried beneath thousands of years of sediment and forgotten history, waiting to rise again?

Jake's hand tightened around the instrument in his grip. His eyes flicked to the holographic readout on his wrist display, scanning the shifting energy patterns pulsing beneath their feet.

"Jake . . ." Rebecca's voice was sharp now.

"I see it," he said, eyes narrowing.

The energy signatures were growing stronger—ebbing and flowing in rhythmic pulses, like the breath of a sleeping giant beneath the surface. The closer they moved toward the central machine, the stronger the fluctuations became.

"These readings are spiking," Jake said. "Whatever this machine is . . . it's still active. And it's waking up."

A low hum resonated through the chamber walls—deep and steady—vibrating in their bones.

Jake inhaled sharply. It was more than just a sound. It was a *feeling*. A presence.

The vibration synced with his heartbeat, thrumming through his chest. It wasn't purely mechanical—it was something alive, as though the stone itself was breathing.

They had spent years chasing this—piecing together fractured texts, decoding forbidden languages, following myths across oceans and continents.

And now, reality had gone beyond even their most impossible dreams.

They were standing at the cradle of it all—at the heart of the cycle that had shaped humanity since the dawn of time.

Jake's eyes darkened, his voice barely more than a whisper.

"Alpha or Omega?" he murmured. "The beginning, or the end?"

A sharp alarm blared through the comms, a high-pitched tone slicing through the silence.

Jake's hand flew to his earpiece. "What the hell was that?"

"Unstable magnetic fields," Naomi's voice came through urgently. She was crouched beside one of the ancient pillars, her handheld scanner flashing red. "The interference is getting worse. Whatever this machine is, it's affecting everything down here."

Jake's gaze sharpened as he stared into the dimly lit chamber, the low hum of energy now unmistakable. The walls around them pulsed faintly, as if the air itself was charged—breathing.

"We need to hurry," he said, his voice tight, clipped. There was no time left for awe.

"John, do you confirm these readings?" Miguel asked, his brow furrowed as he scanned the instruments in his hands. "The pulses, they're rhythmic. Like an energy field. Low-level, but steady. It's awake. Whatever it is—it's *awake*."

John's voice crackled through the comm, calm but certain. "Confirmed. Energy signatures are consistent across all four quadrants. Resonance is building. This system is active."

Jake knelt beside the central mechanism—a massive, monolithic construct of stone, crystal, and what looked like polished metal. He ran his fingers carefully across its surface. The patterns were too intricate, too intentional to be mere decoration. Glyphs overlapped like layered thoughts—a language buried beneath another language.

Across from him, Rebecca mirrored his movements, her hand tracing a different section of the surface. A flicker of recognition passed through her eyes.

"Enki," she whispered. "Here. Carved into the frame. This is his mark."

Jake nodded slowly. "Same on this side. It's everywhere. We're in the right place—no doubt about it."

He stood, turning to the others. "Team, scan everything. Feed all data into the core terminal. Let's keep a real-time sync across devices."

Shirley was already ahead of him, typing rapidly at the portable console they'd brought down. "On it. Uploading direct streams. I'll keep the translation protocols running live. Feed me every symbol, every sequence—we'll make sense of this as fast as we can."

"Good call, Shirley," Jake said, nodding his appreciation. Her foresight was keeping them one step ahead of total guesswork.

Miguel stood guard near the entrance to the chamber, scanning the room with sharp eyes. "Now what?" he asked, tension lacing his voice. "What are we looking for, exactly?"

"Clues," Jake answered. "Triggers. Interfaces. Anything that tells us how this thing works."

"Just be careful," Naomi interjected, her voice tinged with unease. She stood near one of the crystal conduits, studying it but not touching. "We still don't know what we're dealing with. These symbols aren't just language—they're *instructions*. Or warnings."

The entire room seemed to pulse in agreement.

A low vibration began to echo through the floor—subtle, but growing. The lights in their gear flickered slightly as if brushed by an unseen current.

Rebecca moved toward one of the crystalline nodes extending from the mechanism's base. "Jake," she called. "Come here. These aren't just decorative either—they're aligned with the compass points. Four terminals. Four inputs?"

Jake joined her, studying the formation. "A harmonic matrix," he murmured. "They could be receivers. Or amplifiers. Or keys."

Yumi, standing nearby, added thoughtfully, "Or all of the above. If this system interfaces with planetary energy, each of these could be tied to one of Earth's natural frequencies. Like a tuning system. To restore balance—or reset it."

That word lingered. Reset.

Miguel's fingers tightened around his rifle.

"Let's just hope we don't push the wrong button."

Jake looked at them all—the best team he could've ever hoped for. Battle-worn, brilliant, and utterly unflinching.

"We're close," he said. "This thing is responding to us. It's been waiting. But we need to understand it before we risk *activating* anything."

Nadine's voice crackled over comms from the rear corridor. "External seismic activity is rising. We've got maybe two hours, tops. After that, if the fault lines keep widening . . ."

She didn't finish. She didn't have to.

Jake turned back to the mechanism. The hum was growing stronger—almost a low, musical tone now, as if the chamber were becoming a living instrument, tuning itself to them.

"Everyone focus," he said. "The Earth is moving. So are we."

And somewhere deep beneath their feet, the machine began to listen.

CHAPTER 30

Presence

The truth, long buried beneath layers of myth and mis-interpretation, was stark:

Humanity had always been on trial.

The rise and fall of civilizations, the cycles of destruction and rebirth—none of it had been accidental. Beneath the illusion of free will, humanity had existed under quiet observation. The Anunnaki—ancient cosmic shepherds—had watched, guided, and, at times, intervened in Earth's affairs.

And in the shadows of human history, the age-old conflict between Enki and Enlil had echoed again and again, cycling with the cosmic tides. It had always been a test.

Enki, the wise and benevolent, had believed in humanity's

potential for transcendence. He had seen something rare in them—an unpredictable spark of creativity and resilience.

Where others saw chaos, Enki saw possibility.

He had gifted knowledge—writing, agriculture, mathematics, astronomy—not just for survival, but for evolution. His hope was simple, yet profound: that humanity might one day rise above its base instincts. That it could grow beyond war, beyond greed, and earn its place among the intergalactic collective as equals.

But Enlil had seen only entropy.

Where Enki saw promise, Enlil saw a species doomed to repeat its failures. A creature of appetite and destruction.

They built only to destroy. They learned only to weaponize.

He had watched as empires rose, only to fall—their cities swallowed by the sea, their knowledge lost to fire, their monuments buried beneath time. He saw humanity not just as a threat to itself, but to the balance of all things.

And so, time and again, Enlil had enacted the Purifications, each one aligned with natural planetary events. Will humanity come together to heed the warnings? Or will they continue to chase greed and power, turning on one another—fueling wars, endangering other species, and bringing their own planet to ruin? If they refuse to learn, then let the purification cycle return and cleanse them once more, as it has before.

When the great flood consumed the Sumerian world, it was Enlil's hand that stirred the waters. When Atlantis fell beneath the waves, it was Enlil's judgment that sealed its fate. The burning of Rome, the collapse of the Mayan cities, the fall of dynasties lost to time—all were part of the *Celestial Warning*.

Each time humanity approached a precipice—each time it came close to transcendence—Enlil intervened. The test was repeated. The cycle reset.

The Anunnaki would gather. They would debate.

They would weigh the evidence. Enki would argue for mercy.

Enlil would call for judgment. Sometimes, humanity was spared.

More often, it was culled—all but a chosen few—with Enki always trying to soften the blow. But this time was different.

The numbers were clear. The evidence was undeniable. Humanity had reached the edge of the precipice—not just for their species, but for the planet itself. The pollution, the wars, the reckless destruction of ecosystems—it had reached an unsustainable threshold.

The calculations were precise.

The Celestial Warning was there—clear as ever—yet once again ignored by the masses. Civilization was more concerned with appearances, fashion, endless entertainment, and the comforts of technology and luxury. Narcissism reigned. Power and glory were pursued above all else. Humanity had lost its connection to nature, to the Earth itself, setting it marching toward its own destruction.

Only a few could still tune into the truth—like the sky watchers of millennia past. Jake and his team were among them, humanity's last sentinels. They were listening, watching, preparing. But the purification cycle had already begun.

And yet, there was hope.

Rebecca switched spots, her fingertips brushing the lower section of the machine. She frowned.

"These inscriptions . . ." Rebecca murmured, tilting her head. "They're different from the others we've seen."

Jake leaned closer. "Different how?"

Rebecca's brow furrowed as she ran her fingers along the edges of the symbols. "It's not just a warning."

Naomi knelt beside her. "What does it say?" Rebecca's voice dropped. "It speaks of a trial."

Jake's gaze sharpened. "This is it! This is the test we have been looking for."

"Yes, a test," Rebecca clarified. "Only those who carry the knowledge of Enki are permitted to proceed." Her fingers traced the lower row of symbols. "And those who fail . . ." She hesitated.

Naomi's expression darkened. "What?"

Rebecca glanced toward her. "They don't leave."

John chuckled nervously from behind them. "Let's hope that's just ancient superstition."

Rebecca's gaze remained hard. "The ancients didn't waste resources on superstition."

Shirley knelt beside the base of the machine, adjusting the charge on her portable excavation tool. The tool whirred softly as she touched the surface of the stone.

"It's not locked," Shirley said. "At least not mechanically."

Jake's eyes narrowed. "Meaning?"

"It's pressure-sealed," Shirley said. "Designed to respond to a specific trigger, like the one in Atlantis."

"Biometric?" Jake asked.

"Possibly." Shirley adjusted the tool's frequency. "Or something worse."

Jake glanced toward Rebecca. "Options?"

Rebecca swept her light across the symbols. "These carvings," she whispered. "They're not random."

"They're star charts," Naomi said. "But not fixed." Jake's gaze sharpened. "Explain."

Naomi's voice was soft, reverent. "They're shifting.

Recalibrating based on the alignment of the stars. This whole structure—it's reacting to the orbit of Nibiru."

Rebecca's eyes widened. "It's calculating the next degree of approach."

Jake's jaw tightened. "How long until it happens?"

Naomi adjusted the scanner on her wrist. "If this pattern holds in less than 24 hrs. it will be 35% more influential."

Jake's stomach tightened.

"The Mechanism, it's do or die" Rebecca whispered.

Jake stepped toward her, his heart hammering in his chest. His hand brushed the edge of the platform.

A low hum passed through the stone beneath his hand. "It's still active, maybe at half power? Yumi asked.

"Difficult to say" Naomi answered, her voice laced with awe.

Shirley stepped closer, sweeping her light across the room. The shadows stretched unnaturally along the walls.

Jake's fingers traced the edge of it. His breath slowed. The hum beneath his skin was rhythmic—a pulse that seemed to echo through his chest.

Rebecca stepped beside him. "You feel it too?" she asked softly. Jake nodded.

"It's waiting for us to proceed," Rebecca said. Jake's gaze darkened. "Or it's warning us."

They stood in silence for a long moment. The hum beneath their feet grew louder.

Rebecca's gaze met Jake's. "What now?" Jake's hand pressed against the cold stone.

The only way out," he said, eyes fixed on it, "is through."

The choice would shape the future—not just of Earth, but of the universe, of existence itself.

Jake's breath slowed. He thought of the ruins left in humanity's wake—a species given countless chances, only to fall time and again. He saw in his mind's eye the rise and collapse of empires, the endless wars, the relentless cycle of destruction and rebirth. He thought of shattered cities beneath the oceans, of civilizations buried beneath centuries of sand and ice.

He thought of Atlantis.

This was humanity's last chance.

A soft chime echoed through the chamber. Naomi's tablet lit up, glowing with data as the algorithm parsed the ancient inscriptions on the sphere—patterns extracted from Atlantean carvings and symbols recovered from Grecian ruins.

Shirley's fingers danced rapidly over the controls. "Cross-referencing the data sets. The Greek texts and the Atlantean symbols are aligning—forming a third sequence."

Rebecca leaned in, her brow furrowed. "A third language?" Naomi's voice was quiet. "No. A key."

Jake's gaze sharpened. "Show me."

The holographic projection above Naomi's tablet shifted. Three interlocking rings spun into view, forming a complex geometric array. Lines intersected at precise points, threads of light twisting and pulsing in harmony with the machine's resonance.

"It's a command sequence," Naomi said, her voice edged with awe.

The machine's pulse quickened. Shirley's screen flickered with activity. "Deciphering inscriptions; Stand by."

Seconds stretched. Then minutes. Time distorted in the stillness.

The hum beneath Jake's feet deepened. The pulses grew more intricate—no longer random, but deliberate. Structured. They were syncing with the command sequence.

Jake's hand curled into a fist. His breath grew slower, more deliberate, as the symbols on Naomi's screen began to align. The light emanating from the sphere intensified, radiating outward in measured, pulsing waves.

Rebecca stepped closer. "Jake?" A single beep broke the silence.

A phrase appeared on the tablet's screen:

THE GUARDIAN IS DORMANT.
AWAKEN WITH CAUTION.

The chamber fell utterly silent.

Rebecca's eyes darkened. "It was never going to be that easy."

Jake's gaze locked on the sphere. The glowing rings had dimmed, their rhythmic pulse slowing—waiting.

"I hoped we wouldn't have to face this," he said quietly.

Rebecca brushed his arm gently. "We always knew it was coming."

His hand hovered above the activation panel. It trembled. "What if this is what Enlil wanted?" Jake asked, voice low.

Rebecca's expression hardened. "What if it's what Enki was counting on?"

A faint tremor rippled through the floor beneath them. A vibration—soft at first—that deepened into a steady hum.

Shirley's voice cut through the quiet. "We've triggered something."

Jake's eyes narrowed. "What kind of something?"

Her screen flashed—glyphs shifting, forming a new sequence. Rebecca moved closer. "Jake—"

A low, resonant sound rolled through the chamber—a pulse so deep it made the air itself tremble.

Jake's gaze darkened. "It's waking up."

Naomi's hands moved swiftly over the controls. "Let's hope it isn't crabby when it does—"

Jake's hand hovered, motionless above the activation panel. His pulse pounded in his ears. The swirling light beneath his fingertips beckoned.

"Jake," Rebecca said, her voice steady, anchoring him. "We came here for this."

He exhaled, slow and even. His hand began to lower.

The pulse beneath them intensified—faster now, almost frantic, as though the machine itself sensed the moment.

Jake's gaze narrowed.

And then—he pressed his hand to the cold metal. The glyphs ignited.

A brilliant ring of light spiraled outward across the stone floor. The patterns etched into the chamber's foundation lit up in rippling waves.

Jake's breath caught in his throat.

"We've started the sequence," Naomi said.

Jake's hand remained steady on the panel. Rebecca's eyes never left his. "What now?" Jake's jaw tightened.

"We finish it."

A Presence in the Temple

The ground trembled beneath their feet.

A low, resonant sound vibrated through the chamber walls—not mechanical, not organic, but something deeper. Elemental.

Dust and sediment rained softly from the ceiling in thin, shimmering curtains. The ancient ruins, dormant for millennia beneath layers of earth and time, now pulsed with awakening energy. Stone pillars groaned under mounting strain as fractures crept across their surfaces. The stone beneath the Mechanism rippled—trembling under Jake's boots with a slow, rhythmic vibration.

Then came the sound—deep and guttural—echoing through the chamber with a bone-deep resonance. It crawled under their skin, humming through the marrow. It was a pulse older than language, older than thought—older than humanity itself.

"Something's waking up," John muttered, voice taut, barely above a whisper. His fingers clenched around the scanner as the readings spiked violently, outpacing calibration.

Static hissed through the comms. Naomi's tablet flickered—data streams disrupted, overwritten by an electromagnetic surge emanating from the core of the machine.

"It's coming from beneath us," Naomi said sharply. "I'm picking up massive kinetic shifts underground. Something is—"

A violent tremor cracked through the platform.

The Mechanism's light exploded outward in a cascade of pulses. Concentric rings rotated, interlocking with clockwork precision as ancient glyphs ignited along the chamber walls—glowing, alive.

Beneath the Mechanism, the stone began to move.

A grinding roar filled the space—stone against stone, metal against metal—as something enormous shifted beneath the floor.

Rebecca stepped back, instinctively reaching for the hilt of her sidearm. "Jake—"

"I see it," Jake replied, his voice low, steady.

The platform split apart. Stone slabs peeled away with agonizing slowness, revealing a dark, yawning void beneath. A slow spiral of energy rose from the depths—light and dust rotating in a tight, controlled cyclone.

And then—it emerged.

A colossal form rose from the shadows of forgotten history. Metal, stone, and pure energy fused into a single, unified entity.

Its size was staggering. As it ascended, its sheer mass cast long, flickering shadows across the chamber walls, eclipsing the fading light of the Mechanism.

Humanoid—yet distinctly other.

Its towering body was encased in overlapping plates of dark metal, etched with glowing inscriptions that matched those found on the Mechanism. The light within its structure pulsed in rhythm—the same breath, the same heartbeat.

Its face was hidden beneath an ornate helmet, crowned with sweeping bull horns that curved upward like crescent moons. Its eyes glowed cold and pale—not lifeless, but aware. Beneath the helmet, a metallic beard and braided mustache had been sculpted with such precision it seemed woven rather than forged.

Its armor was ancient—interlocking layers of obsidian-like plating inscribed with spiraling geometric patterns. Energy coursed through the veins of the design, casting soft, flickering light into the darkness.

The machine had not been unguarded. This was not a sentinel.

It was a presence.

A burst of static tore through the comms as John's scanner shrieked in protest. He clutched his headset. "Jake—!"

And then—the voice came.

It did not pass through the air. It did not echo from the walls.

It entered their minds.

"WHO SUMMONS THE GUARDIAN OF THE CELESTIAL DECREE?"

The words weren't heard—they were *felt*, vibrating through Jake's skull, digging into the marrow of his bones. The voice was impossibly vast, resonant, and ancient. It transcended sound.

Jake's breath caught. His muscles tensed beneath the invisible pressure of the presence. The others stood frozen, their faces pale, illuminated by flickering glyphs.

He stepped forward. Swallowed his fear.

His hand brushed his sidearm—a reflex, though he knew it would be useless.

His voice was steady. "We are the descendants of Earth," he said. "And we've come to restore what was lost."

Silence.

The figure's eyes narrowed—twin stars of cold, judgmental light.

YOU COME TO RESTORE BALANCE . . . OR TO TIP THE SCALES?

Jake's jaw tightened. "We came to save our world."

YOUR KIND HAS BEEN TESTED BEFORE.

Jake took a slow breath. "And we've endured."

AND FAILED.

His pulse roared in his ears. "Not this time."

The figure's eyes flared with red light. A radiant pulse spiraled outward from the Mechanism, illuminating the chamber in rhythmic waves. The stone beneath Jake's feet thrummed with rising energy.

THEN PROVE YOURSELVES WORTHY.

The Guardian

It towered above them—immense and unmoving. Its surface was a living tapestry of metal and stone, etched with glowing, flowing symbols. Energy pulsed through its frame in a hypnotic rhythm. It was ancient—older than the Temple itself.

Jake stared in awe. The figure was familiar—its likeness carved into the oldest ruins on Earth. He recognized the bull-horned helmet. The beard. The spiral patterns.

"The Bull-Horned Sentinel," he whispered. Rebecca nodded, eyes sharp. "The Enki Guardian."

The light in its eyes burned brighter—cold red fire beneath sculpted metal. Its braided beard gleamed faintly in the glyph-light.

Jake's breath caught. "Enki," he murmured. "God of wisdom. And creation."

The Guardian's head inclined.

I AM NO GOD.

I AM A CONSTRUCT. A SERVANT OF THE BALANCE.

Jake held his gaze. "You were created to protect this place."

YES.

"To guard the Mechanism."

AND TO ENSURE IT IS NEVER MISUSED.

He stepped toward the platform. The Mechanism hummed beneath his palm—ancient, alive.

"If this machine regulates Earth's magnetic field," he said, "then you're here to test anyone who tries to control it."

YES.

Jake's voice lowered. "And if we fail?"

FAILURE RESULTS IN PURIFICATION.

Jake stiffened. "Another reset."

CORRECTION.

He clenched his fist. "And if we pass?"

The Guardian's voice thundered through the chamber:

"ONLY THEN SHALL HUMANITY AT LAST TASTE TRUE FREEDOM BENEATH THE STARS."

Jake's mind reeled.

The ancient texts had spoken of Enki as the giver of knowledge—but the truth was deeper. He had offered humanity a choice. A chance to transcend.

The Guardian was not a protector of power. It was a keeper of balance.

Jake's voice was firm. "Why now?" The Guardian pulsed.

THE BALANCE IS FAILING. NIBIRU'S RETURN HAS ACCELERATED THE INSTABILITY. IF THE MECHANISM IS NOT REALIGNED, THE PLANET'S CORE WILL COLLAPSE.

Jake's breath hitched. "And you believe we can fix it?"

THAT DEPENDS ON YOUR WORTH.

He steadied his hand over the control panel.

"If this is a test," Jake said. "What's the next step?"

A deep hum rolled through the stone. The glyphs beneath their feet brightened, spiraling toward the heart of the Mechanism.

The Guardian's eyes remained fixed on him.

ALIGN THE PATTERNS. RESTORE THE BALANCE.

Jake's jaw clenched. His hand hovered.

Rebecca stepped beside him. "Jake?"

He exhaled. Steady. Calm. Focused.

"We've come this far," he said, and lowered his hand to the glyphs.

The Guardian's light flared.

THEN PROVE YOUR WORTH.

CHAPTER 31

The Mechanism

Justin closed his eyes and steadied his breath.

The symbols etched across the Mechanism's surface glowed brighter—not at random, but in deliberate succession. A language of patterns. A code.

This wasn't just a machine. It was a key. A keeper of balance.

Jake's mind worked quickly, tracing the patterns and aligning them with the star charts and mathematical sequences they had recovered from Atlantis and Greece. The glyphs weren't mere symbols—they were equations. Harmonic resonance signatures mapped to Earth's magnetic field. A planetary algorithm.

He moved with focus. His hands hovered over the activation

panel, fingers mirroring the unfolding patterns, anticipating their order.

Rebecca's voice cut through the hum—calm, sharp. "Jake?"

"I see it," he said, eyes locked on the sequence. "It's a harmonic alignment pattern. If I input it correctly, it'll stabilize the core." Rebecca hesitated. "And if you're wrong?"

Jake's expression darkened. "Then the magnetic field collapses. And the planet dies."

His fingers swept across the glowing interface.

The first ring aligned. Symbols locked beneath his touch, humming with power.

The Guardian's gaze remained fixed on him—silent, watchful. Jake drew a slow breath and input the second sequence. The patterns rippled outward, cascading through the platform like waves across still water.

The pulse beneath his hand intensified. He entered the third sequence.

The chamber shuddered.

Arcs of energy sparked across the walls—chaotic for a heartbeat—then steadied, syncing with the Mechanism's rhythm.

Only one pattern remained.

The final sequence glowed beneath his fingertips. He hesitated. "Jake," Rebecca said softly, her voice grounding him.

He exhaled.

His hand lowered.

The last symbol locked into place.

The rings of the Mechanism ignited—pulses of cascading light spiraling outward toward the chamber walls. Tremors beneath their feet ceased. The vibrations softened, settling into a deep, resonant hum.

Jake staggered back a step, his breath quick and shallow.

The Guardian's eyes pulsed with light.

YOU HAVE PROVEN YOUR WISDOM.

The Mechanism's rhythm slowed to a steady, harmonious beat. The rings rotated in perfect alignment.

The light dimmed—not fading, but stabilizing.

THE MECHANISM IS NOW ALIGNED TO YOUR COMMAND.

Jake exhaled. Relief washed over him—brief, fleeting.

AND THE CHALLENGE SHALL BEGIN.

His gaze snapped to Rebecca.

She stepped forward, her hand finding his arm.

"You got this," she said. Her voice was steady. Certain. Jake turned back toward the Guardian.

Its massive form stood motionless, a statue of ancient purpose. The light within its eyes flickered faintly, watching, waiting.

The Mechanism was fully engaged.

And whatever came next—they had passed the threshold.

The true test had only just begun.

The Challenge

Jake's breath came shallow and fast as the Guardian's gaze locked on him.

The immense figure stood motionless, eyes burning with cold white light—yet Jake could *feel* the weight of its attention. It pressed down on him like gravity—vast, ancient, inescapable.

This was no mere test of intellect.

This was a trial of will. Of perception. Of alignment with something older and deeper than human memory.

Around him, the inscriptions on the Eridu Temple walls pulsed with a dim blue glow, synchronized with the rhythmic hum of the Mechanism. The glyphs—spiraling geometries and ancient sigils—shifted just beneath the surface of the stone, slow and precise, like the movement of stars across the night sky.

They weren't instructions. They were a *language.*

A code.

A map of Earth's hidden architecture—the invisible currents of magnetic fields, tectonic flows, oceanic tides.

Jake could feel it beneath him—a vibration, pulsing through stone and into his chest. A breath.

The machine and the temple were one. Parts of the same planetary system, older than humanity itself.

John's voice broke through, low and tight with tension. "Jake, are you seeing this?"

Jake's hand hovered over the control panel. The vibration beneath his fingertips was steady, almost alive.

"I see it," he said. His voice was calm, but beneath it, there was fear. A razor's edge of uncertainty.

John swallowed. "These symbols—they're shifting."

"They're not just symbols," Jake murmured. "They're harmonic sequences. Keys to the Earth's equilibrium."

Rebecca stepped up beside him, brow furrowed. "What are you saying?"

Jake didn't look away. His fingers floated just above the glowing glyphs. "This machine wasn't built to generate power. It was built to *sustain* it. The magnetic field, tectonics, climate, oceanic flow, it's all connected."

Her eyes widened. "The machine regulates the *planet's* balance."

"A test of understanding," Jake said. "I need to align the patterns. Match the harmonics. If I fail—"

FAILURE WILL RESULT IN THE DESTABILIZATION OF EARTH—AND YOUR DESTRUCTION.

Jake winced. The voice carved its way through his thoughts.

Heavy. Absolute.

He exhaled slowly. "No pressure, then."

The Guardian didn't register Jake's sarcasm. Instead, it tilted its head, like a curious puppy trying to make sense of a command it couldn't quite grasp.

Jake's face paled. "If Earth itself becomes unstable . . ."

A resonant sound vibrated through the chamber—deep, slow, and primal. It trembled through his chest. The Guardian's eyes flared.

THIS PLACE HOLDS THE BALANCE OF THE PLANET. TO COMMAND IT, YOU MUST PROVE YOU UNDERSTAND ITS PURPOSE.

Jake's hand hovered, heart pounding. His mind raced, flicking through equations, fragments of glyphs, star maps from Atlantis and Greece.

"I need time," he said. "This is more complex than anything we've seen."

YOU HAVE TIME ONLY IF YOU EARN IT.

Jake's pulse surged. "And how do I earn it?"

THE TRIAL BEGINS NOW.

The floor groaned. Stone shifted.

Sections of the platform retracted into darkness. The chamber trembled. A grinding roar echoed from below as the ground beneath them rearranged, transforming into a shifting field of elevated platforms—rising and falling in geometric precision.

"Jake!" Rebecca called.

He steadied himself as arcs of blue-white energy leapt across the Mechanism. Platforms emerged from the depths, etched with glyphs that pulsed in rhythmic patterns. The entire chamber was alive—a puzzle in motion.

"It's a sequence," Jake said. "A harmonic pattern."

Rebecca scanned the field. "It's changing the alignment of the machine."

"Or trying to," Jake replied. "It's recalibrating."

John's scanner beeped frantically. "Jake—these readings are off the charts. If you get this wrong—"

"I know," Jake cut in. The Guardian's eyes flared.

ALIGN THE PATTERNS. RESTORE THE BALANCE. OR FACE THE CONSEQUENCES.

Jake stepped to the nearest platform. The symbols danced erratically—out of sync, like instruments playing against one another.

"It's harmonic interference," he said. "The machine is trying to stabilize, but the resonance is off."

Rebecca's hand found his arm. "Then let harmony be woven once more into the fabric of creation."

He traced the glyphs, recalling the patterns from Atlantis, the sequences from ancient Greece. But this went deeper. It wasn't math alone—it was *nature*. Rhythms of tides. Celestial alignments. The pulse of the Earth itself.

He stared at the symbols. Constellations.

Orion. Sirius. The Pleiades. Patterns embedded in human culture since the dawn of civilization. Echoes found in the pyramids—Giza, Teotihuacan—monuments that transcended time.

Rebecca whispered near his ear. "Jake, you can't hesitate.

The alignment window is closing."

He nodded, swallowing his fear. The vibration of the Mechanism filled his bones. It was *alive*.

The Guardian's voice echoed again.

YOU HAVE SEEN THE PATTERNS. YOU KNOW THE KEY.

Jake's gaze fell on three glowing pyramidal icons on the console. He pressed the first—aligning it with a point representing Orion's Belt.

The machine shuddered.

Dust fell from above. The chamber pulsed. Star charts and hieroglyphs on the walls ignited with light.

"What are you seeing?" Rebecca asked.

"It's Orion," Jake breathed. "The layout of the Great Pyramids—it's a star map."

"The Mexican pyramids?" she asked.

He activated another glyph. Three more lights flared. "Teotihuacan. They mirror Orion's Belt too. These sites weren't built to honor the stars—they were built to interface with this."

The Guardian's voice thundered:

PROCEED.

Jake's hands flew across the console. His mind synced with the system—memories, equations, and ancient knowledge flashing like visions behind his eyes.

He adjusted a symbol. It resisted. "It's not holding," Rebecca said.

"The Earth's axis has shifted since they were built," Jake said. "We're off by 0.13 degrees."

"Then compensate." He recalibrated.

A deep vibration surged upward. The console pulsed. Energy rippled through the stone.

"It's working," Rebecca whispered.

Jake closed his eyes, hand steady. This wasn't a machine. It was a living system.

He input the sequence. Symbols aligned, glowing brighter.

The chamber trembled—then steadied.

"They're star charts," he said. "Stellar alignment. The Mechanism is responding to *Nibiru's orbit*—and the outer planets."

Naomi's scanner pinged. "Confirmed—the cycles match the planetary positions."

Jake locked the first symbol. Energy rippled outward. He aligned the second—a symmetrical spiral of light.

The arcs steadied. The field stabilized. He hovered over the final symbol.

"Jake," Rebecca whispered.

He pressed it.

Light exploded outward.

The tremors ceased. The chamber pulsed in perfect harmony. The glyphs aligned. The vibrations quieted into a single, steady hum.

The Guardian's eyes dimmed.

YOU HAVE PROVEN YOUR UNDERSTANDING.

Jake's hand dropped to his side. His chest rose and fell in silence.

YOU HAVE STABILIZED THE BALANCE. THE HEALING OF YOUR PLANET HAS STARTED.

A low, deep thrum echoed from the core. Not mechanical—alive. A frequency that resonated with the Earth itself.

The concentric rings of the Mechanism ignited—silver and blue waves pulsing in concentric harmony. The Guardian stood motionless, his form glowing softly with internal light.

Then the light changed.

White arcs leapt between the Guardian and the Mechanism—a lattice of connection. His etched frame pulsed with ancient symbols—Sumerian, celestial, mathematical—glowing as they synced with the system.

Slowly, the Guardian raised his arms.

A hum filled the air—harmonic, transcendent. Between his hands, a symbol took shape.

The winged disk of the Anunnaki—two symmetrical wings flaring from a central circle—formed from radiant energy. Gold and silver patterns shimmered along each feather, echoing the flow of gravitational fields.

The Guardian's form shimmered.

Light spiraled from the Mechanism, coiling around his body. The winged symbol fragmented, dissolving into golden dust that merged with his frame. He flickered—phasing beyond reality.

Then—he fractured.

Millions of particles erupted—red, blue, gold, silver—swirling through the chamber like a living nebula. They stretched into the walls, the ceiling, igniting every glyph in synchronized pulses of light.

The Guardian was no longer separate.

He had become part of the machine once again. Rebecca watched in awe. "It's rewriting itself."

The Guardian's form dissolved entirely, absorbed into the core. The pulse beneath their feet slowed. The glow across the temple walls settled into perfect balance.

The machine had accepted Jake's command. The sequence was complete.

The mechanism was whole.

Jake's pulse slowed. His hand rested on the console. The rhythm beneath it matched his heartbeat.

"It's balanced," he said.

Light pulsed outward—slow, deliberate. A language written in light and harmony.

Jake's hand slowly lowered from the control panel, his fingers trembling slightly as if still feeling the pulse of the machine. His gaze lingered on the core at the center of the chamber— once dormant, now glowing with a soft, steady radiance. The light was no longer volatile or erratic; it was calm, measured, alive.

He turned, his eyes meeting Rebecca's—wide, glistening, reflecting the same disbelief and wonder stirring in his own.

"We did it," he breathed. Then louder, a smile breaking across his face, "That's it—we accomplished the impossible!"

A cheer erupted from the others. Laughter, relief, and adrenaline surged through the chamber like electricity. The weight of months—years—of pressure finally lifted.

From across the room, Miguel cupped his hands around his mouth and called out, "Is that it, *Jefe*? Did we save the planet?"

Jake didn't answer immediately. Instead, he stepped forward and pulled Rebecca into a tight bear hug, lifting her clean off the ground as she let out a startled laugh.

"Yes, Miguel, we did it. We saved the planet!" Jake exclaims, adrenaline surging through him.

For a brief moment, it was all joy and human connection—raw and unfiltered.

John kissed Shirley while Nadine, Naomi, and Yumi talked over each other, animatedly recapping the final moments: the pulse, the alignment, the activation. Their words tumbled over one another, wide-eyed and half-laughing, as if saying it out loud made them relive the moment.

But the celebration was short-lived.

A shift in the atmosphere stilled them. It wasn't sound, but presence.

They were no longer alone.

The room fell silent as the newcomers advanced, boots echoing off the stone.

CHAPTER 32

Alpha or Omega

Emerging from the shadows of the ancient ruins, another group approached.

Their movements were precise—calculated—as if every step had been rehearsed a thousand times before. They advanced in perfect formation, weapons raised, their dark uniforms devoid of insignia or identity. Black visors and expressionless masks obscured their faces—not merely for concealment, but to erase humanity altogether.

The air thickened inside the subterranean chamber. Dust hung motionless in the dim light, suspended as if time itself had paused to watch what would happen next.

The soldiers held their formation with robotic precision—

unmoving, unreadable. Their armor absorbed the low thrum of the mechanism's energy, and their faceless masks, like black mirrors, caught the faint glint of glowing runes.

They overwhelmed Miguel, who had been guarding the entrance. Forced to drop his weapon, he collapsed to the ground, unconscious, after a heavy blow to the head from the butt of a soldier's rifle.

At the center of it all, Mr. Sloan stood unflinching, like a man carved from ice and intent. His hands were clasped behind his back in studied ease, but every line in his body radiated power—the kind honed over decades, in silence and in blood.

Jake didn't blink.

He couldn't afford to.

Behind him, his team stood at the ready—Rebecca, eyes sharp and lips tight, hand inching toward her holster. Shirley and Nadine were flanking the rear, already triangulating cover positions. Naomi, Yumi, John, and Miguel each waited for the signal they hoped would never have to come.

Jake met Sloan's gaze. "Step away from the device."

"Step away from the device," Sloan repeated, more softly this time, like a teacher tired of repeating a lesson.

But Jake didn't move.

"I won't let you use this machine," he said evenly. "Whatever plan you think you've earned, whatever control you think you can exert—this isn't your weapon."

Sloan exhaled slowly through his nose, like a man enjoying a long-practiced theater.

He stepped forward.

"Mr. Rosen-Fischer," he said, voice smooth as silk and just as dangerous. "You've come a long way. Generations of your family would be so very proud. Truly, quite the legacy."

Jake's breath evened. His heartbeat slowed to match the

machine's steady pulse beneath him. Soldiers tightened formation. His hand drifted toward the reinforced harness at his side, fingers brushing the smooth surface of the control interface.

Sloan continued, almost lazily: "Now, you and your team step away from the Mechanism. No one needs to be harmed."

It wasn't a negotiation.

It was an ultimatum.

But Jake and his team had prepared for this moment.

His eyes narrowed. "This machine was built to *save* humanity—not to become a weapon of mass destruction."

Sloan's boots echoed softly as he moved further into the chamber, flanked by armored silhouettes. He removed his mask, revealing a face carved by war and sharpened by survival. His expression was unreadable. His eyes—unforgiving.

"It's not about saving the world," Sloan said, almost smiling. "It's about deciding who *deserves* to live in it."

Jake's jaw clenched.

Sloan took another step. "You think you're fighting for humanity's survival? You're not. You're fighting for the *privilege* of deciding who gets to survive."

Jake felt his pulse thrum through his bones. Not from fear.

From the gravity of what stood before him—and behind him.

The Mechanism

It pulsed with faint, otherworldly energy—a rhythmic thrum in sync with the Earth's very core. This was no mere device. It governed magnetic fields, balanced tectonic plates, guided ocean currents, and tuned atmospheric rhythms.

In the right hands, it could heal a fractured world. In the wrong ones?

It could become a weapon—turning Earth into a cage. A planetary prison disguised as order.

And Sloan wanted it.

Jake inhaled slowly, letting the silence stretch.

He couldn't match Sloan's forces in firepower. Not here. Not directly.

But brute force wasn't the answer.

Strategy was.

Understanding was.

And truth—wielded correctly—could be sharper than any blade.

Jake glanced once at Rebecca. Then at the others. They were ready. They had always known this was coming.

He stepped forward.

The Trap Is Set

Jake shifted his stance, subtly adjusting the controls on his wrist interface.

Unbeknownst to Sloan, the Mechanism was already synced to Jake's command—access granted just before the final test.

Beneath his sleeve, a thin display glowed with a soft, pulsing light. Lines of encoded sequences scrolled across the screen as he interfaced directly with the system.

Every signal.

Every adjustment.

Deliberate.

Unauthorized users would trigger the Mechanism's auto-defense mode—a failsafe built into the ancient core. Several countermeasures appeared on the screen. Only one was high-lighted, glowing brighter than the rest. Written in ancient cuneiform:

 **The Wrath of Enki.**

Jake studied the symbol. Then let Sloan see it.

He took a step back, feigning strain—his shoulders slumping just enough to suggest fatigue. His fingers danced across the interface, visible to Sloan's soldiers. Letting them believe he was losing control.

"You're too late," Jake said, voice sharp—threaded with just the right note of desperation. "The machine's already aligning to me."

Sloan's gaze sharpened.

A flicker of fear flashed in his pale eyes. Then—hunger.

His mouth curled into a thin, wolfish smile. He raised a hand toward his soldiers.

"Secure the device."

Jake didn't move.

As Sloan's men surged forward, weapons raised, Jake stepped aside. Calm. Focused.

Exactly as planned.

The soldiers stormed past Jake's team, driving them back with force. Sloan advanced to the control platform, his gloved hand brushing the surface of the ancient machine.

The Mechanism hesitated. Then it responded to touch, recognizing authorized users immediately.

The glyphs stuttered, no longer synchronized. Symbols flickered erratically across the core, reacting to sudden interference.

Jake watched.

Sloan pressed his palm to the surface, attempting to force alignment at the same spot Jake had used moments before.

The machine responded—reluctantly. Then, it bucked.

The gravitational adjuster trembled. The chamber shook.

Dust cascaded from above. Debris lifted from the floor and began to orbit in erratic spirals.

Jake's expression hardened. "That's it."

The air distorted as localized gravity began to collapse inward. Plates of stone groaned. The gravitational field warped and twisted—no longer stable, no longer safe.

"You wanted to control it," Jake said, his voice low. Measured. Deadly.

"Now try controlling *that*."

Sloan's eyes widened. The frequency of the Mechanism rose to a shrill, discordant whine. The gravitational field fractured into chaos.

Jake's fingers moved swiftly across his interface. Target profile confirmed.

He locked onto the infrared signatures of Sloan and his soldiers.

The system responded.

The chamber's gravity surged downward—compressing around the soldiers. Movement slowed. Weapons dropped. Their bodies sagged under the crushing pressure of their own momentum and miscalculation.

In a split second, John and Naomi rushed to Miguel. He was alive—disoriented, but okay—and together they dragged him back to the group.

Sloan's knees buckled. He clawed at the machine's surface, straining to rise.

"You think you've won?" he spat, teeth clenched. Jake stepped closer, face calm.

"From where I stand—yes."

The field collapsed further. The gravitational vortex pulled inward, dragging Sloan's soldiers toward the core. Their cries were cut short, swallowed by the rising force.

Sloan screamed—but the sound never left his throat. The pressure crushed it out of him.

His body folded, slamming against the platform. His men lay strewn across the chamber, motionless—buried beneath the weight of their own arrogance.

Jake stood above him.

Silent. Resolute.

"This power belongs to all of humanity," he said. "Not just the few."

The machine's light pulsed once—sharp and final.

Threat eliminated.

The symbols realigned. The gravitational hum softened. The platform steadied beneath Jake's feet.

Balance: Restored.

He turned to Rebecca. His breath came slow, steady—the storm passing through him, leaving behind only clarity.

And then it happened.

A shift—subtle, but immediate. The air felt lighter.

The shadows receded.

The weight in the room—that heavy, invisible tension—vanished.

As if the Mechanism had cleansed the very atmosphere.

Purged it.

Purified it.

"Do you feel it?" Jake asked quietly.

Rebecca nodded. Her eyes softened.

"Yes, I feel such a sense of well-being."

Jake's hand lingered on the surface of the machine. It no longer felt cold.

He looked at her—and finally allowed himself to breathe. "It's finally over. We did it."

The Mechanism pulsed—no longer a weapon, but a beacon. A calm, steady signal radiated from its core, washing the chamber in waves of light. Balance. True balance. Restored.

The Rebuilding

Some parts of the world lay in ruins—but it was not beyond salvation.

The old order had crumbled, leaving behind only the skeletal remains of a world built on division, control, and greed. Shattered cities stood like mausoleums of ambition, monuments to the arrogance that had once believed it could dominate nature without consequence.

But in the quiet aftermath, beneath the fractured sky and among the trembling earth, life stirred once more.

From the ashes of destruction, something new began to rise.

At the center of it all, the mechanism beneath the Earth pulsed steadily—a deep, measured thrum that echoed through the planet's core. The ancient Anunnaki construct, now fully aligned with Earth's magnetic field, radiated a harmonic frequency that rippled outward like the beating of a great, planetary heart. It was never a weapon. It was a guardian.

A planetary shield, calibrated to stabilize tectonic forces when celestial objects passed near the solar system. A frequency anchor designed to deflect meteoric threats. A construct not to control life, but to protect it—to safeguard Earth and its children.

Its signal was pure. It resonated not just through stone, water, and sky, but through the very fabric of the Earth itself.

The balance will remain eternal—so long as humans live in true harmony with the planet. This means not only coexisting peacefully with nature, but also recognizing our role as stewards of the Earth. We must actively seek to live in alignment with other species, honoring their right to exist and thrive, and contributing meaningfully to the ecosystems we share.

Let us offer our highest praise to Mother Earth—our home, our sanctuary, our planet above all.

Rivers once poisoned by greed ran clear, flushing centuries of waste into the deep. Oceans shimmered again, no longer choked with oil or plastic, but teeming with the silent return of forgotten marine life. Forests, once reduced to scars, surged back across hills and mountains—as if the memory of green had only slept.

Even the atmosphere felt lighter, as though the planet had taken its first true breath in a thousand years.

But the mechanism's power went deeper still—beyond the physical, into the consciousness of Earth's people. A resonance. Not control. Not manipulation. Freedom.

It did not command obedience or impose thought. Instead, it lifted the unseen weight that humanity had carried across millennia—the weight of ancestral trauma, inherited fear, cyclical violence. The heavy noise of a species at war with itself, generation after generation.

It was cleared.

And something shifted. Not subtly. Not slowly. Immediately.

People felt it—not like an idea, but like a truth long forgotten. A clarity of thought. A lightness in the soul. Where once there had been fear, suspicion, aggression; now there was stillness. Openness. Connection. To each other. To the planet.

To something far greater than either.

The illusion of separateness—of race, nation, class, creed—dissolved beneath the gentle hum of the mechanism's pulse. It was not erasure. It was remembrance—a return to the knowing that all things are one.

Earth came into perfect resonance—with itself, and with the broader symphony of the cosmos.

And then, as quietly as it had awakened, the mechanism began to sleep. Its pulse slowed.

The concentric rings of light around its core dimmed. The

intricate patterns etched into its surface faded, like breath on glass.

Its work was done. Its purpose fulfilled.

It would rest—until the Earth called again. Humanity had been given a gift. Not of power. Not of conquest. But of understanding. And from that, a new world would be born.

CHAPTER 33

The Stars are Watching

The survivors came from all walks of life.

Scientists who had once unraveled the mysteries of the universe now stood shoulder to shoulder with farmers who knew the language of soil and sky. Engineers and builders worked alongside poets and dreamers, forging a society not from the ashes of war—but from the quiet resolve of shared purpose.

Historians who had documented the rise and fall of empires now collaborated with artists sketching a new future—not one shaped by conquest or capital, but one closer to the heart, shaped by creativity, wisdom, and care.

The borders that once defined nations, the lines that had carved humanity into categories of race, class, and creed, were gone. The governments that ruled by fear had collapsed. Currencies were worthless. The engines of profit had fallen silent.

All that remained was humanity—standing at the fragile threshold of a new era.

At first, there was hesitation. Tension. The ghosts of the old world didn't vanish overnight. Fear still lingered in the hollow spaces between people. Suspicion moved like smoke through broken cities.

But necessity demanded evolution.

And survival—*true survival*—required something deeper than instinct. It demanded cooperation.

Gradually, the divisions faded. What had once fueled conflict—language, culture, philosophy—became the very foundation of their strength. Every voice mattered. Every perspective carried weight. The arrogance of supremacy—the belief that one path, one truth, one people held dominion—was abandoned.

Knowledge became the new currency. And it was shared, not stockpiled. Power was not a throne to ascend—it was a responsibility to distribute.

The survivors built again—not monuments to ego or empire, but cities of belonging. Not fortresses, but havens.

They grew food not for markets, but for nourishment. Technology was no longer the treasure of the elite—it became the tool of the collective. Education was not a privilege, but a birthright. Justice no longer served control—it served equity.

It wasn't perfect. Some clung to the old ways—to the illusion of hierarchy, of dominance, of scarcity. But they were outnumbered. Their voices, though loud, were drowned by the quiet choir of compassion rising in its stead.

Slowly, the balance shifted.

What emerged was not a utopia—but something real. A

civilization not built on fear, but on understanding. A species standing side by side—not because they were forced to . . .

. . . but because they had chosen to.

And that, at last, was what made them worthy.

The Children of the New World

Years passed. Jake stood at the edge of a rebuilt settlement, overlooking the wide expanse of green fields and clear rivers. Beside him, Rebecca's hand was wrapped in his—familiar, steady, and warm.

Their love had been forged in fire, in the heart of upheaval and uncertainty.

But now it was nurtured in the quiet peace of renewal. Together, they had built a home. Not a fortress.

Not a place to defend—but a place to belong.

They had two children—a son and a daughter—born into a world that had never known war, never tasted corruption. A world where kindness was currency, and knowledge a gift to be shared. Where their parents were no longer warriors, but builders.

Their children played not with screens and simulations, but with soil beneath their feet and wind in their hair. They climbed trees, chased each other through tall grass, and laughed beneath open skies. In those moments, they rediscovered a deep, instinctive love for Earth—understanding deeply, that it was not just a place they lived, but a home worth protecting above all else.

Technology had not vanished—but it no longer replaced connection. It was no longer a crutch. It was balance.

Jake's eyes followed his son, who stood laughing beneath the wide shade of a tree as his sister raced around him. The sight was simple—but profound.

Humanity was no longer bound by the chains of consumption and self-destruction.

The cycle was broken.

Rebecca's hand tightened gently. "This is what we fought for."

Jake nodded, his gaze lifting toward the horizon. The sky was deepening into twilight, the first stars piercing the veil of dusk. But they no longer felt distant—no longer cold, silent witnesses.

The stars were guides now.

Destinations.

Humanity was no longer trapped beneath the weight of its mistakes. They had endured. They had risen. They had *learned*.

"We're ready," Jake said quietly.

Rebecca looked at him, a soft smile playing at her lips. "For what?"

Jake kept his eyes on the sky. "For the next step."

He paused. "The stars."

The Anunnaki's message had been received. Their warning *heeded*. The code deciphered.

And humanity had passed the test—not through conquest or dominance, but through wisdom.

Through understanding.

Above them, a faint ripple of light shimmered across the sky, as if something had stirred just beyond the veil of the atmosphere.

The stars flickered—not randomly, but *rhythmically*, like a heartbeat.

Jake smiled faintly.

"They're waiting for us," he said.

Rebecca glanced upward. "Who?"

Jake's voice was soft—filled with wonder. "The universe."

Below, the Earth thrived.

Oceans shimmered like polished glass.

Forests stretched higher, greener, older than memory. The air smelled of clean rain and new life—as if the planet itself had finally exhaled after millennia of tension.

The mechanism was silent now.

But its purpose had already been fulfilled.

Rebecca turned to him, brushing a hand against his cheek. "So, this is just the beginning," she whispered.

Jake looked at her, heart full, spirit quiet.

"For the first time, probably ever" he said, "the future is truly ours to create."

And so, beneath a reborn sky, hand in hand with the woman he loved, Jake knew—Humanity was ready. Ready to rise. Ready to reach beyond the stars. Ready to become something *greater*. The cycle had ended. And from its end, something new had begun. The future belonged to them.

The Very Fabric of the Universe

But the universe was not a place of stillness. It was a vast ocean of opposing forces—positive and negative, light and dark—caught in a constant state of motion. Expansion and contraction, creation and destruction, push and pull—the eternal rhythm of existence.

The ancient symbol of the *Yin Yang* was more than metaphor—it was a reflection of the fundamental nature of the cosmos itself. Harmony was not a fixed state—it was a delicate tension, a fragile alignment of opposites constantly shifting to maintain balance.

Earth had found that balance—at least for now. The mechanism stabilized the planet's magnetic field, restored ecological harmony, and elevated humanity's consciousness beyond the destructive cycles that had plagued them for millennia.

But balance on Earth was only a reflection of a larger pattern. The universe, too, was in flux.

There were civilizations—ancient and advanced—that had mastered the art of balance, weaving their existence into the cosmic rhythm with elegance and precision. They had learned how to coexist with the forces of creation and destruction, riding the currents of galactic entropy without being consumed by them. Others had not.

There were those who had chosen chaos—not out of ignorance, but out of desire. For some, the tension between order and disorder was not a struggle—it was a game. They saw imbalance not as a threat, but as an opportunity. To manipulate. To control. To dominate.

And in the depths of that cosmic struggle, the Anunnaki had always stood at the threshold between order and chaos.

Once gods to humanity, they were not divine—but ancient. A race of engineers, creators, and architects who had shaped the development of countless worlds across the stars. They had understood the mechanics of existence at its most fundamental level—the weave of gravity, light, energy, and time.

On Earth, it had been Enki who had first reached out—gifting humanity with knowledge, language, art, and science. He had seen potential in the fragile species crawling out of the mud and believed they could rise beyond their primal nature.

But Enki had not acted alone.

Enlil had watched from the shadows—skeptical, pragmatic, and ruthless. Where Enki saw potential, Enlil saw chaos. He had always believed that humanity's tendency toward violence and self-destruction would inevitably lead to collapse. He had argued for intervention—for correction—through controlled destruction.

And so, the struggle had begun.

Enki, the creator—the giver of knowledge.

Enlil, the destroyer—the hand of order through force.

And above them both stood Anu—the ancient sovereign of

the Anunnaki, the final arbiter whose hand had guided the fate of countless worlds.

For millennia, they had observed Earth from afar, waiting to see whether humanity would rise or fall. The Purifications had been tests—interventions disguised as natural disasters—enacted when the balance of the planet drifted too far toward chaos.

And now, for the first time, humanity had passed the test.

Jake and his team had proven that balance could be restored not through destruction, but through understanding. The mechanism had not saved Earth. Humanity had.

It should have been enough. But Enlil was not satisfied.

He had always seen humanity as a flawed species—a dangerous anomaly in the galactic order. They were too unpredictable, too emotional, too prone to violence. He had argued that Earth's survival was a mistake—an imbalance that would eventually threaten the larger order of the cosmos.

And now that humanity had risen—now that they had touched the edges of cosmic understanding—they would no longer remain unnoticed.

Earth was no longer just a backwater planet, an isolated experiment on the edges of the galactic map.

Humanity had stepped onto the stage of the greater cosmic order. And there were those who would see that as a threat.

The Council

High above the planetary plane, beyond the reach of human thought, the ancient corridors of Nibiru stirred once more.

The Anunnaki home-world, long hidden in the gravitational shadow beyond the outer planets—had awakened.

Figures robed in deep black glided through halls carved from celestial stone, their faces obscured beneath veils of shadow. The

Council Chambers, silent for millennia, now pulsed with subtle light—faint rhythms of violet and gold breathing along the walls like the heart of a star.

Across the curved chamber, the vast celestial maps carved into obsidian shimmered with life. At the center of the display, one orb glowed brighter than the rest: Earth.

Its orbit flashed softly, stable. Its magnetic field, now aligned. Its anomalies—resolved.

At the head of the chamber stood a solitary figure. Tall. Unmoving. Watching.

His frame was carved in shadow, wrapped in ceremonial armor of polished obsidian, adorned with curved horns that rose like dark crescents from his helm.

Enlil.

His eyes glowed faintly beneath the visor—two cold points of judgment watching Earth's rotation with surgical precision.

His lips curled into a thin, joyless smile.

"Interesting."

Behind him, a second figure emerged from the veil of shadow. same in stature, equal in presence. His silver hair was braided in the traditional style of the Anunnaki priesthood, his face calm, eyes old.

Enki.

"You're displeased," Enki said softly.

"They survived," Enlil replied. His voice was ice. *"Barely."*

Enki stepped closer to the glowing projection. His tone was lighter, touched by something human.

"They survived because they *learned*. They adapted. That was always the test."

Enlil's gaze sharpened. "And now what happens when the others notice?"

Enki's smile faded. "Then they will face the same choice we once faced."

Enlil's tone darkened. *"Humanity is not ready."*

"You said the same about us," Enki replied, almost gently. Enlil's jaw tightened. "This was not supposed to happen." "Perhaps," Enki said, "it was."

A silence settled—heavy, ancient.

Then, from the far end of the chamber, a third presence arrived. He walked with the quiet weight of eternity, draped in white and gold, his carved mask etched with symbols older than language. His hands were folded calmly beneath long sleeves.

Anu.

The Sovereign.

His voice, when it came, was deep, steady, and final. "It seems Earth's cycle has reached its conclusion."

Enlil inclined his head in reluctant acknowledgment. "And what do you propose?"

Anu stepped to the projection, his mask reflecting the soft glow of Earth. He studied the spinning orb—not with wonder, but with the gaze of one who had seen this pattern repeat across galaxies.

"We will wait," Anu said.

Enlil's voice sharpened. "For how long?"

Anu turned slightly, the mask inscrutable. "Until they rise. Or until they fall."

A silence stretched between them. Not tense. Not passive.

Fated.

Enki's hand brushed the edge of the display, fingers trailing over the orbital path of Earth. The projection shimmered, shifting subtly beneath his touch.

"They've earned their place," Enki said. "Not through conquest. Through balance."

Enlil did not look at him. "Perhaps. But you know how this game ends."

Anu's gaze remained fixed on the glowing orb, spinning in silence.

"It does not end," he said. "It only begins again."

The Future Awaits

On Earth, beneath a sky threaded with stars, Jake stood with Rebecca at his side.

The mechanism was silent now—its pulse quiet beneath the stone. The balance had been restored. Humanity had risen.

But Jake knew the truth. Balance was not a destination.

It was a moment—fleeting and fragile.

A breath held between the inhale of creation and the exhale of entropy.

The universe was still in motion—still turning.

And beyond Earth's sky, in the dark corridors of the cosmos, forces watched.

Forces that had not yet cast their judgment. For now, they had earned their peace.

But the stars were watching.

The End

About the Author

Carlo Tonalezzi

From a very young age, I found myself captivated by history, mythology, and the enigma of human evolution. Long before I had the words to describe my fascination, I was already experiencing vivid, recurring dreams—visions of multicolored spheres cascading from the sky. These dreams felt so real that, even within them, I would climb walls just to catch a better glimpse. Something deep within me was already stirring. Then came a moment that would change everything.

It was a quiet Friday night. My father was preparing for one of his regular card games with friends when one of the guests arrived holding a book. I was ten years old. That book was *Chariots of the Gods* by Erich von Däniken. From the moment I turned the first page, I was hooked. It felt like all the swirling thoughts in my young mind—ideas I hadn't yet dared to voice—were suddenly validated. I devoured the book, reading it not once, but multiple times. It was exhilarating to learn about mysterious places and ancient anomalies from around the world. My imagination ignited.

That was the beginning of my lifelong quest.

I started researching obsessively. The deeper I dug, the more I discovered—and the more questions emerged. Every trail led to another: mythology overlapping with history, lost civilizations, unexplained technologies, ancient master builders. But something was always missing. No matter the topic—human origins, religion, sacred architecture—it all lacked conclusive evidence. Many of the mysteries were simply written off as miracles. That explanation never sat right with me. I couldn't stop digging.

Years passed, and my journey continued—until one seemingly mundane event changed everything again.

One day, while attempting to unclog a stubborn pipe in my basement, I made a critical error. As I disconnected the pipe, I discovered too late that it was under pressure. Dirty water jetted out violently, threatening to flood the entire space. In the chaos, I scraped my right hand on a sharp edge. Blood mixed with the floodwater. After finally managing to seal the pipe, I turned my attention to the wound.

Days later, as my hand began to heal, I noticed the scar forming into a strange, unmistakable shape. It resembled a double helix—the structure of DNA. I'd never seen a scar like it before. Intrigued, I began to research the symbol and its implications. To my surprise, I discovered that the double helix is also associated with Enki, a deity I had never heard of. My research into Enki led me to the Anunnaki.

Suddenly, everything started to fall into place.

When you factor the Anunnaki into the equation, the puzzle pieces of mythology, ancient architecture, and so-called religious miracles begin to align. It all started to make sense. My years of disconnected research, scattered dreams, and unanswered questions began forming a coherent picture.

That's when I knew I had to share my journey—not just as a memoir, but as a science fiction story infused with the very real research that has shaped my life. My hope is that this story will ignite in others the same burning curiosity that once overtook me as a ten-year-old with a book in hand.

If you, dear reader, choose to explore what lies within these pages—and follow the threads yourself—it may lead you down a path of hidden truths, ancient mysteries, and perhaps even a redefinition of our human story. It is a path not many take, but for those who do, it offers a deeply satisfying exploration of an alternate history that stirs the soul.

So, what *is* the fine line between mythology and history?

Maybe, just maybe, this book will help you begin to find your own answer.

www.ingramcontent.com/pod-product-compliance
Lightning Source LLC
Chambersburg PA
CBHW070308310726
48976CB00005B/1625